MW00654061

Congrats, Glorianne!

IRIDESCENCE

The Spectrum Series

SPECTRUM
DIFFUSION
CRYSTALLIZED
COVALENCE
IRIDESCENCE
SCINTILLATE (PREQUEL)

SAMANTHA MINA

IRIDESCENCE

BOOK 5 OF A SERIES

The characters, names, and events as well as all places, incidents, organizations, and dialog in this novel are either the products of the writer's imagination or are used fictitiously.

ISBN: 978-0-9991577-4-9

Visit the author's website at **http://www.SpectrumSeries.org** to order additional copies.

For Dianne Becker Tavares
whose passion for Second Earth
burns brighter than a thousand Pits of Fire.

AND

For all the child-soldiers around the world
forced to fight adults' wars:
may you no longer be just
infrared
in our eyes.

PRONUNCIATION GUIDE

Acci: *"AX-ee"*
Arrhyth: *"AR-hith"*
Buird: *"Bird"*
Comat: *"Kaw-met"*
Ichthyosis: *"Ik-thee-OH-sis"*
Leavesleft: *"LEEV-ssleft"*
Lechatelierite: *"Luh-shaht-LEER-ahyt"*
(rhymes with "light")
Nuria: *"NER-ee-ah"*
Qui Tsop: *"Key Sop"*

NORTHWESTERN HEMISPHERE OF SECOND EARTH

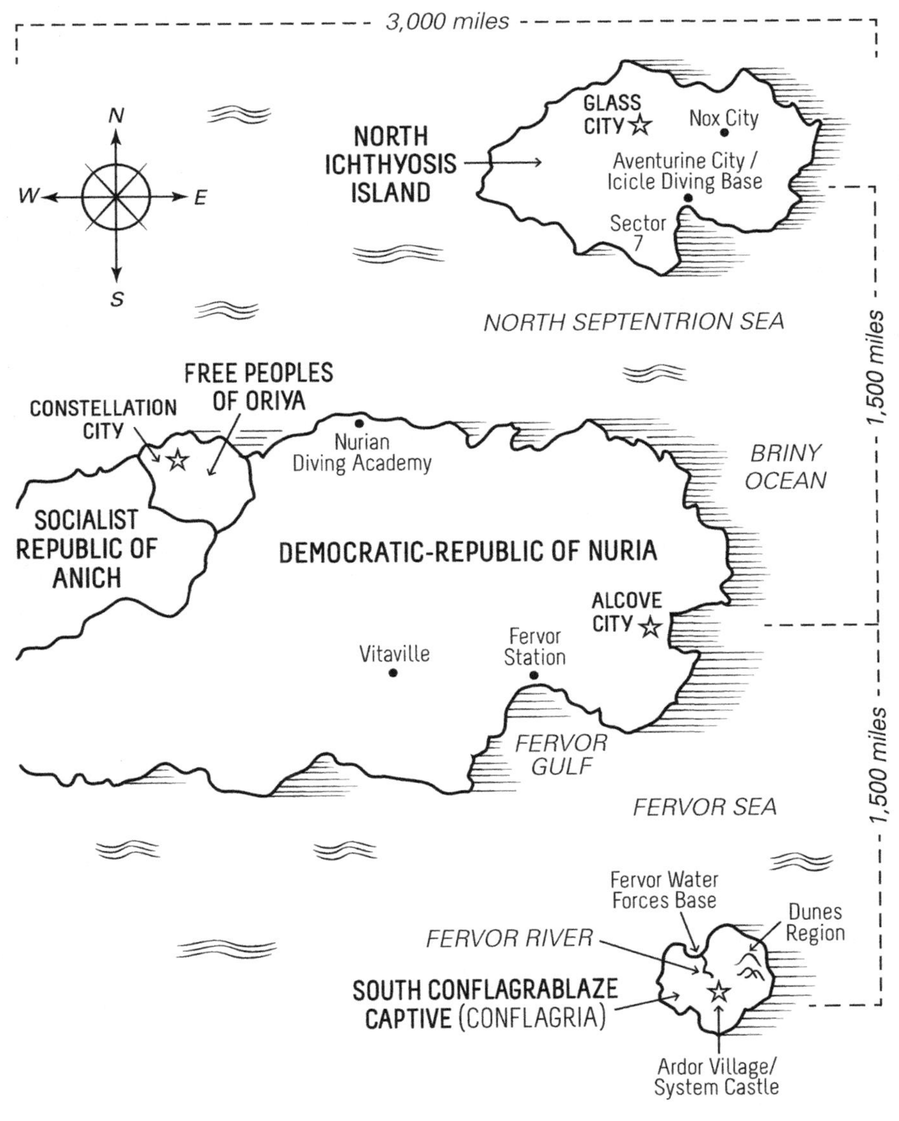

PART I

ENCE: CHILD OF WAR

I am the child without childhood
Never known love
Never heard music
But AK-47s Snipers RPGs
Music that silences

Each time you breathe
God's free air
I am killed in War
Or by War's cousins
I am the child
Whose screams are trapped
In the roofless space of killing fields

—*Excerpt from* Child of War *by S. U. Kamarah*

NURTIC LEAVESLEFT

January seventh of the first age, eighth era.

I turned the key to my mailbox, expecting a handful of ads, catalogues, a couple bills, the usual. But, today, at the bottom of the stack, there was something special. A letter from Oriya, from Linkeree Link. I smiled as I returned to my small seventh-floor apartment, taking the stairs instead of the elevator.

I hadn't seen Linkeree in person since our senior age at the University of Vita. Since then, we graduated from different seminaries; I attended ACBC, Alcove City Bible College, and Ree—just as she always wanted—went to CCA, Constellation Christian Academy, in the capital of Oriya.

At UVA, Ree was valedictorian. As for me, anchorman. Preoccupied by the World Revolt and all its horrific aftermath, I nearly flunked out during my freshman age. Then, during my junior age, my performance tanked thanks to family crises—yes, cris*es*, plural. Not that any of that mattered, anymore. Grades and distinctions. What really mattered was that, against all odds, I was finally certified to enter the mission field. At the age of twenty-seven, I was, at long last, permitted to go on an overseas assignment.

It felt kind of silly and odd, to have to obtain special authorization to travel abroad as part of the Alcove City Aviation Ministry. As a war veteran and longtime delivery and airline pilot, I found nothing particularly special nor daunting about traversing the hemisphere.

I opened Ree's envelope to find a recent shot of her, wedged amongst three notebook pages full of tiny cursive. '*Life with the isolationists has been fun, as always,*' she wrote. '*Being the daughter of the infamous Arnold Link hasn't made going to school in the Authority Nation particularly easy. But, no sea worth sailing is ever totally smooth, right?*'

Right she was. I propped Ree's picture on my mantle, alongside four others—one of my parents; one of me with Ecivon Wen, Tnerruc Ruetama and Scarlet July at the Alcove City train station when I was eighteen; one of Arrhyth Link and Dither Maine at Bay River Secondary swim-team practice later that same age; and one of Ree and I in our caps and gowns at UVA.

Half the people in those photos were dead.

My father had a stroke at the start of my junior age. My mother followed suit soon thereafter, from breast cancer. Finances already shot to hell by the firebombing of the Nurian Trade Centerscraper, my parents left nothing behind for me but a broken heart and thousands in medical debt. My church work and air-delivery job couldn't cover living expenses, student loans *and* my inherited debt, so I got yet another job: piloting for NurroAir, whenever possible. Due to the economic recession, the Trilateral Committee discontinued my veteran's pension long ago. A full-on depression was predicted for the eleventh age. The alliance was in ruins.

And, there was nothing I could do about it. I'd long since given up on trying to save the world.

* * *

I chose the South Conflagrablaze Captive. Everyone at church was surprised I'd select the 'Island of Fire' for my first international assignment, and not just because I was allergic to dust.

"We didn't think you'd want to go there, ever again," the Missions Director, Trys Tor, told me. "Not after... you know..."

Oh, I knew, alright. It seemed that the whole world knew. My life went down in history. Literally. There were books about events I witnessed and people I once knew and loved. Books I'd never read.

"Miss your soldier days, do you?" Trys asked.

I only shrugged, lacking the emotional energy to correct him. He just didn't understand. No one did. I really was through with military life. Forever. If I selected Conflagria for my first humanitarian mission, it wasn't because I was nostalgic for the war. It was because I once promised a dear friend of mine that I'd reach out to her people someday. I was determined to keep my word to her, even if she'd never know.

"You should think of going to Ichthyosis," he went on. "You already speak the language, after all."

The last time I had a reason to utter a word of Ichthyothian, I was twenty. Who knew if I was still fluent, anymore. It wasn't like I had anyone to practice with.

But, Arrhyth Link and Dither Maine—now, they were probably speaking far more Ichthyothian than Nurian, on a daily basis. For the umpteenth time, I wondered how they were doing... and if they were still alive. I hadn't seen nor spoken to either of them since the World Revolt ended. I tried calling their PAVLAKs a few times since then, but the Trilateral Committee apparently severed my link. The Diving Fleet Commander had a personal landline I could still call—and I did know his number, since his quarters were mine, once upon a time—but, I was pretty sure that

Inexor Buird would hang up in my face, if I rang him up to ask for or about my friends.

By now, I wasn't sure what I'd even say to Arrhyth or Dither, anymore. They were in their late twenties now, like me. They'd be nearly forty by homecoming, if everything went according to plan, which it never did.

* * *

Conflagria wasn't exactly a popular choice, among my fellow missionaries. I was placed on a 'team' of only two others—fellow twenty-something ACBC grads Ayden Long and Dylan Minn. No one else was brave enough to join us.

On January twenty-fifth, mere minutes after arriving at Conflagria's northern shore, we understood why.

'Chaos' wasn't a strong enough word to describe what we saw. The number of sick and homeless mages haunting the paths seemed to have tripled since I was here last. Criminal activity wasn't only ignored, but apparently expected—heads didn't even turn when unspeakable stuff happened in broad daylight. We could hardly walk a block without running into some sort of scary sight—someone being mugged, beaten, raped.

When I was here in the nineties, I faced all sorts of terrors. But, this was the first time I'd ever witnessed an attempted rape, in person.

Unlike everybody else in the vicinity, I refused to turn a blind eye. I grabbed the attacker by the neck.

Dumb move. I wasn't dealing with any old joe, I was engaging in hand-to-hand combat with a Conflagrian mage, while unarmed myself. And, it turned out, he was a leg mage. With one swift kick, he knocked me to the sand.

I woke up some time later to the sight of a splintered wooden ceiling. Head throbbing, I struggled to sit up, slowly realizing where I was. The lobby of Fourth Cabin, a Red stronghold.

Or, at least, what *was* Fourth Cabin, back in ninety-four; I had no idea what this place was used for, nowadays.

"Huh?" I gaped.

"Hey, there, Nurtic Leavesleft," came a female voice in accented Ichthyothian. "I didn't think it was possible for you to get any taller, but I stand corrected. You're taking up the whole floor."

Squatting before me was none other than a twenty-four-age-old Fair Gabardine. She looked just like my memory of her, except her eyes had a new sort of droop to them. Ayden and Dylan stood a couple paces back, sweaty and worry-struck.

"Fair," I breathed, brain scrambling to find the Ichthyothian words, "good to see you, again."

Her white hair autonomously leapt over her shoulders. "I see that you're still the same wide-eyed, well-meaning, dumb-as-a-dragon troublemaker as ever before. Lucky that I came across you and your team, when I did." Her oil-black eyes rolled. "Times have changed here, my friend. You can't just go around, sticking your pointy nose in other people's business."

"Other people's business?" I sat up. "That guy was trying to rape someone, out in the open, and you expect me to just walk on by?"

"Yes. I can tell that you haven't been around, in quite a while. If you try to stop every crime you stumble upon, you'll be dead in a day. Tincture, you almost got killed in the first *hour*."

"I was sent here to help people," I swallowed, "but, I don't even know where to begin."

"On a church mission?" she asked, brow cocked.

I nodded. "Until the end of May."

She snorted, "Good luck."

"Scarlet July would throw herself into the Fire Pit if she could see what's become of her country," I murmured, sadly.

I watched as Fair's face warped with my words. "Um, don't say things like that too loudly; I don't know what's going on in the Nordic world right now, but on *these* shores, Scarlet July's name carries somewhat of a… mixed legacy."

I blinked. "Mixed legacy?"

She inhaled. "By now, a lot of people—more than just the original System-supporting crowd, I mean—kind of resent her for taking away Conflagria's chance at 'utopia.' So, there's been talk of attacking the spectral web, to break her aura's hold on it. Well, more than just talk…"

"No," I gasped.

"Communication with her frequency has already been attempted, countless times; mages have linked their minds to the web's currents and asked her, *begged* her, to let go. But, either she can't hear them, or she does but refuses to obey."

"Of course, she won't," I fiercely retorted.

"Which is why there's a nationwide effort to figure a way to *force* her to."

What? Scarlet's wavelength was intertwined with that of every mage, which begged the question: "Wouldn't that backfire bigtime? Wouldn't attacking her magic potentially compromise your own?"

"It could leave us spectrally crippled, yes. But, at this point, many don't care."

"Many," I echoed. "What about you? Do you care?"

There was a pregnant pause.

"Nurtic, please try to understand what we've been going through—"

"I can't believe you!" My chest instantly filled with red-hot rage as I hadn't felt since the mid-nineties, when I was still deeply entrenched in world affairs. "You want to diffuse your dead best friend?"

"I know how horrible that sounds," she piped, "and, believe me, I wish with every photon in my frequency that we didn't have to do this. But, if the wars have taught us anything, it's that sometimes we must turn to the last resort—"

"You're helping them, aren't you?" I cut across her. Fair was a genius spectroscoper; with her on the job, Scarlet was in imminent danger.

Ayden and Dylan, who couldn't understand a word of our conversation, stared at us in shock and awe. I doubted they'd ever seen me so upset.

"Nurtic, I'm the only spectroscoper in their ranks with a lick of compassion for Scarlet. So, my participation is in her best interest; I'm trying to find a solution that'd harm her wavelength the least. I don't want us to diffuse it completely, I only want to injure it, making a portion of it inactive. The portion that controls her will, so we can—"

The portion that controlled her *will?* "So, you can fully restore the evil dictatorship you fought against for ages," I spat, getting to my feet and dwarfing her with my nearly-seven feet of height. "If this is what's become of Conflagrian society at large, my team ought to pack up and go right now, because you all deserve to burn in the Fire Pit."

Fair stood, backing away from me. "This is so unlike you, Nurtic. I never thought I'd see you so—"

"Well, *I* never thought I'd see Scarlet's closest friend willingly bow to the evil System, setting out to slaughter her aura!"

Clearly thinking that I was about to get physical, Ayden and Dylan grabbed me. But, having just awoken from an unconscious stupor induced by an angry leg mage, I knew better than to attack a trained magical warrior with my bare hands again.

"It's easy for you to get all self-righteous and indignant," Fair growled. "Where have *you* been since the World Revolt went under? In your perfect little middle-class bubble, studying at elite schools and going home for holidays to mommy and daddy—"

"You have no idea what you're talking about!"

"What do you want from me, Nurtic?" she thundered. "You think I *want* to injure Scarlet's aura? Of course not, but what alternatives do we have? We've just got to end the chaos, before it kills us all. When given the choice between death, or life for a heavy price," she threw her arms up, "heaven forbid, my people choose to live. It's a *dilemma*, Nurtic—something you privileged Nordics can go your whole lives without facing once!"

I stayed put for a while, digesting Fair's words, Ayden and Dylan's hands still on my shoulders. And, I began to feel overwhelmed by that all-too-familiar mix of emotions that characterized my soldier days. The feeling of... responsibility. The hunger to solve the impossible. The longing to *do something*.

But, I was only one man. Conflagria needed the attention of the world. There was nothing that I, Nurtic Leavesleft, could do to for magekind at the moment but press on with my short-term trip, touching only a handful of lives. And, then, I would leave the island forever, knowing that it was willingly condemning itself to tyranny and oppression. Maybe, twenty-age-old Nurtic believed that one man stood a chance of making a difference for millions. But, that boy was long dead.

* * *

May twenty-fourth. Our last night here.

Our plane was parked near camp, its storage compartment almost empty now that we'd distributed all the food, clothing and medical supplies we came to give away.

Tense and sweaty and anxious, I couldn't sleep. Barefoot but otherwise dressed, I crawled out of our tent, trudged across the beach and waded in the Fervor Sea, mud-brown like the night sky. It'd been maybe six ages since I last swam. Since the World Revolt ended, I generally stayed away from beaches, ports or even pools; they all reminded me too much of war. The water was hot and frothy. It lapped my ankles and reddened my flesh. But, I hardly felt a thing.

I found myself thinking about the summer day, nine ages ago, when Commander Cease Lechatelierite led the Diving Fleet all the way down here to Fervor for the first time, ultimately kamikazing into an enemy base. Lechatelierite expected to die, that day. It was a miracle that he survived the crash. Wiping my eyes in my left sleeve, I pondered the magnitude of despair that could possibly compel a seventeen-age-old boy to try to throw away his life, just like that.

Without bothering to remove my clothes, I took a deep breath and dove in, headfirst.

My eyes burned, so I closed them and swam blind. I swam and swam and swam, heading nowhere fast, like I was trying to escape from something. Like I was trying to leave this whole world behind, this world with all its miserable problems I couldn't solve. I thought of the starving mage children haunting the villages and the rapist I attacked on my first day here. After some time, I returned to land, face salty from both tears and seawater. And, I wondered, not for the first time since Scarlet's death, when or if the true Multi-Source Enchant would come to this godforsaken planet.

Drying off, I ran through the Dunes, eventually stumbling upon a graveyard. I was surprised; considering all the random corpses spewed across the paths, I didn't know that Conflagrians bothered with proper burials, anymore.

Every wooden grave was inscribed, except one. The smallest stump in the field—all the way in the back-right corner—only bore a diagonal red slash. Immediately, I knew who it must've belonged to. With her 'mixed legacy,' it would've been unwise to openly display her name, inviting enemies to dig up and disgrace her body.

I wasn't in the mood to see this. I wasn't sure that I could handle an emotional assault, right now. But, despite myself, I walked right up to the pathetic thing and dropped to my knees.

"So, this is what they gave you, huh?" I scooped a fistful of coarse sand; it filtered through my fingers. "Reminds me of Cease Lechatelierite's tomb. Flat. Small. Marked, but not easily noticed. Buried in snow." Leaning forward, I touched the crimson line. "So, here I am, Scarlet, as promised. Seven ages ago, I said that I'd be back one day. I just never expected our reunion to be like this. I was hoping for more of a two-way conversation." I inhaled the humid air. "Anyway, I just want to say… I'm sorry. For everything. For what's become of your country. For the way your people disparage your name. For the way they're working to diffuse your aura, tearing apart the spectral web… Oh, Scarlet, even Fair Gabardine's turned her back on you," I gasped sharply, as though stabbed. "Forgive them, Scarlet. They're desperate, and they don't know what they're doing." I paused to blow my nose in my damp shirt. "I'm not the same guy you served alongside, Scarlet… and, I hate to say it, but losing *you* was the straw that broke the scabrous's back." I stared up at the murky sky. "I guess you could say that I've learned the price of irrational optimism, by now. Now, I know better than to blindly believe that good always prevails over evil. Like, I don't know if the System's diffusion team is going to succeed, but I'm scared they will. Really scared. Because they have Fair on their side." I swallowed. "Scarlet, she was your best friend. Your right hand. I know everyone thinks that it's impossible to communicate with your aura, but if you can hear me right now, I beg you to appear to Fair in a vision or dream or whatever it's called and convince her to stop. Because, I can't change her mind. I talked to her and got nowhere. I never get anywhere, with anything, no matter how hard I try—it took me the entirety of my adult life thus far to accept that. Yet, if I could, Scarlet, I'd do anything, just for you. I'd give my life, to make all your dreams come true. At the very least, I wish that I could stand at the top of a mountain and scream loud enough for the whole earth to hear, but it seems like no one has ears, anymore. If I could, I'd write everything down, Scarlet, your whole story, for the world to read. You and Cease Lechatelierite and the son you were supposed to have and the international war and the Red Revolutions and the World Revolt—everything. I'd make everyone see it all, clearly. Your motives. What you tried to do. How humanity misinterpreted it. Where it went wrong and why. What can be done to make things right again. But, Scarlet, you may think I have a 'way with words,' but I still can't tell *this* story, because I don't know enough to do it justice. We've been through a lot together, but I can't speak for you. I doubt anyone could." I clambered to my feet, trembling a little. "Whatever you do, don't let go of the spectral web. Warning you about Fair is the only help I can give you anymore, because I'm done with all this. I hate to turn my back on you like the rest, but I quit being a hero, long ago. It's my first time visiting you, Scarlet, but it's also my last. I don't expect to ever return to this island. Sorry."

I took a few steps… then, turned right around.

"One more thing," I said to the red paint. "I never told you this outright when you were alive, but I think you were able to tell, anyway: I loved you, Scarlet. I still do. You *and* your son."

With that, I left the graveyard without looking back.

AMBREK COPPERTUS

Conflagria didn't have room for me anymore, that much was certain. I was the most despised and hunted man in all the land. The Reds hated me for betraying their trust and killing their beloved leader, while the System hated me for unleashing the Multi-Source Enchant's aura upon the spectral web.

Not that belonging to either camp got you anywhere, these days—both sides could hardly accomplish a damn thing. The island was far from polarized, anyway; the masses weren't neatly divided between Reds and System-supporters, anymore. There were plenty who seemed to change their minds constantly, picking sides according to what got them more taro on the table, this week. There were many who knew full well what they believed but could hardly stand to stand for it anymore, because of what it cost. There were those who were so sick of it all, they just wanted out, yet had no choice but to keep on breathing, at least for now. There were some like Fair Gabardine, who wreaked serious havoc no matter where they went or what they did, because they were the tragic combination of brilliant, powerful, troubled and confused. And, then, there were the apathetic and amoral ones who didn't give a dragon turd for Conflagria's future, as long as they could spend the rest of their days far away from everything and everyone political, burying their heads in the sand like baby scabrouses. These 'neutrals' were the Sand Dune Gypsies. When I had nowhere to go, they took me in and allowed me to blend into the background, uninterested in my identity and past, simply endeavoring to make use of my survival skills and strength, for the greater benefit of the tribe.

Since Scarlet's death, as I hid out in the Dunes, I slowly came to see the errors of my ways. With time, I went from regretting how my beliefs and actions had to hurt Scarlet… to actually regretting having served the System, in the first place. This change of heart didn't happen easily or overnight; it was the product of a series of visions that Scarlet's aura delivered to my mind through the spectrum, over the course of several ages. She gave me memories—hers, Cease Lechatelierite's, and that of a handful of other mages and Nordics who were touched by the wars. They were powerful, eclectic stories. They were striking enough to make the truth abundantly clear, even to someone as screwed-up as me.

But, the moment I decided that I was fully and firmly persuaded beyond a shadow of a doubt—roughly an age ago—the visions abruptly ceased. Apparently, once I'd learned my lesson, Scarlet no longer felt the need to speak with me, at all. Her work was done. On one hand, I was relieved that I could actually sleep at night without being haunted—typically, the dreams she gave me were far from pleasant, especially since many involved my betrayal of her. But, on the other hand, I was sad that I no longer got to communicate with her aura. I missed her.

Someday, I wanted to find Scarlet's son and tell him everything. I remembered the hatred that I thought I saw in the baby's uncanny eyes, when he looked at me for the first time. The very memory made me shiver. Having Scarlet's forgiveness wasn't enough for me, anymore; I needed it from her child, too. One day. Only then, would I truly be free.

NURTIC LEAVESLEFT

May thirty-first.

"Lunchtime!" I called. Apparently, those were the magic words around here; the kids immediately flocked over.

Having just returned from Conflagria, I kept busy by working at the church orphanage and flying for NurroAir and Frost's Delivery Service. Today was my first day at the institute. The last time I interacted with young children was during my brief stint as a second-grade teacher's assistant at Vitaville's 'K-12,' when I was twenty. But, the two groups of kids couldn't be more different. At the public school, the vast majority of my students were from middle-class nuclear families. For the most part, they had parents who loved them, siblings who played with them, hot meals every evening and warm beds each night. Their concerns revolved around who dressed better and whose toys were nicer. But, here, no one had the luxury of fretting over fashion or possessions. These boys and girls only worried about their bellies.

The facility was horribly under-funded and understaffed. Currently, there were forty residents, ranging in age from four to eleven. Today, I was in charge of half of them. Which meant that I now had one pot of soup and two loaves of bread, to divide twenty ways. Two slices apiece would have to do. Once I was done serving, however, I found leftovers at the bottom of one of the bags. Did I miscalculate, or was someone missing? Uh oh, did I lose a kid in my first hour on the job?

"It ain't fair that we got the same amount when I'm so much bigger!" the shout of a ten-age-old boy wrenched me from my thoughts. He glared at a toddler who looked about ready to wet her frayed skirt. With a single swipe, he knocked her bowl to the floor.

In a flash, I darted over. "What's going on, here?" I demanded.

The boy turned, regarding me with scared eyes. Apparently, he was only brave when picking on little girls.

"N-nothing," he sputtered, gaze dropping to his ratty shoes. "I-I'm sorry; I'll wipe it up. And, she can have mine."

I was surprised by how quickly he stood down. I guessed that my nearly-seven-foot stature may've had something to do with that.

"What's your name?" I asked him, voice softer.

"Acroph," he answered. "I'll go get some paper towels, now." And, with that, he scurried off.

"Is that my portion?" came a snarl from behind.

Startled, I turned and saw what must've been the twentieth kid of the pack. He looked not a day older than five. The door behind him was wide open. I blinked. How did he manage to come in and walk *right* up to me, without my noticing? Ex-divers weren't exactly easy to sneak-up on.

He gave me an acidic stare, scrawny arms folded tightly across his bony chest. His fierce grey-green eyes were far too large for his pointy face, and his ruddy skin was stretched tight across his high cheekbones and sharp jaw. His delicate features were overwhelmed by a great mop of greasy mud-brown hair that looked like it hadn't been washed in months. His shirt was sweat-soaked, yet his arms were well-goosebumped. His jeans were torn, revealing a fresh knee scrape. Scars decorated his arms and cheeks.

I smelled trouble.

"Nice of you to show up for lunch, after all," I said, mildly. "Unsupervised outdoor playtime isn't allowed. From now on, make sure you wait until we're ready to go as a group."

"From now on, make sure you pour the soup properly," the child responded, his tone a perfect mockery of my own. It was flabbergasting that someone so young could have such refined vocal control. "The container's got one-hundred-twenty ounces. There's twenty of us, which means that we each get six."

I froze. The pot was on the counter, far too high for him to see inside. How did he know that it was empty?

Moreover, who taught him to multiply and divide?

"How old are you?" I asked, curiosity getting the better of me.

He cocked his angular chin. "Seven."

He was older than he looked. But, still.

"How'd you know that there's no soup left?"

"So, I'm right," he growled. "You didn't leave any for me. Bastard."

"Watch your tongue," I warned, "and answer my question. Were you guessing?"

"No, I can just tell by looking at everyone else's bowls. They're too full."

What? He could tell that there was an extra *third* of an ounce, in each of the other nineteen bowls?

"What's your name?" I asked, grabbing my clipboard.

"Ence."

I could easily and instantly spot him on the long roster... because he was the only one without a surname. Huh?

"Are you going to quit gaping and get me some lunch, already?" His foot stomped.

"First, we need to clean off that new blister of yours." It looked awful. For heaven's sake, most children his age would've been bawling from the pain, right about now.

"No, I'm *eating* first. And, in case you're wondering: no, it doesn't hurt. Not much, anyway. I'm tough for my age."

What was he, a mind-reader? "Well, sit down, then," I resigned, figuring that he wouldn't cooperate until he had at least a couple bites in him. I was no stranger to the pangs of starvation and the desperation it could stir. "We have bread left."

"You better save some soup, next time."

"No, you better *be* here when I'm serving it, next time."

"Or else, what? You don't know how things work, around here. I *always* get what I want."

He approached the table. But, instead of sitting in the one empty seat, he walked up to the largest boy in the group.

"Give me your soup, Ckipno," Ence ordered, voice sharp and convicting.

And, this, ladies and gentlemen, was the big kid's cue to beat the snot out of the nervy little twerp. But, to my surprise, no violence ensued. Not even a word of opposition was spoken. Ckipno, quickly and quietly, handed Ence his bowl.

What in the world?

"I'm full," Ence announced, after maybe three bites of bread and two gulps of soup. For all his fierce insistence to get 'enough' food, he sure had a tiny appetite.

"Can I have the rest back, then?" Ckipno pleaded. "I mean, only if you're not going to eat it?"

With a malicious grin, Ence stood and dumped the remainder of his meal on Ckipno's head. Now, I was positive that Ence was going to get a beat-down. But, Ckipno just sat there for a moment, blinking the sludge from his eyes, before quietly heading for the bathroom. As he left, I noticed that his right hand had only four fingers.

"On your feet, now," I shot at Ence. "Get up and clean the mess you made. And, when Ckipno comes back, you're apologizing to him."

"I don't apologize to *anyone*," Ence roared.

"We hardly have enough food, as it is. To waste it like this is—"

"I don't care. I wasn't even hungry, to begin with."

"But, *you* aren't the only one here. Show some consideration." I paused. This was getting weirder by the second. "Why did you ask for his soup if you weren't hungry?" I couldn't help but croak.

"Because I can."

Incredible. I was only beginning to understand the group's self-established hierarchy. Somehow, this little boy managed to work himself up to the top of it. How?

No. Considering Ence's size and age, that was hardly likely. Just because he had control over *one* child didn't mean that he was the leader of the entire pack. There was probably something special about Ence and Ckipno's relationship that I didn't yet know about. A debt to repay, perhaps. Yes, that had to be it.

Ugh, what was I doing? Analyzing these kids and ranking them, like they were my soldiers! My job here wasn't to hunt for leadership ability and bolster a chain-of-command. My job was to *dismantle* their ridiculous bullying system to help forge a safe environment for everyone.

Once mealtime was over, my group joined the other twenty for outdoor playtime, freeing me to tend to Ence's scrape. But, instead of following me to the bathroom when I asked him to, Ence chose to sprint right past it, diving into an adjoining hallway.

"Get back here, right now!" I called after him. Suddenly, my calves felt a powerful kick. I spun around.

It was Ence.

How did he get there!?

"Ence!"

He ran behind me and leapt onto my back. I had a hunch that it wasn't a piggy-back-ride he was after. I hesitated. I couldn't get physical with a seven-age-old. Using a little force with six-age-old Comat Acci was different—he was an Ichthyothian soldier, unafraid to wield his dangerous training in hand-to-hand combat. But, Ence wasn't military. Ence was a young boy at an orphanage. A troubled civilian boy.

Wrapping both his arms around my throat, he leveraged his weight to throttle me. His legs thrashed wildly, kicking my lower back and side until I actually felt a little bit of vomit creep up my esophagus. And, then, he leaned in and bit my neck, like a snake. Hard.

I wouldn't dare strike him, but I sure had the right to protect myself. Ence may've been a seven-age-old civilian, but he was still—I couldn't believe it—apparently capable of inflicting real harm. I took hold of his arms and began carefully prying them off. His grasp was unbelievably strong. Suddenly, he let go on his own volition and swung backward like a gymnast, head hanging between my legs. And, he turned and bit my thigh, through my jeans. With my left hand, I unwound his legs from around me, but instead of falling to the floor in a heap, Ence flipped over and landed on his feet, catlike.

His silver-jade eyes were triumphant. He spat out a wad of denim and flesh, on the carpet. And, he smiled.

Holy crap, this kid was freaking crazy.

Then, to make matters spookier, his grin turned to chuckles. I didn't know what to do. I'd never dealt with such violence from someone so young, before. Even Comat Acci had some self-restraint. Comat had a sort of professionalism about him; he knew when to stop. He never drew blood.

But, Ence did. And, laughed about it.

"Come on, Nurtic," he said, though he wasn't even around when I introduced myself, "why do you think Ckipno gave me his soup, when I demanded it?"

My pulse quickened. "Why?"

"Look closely at his right hand, next time."

No way. "You *tore* his *finger* off?"

"Good job; you're the first to figure it out." Ence winked. "Nobody else knows. I made him tell everyone that he closed a door on it. I warned him that I'd take another off, if he ever spills the truth. That goes for you, too." He touched my knuckles. "You're lefty, though, correct? I could tell, from the way you fight."

I snapped my hand away from him, heart hammering in the region of my Adam's apple. Ence was dangerous. Criminal. He didn't belong at an orphanage, he belonged in a juvenile correctional facility. He was a loose cannon in need of personal thirty-six-hour surveillance.

"Get in the bathroom, now," I ordered, intensely relieved when he actually obeyed. I exhaled through my nostrils.

Our struggle hardly lasted a minute, yet Ence was still able to detect something as subtle as my favoring a particular side of my body. I was stunned… and impressed. He had the eyes and instincts of a soldier.

Ugh, there I went again, evaluating potential military prowess! I really needed to stop doing that. Ence's scary behavior wasn't supposed to wow anyone.

But, there was no denying that the boy was exceptionally bright. And, he knew it. He relished the power it gave him. He enjoyed watching everyone bend to his will. He didn't take Ckipno's food because he wanted to eat it, but because he enjoyed watching the kid squirm. I supposed, in a place like this, someone as quick-witted as Ence felt like he had nothing better to do with himself. It was tragic, how his intelligence was being ignored here, wasted, allowed to run amok. He needed rehabilitation and direction. His energy and brilliance needed to be channeled constructively, into something other than terrorizing and manipulating.

In conclusion, Ence needed to be adopted. Of course, all of these children needed and deserved that, but Ence's situation seemed like an emergency to me. Right now, he was on track toward a future of violence and crime, and the longer he went without help, the tougher it'd undoubtedly become, to reverse that transformation. Sooner than later, Ence needed a home where he'd receive the attention he desperately craved, so he wouldn't feel compelled to do terrible things just to feel special and get noticed. He needed love to mellow him out and make him content. And, instead of the low-budget, multi-generational large-group tutoring that the orphanage provided, he needed to be sent to good schools that'd challenge him and foster his genius, so he wouldn't resort to creative torture to exercise his restless mind and body.

Anyway, the first-aid kit was kept in a storage closet, one door down from the bathroom. In seconds, I grabbed it, stepped back into the hall… and abruptly stumbled to the floor. I was nonplused; I hardly ever tripped. My military training made me too vigilant to get surprised by benign things like carpet bumps or uneven tiles.

I got up and entered the bathroom. Ence was sitting on the sink like a statue, awaiting me like a good little boy.

Uh oh.

As if on cue, he whipped out a bottle of antiseptic from nowhere and squirted me in the face. Miraculously, I managed to close my eyes in the nick of time. So, instead of blinding me, the chemical only stung my lashes. Lids still scrunched, I turned on the faucet and ducked my head beneath the spout, to the sound of Ence's gleeful chortles.

I snapped the water off, wiped my face in my shirt and snatched the bottle from Ence's hands.

"Funny prank, wasn't it?" he cheerily asked.

"You could've blinded me. I think this surpassed the level of 'prank.'"

Where did he even get the bottle, in the first place? I had the first-aid kit!

But, when I opened it, I found the contents loose, like something was missing. The antiseptic, of course. How did he do it? *When* did he do it?

While I cleaned his wound, he stayed quiet and still. Any other kid would've yelped from the burn.

"Where and when did you get the bottle?" I demanded, after a full minute of silence.

"I dunno."

"Yes, you do."

He shrugged, a satisfied smile creeping across his face. "I got it out of the kit, right before you reached the closet. I'm quicker than you. I'm quicker than most people."

So, in a matter of seconds, he managed to open the closet, retrieve the kit, remove the antiseptic, close the kit, put it back in the closet, head for the bathroom, and hop onto the vanity... without my noticing. That wouldn't just require superhuman speed, but total invisibility. Ence was obviously lying.

I was about to bandage up his knee when I noticed that his cut was now barely more than a scratch. I stared. I knew that kids healed relatively fast and all, but... what on earth?

"So, what were you doing outside, anyway?" I asked. A big wrap wasn't necessary anymore—a little band-aid would do the trick.

Ence kicked me in the gut, knocking the kit and all its contents to the floor. For heaven's sake, I hadn't been taken by surprise so many times in one afternoon since my diver days. I wasn't sure how to respond, anymore.

"That," he said. "That's what I did outside."

I slowly found my vocal cords: "What? Kicking?"

He nodded. "Loads of people on the streets love a good brawl. Homeless bozos, high-schoolers skipping class, even gang-members, if I'm lucky. I don't like the drunks, though. They're too easy."

This scrawny seven-age-old picked fights with random city-folk for fun? Normally, I wouldn't have believed it for a moment, but Ence had already rapidly proved that he was the absolute farthest thing from normal.

"Don't you *ever* do that, again," I breathed, hollowly. "You're playing with fire."

His enormous eyes rolled. "Come on. I've gone out at least a couple times a week, since I was five."

"You have?"

I was flabbergasted. Apparently, stealing soup from big kids wasn't enough of a thrill for Ence. He was practically begging to be killed. No wonder he had so many scars, all over his body.

Not only was he banged and bruised, he was dirty. Positively covered in filth. Especially his hair. I couldn't even tell what color it was supposed to be, so much it was caked in grime.

"Ence, when was the last time you showered?" I asked, rolling his pant leg back down.

He hopped off the sink, landing on my left foot.

"Bath-time's the best time to sneak out."

And, with that, he smirked and took off down the hall.

NURTIC LEAVESLEFT

It was a beautiful June afternoon. Sunny and seventy-two degrees. After lunch, I took the kids outside for recess, in the field behind the building. We didn't have a playground with swings or slides, but we did have a small grassy area and some tennis balls, basketballs, hula-hoops and jump-ropes.

They engaged in various games of tag, catch, duck-duck-goose, foursquare and the like. I watched Ence as he played with the other children. Apparently, his authority didn't just extend over Ckipno; he was the leader of the whole pack. The others *always* obeyed him, no matter what. Why? It made sense that Ckipno would fear Ence, considering their special history. But, what about the others? Did Ence do something horrible to *each* of them? I shuddered at the thought.

As recess wore on, I could see that Ence had more than just their fear. He had their respect. They seemed to admire him. They were in awe of him. They voluntarily sought him out, asking what they should do next. They craved his guidance. They *wanted* to subordinate themselves to him. And, Ence was happy to oblige. He gave commands in a frighteningly-authoritative voice, tenor bizarrely compelling and magnetic.

When Ce Repla, a fellow staff member, took Ence for a bathroom break, I decided to do a little prying, against my better judgement. I asked the children why they followed Ence.

They stared back at me, confused.

"What do you mean?" asked a blonde eight-age-old. She was incredulous, as though I'd posed an outrageous rhetorical question. Her tone seemed to say: why *wouldn't* we?

"Well, why's he always the leader of all your games?"

"Because he knows what to do," answered a ten-age-old.

I blinked. "But, doesn't anyone else?"

"Not as good as him."

"So, you do what he says because he's smart?"

Everyone exchanged confused looks. Apparently, I was challenging the way things were *supposed* to be. Ence was *meant* to be charge; that was simply the way it worked, around here. Human beings—children in particular—were creatures of habit, and my questions were forcing these kids to consider what appeared to be a deep-seated unspoken rule.

"Well, not only that," another boy said, "but, it's just… better to be on his side."

Those chilling words were met with widespread nods and murmurs.

"You're afraid of him," I commented.

There was a heavy pause.

"Well," the blonde girl piped, "it's more like… if he thinks you're good at something, you must be *really* good at it."

"He's a judge," I offered.

She chewed her lip. "Sorta. You care what he thinks of you because… he just knows, you know?"

The others were nodding, again. Incredible. So, Ence was a born commander. Ugh, no, not a born *commander*—this wasn't the military. In the civilian world, the proper word was 'leader.' Ence was a born *leader*.

"You want him to approve of you," I suggested.

"Yeah, kinda. But… different. More."

More. "You want him to love you."

At this, they all had a good laugh.

"Naw, Ence loves *nobody*," Ckipno chimed. "He doesn't even *like* people. He can hate, though. And, when he hates you, you don't want to exist no more."

Ence returned at that moment and, from his narrowed eyes and furrowed brows, clearly suspected that he was being talked about. Immediately, everyone zipped back to their activities, trying their best to seem inconspicuous.

Goodness, he had such power over them. The degree of control he had was scary.

In that freakishly-convicting voice of his, he now ordered the kids nearest to him to join him for a round of foursquare. Of course, they dropped whatever they were doing and scurried over.

One interesting thing I noticed, as I watched Ence move about, was how very… *uncomfortable* he looked, all the time. He was always agitated, sweating, fanning himself. One would think it were ninety degrees out today, not seventy. Stranger still, he paradoxically kept sneezing, shivering and rubbing his well-goosebumped arms. Was he hot or cold?

Everybody played nicely for about ten more minutes… until the backwall hose found its way into the kids' hands. One boy aimed it at Ence, giggling and squealing. In a single second, Ence lunged at him, wrenched it from his grip, got him in a headlock and pointed the spout right at his ear. In a flash, Ce and I seized the hose and tore the two children apart, but it was too late; the damage was done. Ence's victim had to be rushed to the hospital.

After dinner, I pulled Ence aside, but no matter what I said or did, he wouldn't engage. He didn't even yell or get violent. He just sat there and stared at the wall, deadpan gaze transfixed. I looked helplessly into his acidic unblinking eyes, into their fiery silver-green lucidity, desperate to see some humanity in them.

Ence didn't speak a word for the rest of the evening. And, he wasn't around when everyone hit the showers, though I swore I never saw him leave.

ENCE

I saw everything. I mean, everything. I saw the ladybug on the wall across the hall right now, how many spots it had on each wing. Three on the left, two on the right. I saw every little movement within a thousand-yard radius, all the time; I was able to just sense it, detect it. I could hardly sleep because of it. All night, every night, I lay awake, seeing, watching, waiting. For what, I didn't know. I saw in the dark like it was day. I liked to watch the others sleep—their motions, how often they tossed and turned, if they ever mouthed anything, whimpered, whispered, cried, shook. I thought about what these behaviors meant and how I could use that intel against them if the need aroused, which it usually did at some point. Kati always sucked the corner of her blanket while she slept. I wondered how many shreds I could tear that blanket into, just to see how she'd react. She'd cry. Yeah, she'd bawl like a baby. But, I couldn't just destroy it for no reason. I had to save this info for future reference. Store it in my mental arsenal. Who knew when I might need it, to get something from her. Maybe, I could use it to figure out what everyone was talking about yesterday when I came from the bathroom and saw them all huddled in the field. I knew they were talking about me. Why? It was Nurtic's fault; he was trying to incite everyone against me. I knew he was. He was threatening my place here, trying to usurp me. Why? Who gave that bastard the right to do that? I mean, he just came around one day, completely new, and tried to be the boss of everybody. I hated him. Hated him. Hated. Him. I wanted to do to him what I did to those random guys on the streets. When I attacked, those guys sometimes retaliated by holding me upside-down, or kicking me around, or trying to do stuff to my crotch, but I always outmaneuvered them in the end. They were bigger than me but I was faster and smarter than them. I was faster and smarter than most people. But, Nurtic obviously thought that he was smarter than me. Well, I didn't think so, but I had to admit that he had some serious reflexes and he sure knew how to fight. I liked to attack him just to see how he'd defend himself, so I could learn his moves. Because I didn't just see everything, I *remembered* everything. I was able to replay stuff in my mind as many times as I wanted, like a movie. So, I kept a record of all Nurtic's actions. I watched everybody, of course, but especially him. And, I was learning quick. I'd be able to outmaneuver him soon, if he kept showing me everything. He was so stupid to show me stuff, they all were. They thought I couldn't see, but I saw *everything*. But, just like I was always watching Nurtic, he always seemed to have an eye on me. Always. Why? What did he want? He clearly wanted something from me, something more than just to dethrone me, and I had to figure out what that was. I was in danger until I found out. I had to know what everybody was thinking, all the time, especially about me. I was usually able to discern it, just from watching people's behavior and listening to their words. Like, when I went to court a couple ages ago, threatened with juvenile detention for the whole 'stove' incident, I was able to determine what the judge wanted to hear just from watching him, just from listening to the questions he asked and figuring out what they *really* meant. And, then, I said it, exactly what he wanted to hear, and got the reaction I was after. Innocent. It was all an accident, of course. But, Nurtic was difficult to understand, more difficult than everybody else. Why did he ask so many questions? I still didn't know all his motives, and I couldn't stand the fact that I didn't know. I was supposed to know. I was supposed to know everything. I answered some of his inquiries, because it got him scared. I could tell, even he was sometimes afraid of me. Even Mr. War Hero Pilot Wonder Boy. Good. That was the way things were meant to be. Because, I never stopped. I couldn't be stopped. Even when I got hurt, I didn't stop. Like, whenever I got a scrape, the blood went away, real fast. Sometimes, it went away in seconds—so much faster than anybody else. Sometimes, I slashed myself on purpose, just so I could watch the cut almost instantly scab up and heal, right before my eyes. I didn't mind the pain; it was fun, actually. Pain was fun when I wanted it to come, when I knew it was coming. Like, when I went downtown. I was always looking for it, then. But, when I didn't want it, it wasn't fun. Like when Nurtic swabbed my wound one too many times with the hydrogen peroxide stuff. That wasn't right. He was going to pay for that. And, I didn't like that I constantly felt some measure of pain, just from the environment. I couldn't stand the weather, especially at this time of age. Everyone was always like, 'OOOH, WHAT A BEAUTIFUL DAY!' whenever it was in the sixties and seventies, but I couldn't stand it, I just couldn't *stand* it. To me, it felt like hot... cold... hot... cold... hot... cold... hot—cold—hot—cold—hot—cold—hotcoldhotcoldhotcold hotcoldhotcold—HOTCOLDHOTCOLDHOTCOLD! And, I wanted to scream and tear out my sweat glands and my goosebumps and my hair. I felt waves of that pain, even right now. It bothered me, almost continually. The only times it stopped was in the middle of summer, during those weeks where it got so hot that everyone else was dehydrating and passing out, or those few days in the winter when it snowed and everyone scurried inside like scared puppies. I *liked* those days—*those* were the days I wanted to go out and play—but no, everyone *else* was uncomfortable unless the weather was so-called 'moderate,' so we had to stay indoors, we all had to stay in the seventy-degree room, relaxing and having fun while Ence suffered, while Ence sneezed and shivered and perspired and wanted to die. I said I wanted to go out, I *needed* to go out, but they all looked at me like I was crazy and said I was just being difficult, but they didn't *understand.* I was different than them and I didn't know why. I was different in lots of ways. Like, people always thought that I was really quick, always saying stuff like, 'Ence, where did you go? How did you get there, Ence?' Sometimes, I walked right by people and they looked directly at me, almost *through* me, then claimed that they didn't have any idea where I was. It was like, whenever I didn't want to be seen, they just... didn't see me. Like, I could make myself invisible, whenever I wanted. I wanted to get the antiseptic from the first-aid kit before Nurtic did, so I walked right past him and took it out without him seeing. Then, I decided to try something else, too—I sat down and stuck out my leg and tripped him, yeah, he fell real hard, so hard that I had to stop myself from laughing out loud and blowing my cover. I loved using my unusual abilities to my advantage. Sometimes, though, I hated being different. Like when my differences hurt. Sometimes, my eyes felt like they were burning up. I could just be sitting there or running around or sleeping or doing whatever when they'd suddenly start pulsating in their sockets and stinging like acid. Sometimes, when I concentrated real hard, I was able to will the pain away. I liked that, I liked being in control. But, other times—most of the time—I didn't know how to stop the burn or control the surging heat, and it shot through my body like all of me was on fire, especially my eyes, throat and scalp. It made me want to scream, scream, SCREAM, but I usually held it in. Yet, sometimes, it got so bad, I had no choice but to scream. Which frightened everybody a whole lot. They all said that I had a really loud and powerful voice. They said that my voice scared them bad. Good, let them be terrified. Let them try to feel even a sliver of the agony that I always did; I didn't care if they thought I was crazy, because maybe I was. But, no, I didn't want anyone's help. Especially Nurtic's.

NURTIC LEAVESLEFT

Ence had rather unusual hair. I always thought that it was a mousy shade, but apparently it was only the build-up of filth that ever made it appear that way. Since getting hosed during recess last week, its real color got more exposed. Or, should I say, color*s*, plural. Some locks were velvet-red, from root to tip. The rest was deep brown, almost black. From a distance, his hair gave the impression of being auburn. It was almost… iridescent. And, its texture was also quite odd. No longer matted down, it was wiry, stiff and stubbornly messy. In direct sunlight, it was shiny as a mirror. It seemed to have a life of its own, swishing and bouncing with Ence's every motion.

With his grey-green eyes, red-black hair, ruddy face, angular features and precautious countenance, Ence was definitely the most noticeable boy at the orphanage. Whenever prospective parents came around, they were quick to spot him.

Then, dismiss him.

Ence's roughneck attitude might've served him well if he were a street urchin, fighting to survive on his own. But, at an orphanage, his nasty behavior shot him to the bottom of the totem-pole; no one wanted to adopt him. Most prospectives didn't take the time to notice his intelligence, strength or potential. They just took one look at his angry scowl, wrote him off as a troublemaker, then moved onto the next possibility.

Not that I could totally blame them. They were looking for a child to raise, not a wild animal to tame.

And, Ence sure wasn't helping himself. He seemed *extra* belligerent whenever we had visitors. He'd shout and run around and break things, broadcasting every unruly facet of his character. Ence may've been one of the smallest kids in the pack, but he certainly wasn't the youngest; I was starting to think that the only way he'd ever get adopted before reaching adulthood would be if visitors dropped by while he was asleep. Not that he slept much, in the first place—I spotted him lying awake on many an occasion.

"He's energetic," I once told a middle-aged couple, feeling like a used-flivver-salesman or a pound worker. "Amazing athleticism."

"Is it athleticism or aggressiveness?" the wife jeered, turning her back on me.

It was low, the way we had to practically sell these kids, listing their traits like features of a sports-flivver. For heaven's sake, they were *children*, not merchandise. Children could grow, learn, change. Children responded to their environments, reflecting the love and attention that they received. Children weren't fixed entities with permanent, inalterable qualities. Ence may've been volatile *now*, but he didn't always have to be. He needed nurturing and a second chance.

Today was the third time this summer alone that prospective parents came around. And, the moment the first couple entered the building, Ence threw himself to the floor and started shouting at the top of his lungs, like a thousand revving jet engines. I'd never heard anyone—neither child nor adult—yell so loudly.

Hastily, I pulled him to his feet, ushering him out into the hallway.

"What do you want?" he cried, rubbing his bloodshot eyes.

"I was about to ask *you* that." I knelt so we were face-to-face. "If you keep throwing temper tantrums every time we have visitors, you'll never get to go to a good home. Don't you *want* to get out of here?"

"Yes, of course," he moaned.

"Then, what's the matter?"

"My eyes!" he hollered, scrunching them shut. "They're burning, oh, they're burning; I can't stand it!" And, he screamed yet again, emitting a blood-curling shriek that sent shivers through my whole body.

"What's going on, here?" came a voice from behind. I turned. It was Neg Selepoh, the orphanage manager. "It sounds like someone's being murdered. You're not creating a very welcome ambiance for our guests." His arms folded. "Either cut it out or take it outside." And, with that, he turned and stalked away.

Ence darted for the nearest exit; apparently, he decided to take Selepoh's suggestion literally. Tailing him, I scooped him up and turned right around. Of course, he flailed like a baby scabrous, inverting in my arms. When he flipped over, something slipped out from under his shirt, dangling from his neck. It was a little silver medal, suspended on a black-and-blue ribbon.

A Silver Triangle. I stared. I had one myself, stowed in my viola case.

I carried Ence inside, where everyone gave us disdainful looks. The second I set him on his feet, he tucked the medal back under his clothes, protectiveness in his lime-slice stare. My mind spun like a propeller. How on earth did Ence get his hands on a Silver Triangle? Did he steal it? From who? Where? High military honors weren't exactly common. Then again, maybe, he didn't take it directly from its original owner. Maybe, he got it from one of the interesting characters he consorted with on the streets.

Or, maybe, it belonged to one of Ence's biological parents, a soldier who got killed in the war. The problem with *that* theory was that Ence didn't even have a documented last name, which meant that he couldn't possibly be the son of a renowned vet. Could he?

The moment I got home in the evening, I snatched a cup of plain yogurt from the fridge—my dinner—and zipped to my laptop to do some prowling. But, before I could open a web browser, an instant-messenger window popped up:

> LinkX2: boo!
>
> Automated response from Born2Fly: I am away from my computer right now.

I stared at the screenname, slowly pulling my spoon from my mouth. It was unfamiliar—not in my contacts—but, I knew that there was only one person it could possibly belong to. Link times two. Linkeree Link.

I thought it odd that Ree would choose a screenname that capitalized on the redundancy of her real name—something she hated. I changed my status from 'away' to 'available.'

> Born2Fly: hey ree! Long time no talk. didn't know u had IM?

Throughout high school and college, Ree always refused to use messenger apps and social media, despite the urging of all her friends. She said that she considered such things as time-wasting distractions.

> LinkX2: i didnt till now
>
> Born2Fly: what made u finally cave?

For the next several minutes, the words '*LinkX2 is typing*' intermittently flashed at the bottom of the window. Just how long of an explanation was she writing?

LinkX2: did u disconnect ur # & change ur email?

And, that was it. She took all that time to come up with one short sentence. Since when was Ree so intimidated by *me?*

Born2Fly: yes, sorry ☹ i couldn't really afford both net & phone so i had 2 pick. church lends me a satellite cell whenever i travel anyway. as for the email and sn, i dunno, just felt like time 4 change

LinkX2: well when ur emails bounced & ur # didnt work, i joined messenger 2 find u. i had a very awkward convo w/ a random 'LeftyLeaf' i thought was u, LOL

Born2Fly: lol, yipes

LinkX2: then i called ur church. it took some prodding but some1 from aviation ministry finally agreed 2 pass along ur info

I was surprised by the lengths that Ree went just to get in touch with me. Suddenly, I felt intensely guilty for leaving her in the dark, neglecting to tell her that I'd disconnected my phone, changed my email address and got a new screenname. I'd completely forgotten about her.

Born2Fly: that seems like lots of trouble 2 go thru

LinkX2: its ok, worth it 2 talk 2 u

Born2Fly: im really sorry ree ☹

How empty those typed words looked. How pathetic that emoticon seemed. For a moment, I wished I had a phone again, just so I could call her and apologize with my own voice.

Then again, I didn't really have time for a chat—no matter the media—right now. It was getting late and I had an early delivery to Glass City, Ichthyosis, in the morning. I needed to finish what I came online to do, so I could go to bed.

LinkX2: its ok. im not mad or anything

I opened my web browser, where I searched for the names of every Nurian Silver Triangle recipient.

There was only one. Me.

LinkX2: u there?

I minimized the messenger window. I knew I was the *first* Nurian to receive a Silver Triangle, but I didn't think I was the *only* one. Did Ence's medal belong to an Ichthyothian, then? I broadened my search to include all recipients:

Captain Terminus Expiri Lechatelierite
Admiral Oppre Is Sive
Commodore Rettahs Krad Slous
Colonel Autoero Augustus Austere, Sr.
Commander Cease Terminus Lechatelierite
Commander Nurtic Ehud Leavesleft

And, that was it. I was stunned.

One by one, I considered each name on the list. I ruled out Terminus Lechatelierite since Finis Lechatelierite was his only offspring, not to mention that the Captain died decades ago, when Finis was little. I eliminated Oppre Sive and Rettahs Slous because neither of those men ever married or had any kids at all. As for Autoero Austere, he had just one—a son around my age who was currently active-duty at Icicle.

That left Commander Cease Lechatelierite. But, I knew all too well what happened to *his* baby.

Ugh, what was I doing? Wasting time. It was obvious that Ence wasn't the child of an honored officer. He didn't even have a *surname*, for heaven's sake. The medal was probably a fake that Ence nicked from some street urchin.

I threw away my empty yogurt container and closed the browser. Behind it, Ree's messenger box awaited.

LinkX2 is away at 35:07:25

LinkX2 returned at 35:20:12

LinkX2: im leaving on my 1st official int'l mission 2morrow & just wanted 2 say bye b4 going

LinkX2: u never told me how ur trip 2 conflagria went

LinkX2: im going 2 the anichian jungle

LinkX2: for @ least 3 mo, prob w/o net access. then im moving to seaview city, nuria, a few hrs from u

LinkX2: ill talk 2 u when i get back k?

LinkX2: k?

LinkX2: nurtic?

LinkX2: respond when u can

LinkX2 is away at 35:25:07

LinkX2 returned at 35:44:23

LinkX2: i miss u

LinkX2 signed off at 35:44:29

I was about to close the window, but instead, I found myself clicking into the text-area.

Born2Fly: miss u 2 ree

LinkX2 is offline

Born2Fly: i know

LinkX2 is offline

I shut my laptop and went to bed.

FAIR GABARDINE

Exhausted from the day, I tossed fitfully in my tarp, drifting in and out of consciousness… until I suddenly got overcome by a swooping sensation, as though falling from a cliff. I flailed and kicked to no avail, until I found myself floating in a dense cloud of darkness.

This was the start of a vision, I realized. Oh, Tincture, was I going to see Cease Lechatelierite again? The thought filled me with dread. I wanted to cry. I wanted to scream. I wanted to vomit.

"Fair, calm down; it's only me," came a small female voice.

I opened my eyes—a strange thing to do when I thought they were already open—and, sure enough, it wasn't Lechatelierite standing before me. It was another phantom from my past, frozen at seventeen. My breath caught in my chest. I tried to flee, but the black clouds held me in place. I couldn't even blink, anymore—my lids were stuck open. I wanted to cover my face with my hands, but my arms abruptly grew heavy as hobnail tails. I was trapped. Trapped in front of the very last person I wanted to see.

"I know why you want to run," she said, tormenting me with her painfully-familiar rosy features and glassy green eyes.

"Please, Scarlet, I can't take this, right now," I whimpered.

"You're one of the most brilliant people I've ever met, Fair, have I told you that?" she whispered. "You're a genius.

And, I'm not just talking about spectroscopy. You're street-smart, too. Cunning. I've always admired you."

"Stop," I gasped. Somehow, her praise wounded me worse than any scathing accusation. I deserved to be cursed, hated, called a traitor. But, no, that wasn't Scarlet's way. Scarlet found worth in even the lowest of people. She loved her enemies.

And, that's what I'd become, since her death. Her enemy.

"It's the truth," she continued. "But, you're allowing your extraordinary mind and talents to be abused. Twisted. Exploited. You've let yourself become a tool—no, a weapon—in the hands of a corrupt tyranny." She took a step forward. "I know you're capable of killing me." Her quiet words pierced my eardrums like hot knives.

"Y–you're already dead," I blubbered.

"You'll figure out how to diffuse my aura sooner or later, I know you will. You're probably the only person who could; with our lingering spectral connection and your exceptional scientific mind, you'll find a way." Her tone suddenly grew desperate as she added, "But, don't go through with it, Fair, please. I beg you."

To my horror, she got to her knees, just as Cease once did when his aura visited me seven ages ago. In an instant, humiliation struck me like a whip of burning hair.

"I loved you, Fair," she spoke to my feet. "I never stopped loving you, even when you sold me out to the System on July twenty-fifth of the eighty-seventh age. Even when I saw you clad in the orange and green of the System Water Forces in July of the ninety-third age. And, yes, even when you wanted my unborn son dead, throughout my entire pregnancy in the ninety-fourth age. Even when you demanded that I kill him. You were my first friend—at times, my only friend. You were there for me when I was condemned at my Circle Trial in the eighty-third age. You fought alongside me during the Red Revolutions and the World Revolt. You were my sister, Fair. My family."

"And, you aren't Scarlet!" I yelled. "You're just a blob of photons, taking on her shape, to manipulate me!"

Her face lifted. "No, Fair, I'm not just a random spectral haze. I'm *her* spectrum, with *her* memories, acting according to *her* will. I'm what you want to diffuse. I'm Scarlet July. And, I'm pleading with you not to murder me."

I couldn't take this, anymore. "S-scarlet," I choked, "Scarlet's aura, or whatever the hell you are, I don't want to hurt you." I shook, head to toe. "I really don't. I-I know I'm being used; you're right. I don't agree with the System today any more than I did back when I was a Red. But, I don't know what else to do. I just want to end the pain. You don't walk these dusty paths, anymore; you can't possibly understand what life has been like here, for the last few ages. If you can believe it, everything is even worse now than when you were around. Far worse." I swallowed, horrible memories washing over me. "Nurtic Leavesleft—remember him? He's part of an aviation ministry, now. In January, he came here with a couple Nurians on a humanitarian mission, and I told him that he might as well pack up his plane and turn right around, because magekind is beyond help. Beyond just needing cute little care-packages of food and medicine. The island needs to be flooded, or burned to the ground, or bombed to pieces, then started over. But, we can't do that. We have no choice but to find a way to fix the mess we're in. And, nothing in our nation's history has ever come close to doing that... except the System. They alone were able to give our people the illusion of happiness and comfort."

"Illusion," Scarlet murmured bitterly to her knees.

"Yes, I'm aware that's all it ever was. An impression. Spectral ecstasy, if you will. But, we're in total despair. I've got to do something, before it's too late."

"The Red Revolution," she breathed, "is something."

"The Red Revolution is all but dead."

"Not if you return to it."

"No." I shook my head. "I'm not who the Reds need. I can't make people follow me to the ends of the earth, the way you could. I can't fill your sandals, Scarlet. I'm a spectroscoper. A scientist. I work with numbers, elements and natural laws—things that are measurable, predictable, quantitative. I can't deal with the erratic, ethereal world of politics and persuasion and rallying people. I can't put my faith in others the way you did, and people sure as hell don't trust me the way they trusted you. You had the gift of inspiring allegiance. More than allegiance. Love. Throughout your Red Revolution, any one of your men was willing, without hesitation, to take an arrow to the heart for you, if need be."

"I obviously wasn't *that* good of a leader if my own sister was so quick to betray, upon my death," Scarlet retorted. "The type of leader that you speak of would've left too great a legacy to fade in a mere handful of ages."

I bit my tongue so hard, it bled. The guilt was overwhelming. My face burned like I was sunbathing in the Fire Pit.

"I–I do still love you, Scarlet," I squeaked like a little girl who just scraped her knee. "When I said your Reds were willing to die for you, I was including myself in that. My love and dedication to you, back then… I don't really know how to describe it, but I'll try. Since you've always been a leader, I wonder if you even know how it feels to *be led* by someone so… so *consuming*. How it feels to have so much faith in another human being that you're ready, at any minute, to throw yourself before a torch for them. To put their word and will before your own. To love them more than family, more than anything and anyone else you ever loved."

Her crimson lashes were dotted with tears. "Yes, Fair," she croaked, "I do know how all that feels. I wasn't always a leader. I was once in someone *else's* army. And, I never dreamt of betraying him, not for a second."

Right. Of course, Scarlet would know exactly what I was talking about, because she was also once willing to follow someone to the bottom of the sea. Except, unlike me, she actually stayed steadfast in her commitment, to the point of death. She was willing to single-handedly raise her beloved's covalent child, in the middle of a war, against all odds. Her life would've been easier—in fact, it probably wouldn't have ended, yet—if she didn't try to keep her son. She gave up everything for Cease Lechatelierite and his legacy.

"Actions speak louder than words, Fair. It's obvious that you aren't as devoted to me as you say. My assassin is now more of an ally to me than you."

At that, I dropped to my knees and cried out like a wounded scabrous.

Mercilessly, she continued: "Our relationship aside, your loyalty to your *nation* should be enough to stop you from using your genius for evil. Regardless of your feelings toward me, you wouldn't work to diffuse my aura if you truly love Conflagria. If you truly love peace."

"But, I *do*," I protested. "That's *why* I'm doing this. I used to believe that you were the one, Scarlet. I used to believe that you fulfilled the prophecy when you bound the spectral web. But, now, as I'm watching Conflagria crumble, I realize that can't be the case. It just can't. Because what you did brought about everything *but* peace."

"That's because my work didn't finish the job, it only started it. Cease and I took Conflagria on its first couple steps, on the long road to peace. By ending the Crystal and binding up the spectral web, we paved the way for the Red Revolution, which *could* ultimately save the island."

"Says who?" I roared. "The Red Revolution never accomplished a damn thing. In all of Conflagrian history, *nothing* has ever brought about any semblance of peace except the System and its spectral direction."

"Spectral *direction?*" Scarlet stood. Now, *I* was the one kneeling before her. "Is that your euphemism for ruthless mind-control?"

"It will end the civil war. It will stop mages from slaughtering each other. Please, let go of the spectral web. Please."

"Why, so you can spare yourself the guilt of knowing that you're slaying your best friend a second time?" she hissed.

"Please, Scarlet, I beg you. For your country."

"No, Fair." Her green eyes reflected disappointment so deep, so striking, I wanted to evaporate on the spot. "You'll have to kill me."

With that, I felt her presence begin to ebb.

"Wait!" She couldn't go—not yet, not like this! "How come you never appeared to me, before now?"

Her grief-filled gaze scoured the top of my head. "I only showed up today because a loyal friend recently bowed before my grave and asked me to—a true friend, with a pure heart, who loves me the way that you falsely claim to. I wouldn't have chosen to visit you, on my own volition." She slowly inhaled. "This is the last time I'll ever appear to you, Fair. I'm sorry it has to end like this."

And, with that, she vanished.

I leapt up, reaching helplessly in the darkness, but it was too late. Overcome once more by the falling sensation, I awoke on the floor beside my overturned tarp, cold and heartbroken and alone.

NURTIC LEAVESLEFT

June twenty-first, seven o'clock.

"Nurtic? What are you doing here?" asked Selepoh, the orphanage manager. I'd been sitting in his office since dawn, awaiting his arrival. I felt a bit anxious because I had a passenger flight to Atlas City in only two hours. "You have the day off." He eyed my NurroAir uniform. "I'd tell you to go enjoy it, but it looks like you have other plans."

I nodded. "I have a flight, later this morning. But, I wanted to speak with you, first."

"Just how many jobs *do* you have?"

"Three. Frost's, NurroAir and here." Because those student loans and inherited debts certainly weren't going to pay for themselves.

"How do you manage that? Do you eat and sleep?"

I shrugged.

"You must really love to fly."

"I do."

He chuckled. "You know, I always wondered why someone like you would go into the Diving Fleet instead of the Air Force."

He was right—under normal circumstances, the Air Force would've been my first choice, my natural inclination. But, my circumstances were far from normal.

"I wanted to serve under Commander Cease Lechatelierite," I answered, simply. "I wanted to meet him and see his genius in action, up close."

"Was it worth it," he somberly asked, "everything you've been through?"

"Oh, yes. Though it certainly left scars," to say the least, "I wouldn't trade my diver days for anything. I only wish I had more time with him, you know?"

His head shook. "No, I really don't. My family used to live in Vitaville, several ages ago; my daughter attended your little assembly at the public 'K-12.' Poor Shelli had nightmares for weeks. You've learned your lesson by now, I hope? You haven't been telling colorful war-stories to my orphans, have you?"

"Oh, no, sir," I assured him. "But, only because they haven't asked."

"It's a good thing I know you're joking. These kids have enough to deal with, as it is. Their imaginations certainly don't need stimulating in that area, if you know what I mean—especially Ence's."

"Speaking of Ence," I jumped on the topic, "he's the reason I came to speak with you, today. I was wondering if I could ask a few questions about him?"

"Sure, I suppose. What's on your mind?"

I chewed my lip. "Well, firstly, I noticed that Ence is the only kid here with neither a surname nor a birthdate listed in his records."

"That's because his parentage and birthday are unknown." His tone seemed to imply: *no duh.*

"But, why? Where did he come from? How did he wind up here? Did he used to live on the streets?"

Selepoh gave a wry chortle. "I understand why he'd give off that impression. But, no, Ence was brought here as an infant."

"So, you *do* know when he was born?"

"Not the exact date." He sipped his coffee. "We estimate late in ninety-four or early in ninety-five."

"So, he's not seven yet."

"Soon. Ence likes to round up."

"Who brought him here? And, from where?"

"Social services brought him from the local hospital."

"So, he was born at the hospital? How come his parentage is unknown, then? I mean, the mother had to have been admitted at some point, right?"

Selepoh took another sip. "I honestly have no idea, Nurtic. My job is to take care of the kids given to me, until they're adopted or grown. That's it."

"The hospital must know *something*. But, before I try to go digging through birth records and such, I need to know if 'Ence' is even his real name, because it sure doesn't sound like one to me. It strikes me as a nickname. Did he arrive here with it? Did the church staff decide to call him that? Who named him?"

Selepoh was starting to get frustrated. "Nurtic, I've seen dozens of children pass through this facility in my lifetime."

"You don't have any idea, at all?" I insisted.

He plunked down his mug. "No, I don't. My speculation is, if not his mother, maybe a social worker named him. We usually don't do that here."

"If he was named *after* leaving the hospital, then my search just got a whole lot tougher," I murmured.

He exhaled through his nostrils. "Why are you so curious about Ence, anyway?"

It was a good question. Why *was* I so invested in Ence? There were around forty children here, each with their own unique talents and abilities. Why was I always watching Ence in particular, hungry to help him out, hoping that he—of all children—would get adopted, as soon as possible? There had to be more to it than the fact that he was the perfectly-tragic hybrid of brilliant and lost. I'd met many brilliant-but-lost people in my life, and I didn't always feel toward them the way I instantly felt about Ence.

"I don't know," I replied, "there's just… something about him. Something familiar, something that draws me to him. It's like I've known him for a while, though we've only just met, of course. And, I'm not sure if you've noticed, but he has an extraordinary mind. Amazing potential."

"Potential? The boy's smart, I'll give you that, but he's also… how do I put this?" Selepoh's fingers drummed the desk. "He's not a good person."

Fury pricked my chest. Ence had anger-management issues, sure. But, it seemed rather inappropriate for the facility owner to talk about one of his own kids, like that. To write Ence off as if the character flaws he had now, at age six, were what he'd inevitably take to his grave.

"Excuse me, sir?" I coldly asked.

Selepoh's face was solemn. "He killed someone, Nurtic. Two ages ago, when he was not yet five."

All the air seeped from my lungs. Selepoh didn't mean that literally, did he? It was just a tactless expression. Hyperbole. Right?

"S-sir?"

"The orphanage almost got shut down, because of what happened. It was a real scandal and we paid a heavy price. But, Ence? He was declared innocent, because he knew how to answer every question thrown at him by all the judges and psychiatrists who got involved. The jury determined that it was all just a tragic accident. But, personally, I was never fully convinced of that."

This was too much. Ence was aggressive, yes, but he was only supposed to be a prankster, a bully. Just a restless, undisciplined, un-nurtured kid with more energy than he knew what to do with. Not a killer.

"H-how did he do it?" I sputtered, pulse pounding like a semi-automatic. "*Who* did he do it to? Was it premeditated? Was it in cold blood?" I was screaming inside.

"I do believe that circumstance played somewhat of a role. So, no, I don't think Ence intended to end a life, that day." Selepoh took a deep breath. "The victim was another boy here, only a couple ages older than him. Timothy Vic was his name. The two of them were alone in the kitchen when I heard raised voices through the wall. So, I came in and found Vic, burning to death, while Ence just stood there, *glowering* at him. Such ferocity in the gaze of a four-age-old… I hadn't thought it possible." His lids scrunched. "How Ence managed to reach the dials up on the gas stove is beyond me. The courts deemed it accidental manslaughter." He opened his eyes, and they were glazed with terror. "But, they didn't see what I saw—the fury and hatred on Ence's face. I don't think that Ence set out to murder someone that morning, but I do believe that he meant to cause serious harm."

I looked away, sick inside. Whether Ence acted on impulse or according to an agenda, the fact of the matter was, at age four, he was capable of killing another human being. Another child. My head rested in my hands.

Fire. My mind couldn't wrap around it. Ence literally burned a kid alive.

In that moment, I realized that Ence did indeed have that deep-set look of one whose naïveté was stolen, far too early in life. It was a look that I was used to seeing only in the mirror and in the stoic stares of my fellow veterans—a look that conveyed a certain weariness of the soul. I saw it in Ence all along, but didn't recognize it for what it was, until now.

Selepoh's hands clasped together. "Psychiatrists, therapists, doctors—nobody has been able to get through to him and instill lasting change. He knows how to answer their questions so that they leave him alone, but he never actually takes any of their words to heart."

I was silent.

"Nurtic, I know you want to help him," he went on, "but, I don't want to see you waste your time or get your hopes up for nothing."

"I'm sorry, sir," I said, harshly, "but, I'm not ready to give up on him. He's six. It's too early to decide what does or doesn't 'work' on him."

Selepoh's bushy brows shot to the rim of his receding hairline. "Look, Nurtic, it isn't your job—or mine—to *save* anyone. Our job is to run this facility until someone comes along, to adopt these kids." His arms folded. "Though, I pity whoever chooses Ence—God have mercy on their souls," he dryly added.

"With all due respect, sir, I completely disagree with you." My voice was low. "I don't think we're just meant to keep these kids alive until they're no longer our responsibility. Right now, we're not their *owners*—like they're pets or real estate or something—we're like their *family*. And, family does more than just keep their members alive. Family nurtures, cares and loves. If you want to call that 'saving,' then fine."

"Nurtic, sacrifice is great and all," he countered, "but, not if it's the only thing you ever do. You've spent your entire life giving, giving, giving, without ever stopping to refill your own well. I look at you and see a young man who's been dealt a rough hand in life, a scarred veteran who's lonely and sad and looking for a new project—something that'd ultimately yield satisfaction and happiness, to all parties involved. Well, I've got a bit of advice for you: look elsewhere. Not at

Ence. He'll just disappoint you. Hurt you. Heaven knows, you don't deserve another moment of pain."

I got to my feet. I had nothing more to say to a man who obviously didn't give a used catheter for Ence's well-being. He'd be no help to me, in my endeavor to change the boy's life.

"Thank you for your time, sir," I said, stiffly. "I'll see you on Monday."

With that, I left his office with that all-too-familiar blend of ambition, curiosity and hope, burning in my heart. Despite everything I just learned about Ence, I still had faith that he could become great. I still believed that his humanity could be salvaged. If *we*—the only adults in these orphans' lives, the closest thing they had to parents—didn't believe that they were worth the time of day, who would?

Maybe, Selepoh was right and I just wanted a new project to inject a little light and purpose into my mundane life. Well, what was wrong with that? And, what better hope could I have, than a child?

NURTIC LEAVESLEFT

July first.

"But, why, sir?" the woman behind the special-services counter asked me, skeptically. "Are you a social worker? An investigator? Has there been an incident of neglect, abuse, kidnapping or fraud?"

"Oh, no, ma'am, nothing like that," I quickly reassured her. I was at the Alcove City Hospital, pursuing access to the birth records of the ninety-fourth and ninety-fifth ages. "I work at the orphanage, just down the street." I showed her my badge, on my lanyard. "You see, there's a kid under my care with no surname, but I was told that he was brought from here, nearly seven ages ago. I just wanted to—"

"Ah, a home-grown private." She gave me a tired smile. "Room seven-two-five. Mrs. Hope Cede should be able to assist you."

"Thank you." I paused. "Where may I find the stairs?"

"The elevator is down the hall, to your right."

I was too anxious to wait for an elevator. "What about the stairs, ma'am?"

She blinked. "The record room is on the seventh floor. You want to climb seven flights of stairs?"

"I'm in a hurry."

She stared at me for several more seconds.

"Second door on the left," she said, faintly.

I jogged up and found room seven-two-five already open. Inside, I came across an aged lady with deep-set blue eyes and a grandmotherly face, busy rifling through an open file cabinet. Mrs. Hope Cede.

"Cabinets?" I breathed, blankly. "Paper records, in *this* era?"

She gave me a wrinkly grin. "Everything has also been digitized, of course. But, alas, the desire for paper endures. There's something about a physical birth certificate that appeals to a mother."

I laughed. I decided that I liked her already.

"Just photocopies here, of course. The originals are with the families." She adjusted her wispy white ponytail. "How may I be of assistance, Mr. Leavesleft?"

I frowned. "Well, I was about to introduce myself, but I guess that isn't necessary."

She gave a crackling chuckle as she shook my hand. "Find me a city-dweller who *doesn't* know who you are, then you can introduce yourself all you want."

"This isn't exactly a small town, and I didn't exactly come home yesterday. I'm sure I could find plenty who fit that description. Just now, the lady at the special-services desk asked me for ID."

"She's new, in these parts." Hope gave me a wink. "But, I've lived here since graduating nursing school, decades ago—just don't ask how many decades, Mr. Leavesleft."

"Call me Nurtic."

She beamed. "What can I do for you, Nurtic?"

"Well, I came here today to research the parentage of one of the children currently living at the orphanage I work at. He doesn't have a surname, but I was told he might've been born here."

"How strange," Hope commented. "What age?"

"Either ninety-four or ninety-five. Not sure."

She directed me to a rather ancient-looking computer terminal. "Search away, my friend. Just be sure to include 'birth' or 'obituary' in your keywords. If I catch you snooping around any private medical files—anything *outside* of public birth or death announcements—I'll throw you out in a hot second, no matter how tall, dark or handsome you are, got that?"

I saluted her, jokingly. "Yes, ma'am."

Her grin widened further still. "I'll be in the back, if you need me."

"Thank you."

I opened the directory and typed 'birth,' 'male', '94th age' and '95th age' into the search filters. There were over twenty-thousand results. I stared. Twenty-thousand? This hospital got a lot more traffic than I thought. I tightened the window to November of the ninety-fourth age through February of the ninety-fifth, but still got four-thousand-three-hundred-fifty-five results. I took a deep breath. This was going to be a long afternoon.

I narrowed the search to those with 'ence' in their first names. The computer regurgitated a couple hundred Spencers, Clarences, Cadences, Florences, Torrences and the like. One by one, I plugged their surnames into the obituary directory and found that, though seven of the birth-mothers died in labor, all the babies still had living fathers or relatives to go home with. None wound up at the orphanage.

Maybe, Ence was named later on in life, after all. I cleared the filters and tried searching for a kid who could've possibly left the hospital totally unnamed.

No results.

Dispirited and out of ideas already, I mindlessly retyped some earlier keywords so I could start all over: 'male,' 'November 94 - February 95' and 'Ence.'

Sixteen-thousand-seven-hundred-twenty-four results.

Whoa. How come the number suddenly quadrupled? I checked my filters and realized that I'd forgotten a key one: 'birth.' So, this list contained *every single hospitalization* of an 'ence' in that timeframe.

This was forbidden territory. Uneasy, I glanced over my shoulder. Hope seemed completely buried in her work.

I looked back at the monitor. The very first result was about an 'Ence.' Not a Sp*ence*r nor a Cad*ence* nor a Flor*ence*. Just 'Ence.'

It was the only one.

My heart thudded. I clicked on the record, anxiously waiting for it to load. After fifteen suspenseful seconds, a note popped up:

> *'Entered on 1/25/95 at 01:25:07 by Hope Faith Cede: Male child, est. 2 wks old & 2 mos premature, was brought in by an unidentified man on 1/8/95. Authorities believe that the child may be a kidnapping victim. Named 'Ence' by patient #87725. Ence is now a ward of the state.'*

My eyes lifted from the screen. This was it. This was the right one, my Ence. It had to be. I glanced back at the header. The note was entered on January twenty-fifth of the ninety-fifth age, by Hope Faith Cede.

Hope Cede.

Holy crystallines.

"Ma'am, can you come here for a minute?" I called, voice unusually high.

"Do call me Hope," she said cheerfully, arms full of folders. She plopped down the stack and walked over.

"Hope," I pointed to the computer, "I think I found him."

Settling beside me, she squinted at the screen. Her lips parted.

"I remember that day," she half-whispered, "always will. Strangest workday of my life. I was in the lobby that afternoon when a young man in an odd costume came inside and placed an infant in my arms."

"Just like that?" I breathed. "A strange man just... walked up to you and handed over a two-week-old?"

She nodded. "I tried to speak with him, but he didn't seem to understand a word. No idea who he was or where he and the child came from."

I chewed the inside of my cheek. "I don't think that the story the authorities came up with adds up. If Ence were a kidnapping victim, he'd have parents worth blackmailing. Parents who'd be looking for him, willing to pay some sort of ransom. Parents the authorities would restore him to, in the end. So, I doubt that anyone was kidnapped; I'd guess that Ence's family gave him away, voluntarily." I swallowed. "You said the man didn't understand Nurian, right? There *was* a community of displaced Ichthyothians living around here at the time, because of the Spectral Hurricane. Perhaps, Ence's parents were Ichthyothians who just lost everything in the storm, rendered unable to afford a kid, so they abandoned him."

Hope's head shook. "The man I met couldn't have been impoverished, because he left in an airplane. A small private plane. He was the one flying it—hopped right into the cockpit and took off."

"What?" This tale was getting more twisted, by the second.

"The craft was nice," she went on, "the pilot looked well-fed, and the child wasn't starving either. He was small and sick, yes, but only because he was obviously very premature."

I let out a frustrated sigh. "Maybe, the pilot isn't the father. Maybe, the parents gave the baby to the pilot, to do their dirty work?"

"These poor, desperate parents sure have fine connections. Connections willing to risk a lot for them."

Good point. "What did the plane look like?" Had to start somewhere.

She bit her lip. "It's been nearly seven ages, Nurtic."

"You must remember *something*," I pressed.

She blinked. "Um, it was grey."

That didn't narrow the field much. "Any special markings?"

"Well... yes... I believe there was something on one of the wings..." She scratched her forehead. "Something blue."

"A blue triangle?" I sat bolt upright. "It's from the Ichthyothian military." I rubbed the back of my neck. "Ence has a medal, just like mine. A Silver Triangle. I thought that it must be a fake, but if Ence is connected in some way to the Ichthyothian military, then..." Then what? I snapped my fingers. "Maybe, the pilot was an active-duty soldier who wanted to dispose of the evidence of his 'emotional protection' crime—his newborn—so, he flew to a random hospital in another country and—"

"The man wasn't in military attire," Hope interjected. "He was wearing some sort of... flowing green gown."

"What?"

A robe. A colorful robe. The man was dressed as a mage. Now, what could I make of *that?* A Conflagrian mage, flying to Nuria in an Ichthyothian warplane. With a baby.

"Nurtic, aren't Ichthyothian soldiers taught to speak Nurian?" Hope asked.

"Yes. Civilians, too." Nurian was the closest thing Second Earth had to an international language, and most Ichthyothian public schools made sure their students became somewhat proficient.

"Well, like I said, this man definitely didn't understand me."

I shrugged. "He may've been playing dumb. He probably figured that he'd have a better shot at getting away with everything if he stayed silent and disguised."

"He had one hell of a disguise, yes, but he didn't keep quiet. He kept saying a name, over and over."

"Ence's name?" I pounced. "He's the one who gave Ence his name?"

"No, no, he said the name of a patient here, at the time. We brought the baby to her and *she* named him."

"Right. Patient eight-seven-seven-two-five," I breathed, glancing at the screen. "Who's patient eight-seven-seven-two-five?"

Without asking, I brazenly reached for the keyboard and entered the number.

Qui Tsop Lechatelierite.

I stared. It was Cease Lechatelierite's mom. I'd met her before, in August of the ninety-third age, when I flew her and her husband, Finis, to Ichthyosis to visit their son for the first and only time. Finis passed away in the Centerscraper firebombing and Qui followed suit soon thereafter from radiation poisoning.

So, Ence was, in some way, connected to the Lechatelierites, after all. How? From reading *The Legacy of the Lechatelierites* in high school, I knew that their family was a small one. When Finis, Qui, Cease and Commence all died in rapid succession, the Lechatelierite bloodline came to an abrupt end. What other ties, if not blood, could Ence possibly have to that family?

NURTIC LEAVESLEFT

July seventh.

It was the hottest day of the age, thus far—about a hundred degrees—and the orphanage's air-conditioner was broken. The children, nursing cold tap water, all sat around the one working fan we had. It rotated back and forth, giving each kid about half a second of air before moving on. Outdoor playtime was cancelled on account of the weather. No one complained.

Except Ence. Of course.

"It's a beautiful day," he fiercely declared. As usual, his voice was much too loud. "I want to go outside."

"It may *look* nice, from in here," I said, "but, if you actually go outside, you won't like it, believe me. It's about twenty degrees hotter, out there."

"Exactly!" His foot stomped. "That's the kind of weather I like best!"

"Really?" Obviously, it wasn't—he was just objecting for the sake of objecting, because he thrived on argument and confrontation. Bickering was his favorite pastime, next to beating up street thugs, tearing off fingers and burning his peers alive.

"Yes!" he shrieked. "I need to go outside! You don't understand, it hurts to be in here!"

Oh, boy. "It *hurts*, Ence?" Getting a bit melodramatic, were we? "Come on, let's sit down with the others."

"It's a hundred-two, right now—that hardly ever happens!" He let out a frustrated roar. "It's my chance to finally feel okay; I can't miss this! It's one-oh-two!"

"How do you know that?"

"The thermometer!"

There was a tiny old-fashioned mercury thermometer taped to the lobby window, maybe fifty feet away.

"When did you check it?"

"Right now. I can see it, right now. It says one-oh-two."

I sighed, internally. "I'm sure it does, Ence."

"What, you don't believe me?" His arms flailed. "It says so, *right there*, right now!"

To humor him, I trekked over. And, sure enough, he was right. It was exactly one-hundred-two degrees.

"Alright, when did you go look?" I demanded, the moment I was back.

"I can see it from here," he repeated with a straight face.

He was making me very tired. "Okay, Ence. Whatever you say. Now, sit down."

His feet stayed planted. "What, can't you see it?"

"That's enough." He had to learn that lying wasn't a game. It was okay to joke around every now and then, but not *all* the time. It seemed like Ence lived for deception.

"You *can't?*" he repeated, incredulous. Boy, did he sound convincing. He was such a skilled voice-actor. Such a master of tone.

"Come on, I know that you must've walked over there when I wasn't watching. You have a knack for sneaking around."

"But, I didn't go anywhere this time, really. I can read it, from right here. It's obvious. Look, it just went up to one-oh-three!"

For heaven's sake. "I don't care if its one-oh-two or one-oh-three or one-fifty-three. The fact of the matter is: it's too hot to go outside, so you're not going outside, period. Now, come on, everyone's waiting for us to start the game. We're going to play story-chain."

"I hate memory games," he spat. "They're boring."

Again, he was being defiant, just to be defiant. It was getting old, fast.

While everyone else clambered to get a better spot in front of the fan, Ence sat down directly behind it, where its rotation didn't reach. Fine by me. As long as he didn't faint from heat exhaustion, he was free to punish himself, all he wanted.

"Alright, everyone, it's time for story-chain," I announced. "Rule recap: we're going to collectively tell a story with each person adding one detail, on their turn. The challenge is that you have to recite the entire storyline before adding your part." I'd never seen the kids play this particular game, before—it always seemed to happen on my colleagues' watch. I wondered what they'd come up with. "Who'd like to begin?"

Immediately, everyone threw a hand into the air. Except Ence. Of course. He just stared at the floor with his arms folded across his hollow chest. I randomly picked Acroph, sitting beside him.

"We're going to go around the circle *this* way. Clockwise," I instructed.

"There once was a boy named Ciladus," Acroph opened.

"There once was a boy named Ciladus who liked to ride his bike," the girl to his right continued.

"There once was a boy named Ciladus who liked to ride his bike. He rode all around town," the next child added.

"There once was a boy named Ciladus who liked to ride his bike. He rode all around town, searching for his sister."

"There once was a boy named Ciladus who liked to ride a bike. He rode all around town, searching for his sister. Her name was Rlet."

"There once was a boy named Ciladus who liked to ride his bike. He rode… all over town… looking for his sister. Her name was… Rlet. She ran away because her brother was being mean to her."

The story went on for some time, after that. It wasn't long before the kids began seriously stumbling, forgetting things, pausing for lengthy stretches, and saying lines out of order. I often had to help out, in order to keep the story going.

At last, we made it to the very last child in the circle. Ence.

"There once was a boy named Ciladus who liked to ride his bike," Ence said, quickly and monotonously. "He rode all around town, searching for his sister. Her name was Rlet. She ran away because her brother was being mean to her. He'd been calling her names, but now he wanted to apologize. She ran to the city park. When she was there, she met a fluffy dog. She named the dog Oby. Oby liked to play fetch. Rlet played fetch with Oby, all day long. Rlet took Oby home, that night. Then, she had an idea. She made the dog chase her mean brother across town. While he was gone, Rlet took Ciladus's bike and hid it by the creek. It accidentally fell in. Rlet jumped in the water to rescue it, but she couldn't really swim. The dog chased Ciladus to the creek and Ciladus saw what was happening to his sister."

The kids burst into applause. Ence had recited the entire chain without so much as a pause for breath.

"You're not done yet, Ence," I said, grinning. "You have to add a sentence or two of your own. Come on, finish off the story."

He raised his chin, locking eyes with me. If looks could kill, I surely would've been reduced to a pile of ashes on the floor, at this very moment. You'd think that I were asking him to scrub toilets with his tongue, not give the last line to a silly game we that were playing for fun.

Everyone giggled excitedly, anticipating the conclusion to their winding tale.

"Oby watched as Ciladus jumped in to rescue Rlet," Ence said, still glaring unblinkingly, "but, Ciladus didn't know how to swim either, so they both inhaled water and suffocated and died."

Immediately, all laughter in the room ceased. Some of the more sensitive children looked rather distraught over the fate of their beloved characters, while others seemed irritated that Ence ruined the plot that took them so much time and effort to construct.

I cleared my throat. "Well, um, thank you, Ence, for that... dramatic ending. So, who'd like to begin our next story?"

"This game is dumb," Ence declared—loudly, of course. "I hate it; there's no point to it—"

"Thank you, Ence," I cut him off. "Kati, would you like to start?"

"Do you all want to hear our story from last week?" Ence continued, belligerently. "There once was a girl in a pink dress who loved ice cream. Her name was Tomen and she had long blonde hair. She liked to wear her hair in braids. One day, when she woke up, her braids were missing. She was very sad about that. So, she decided to search for them. She went to the lake. They weren't there. She went to the park. They weren't there, either. She went downtown. They still weren't there. Then, she went to the ice cream store, and sure enough, they were sitting next to a big cup of strawberry, her favorite flavor. She put her braids back on and ate the ice cream."

Once again, the kids started exclaiming and clapping.

"Whoa, I can't believe you remember the whole thing, from *last week!*"

"Wow!"

"Amazing!"

"How about I finish that story, too?" Ence yelled, overpowering all the enthusiastic chatter. "Tomen's braids decided that they didn't like ice cream, so they wrapped themselves around her neck, causing her to choke and throw it all up. She kept vomiting until she puked blood all over her frilly pink dress and died."

Screaming, Kati covered her ears with her palms. A few of the younger kids followed her lead.

"Want to hear our story from the week before last, everybody?" Ence bellowed, voice like a thunderstorm. He got to his feet. "I can make a special ending for that one, too!" At this, some of the children actually started sobbing. "There once was a green alien named Zed. He lived on an orange planet called—"

"That's *enough!*" I shouted, and everyone went silent, even the criers. "No more stories, no more special endings!" I checked my watch. "It's time for lunch, anyway." I was glad that I had to leave soon, for a delivery flight. I'd had my fill of Ence's temper, for one day. Any minute now, Ce Repla would come and relieve me from duty.

Immediately, there was a stampede to the kitchen.

"If you just let me go outside, I wouldn't have had to do that," Ence growled at me, when his turn came. He was the very last one in line—everybody else was already sitting down and eating. Ence, however, never seemed to get hungry. He apparently didn't mind delaying his meal all the more, just to try and pick a fight with me.

"Ence, you didn't *have* to do anything," I answered, pouring him the remains of the soup. "I don't even know what to do with you, anymore. You turn everything into a scene, no matter what. What exactly do you want? What are you trying to accomplish? You're angry, all the time. *All the time*. I've never met anyone like that, before."

Well, that wasn't exactly true. I'd witnessed some serious fury in my lifetime, but the people expressing it usually had real reasons to be upset. Like Commander Cease Lechatelierite. If there was anyone on Second Earth who had a right to be chronically stressed and angry, it was him. He was like a wind-up toy that'd been cranked, one too many times. But, he knew how to channel his righteous indignation into his work. He had discipline and drive. He didn't just go on random destructive rampages for kicks and giggles.

That was what Ence was missing: something to put his radical energy into. A purpose.

"I already told you what I want," he grumbled. "I want to go outside."

I thought about Hope Cede and the hospital and all the mystery surrounding Ence's origins. If everything happened for a reason, then God must've had something special in mind when He brought Ence to Nuria in that Ichthyothian warplane. There was no way that Ence was just meant to spend the rest of his days barely scraping by, bent on inflicting pain on everyone around him.

And, what was *my* role, in Ence's story? To watch his childhood go to waste, beating him down with 'don't do this' and 'don't do that' until his brilliance gave way to insanity? Ence needed intellectual stimulation and individual attention, neither of which he'd get as long as he stayed here. If Cease Lechatelierite wasn't given military training, a war to fight, a fleet to stand behind him, and a second-in-command whose gifts perfectly complimented his, what would've become of his life? Would he have still achieved the impossible? Probably not. Because it wasn't enough for a person to simply *have* talent. Talent needed to be stimulated, cultivated, directed toward something worthwhile. If the World Revolt taught me anything, it was that true progress rarely occurred in isolation. Ence was intellectually and emotionally isolated, here. He needed to be actively worked with, raised up.

The problem was, I didn't know how to really help him. I worked here five days a week, but still felt like I wasn't making a substantial difference in any of these kids' lives. All I did, day-in and day-out, was feed these children stale bread and lumpy soup, play some silly games, and proctor Ence's temper tantrums. I wasn't solving anybody's problems. As usual.

"You wouldn't be able to stand it, if you went outside," I answered Ence, wearily.

"Would too."

"You're sweating waterfalls in *here*, where its significantly cooler." I fished the last two pieces of rye from the bottom of the bag.

"But, I'm shivering too. I've got goosebumps, everywhere. See?" His arm lifted and, sure enough, all the tiny red and black hairs were standing at attention like little soldiers. "I'm hot and cold, at the same time." Something in his eyes flickered. "I need to go outside where I can be comfortable; why won't anybody understand that?" His hands gripped his hair as he screamed, "I can't stand it, I can't STAND IT!"

The slices of bread in my hands… were on fire!

Calling out in surprise, I dropped them on the floor and stomped the stubborn flames until nothing remained but a small pile of black dust.

Everyone stared at us with open mouths, lunches forgotten.

Chest heaving and eyes bloodshot, Ence took off down the hallway, zipping past Ce, who was arriving for his shift.

"Hey, Nuric," Ce greeted me, sounding bored. "Ence is being himself, I see?"

"I'll take care of it," I muttered.

I ran out into the one-hundred-plus-degree sunlight and found Ence spread-eagled on the lava-hot pavement, gaze wide and face tomato-red.

He stared directly at the sun.

"No!" I gasped, blocking his light. "Ence, what do you think you're doing? You can go blind!"

I stooped, but he shrank away from me. "I won't go blind. I do this, all the time."

"Do what?" I breathed. "Look at the sun?"

"Yeah. When I feel weak, it gives me energy." Curling into a fetal position, he moaned, "I feel so bad, right now. Like I'm dying. I always feel like that, after I make a fire. I can hardly move."

"Come on." I touched his shoulder. "Off the tar, before it cooks you." If it didn't already.

"I just said I can't move," he faintly insisted.

I scooped him up and, for once, he didn't put up a fight. In fact, he remained limp as a ragdoll, in my arms.

"Please don't take me inside, Nurtic, please, I need the heat, please, Nurtic, please," he whimpered. "I don't want to go inside, I'll die if you do, it hurts, oh, how it hurts…"

He was delirious, probably from dehydration or heat exhaustion. Cradling him, I kicked the door open and hurried into the lobby. Instantly, his lids scrunched as he fell silent. I laid him in his bunk and fetched him some water.

"Ence," I stroked his arm, "Ence, get up for a minute; you need to drink this."

No response.

"Ence." I shook him.

Still, nothing.

I plunked the glass down. Then, I poked and pinched him, a couple times.

He didn't wake.

Fear prickled through me. I felt his neck for a pulse. It was slow. Dangerously slow.

On the brink of panic, I spontaneously did the most irrational thing imaginable: I lifted Ence from his bed… and ran back outside. Sure enough, the second I stepped into the blazing sunlight, his body jolted. I gently set him on the pavement. He lay there for a while, panting with an open mouth as his jewel-like eyes scoured the sky. At long last, he laboriously pulled himself upright.

I didn't know what to make of any of this. Nothing made sense. I was dimly aware that I was late for my delivery but, at this moment, I didn't care.

"Don't take me back in," Ence mustered. "Not yet, please; I'm still weak. I always feel sick after making a fire. I didn't mean to, really," he pleaded, looking up at me. "I was just upset, and it happened. I was mad, and the next thing I knew, the bread was burning up. I didn't want it to. It was the same thing with Tim. I didn't want to hurt him, either. I swear."

Tim. Timothy Vic. Ence was speaking of the boy he killed two ages ago, in a fit of rage. The one he burned alive.

Not with a stove.

"Make a fire," I echoed. "You can… *create* fire. Yourself."

"It even burns me, sometimes. Inside." He rubbed his eyes.

Eyes.

Selepoh said that he'd entered the kitchen to the sight of Tim Vic writhing on the floor while Ence stood over him, *glaring*.

Ence was a Conflagrian mage. An eye mage.

All the air instantly evaporated from my lungs. Of course. How come I never connected the dots before? The pilot who brought Ence to Nuria wasn't an Ichthyothian in disguise, he was a mage. A mage flying an Ichthyothian plane—*Scarlet July's* plane—in January of the ninety-fifth age, shortly after Scarlet got killed, to bring him to Qui Tsop, then the sole living member of the Lechatelierite family. And, Qui named him 'Ence'… *Comm*ence.

Ence was the child of Cease and Scarlet.

My stomach disappeared. Yes, Ence did indeed have his parents' energy, brilliance and minuscule stature. He had Cease's temper and Scarlet's perfect memory. He had Cease's angular face and pallor, but with Scarlet's delicacy and ruddiness. He had Scarlet's wiry hair texture, but with Cease's tousle. And, most striking of all, he had glassy grey-green eyes and red-black hair, a striking mix of them both. No wonder the kid seemed so familiar to me, upon first meeting.

I felt dizzy. This couldn't be. I'd seen countless images of Scarlet's butchered body. Both mother and son were slaughtered, brutally.

No. The baby's corpse was never found. The baby was only *presumed* dead because no one believed that a preemie would make it out of that bloodbath alive. Well, if anyone could survive the impossible, it'd be the progeny of the most powerful mage in history, right?

Ence was staring at me. Staring at me, staring at him.

"Nurtic?" he croaked, adjusting the black-and-blue ribbon around his neck—obviously, Cease Lechatelierite's Silver Triangle.

I somehow managed to find my voice: "How are you feeling, now, Ence?" Yes, how are you feeling, Commence July Lechatelierite, orphaned child of war, covalent son of the two greatest military figures to walk Second Earth… how are you feeling after using your eye-magic?

"Better. But, still tired." He looked away when he said this. Of course, he'd hate to admit weakness.

But, why would the offspring of the Dual-Source Enchant get so wasted from such a minor magical exertion? He didn't even possess a noticeable aura. Was that just because he was young and untrained? Were we too far from the Core Crystal? Neither of those factors ever hindered Scarlet. Maybe, covalence was to blame for Ence's spectral shortcomings?

I retrieved my cell from my pocket—I'd long since cancelled my service, but I could still pick up wi-fi. "Ence, I was wondering if you could read something for me?" I asked, slowly. Heading down the driveway, to the outskirts of the facility's wireless network range, I pulled up a random bible passage and turned the screen toward him. "From the top, please."

His auburn brows furrowed. "Why?"

"I just want to know if you can see the words from where you are."

"Of course, I can."

"Ence, I'm on the opposite end of the drive."

"So, what?" He lay back down.

He really didn't think that there was anything special about his vision? If so, all I had to do to make him cooperate was appeal to his ego…

"*No one* should be able to see the words from where you are," I sighed, theatrically.

As I expected, his pride got the better of him. "No one?" He sat up.

My head shook.

Eagerly, he stood. "*The wolf also shall dwell with the lamb, and the leopard shall lie down with the kid; and the calf and the young lion and the fatling together, and a little child shall lead them*," he read Isaiah eleven-six.

Incredible. Not only could he see the words, he was able to recite them quickly, without so much as a stutter. Most kids his age, even the middle-class ones in good schools, typically couldn't read at such a high level, not so smoothly. Did Ence also inherit his mother's linguistic talent?

I walked back over to him, pocketing my phone.

"Ence, could I ask you a few questions?"

His mouth went hard. "Why?"

"Well... I think I may have an idea about... who you are."

"What do you mean, who I am?" His citrus stare narrowed. "I know who I am. I'm *me*. Why're you always trying to psycho-analyze me, like some quack?"

My head shook, again. "It's not like that. What I mean is, I might know something about your origins. Where you're from. Why you're here instead of in a regular home with a family." I needed to spike Ence's curiosity, to get him to work with me. "Haven't you ever wondered why you don't have a last name? Or, who your parents are?"

"I'm an orphan. I've got no parents. Knowing who they were or why they abandoned me won't do a damn thing. They're gone; there's no point in dwelling over it."

"Abandoned you?" I echoed. That was quite a conclusion to jump to. "Why would you assume that?" While it figured that he'd want to keep up the tough-guy act, I surely didn't expect him to actively *resent* the parents he never knew.

His vine-thin arms folded. "You know something. Spill."

"I don't know anything for sure and I don't want to get your hopes up for nothing. But, I promise that if I can confirm my suspicions, I'll tell you everything. But, to get there, I'm going to need your help."

"You expect me to help you when you're keeping secrets from me?"

"Ence, fighting me does neither of us any good. I'm the one conducting the investigation, so if I'm stuck, you're stuck."

"Fine," he spat. "How can I possibly help? I don't know anything about my roots; I've been *here*, all my life."

"Not *all* your life. You weren't born at the orphanage. You were brought here, at some point."

There was a pause.

"I've been here since infancy. No one can remember being a baby," he said, flatly.

"*You* might. After all, you could effortlessly rehash every detail of the old story-chain games." I was hoping that Ence could provide more of a description of the pilot who brought him to Nuria. All Hope Cede managed to recall was that he wore a green robe.

"Yeah, but that's relatively recent stuff," he protested.

"Ence, you're arguing with me for the sake of arguing. If you just stop and actually *try* to do this, you might be able to."

He fell silent, perching on the ground for minutes on end, body rigid with concentration. I waited patiently, ignoring the sweat pouring from my every orifice.

At last, he spoke up: "What comes to mind... I don't know if it's real or just my imagination. But, it shows up in my dreams, a lot." He hesitated. "Eyes. A pair of gold eyes, watching me. They looked almost... scared."

Gold eyes. And, a green robe.

Of course.

Ence must've seen the recognition flash across my face, because then he piped, "What does that mean?"

"I'm not sure, yet. But, like I said, I'll tell you everything I know, once I'm certain. It won't be today." And, before Ence could object, I hastily plowed on: "So, you can generate fire. Is there anything else... out of the ordinary... that you can do?"

He blinked. "Out of the ordinary?"

"You know, anything that'd be considered… supernatural, perhaps?"

I swore I could see Cease Lechatelierite's ice crystallize in his eyes. "What does this have to do with where I'm from?"

"Everything."

He instantly caught on: "Are you trying to say that I'm one of those *fire-savages?*"

"Ence, that's a racial slur. Mages. They're called mages."

These days, Conflagrian mages were the antagonists of every book, movie and TV show. Portrayed as barbarians and bloodthirsty terrorists, they were the monsters of children's nightmares and the butt of crude jokes on late-night talk-shows. Scarlet July's name was legend, but she was considered a sort of exception to the rule. A 'civilized mage.' An anomaly. Scarlet was depicted as the only sound mind in a nation of dangerous cavemen.

And, now, I was telling Ence that he might be one of them.

"Ence, I need you to trust me. I need you to answer my questions even if they seem crazy to you right now, okay? Together, we can get to the bottom of things. So, please tell me, is making fire the only special thing you can do?"

He thought for a while, staring hard at the sun like only Scarlet July could. "I can hide real good," he whispered, as though worried that the trees might overhear. "Sometimes, I can walk right in front of people without them noticing. It's like, whenever I don't want to be seen, I'm not."

He had the ability to destroy others' visual perceptions of himself. That was another one of Scarlet's specialties. It explained a lot, like how he managed to slip out for his little forays in the street.

Humming, I nodded.

He scowled. "How's this helping you research my origins? Sounds to me like you're just scamming on my arsenal, so you can gain the upper hand."

It was funny that Ence would speak of tactical advantages. He didn't know just how much those words reminded me of his father.

"Really?" I gave him a weary glance. "Why do you still insist on treating me like your enemy? Are we at war with one another, for you to speak of strategic intelligence? Are you actually dumb enough to think that I'm doing all this just so I can better assert my authority over you? I'm so late for my delivery flight right now, I'm risking getting fired from a job that I desperately need. For you. Because you're important to me. So, quit biting my head off, will you?"

He muttered inaudibly, fiddling with his collar.

"Could I please see that?" I suddenly asked.

"What?" His hand snapped away.

"Your necklace."

Reluctantly, he pulled it off. I took it from him—not without enduring a scathing glower—and carefully examined it.

"When did you get this?" I slid my thumb across the medallion. "And, where?"

"I don't know. I've always just… had it. It's the only thing I've ever really owned, you know? So, I protect it. Never take it off."

It was definitely authentic. Exactly like mine, except scratched and dirty from nearly seven ages of continuous wear.

I handed it back. He quickly put it on and tucked it under his shirt, breathing a literal sigh of relief.

"How are you feeling, now?" I noticed that he no longer looked exhausted. Quite the contrary; he could hardly sit still.

"Restless."

The heat restored his depleted spectrum.

"Come with me." We went over to the grassy field, where I retrieved a fallen tree branch. "Can you set this on fire?"

He blinked. "You mean, like, right now? On purpose?"

"Yes."

He glared at the branch for an entire minute, then finally declared, "I can't do it."

"Try harder."

He squinted at it again, holding his breath until his face purpled.

Nothing happened.

I tossed it aside. "Let's try something else. Walk around without my noticing."

He circled me.

"Can you see me?" he called, quickening his pace to a run.

"Yes."

He gave it another loop.

"How about now?"

"Still, yes."

He changed directions.

"Now?"

"Yes, I'm sorry. Alright, let's shake things up a bit. Let's race down the driveway," I suggested. "You want to beat me, and you don't care what it takes. Trip me, hit me, kick me—it's all fair game. Okay?" Maybe, I had to trick the magic out of him.

"Am I dreaming or did you just *ask* me to prank you?"

"Today's your lucky day. On your mark... get set... go."

I jogged. A couple yards from the finish-line, my foot caught on something. I landed heavily on the pavement, jeans tearing. I'd never been so happy to fall so hard.

From several feet behind, there came peals of laughter. "Oh, man, I only wish I could take credit for that!" Ence howled.

My cell lay on the ground beside me, screen shattered. Ence didn't do a thing; I stumbled on my own accord.

Well, I supposed I had my answer, nonetheless: he didn't have conscious control over his magic—it was all instinctive.

"What's going on, here?"

We turned and saw Selepoh storming toward us like a hobnail on a rampage. He grabbed Ence's wrist.

"Always up to no good, aren't you, boy? Mr. Leavesleft was supposed to be gone, half an hour ago!"

"Oh, no, sir, he wasn't giving me any trouble," I quickly interjected, and Ence shot me a grateful look.

"We were reading from Isaiah," Ence chimed. "*The wolf also shall dwell with the lamb, and the leopard shall lie down with the kid—*"

"That's tomorrow's verse-of-the-day." What were the odds? "Have you been breaking into my office, again?" Selepoh growled.

Again?

"No," Ence squawked.

"Really? Because you've got a nasty habit of creeping around. You're a liar and a sneak, that's what you are."

"Sir, we really were just reading and talking," I interjected. "He didn't break into your office."

Selepoh gave me an incredulous frown. "Why are you covering for him, Nurtic? I understand that he's your little community service project and all, but I never thought I'd see *you* stoop so low."

Little community service project? Ence's eyes flickered at the phrase, hurt and betrayed. Not by Selepoh. But, by me. So, he believed Selepoh's words. And, if there was one thing that Ence hated most, it was feeling controlled or manipulated. Now, Ence was inclined to think that I was using him for my own ends. *I* wasn't helping *him* out; *he* was *my* project. My experiment.

It took a lot to get him to start trusting me in the first place and, in an instant, all my hard work probably came undone. Today, he was willing to share his secrets and memories with me. He even let me hold his medal. Never again, I'd bet. From now on, he'd likely be suspicious of me. He'd doubt my motives and actions. Censor his answers to my questions. Guard his 'arsenal.' I blinked sweat from my eyes. All I wanted to do was help him!

Of course, that was all I ever wanted to do, wasn't it? Help out. Solve everyone's problems. Save the world. When would I learn?

I departed for my delivery, mouth bitter. As I flew much too fast, I tried hard to recall a single time that I'd managed to actually help someone without hurting them in the process. I drew a blank. It seemed like everything I touched always turned to dust.

NURTIC LEAVESLEFT

July twenty-fifth.

It was dawn and Ence was nowhere to be found. Shocker.

"I don't get it," Ce Repla growled. "Why wouldn't he wait until *after* breakfast to run away?"

"Because it's easier to slip out while everybody's still asleep," I answered. "And, it's not like Commence ever actually gets hungry, anyway."

Ce nodded. "Ain't that the truth—wait, *what* did you just call him?"

I resisted the urge to kick myself. "Um…"

"Commence? Is that his new nickname or something?"

Ah, if he only knew. "Never mind that; I'll go find him," I quickly said, turning on my heel.

It was a steamy morning; a yellow haze already hung in the air, foreshadowing a true sticky scorcher. A perfect day for a Conflagrian mage.

I knew where I'd find him: the dreary graffitied alleyways that smelled of alcohol, vomit and urine. Alcove City had plenty of those, but Ence's favorite was Anaco Avenue. I found little difference between the state of things there—a street in the capital city of the most prosperous democracy in the world—and that of the impoverished, war-torn, third-world nation of Conflagria. Scarlet, if you only knew the sort of things your son did for fun…

"Hey there, hottie," called a sultry voice, the moment I hit Anaco. It was a gaunt blonde wearing black fishnets over hot-pink underwear. Her face was caked with inordinate amounts of makeup—glitter powder, red lipstick, black mascara, purple eye-liner, the works.

A man with platinum hair stepped out in front of me, practically blocking the entire passage with his bulk.

"Whatcha doin' here?"

Military training or not, I knew better than to provoke the likes of him.

"Just looking for someone."

He gave me a yellow-toothed grin. "You came to the right place, then. I've got plenty. Whatchou in the mood for? I believe you've already met Eidnolb—if you want a screamer, she's the one."

I blinked. "Not exactly what I meant, but thanks anyway." I turned.

"Hey!" He caught my shoulder, roughly. "Ain't nobody enters *my* turf without makin' their intentions clear," he boomed, odorous breath withering my lungs. "If you ain't here for one of my girls, whatchou up to? You tryin' to move in on my territory witchour own business?"

"No," I answered, calmly. "Just passing through."

"*What for?*" My arm was going numb.

"Like I said, I'm looking for someone. A child."

He snorted. "You a pedophile? 'Cuz, if so, I ain't got nuthin' fer the likes of you." His blue eyes narrowed. "Heeeey, you're that *pilot* boy, aintchou?"

For once, I was actually grateful for my so-called 'fame.' "Nurtic Leavesleft," I said, dryly. "Nice to meet you."

He released me. "You lookin' for that scrawny redhead, by any chance?"

Ah, so he *did* know Ence. I wished I could say I were surprised. "Yes, have you seen him?"

"One too many times. He looked a bit young to be a customer, but he asked for a girl a short while ago 'n' offered his medal to pay. So, I let 'im see Mari, but it turned out that he didn't want nothin' *normal* from 'er. He beat 'er ass senseless while howlin' at the top of his lungs 'bout how wrong it is fer people to screw around 'n' make babies they ain't gonna raise. When I came 'round 'n' saw what he was up to, I took care o''im." The man gave a sinister laugh. "He ain't never gonna come back 'ere again, that's fer sure. That is, if he e'er manages to leave. Can't walk too good, no mo'. I didn't want to kill 'im 'cuz, ya know, it's more fun to watch 'im writhe."

My stomach jumped up my esophagus. "Where is he?" I demanded.

He chuckled again, and it took my every ounce of self-control not to introduce his blonde mustache to my sneaker. "Shouldn't be too hard to find. Like I said, he ain't goin' nowhere."

Terror-stricken, I took off at a run… and, sure enough, found Ence farther down the ally, battered and bleeding beside an overturned garbage can. His left ankle was obviously twisted. My breath caught in my chest.

"Ence!"

His watery eyes looked up at me.

I stooped to pick him up, but he took me by surprise by kicking my face with his good foot. Blood spurted from my nose.

"Go away!" he screamed.

"Ence, we need to get you out of here, right now," I hissed.

"Come to rescue your little *community service project?*"

His pride would have to wait. I forcibly scooped him up and hightailed back onto the main road. Scandalized looks followed us as we blew past. With my fountain-nose,

I probably looked like a psycho kidnapper. Thankfully, though, no one tried to stop me.

"I tried to set him on fire," Ence whimpered, lips by my ear, "the pimp guy. When he was beating me up, I tried to ignite him, but the flames didn't come out. It never works, when I want it to. Only when I don't."

I burst into the orphanage. Selepoh, Ce and all the kids stared at us with mouths agape.

"Hospital, Ce. Now," I ordered.

"I'll bring the flivver around," Ce breathed, jumping up.

"No," Ence croaked, "Nurtic, I'll heal myself. I always do. Once I get my energy back, I'll just—"

"You may be able to take care of your scrapes that way, but your ankle needs professional medical attention," I whispered back.

"How do you know?"

Well, Ence, because that's how your mother's magic worked. "Just trust me on this one."

He looked away. "I didn't want to be rescued, you know."

"Really?" While Selepoh supervised the rest of the children, I took Ence to the bathroom so I could dress the deep slash across his face—at the rate it was bleeding, I didn't think it could wait until his aura rebounded, nor until we got to the hospital. "So, what exactly *was* your plan to get out of there? You can't walk."

There was a pause. "By you," he added, quietly. "I didn't want to be rescued by you."

Silence.

I heard the honk of Ce's flivver. Cheek bandaged, I carried Ence outside and set him in the backseat. Then, I went to clean the mess we'd left in the bathroom. Ence managed to get blood all over everything—the floor, sink, counter, a couple towels.

Towels. I stared at them, heart hammering against my Adam's apple. And, then, I went to the kitchen to retrieve a plastic sandwich bag.

* * *

In the evening, after Selepoh went home, I used the facility's landline to make a long-distance call. I knew those weren't allowed, but I didn't have phone-access otherwise and, in my opinion, this was an emergency worth a pay-dock and some scolding from my employer.

"Hello?" came an Ichthyothian voice.

"Commander Inexor Buird?" I chirped.

"Who is this?" he demanded.

"It's Nurtic Leavesleft, sir."

There was a stunned silence.

"Leavesleft? What's going on? How did you get this number?"

He clearly forgot that his line used to be mine. "Sir," I began, "I know we haven't spoken in nearly seven ages, but I need your help with something. It's serious."

"What is it? What's wrong?"

"Don't be alarmed, sir; it's got nothing to do with the war."

"Well, then, it's got nothing to do with me. Good day."

"Wait, no, don't hang up! Please, sir, it's important. You're the only person I can trust with this. And, not to mention, you're the only one with the resources I need, to figure things out."

Inexor cleared his throat. "You've got thirty seconds to explain what the hell you're on about."

"Well, first, you've got to promise to keep this between us."

"I will promise no such thing. Either speak now or I'm disconnecting this call and blocking your number."

Very well, then. "Sir, I have… a blood sample. I need a blood-spectrum-content analysis and—"

"Sorry, but you don't need Icicle for that," he interrupted, crossly. For heaven's sake, was he always this snappy? "You could get that done at the Nurian Diving Academy. I'm sure they'd be happy to do your bidding; I mean, it's been seven ages since your discharge and all of Nuria is *still* kissing your ass. Now, if you're done wasting my time, I'd like to—"

"And, I'd also like a gel electrophoresis test."

"I'm not a doctor," he grumbled. "Translation, please?"

"It's a type of DNA test usually used to determine parentage."

"Again, you don't need Icicle for that. You don't even need a military hospital. Besides, we've only got our own soldiers' DNA on file."

"What about ex-soldiers?"

"Them, too."

"Even ones who served seven ages ago?"

"Well, we don't really throw anything away, so I suppose so."

"Good. Because I need to see if the sample I've got matches up with Cease Lechatelierite and Scarlet July."

There was a very pregnant pause.

"Is this some sort of joke?" he roared.

"Do you really think I'd make an exorbitantly-expensive long-distance phone call to the Leader of the Nurro-Ichthyothian Resistance for kicks?"

"How old is this blood sample?"

"A few hours."

There was yet another pause.

"Leavesleft, what's this all about?"

I took a deep breath. "Sir, I think Scarlet's child might've survived. The baby's body was never found at the scene, after all. You saw the pictures."

"Oh, yes, I sure did, and I could barely tell what the hell I was even looking at, because all I could see was a bloody fly-ridden heap of dragon dung."

"Sir," I objected, stricken.

"Leavesleft, the fetus was extracted from her womb two months before he should've been born, and not by a surgeon with a scalpel in a sterile operating room, but by a lunatic assassin with a rusty sword, on the floor of a filthy cabin."

"Commander, I work at an orphanage in Alcove City where there's a six-age-old with a perfect memory, inexplicable magical powers, a Silver Triangle and a really familiar face."

"What?"

"He doesn't have a surname; he just goes by 'Ence.'"

"Ence?"

"Scarlet's son was supposed to be '*Comm*ence.' Somehow, since his birth, his name got truncated."

"How do you know what Scarlet's son was supposed to be named? She never told anybody."

"She told me. And, one other person."

"Who?"

"Cease Lechatelierite's mother, Qui Tsop. I did some digging: turns out, when Ence was two weeks old, he got dropped off at the Alcove City Hospital where Qui was temporarily inpatient—dropped off by a green-robed gold-eyed man flying a Nordic warplane."

"What?"

"Ambrek Coppertus in Scarlet's aircraft."

Inexor exhaled, loudly. "This is a lot for me to handle, Leavesleft. And, I don't mean emotionally. What you're telling me… if it's true, it can change… well, a lot of things."

"Everything." I rubbed the back of my neck. "So, will you run the tests?"

"Yes. When will you send over the specimen?"

I definitely wasn't trusting the transportation of something this important to a third party. "I'll fly over and hand it to you, myself. I have a delivery to central Ichthyosis in the morning; I could stop by Icicle on my way, if you give me clearance to land."

"You'll have clearance, but I can't guarantee that *I'll* be around. The System doesn't give advanced-notice before attacking, you know. But, if I'm out at sea, ask for Nurse Insouci Raef. She can be trusted with this."

"Alright." I breathed out. "Thanks, sir."

"Don't thank me until you get the results."

"How will I get them? No post or email."

"Well, is this your number?"

"I actually don't have my own number, anymore. I'm calling from work. It's a shared line, though. You or whoever's going to call back will have to be totally certain that I'm the one on the phone, before saying a thing. And, if I'm not around, just call again later. No messages."

"Of course."

"I appreciate this, sir. More than you know."

There was a tense gap, followed by: "I don't mean to sound heartless, Leavesleft, but I'm not entirely sure how I want this to turn out. Because, if you're right, Second Earth will never be the same."

NURTIC LEAVESLEFT

August sixth.

The phone rang and Ce was the one standing nearest to it. Great.

"I'll get it," he called, automatically.

"No, that's okay!" I leapt to my feet.

Ce gave me a weird look as he headed for the wall. "I don't know what's gotten into you, lately—you go crazy, every time it rings." He snatched up the receiver. "Alcove City Orphanage, Ce Repla speaking... Who may I say is calling?... Just a moment, please." He looked up. "It's for you. It's a lady from the *Ichthyothian Diving Fleet.*" He grinned. "They're issuing a draft and need you to head over, stat."

"Very funny." My pulse jumped as I took the phone from him and slipped out into the hall. "Hello?"

"Mr. Leavesleft, this is Insouci Raef, a nurse from the Icicle Base Hospital. You delivered a blood sample on July twenty-sixth, requesting a blood-spectrum-content analysis and a gel electrophoresis test; is that correct?"

"Yes, ma'am."

"I have the results, whenever you're ready."

I was as ready as I'd ever be. "Shoot, ma'am."

"The subject's blood-spectrum-content is point-seven parts-per-milligram."

Point-seven? Good grief, that was awful. "What about the DNA test?"

Raef didn't miss a beat: "It's a match."

My world stood still.

"Th-thank you," I breathed.

"You're welcome, sir. Have a good afternoon."

"You too. And, remember, this stays between you, me and the Commander. I'd like the boy to have a normal life. That's all his mother ever wanted for him."

"Of course, sir."

I nodded, though she obviously couldn't see. "Thanks again."

"Mr. Leavesleft?" she piped, a second before I could hang up.

"Yes, ma'am?"

"I'd just like to… to thank you for finding him." She sounded throaty. "It would've meant a lot to Scarlet, to have you in her son's life."

I smiled to myself. "It means a lot to me too, Mrs. Raef. Have a nice day." Heart heavy, I pushed 'END.'

Seconds later, the phone rang again. For a wild moment, I wondered if Raef was calling back to tell me she'd misread the results and Ence actually wasn't who we thought he was, after all.

"Hello, Alcove City Orphanage, Nurtic Leavesleft speaking."

"It's Commander Buird," said a hushed voice. "Did Raef just call you?"

"Yes, sir."

"She gave me the news, right now. I can't *believe* that he's still alive. I can't believe that he's been in Alcove City, all this time."

"Yeah, me neither." I knew there had to be more of a point to Inexor's call. He wouldn't ring me up just to muse or marvel.

"But, there's something I really don't understand, here," he said, right on cue.

"What's that?"

"His BSC. It's too low. The average mage has at least a three-point-four."

"Commence is only a kid."

"Even so. At his age, he should have a two-point-five or something. Not to mention, he shares genes with the strongest mage in history. Scarlet's BSC was a ten-point-oh. So, a *point*-seven? That hardly qualifies as a mage, at all. The tiniest spectral exertion would knock him out."

"Well, sir, it kind of does. He doesn't seem to have conscious control over his powers, either. It's more like... things happen *to* him, if you know what I mean."

Inexor whistled. "I thought any offspring of Scarlet's would have multiple sources."

"Me too. But, he's not showing any signs of possessing a second source."

"Yeah, because he hardly has the photons for *one*."

"I can't even discern the color of his frequency. I mean, Scarlet once told me that it was iridescent—red and black—but, honestly, I don't see it. At all. He might as well be infrared." I gnawed my lip. "I don't know, maybe this was stupid of me to ever consider but, as soon as I got a hunch who he was, I began to hope that... well..."

"You began to hope that he's the one. The mage the prophecy's about," Inexor quietly finished for me.

I was glad that he couldn't see my cheeks burn. "Yes."

"Leavesleft, can I tell you something?"

"Of course, sir."

"I was hoping for that, too."

Silence.

"So, um, what's he like?" Inexor blurted. "I know that it's none of my business," he added sheepishly, as though it were odd or inappropriate to be curious about his dead best friend's long-lost son.

I smiled. "Brilliant. The schooling here at the orphanage isn't too great, but I'm not talking about book-smarts. I mean, he's just *brilliant*. Sharp. Quick. Cunning. He's a natural leader, too—the other children follow him, religiously. Physically, he's tiny; he definitely inherited his parents' small stature. Currently, he's only about three feet tall. No idea how much he weighs, but I'm pretty sure my backpack is heavier. Yet, he's strong. The strongest kid I've ever met."

"Wow."

I shifted on my feet. Time for the flipside. "He also has zero self-control. He's aggressive, paranoid and short-fused. Causes scenes on a regular basis. Bullies all his peers, indiscriminately. Goes out on the town to pick fights with strangers then comes home all bruised and bloodied. And, oh yes, he once killed a kid in a fit of rage, when he was less than five ages old."

"Ah," Inexor said, "well, I guess you've got to take the bad with the good."

"What're you talking about?" a boy's voice called, from the opposite end of the hall. I wheeled around.

"Ence, what are you doing here?" I hissed, switching to Nurian. "Go back inside."

"Is that him, right now?" Inexor asked, hungrily. "Wow, he sounds a lot like Cease—or, how I think Cease *would've* sounded if his Nurian accent weren't so horrible. Did you know that Scarlet once wrote in her log that she thought Cease was turning into a throat mage?"

Ence wobbled on his crutches. "You're talking about me, I know it."

How on earth could he tell? We were speaking Ichthyothian! "I should probably go, Commander," I said to Inexor.

"Looks like you're about to have another *scene* on your hands," Inexor chortled. "Just don't let him strangle you with his hair, okay?"

There was that good old base-raised humor.

"Good-bye, sir." I ended the call.

Wait, strangle me with his hair? I frowned. Inexor assumed the wrong source.

"*Sir?*" Ence echoed. 'Sir' was the same word in Nurian as it was in Ichthyothian. "Who were you talking to?"

"Go back in, Ence," I said. "It's not okay to eavesdrop."

He didn't move. "You were talking about me, to someone else. To a 'sir.' A *superior*. I want to know who it was, and what you guys were saying about me."

"Ence, you're fully aware that I'm in the process of researching your origins. And, I already promised to let you know everything, once I find out."

"You did find out. Right now. I can tell." He hobbled down the corridor. "I'm ready to know, Nurtic."

I watched his sharp face, closely. He was ready to know. But, was I ready to tell him? Was the world ready for the son of Cease Lechatelierite and Scarlet July?

NURTIC LEAVESLEFT

"Come with me," I told Ence. "Let's talk outdoors."

He obliged, following silently. He settled on the pavement, propping his injured ankle. I plunked down beside him. He stared at me, expectantly. Where to begin?

"Ence, could I see your necklace, again?"

He hesitated for a moment, then slowly pulled it off and handed it over.

"Do you know what this is?"

"A medal."

I nodded. "Not just any medal. It's a Silver Triangle from the Ichthyothian Diving Fleet. The highest honor a diver can receive. It belonged… to your father."

Ence blinked.

"Your father is Commander Cease Terminus Lechatelierite."

He blinked, again. "Okay."

Okay? "Ence, do you know who that is?" I spoke, slowly.

"Of course, I do," he answered, stiffly. "He fought in the Ichthyothian Resistance."

"He *led* the Ichthyothian Resistance."

"I know."

I didn't know what to make of Ence's bland reaction. He was usually such an emotive person, so I expected more… well… *emotion*.

"Cease Lechatelierite married your mother on May twenty-fourth of the ninety-fourth age," I went on, "the day before his life was taken in combat. His wife was his Second-in-Command, Scarlet Carmine July."

"Before you ask: yes, I know who that is, too," Ence interjected, tone flat. "I *am* vaguely aware of major historical figures, thanks."

"In that case, I'm sure you've discerned that you've inherited a few of her spectral gifts, like your vision, memory, invisibility and eye-fire."

Ence looked almost bored.

"Seven months after your father passed away, your mother also did."

"Scarlet July was assassinated," Ence belligerently blurted. "Cut the 'passed away' crap. I hate euphemisms."

Very well, then. "Scarlet July was seven months pregnant with you when she pass—was assassinated, but you survived. Your birthday is December twenty-second of the ninety-fourth age. You were brought to Alcove City a couple weeks after you were born, to live with your grandmother, Qui Tsop Lechatelierite. At the time, she was your only living relative. But, she never got to raise you because she passed aw—died from radiation poisoning, following the 'Cobalt-60 Project' scandal. Which is why you wound up here, at the orphanage." I looked down at my hands, folded in my lap. "Your mother and I used to be comrades-in-arms. But, we were more than that. We were friends. So, she once told me what she was going to name you. It turns out that 'Ence' is only an abbreviation. Your real name is Commence. Commence July Lechatelierite."

Ence neither moved nor blinked. I might as well have been relaying this week's forecast.

"In your mother's final months, I promised her something. I said that I'd help take care of you, once you were born. And, now that I found you, I'm not going back on my words." I inhaled. Here went nothing: "Commence, I want to adopt you. I want to give you a real home. I'm not exactly well-off—far from it—but, I guarantee that life with me will still be much better than what you've had here. I'm a missionary and a pilot. You'd get to come with me on my adventures. Travel the world."

Ence looked down at the pavement. As much as he might've hated me, he didn't immediately object, as I half-expected him to. After all, he craved self-advancement as much as the next person, and he recognized that I could open quite a few doors for him.

"Well… I guess that'd be alright," he finally said, after several suspenseful seconds. "I'd like to get out of here."

I grinned. "Great."

Ence didn't smile back. "When can I move in?" he asked, businesslike.

Adoption in western First Earth countries was an exorbitantly-expensive and time-consuming legal process. My, how times have changed. These days, thanks to the endless war, there were so many orphans haunting the streets, the Nurian law pretty much allowed prospective parents a free-for-all. Basically, as long as you weren't a rapist or a serial killer, you could adopt all the kids you wanted.

"There's some paperwork involved, but Mr. Selepoh would probably let you come home with me today. That is, if you don't mind sleeping on the pull-out—I obviously don't have a bed for you yet, but we can get one tomorrow."

Grabbing his crutches, he hoisted himself up. "Okay," he said. And, with that, he hobbled back inside.

* * *

Ence's stoicism lasted the rest of the afternoon and evening. But, at night, when I brought him home and left him alone to go to sleep, he broke down. From outside his barely-cracked door, I saw him hurl his Silver Triangle against the wall, yank out fistfuls of hair, punch the couch and throw himself down on the carpet. And, last but not least, he did something I never saw him do before. He cried.

* * *

Insomnia. I lay in bed, mind chasing one stream-of-consciousness after another. I thought a lot about Ence's parents. Mainly, I thought of Cease Lechatelierite… which was odd because, between the two of them, I usually preferred to think about Scarlet July. Scarlet and I had a lot of history—history that I rarely shied from mulling over. But, tonight, I found my mind dwelling on Lechatelierite. On how little I actually knew him.

Once upon a time, I felt an allegiance to him so strong that I was honestly willing to take a bullet for him, at the drop of a hat. My commitment to him was only rivaled by my dedication to God and my country. It all seemed rather strange and frightening to me now, because Lechatelierite and I hardly ever had a real relationship to begin with. How did he do it? How did he stir my convictions like that? Scarlet and I had a substantial friendship, with mutual vulnerability. The strength of my feelings for her made sense. But, Lechatelierite? Lechatelierite never let anyone get close to him, except perhaps Scarlet and, for a time, Inexor Buird. How did he manage to instill such undying devotion in the hearts and minds of his subordinates, without ever letting us in?

I only had one private conversation with Lechatelierite, throughout my entire service in the Diving Fleet. It happened on the eve of his arrest. That day, he announced that I'd be his successor.

I was up late with diarrhea, that night. My fear of taking command manifested itself in a two o'clock bathroom trip. I was on my way back to the barracks when I came across Lechatelierite, pacing the dark corridors alone.

He looked upset. Well, he certainly had every right to be.

"Hello, sir," I greeted him, cautiously.

To my surprise, he didn't just nod curtly and continue on his way, as he usually did whenever we ran into each other. Instead, he actually stopped and gazed up at me, silver eyes struggling to focus on my face.

"What are you doing here, Leavesleft?" he asked in his heavily-accented Nurian. "I don't believe it's your turn to be on watch."

I supposed, without his visual band, he couldn't tell in the darkness that I was wearing pajamas. "No, I'm not on watch, sir. I was just returning from the restroom." The moment the word 'restroom' left my lips, I regretted it. Lechatelierite would obviously understand what *that* meant, at a time like this.

"Nervous?" he asked, bluntly.

"Yes, sir," I admitted.

"Don't be. I have complete confidence in you," he declared, shocking me to the core.

"Thank you, sir," I breathed.

"Last summer, when you were fresh out of school, I wouldn't have made you the officer of unit two, if I didn't think you had remarkable potential."

My pulse hammered so hard, I was positive that he could hear. "Thank you, sir," I repeated.

He grew pensive. "And, to think, you almost didn't get chosen for diving, at all."

Wait, what? He took me from elated to crushed in about three seconds flat. I froze.

"The Air Force Academy wanted you," he clarified. "Though you did well on the swimming tests, a lot of the examiners believed that the Air Force would've been a better fit because your pilotry record was among the best they'd ever seen. The debate wound up escalating all the way to Air Force Commander Rai Zephyr and me. I said something like, 'Well, if the man *can* dive, let him dive. I need good pilots, too.' And, that was that." He blinked. "Now, a mere age later, the entire fleet is about to be yours."

The commanders actually *fought* over me? No way.

"This will always be *your* fleet, sir," I firmly said. "I'll never be anything more than your substitute."

His head shook. "You're too heavy-handed when you give praise, Leavesleft. It makes you sound desperate. If you treat your subordinates that way, they'll never take you seriously." He looked me up and down. "I hope I'm not wrong about you."

"You aren't, sir. I promise."

"Good," he grunted.

There was a pause in which he just *stared* at me, with neither blink nor expression. I had no clue what went on in his head, when he regarded me that way. It was incredibly unnerving.

"It's been an honor to serve under you, sir," I broke the silence. "Truly."

Was that a hint of a smile in his iron eyes? "Goodnight, Leavesleft."

"Goodnight, sir." I saluted.

I tossed in my bed again, the memory receding. Lechatelierite was a good man. He trusted me with everything that he'd worked his whole life to build.

I got up and went to get a glass of water, though I wasn't really thirsty. I sat down at the edge of my bed and sipped, muscles tense. Wiping my face in my left sleeve,

I randomly started thinking about attachments and goodbyes and separations. It seemed as though, throughout my adulthood, I was always leaving someone somewhere for something. I was constantly heading here and there, inevitably leaving someone or something behind. I was a globetrotter. Ever flying away.

Ence was going to like that life. He was the adventurous type, eager to do and see and experience. Finally, with me, he'd get the chance to channel his energy into something productive. All his life, he'd been *re*active, but now, he'd have the opportunity to learn to become *pro*active.

And, hopefully, as Ence grew up in my home, he and I would grow close. I knew that when he agreed to the adoption earlier today, he was only thinking of self-advancement. But, I hoped that maybe, just maybe, as the ages rolled by, he'd mellow out and really come to see me as his dad.

So, that's what this came down to, huh? I wanted someone to love me. Someone to come home to, after my hard days. Someone to miss me when I wasn't around. Hmm. So, my motives were selfish, after all.

When I was a freshman at UVA and a co-leader of the Tri-Nation Campaign, I was either leaving Scarlet behind to head to Nuria, or leaving Ree behind to head to Conflagria. So, someone always *was* missing me. Missing me, and feeling pain because of it. Was that how things had to be? Was I either loved but hurting someone, or lonely but hurting no one? Which was better?

I placed my cup on the nightstand and lay back down, thinking about relationships and how they were always double-edged swords. 'Better to have loved and lost than never to have loved at all,' the old saying went. Was it true? All my life, I wanted to believe so. But, now, I couldn't help but think of how Scarlet July would probably still be alive today if she never fell in love with Cease Lechatelierite and had his child.

No, that wasn't fair of me. Ence's life was a gift, and I was grateful for it. Which meant that I had to be glad that Scarlet and Lechatelierite once loved one another. Everything happened for a reason.

Everything. Even bad things. Even pain, death and separation. Even the brief marriage of two radically different people who never could've made a life together anyway, no matter how hard they tried, simply because of the cruelty of this isolationist world.

For some reason, *that* made me think about August seventh of the ninety-third age—the day Scarlet and Fair left Icicle for the First Red Revolution. I'd volunteered to fly them over. Fair and I were on our way to meet up with Scarlet in the mess hall when I spotted something from the cafeteria doorway that was none of my business: Scarlet and the Commander with their arms entangled, kissing like their lives depended on it. To say that I was shocked would be the understatement of the era.

I'd immediately whirled around and blocked Fair's path, blurting, "How about we head straight for the ship and wait for Scarlet there? She's still saying bye to people, and I don't want to interrupt."

Fair blinked. "I don't hear any voices. Everyone's probably gone and Scarlet's wondering where we are."

"No, everyone isn't gone, yet. Come on, let's go out the back."

Narrowing her eyes, Fair pushed passed me.

"Hey!" I croaked.

She stopped dead in the doorframe, face contorting at the sight of Lechatelierite and Scarlet really going at it, faces mashed together. Fair threw off her hood.

"That son-of-a—"

"Fair, no!" I grabbed her hair, before she could use it to decapitate anybody.

"Get off me!"

I literally dragged her down the corridor. "Come on, it's not like he's holding her against her will." I knew what'd happen if a man *were* to try to take advantage of Scarlet; Amok Kempt almost met the same fate as Timothy Vic. "So, Scarlet must really care for him."

"How could she, how *could* she," Fair raged, "kiss the guy who tortured me! For Tincture's sake, I'm her *best friend!*"

Now, as I curled into a ball at the corner of my bed, I wondered for the gazillionth time how Scarlet did it—how she managed to get Cease Lechatelierite to let her in. How the two of them managed to take their illegal affair all the way to covalence. Scarlet sure was a rebel to the core. Crazy odds and risks didn't scare her away from anything, did it?

As for me, I'd already figured out how my human connections tended to unfold. I scrunched my lids, face planted in my pillow. It was probably a good thing that no one loved me, not even Ence. That way, no one got hurt.

Except me.

NURTIC LEAVESLEFT

August seventh.

"Commence!" I knocked on his door. "Breakfast."

He opened up. His cheek bore a clear carpet imprint.

"Pull-out couch was *that* bad, huh?" I laughed, though I knew what *really* happened, last night.

He crutched right past me, without a word.

I followed him to the kitchen. "Well, the good news is that I'm getting you a real bed today, along with anything else you may need. I took the day off from work—all three of my jobs, that is—to get you situated."

He sat down at the table, silent and staring.

I put a toasted bagel on his plate. "Commence?"

His acidic eyes settled on mine. "My name's Ence," he said, stiffly. "That's what I've been called for seven ages."

I grinned. "You're not seven, yet. Your birthday is in December—and, this age, it'll be properly celebrated, might I add."

"That's not the point!" he shouted, knocking his plate to the floor. "Don't ever call me 'Commence' again—I hate it! If my *parents* wanted to give me a name, they should've stuck around long enough to call me by it! They shouldn't have abandoned me!"

"Nobody abandoned you," I calmly said. "Your parents died in combat, serving their countries."

"Exactly! Soldiers have no right to bring kids into their screwy circumstances, in the first place!"

"Ence, that's not—"

He jumped up on his good foot. "Maybe, people should think twice before having babies if they're in the middle of a great big international war! There'd be a hell of a lot less orphans in the world! Less children suffering because of adults' negligence and stupidity!" His whole body shook.

"Ence, I knew your parents," I quietly said, "and they were anything but negligent or stupid. They were the most brilliant and caring people I ever—"

Suddenly, my shirt... was on fire! Before I could throw it off, something red and black swung from Ence's head, striking me in the chest, snuffing out the flames. Then, as rapidly as it came, it retreated, shrinking like an elastic sheet.

It was Ence's hair.

Without warning, he crumpled to the floor, lids shut and face glacier-white.

* * *

Ence spent the rest of the day paying dearly for using both of his sources back-to-back; he lay by the lit fireplace, wrapped in a blanket, sipping soup and hot coco while falling in and out of consciousness.

Despite covalence, Ence had a second source after all, like his mother. I couldn't believe it.

And, then, I thought about his voice. I thought about his astounding mastery of tone. He had extraordinary vocal control. The ability to almost paralyze or hypnotize with his words. Like his father.

I chewed my lip, anxiety pricking my chest. Maybe, Ence wasn't just a dual-sourced mage. Maybe, he had spectrum in his eyes, hair... and throat. Maybe, he was a multi-sourced enchant. *The* Multi-Source Enchant.

* * *

My apartment was hot and smoky from keeping the fireplace running all day and well into the night. Dizzy and exhausted, I yanked open my bedroom window, leaned over the edge and inhaled the humid August air. Wails of city traffic grated against the blur of whizzing lights. I titled my head back and squinted at the few stars managing to poke through the thick grey curtain of the sky.

When Scarlet died, so did a lot of my naïveté and optimism. As the ages slipped away, I felt my heart progressively harden as I struggled with several of the beliefs that I'd always clung to since childhood—mainly, that everything happened for a reason and that good always prevailed over evil in the end. And, the more time passed, the more I doubted that the Multi-Source Enchant would ever come.

Commence lit a spark of hope in my heart, but it was a small spark. What if he was just another false alarm, like Scarlet July or Spry Scintillate? Scintillate, Scarlet's grandfather, was a leg mage with a hint of hair spectrum. Mage society hinged its hopes and dreams on him… until he failed spectacularly, leaving the System to cover his tracks. Scarlet spent her entire life trying to decipher the prophecy, frantically doing everything and anything in her power to solve the planet's many ailments. There was no denying that she accomplished a lot for mankind during—and, even after—her short existence. Consequently, many believed that the prophecy really was over and done. But, I didn't. I loved Scarlet dearly, but I couldn't convince myself that she was the one, because she never actually had confidence in any of her prophetic interpretations and because, even after all her hard work, Second Earth was still very much in shambles.

Ence may've had multiple sources—more than Scarlet or her grandfather—but, he was weak. Weaker than normal single-sourced mages his age. There was no gentle way to put it: Ence was spectrally inept. I saw no trace of the iridescent aura that Scarlet claimed he had in the womb. I wished I could help him with that, but I didn't have the faintest idea how. I couldn't offer him a magical education. Conflagria was in ruins; I couldn't exactly send him abroad to study at the Mage Castle.

I wanted so badly to believe that the prophet would come, that the earth still had a reason to hope for better days. But, as I went to pile another blanket atop Ence's shivering frame, my heart couldn't help but sink even lower.

NURTIC LEAVESLEFT

By midday, snow began to fall. While snow in early November wasn't unheard of, it wasn't exactly the norm, around here. Southern Nuria only tended to get wintry from December through March.

I wondered how Ence would handle it, coming home from school. He hated autumn, constantly on the brink of hypothermia. I imagined that winter would be an absolute nightmare for him. But, alas, when I opened the door, I was greeted by a snowball in the face. Ence laughed, wiping his bare hands on his jeans. His backpack, coat, scarf and gloves lay abandoned in a heap beside him.

"Ence?" I breathed, blinking slush from my eyes.

"I'm gonna stay outside for a while!" he cried, kicking his gear inside. "Weather's too good!" And, with that, he turned on his heel and took off, back down all seven flights of stairs.

He explained to me later in the evening that he loved both weather extremes, not just heat. Ah, the wonders of covalence.

"I'm good with anything but so-called 'moderate,'" he said over his pre-algebra homework.

Unlike Scarlet, he couldn't spare a photon of spectrum to control his body-temperature. So, the window above his desk was now wide open, blasting us with icy air. And, for the first time since he moved in, the fireplace was dark.

"Mind if we keep your room door closed whenever you need to crack a window in the middle of a blizzard?" I asked, dryly. I didn't exactly enjoy freezing as much as he did. It'd been many ages since I lived in Ichthyosis.

"Sure," he said, mischief in his smile.

Of course, after that, Ence insisted on reopening his door whenever my back was turned, just to spite me. He thought it was funny when I caught a cold.

"Do you know how uncomfortable it is, to wear a flight-mask with a runny nose?" I asked him.

"No," he retorted, "I've never flown before."

I sniffled. "Well, you certainly aren't encouraging me to let you near my plane, anytime soon."

Flying had become a touchy subject since Ence hit middle school, a couple days ago. Allow me to backtrack a smidge and explain how a six-age-old managed to *get* into middle school, in the first place.

Once the adoption was finalized, I enrolled Ence in Bay River Elementary, whose school-age started the first week of October. Though he was extraordinarily gifted, the poor quality of his prior education coupled with the absence of certain 'normal' life experiences landed him in the fourth grade. However, within a day or so, it became evident to Ence's teachers that his critical thinking skills far outstripped that of his nine and ten-age-old peers. Not to mention, he never needed review. He absorbed information like a thirsty hobnail, with ferocious enthusiasm. By the end of his very first week, he was permitted to take another battery of exams, prompting an immediate transfer to the fifth grade.

Soon, it became a pattern: Ence would enter a grade-level, breeze through it, take another set of tests, then get bumped up again. In under a month, he soared from fourth to seventh grade. Now, Ence attended Bay River

Intermediate, where he likely wouldn't stay for more than a fortnight.

While Ence still remained somewhat of an aggressor, the frequency of his tantrums diminished with his increasing workload. Just as I predicted, all he really needed to (somewhat) mellow out were some real challenges—and, not just academic ones. It wasn't long before he found his true athletic callings: karate and swimming.

I saw it coming from a mile away: Ence's love of sparring and swimming would ultimately lead to the development of a certain desire. Indeed, Ence asked me about Bay River Intermediate's Junior ROTC Program last night, roughly thirty-six hours into his middle-school career.

"I already love the water," he had told me, eagerly. "And, you can teach me to fly. So, once I graduate from high school, I can go to the Nurian Diving Academy."

"No ROTC and no flying lessons," I said, flatly.

"But, it's what I want!" he cried.

"You're too young to know what you want."

"I'm a *Lechatelierite!* It's in my blood!"

"Cool down," I said, as he struck me in the shin. "You might set off your eye-fire."

"Good! I'll watch you burn!" he screamed, kicking me in the gut.

"Do I *really* need to remind you how sick you get after using magic? If you have to stay home to recover, how will you finish off seventh grade by Friday?"

"I don't care! I HATE YOU!" He jumped onto my back like a feral cat.

I peeled his arms from around my neck. "I wonder what the ROTC admins would say if they saw you, now? You don't have a fraction of the discipline it takes to be a soldier."

"You'll see!" He thrashed. "One day, I'm going to be the boss of everyone! I'll be a commander—but, not like my *parents*," he spat.

Ence couldn't go a day without finding some reason to rail against Scarlet and Lechatelierite. His hatred for his parents was astounding.

"You don't have the *loyalty* it takes to be a soldier, either," I added, sadly.

"You'll see," he growled again, intense voice so much like the father he despised. "Just wait, I'm going to be there when the alliance wins the war!"

I slammed my open palm against the wall, causing Ence to literally jump. Congratulations, I thought, you're the first person since Fair Gabardine to really get under my skin. The first person in months to fully spark my fuse.

"You don't get it, do you?" I shouted. "Wars can't be 'won'! Wars *end;* they're never won. When all's said and done, each side's left with a pile of body-bags, and the side with less *calls* itself the 'winner,' while in reality, they're both sore losers. And, you know who loses the most? Who loses *every time*, no matter the documented outcome? The soldiers. The soldiers who survive. The soldiers who have to go on living, day after day, age after age, in the wake of everything that's been lost!" My chest heaved. "I'm sorry, Ence, but your mother once told me that she wanted to keep you away from the Ichthyothian military. All she *ever* wanted is for you to have a normal life, free from the trauma that she and your father experienced. And, I'd be damned if I let her down, one more time."

Ence said nothing. He stared at me, eyes almost aquamarine in the fluorescent light. Then, without a word, he retreated to his room and slammed the door.

ENCE LECHATELIERITE

I couldn't stand it, anymore. I was going to go crazy if I spent one more day with Nurtic Leavesleft.

Yeah, yeah, I was an ingrate. Just this past summer, I was scraping soup bowls at the Alcove City Orphanage, but now, I lived in a real apartment and ate three full meals a day and attended a good school where I got to learn algebra and go swimming. I wouldn't have been able to get this far without Nurtic, so I ought to thank my lucky stars for him, right?

Well, guess what? I didn't ask to be put on this godforsaken earth. I didn't do anything to deserve all the crap I'd swallowed since birth. And, I didn't see why my spoiled-rotten peers deserved more than me. On the contrary. Why did they get to grow up in nice homes with parents who answered to their every need, while I spent my first six ages wasting away in some sewer-hole? The complaints that I heard from my classmates made my blood boil. Like, my second day in fourth grade, one girl actually whined at lunchtime, 'Oh nooo, mommy packed peanut butter and grape jelly when I *told* her I only like strawberry!' I jumped up, grabbed her sandwich, split the slices open and threw them in her face, growling, 'There are kids in this world—in this *city*—who've never even *tasted* jelly before!' That got me in big trouble, but I didn't care. I'd eaten nothing but dry bread and soup for nearly seven ages and my growth seemed stunted because of it. Now, no matter how much I exercised, I still stayed shorter and thinner than everybody else. Everyone was so big and fat, compared to me. So squishy. Their bodies were like pillows.

So, yeah, *they* were the ingrates, not me. Why did I have to go through hell to get this far while everybody else got everything handed to them since the cradle? I wanted to scream at the unfairness of it all, at how society pampered some and neglected others. Moreover, I wanted to change that. There were so many things in this world that needed fixing. I believed that nothing should ever be left to chance, that everything should be controlled. One day, I was going to be the one to control it all, ensuring that power and opportunity were given to the deserving.

If the world worked right, I wouldn't be in Alcove City right now, spending my days sitting in a classroom with a bunch of listless idiots who had a hard time with simple linear functions. Though the life I had now was way better than what I had at the orphanage, it still wasn't enough for me. I wanted more. I *needed* more. The desire was like a sticky fire in my gut. I couldn't extinguish it. I couldn't ignore it. I was meant for greater things. And, I was going to get those things with or without Nurtic's help.

No, it had to be without. Because Nurtic was part of the problem. He was holding me back. He was a micro-manager. He was like: let's see if I can make Ence into a perfect little boy, doing only what I want him to do, thinking only what I want him to think, breathing only when I want him to breathe. Well, I couldn't bear to be his pawn, anymore.

I wanted to do ROTC, but of course, Nurtic said no. Initially, he even objected to the *swim team*. He was always like, 'Oh, I used to play lacrosse and I loved it; why don't you give that a shot?' or 'You're such a fast runner, maybe you should try track and field.' See how paranoid and controlling he was? I wasn't even thinking about the military when I initially decided to try swimming in the fourth grade. But, Nurtic had that fear in mind, from the start. That's why he always kept me away from his plane, even before I began asking him to take me up in it. I lived with *Nurtic freaking Leavesleft* and I'd never ridden an *airplane!* That was like being the heir of the Adip Café franchise without ever tasting coffee.

Nurtic knew how smart I was; he knew that if he ever took me flying, I'd be able to figure out how to do it myself, just from watching him. Nurtic knew what I was capable of. He knew my arsenal, inside and out. Because, once upon a time, I trusted him and told him everything. Never again would I reveal myself so fully, to anyone. I learned my lesson: anything I shared with others could always wind up getting used against me. I had a hunch that Nurtic knew more about my past and my parents than he let on. He was keeping secrets from me. Secrets *about me.* That wasn't right.

Nurtic was holding me back. Hell, this whole country was one big cage. Nuria, the Great and Mighty Democratic-Republic. The Frontier of Freedom and Opportunity. What a joke. This nation was doing nothing but tying me down. I found everything about it oppressive. Especially the weather. Save for a few days in the summer and winter, I couldn't *stand* the weather. My strength was measured by my proximity to a fireplace or space-heater. Nurtic said that my mother could magically regulate her body-temperature. Well, I couldn't do that because I didn't have nearly as much spectrum as her. And, that was *her* fault—she married a magicless Nordic, gave birth to a covalent freak, then left that kid all alone an inhospitable country where he'd never belong. I hated being weaker than everybody else and, as long as I stayed here, I always would be. Every day, I fought to pretend to be fine when, in truth, every breath I took was like a stab in the lungs. No one at the orphanage really noticed or cared that I'd sweat and shiver at the same time. But, in public school, I was being watched much more closely, by everyone. Peers. Teachers. Administrators. They all noticed. They insisted that something was wrong. They forced me to go to the school nurse. It made people suspicious. It made people ask me questions. Questions I couldn't answer. Questions I wasn't *supposed* to answer. Nurtic said that I couldn't tell anyone who I really was. I had to let everyone go on believing that the son of Scarlet July and Cease Lechatelierite was dead, so I wouldn't get dragged into the international conflict. My existence was a scandal. Revealing my parentage would endanger me. It would give me many enemies. As long as I wanted to live a 'normal life,' no one could know the truth.

But, I was tired of hiding. So very tired. One day, I was going to stop hiding. But, I had to be careful about it. Wait for the right time. Tell it to the right people. Use it to my advantage, to get what I wanted. To get all the power and opportunity I needed to change this world into what it was supposed to be. My identity was part of my arsenal. It was intel that I had to use wisely.

Another obstacle I faced everyday was my spectrum. It controlled me. I hated being controlled, by anyone or anything. I wanted control over *it*. But, as long as I stayed in Nuria, I couldn't get any mage training. Nurtic once told me that Scarlet July never went to magic school; she taught herself. But, her powers were naturally a lot stronger than mine, which meant it was probably much easier for her to self-educate. *She* didn't feel sick every time she tried to light a mere candle with her eyes. *She* didn't writhe in pain from random unfettered photon surges. She had a BSC of ten-point-oh, not a *point*-seven; she was able to regulate her frequency. She could prevent it from attacking her own body. And, she could teach herself to use it, not only because her aura was strong, but because she got to spend her childhood watching other mages in action, all around her. She learned from observation, they way I liked to learn. But, I had no one to watch. That was, as long as I stayed here in Nuria.

My parents. This was all *their* fault. Two war leaders—two teenage soldiers living under the gun—had no business having a son. They had no right to bring a covalent child of war into this world, at the mercy of point-seven parts-per-milligram.

Just last week, Nurtic and I were arguing (yet again) over the crime that my parents committed by having a child. Nurtic fiercely defended them, saying how they never *meant* to cause me any harm, that it wasn't their fault that they got killed in combat, that they would've lovingly raised me if they survived the war. I'd heard about the Laws of Emotional Protection and I agreed with them, not because I thought relationships were 'mentally compromising' or any of that stupid psycho-babble, but because sexual relationships often led to babies. And, active-duty teenage soldiers certainly had no business making babies.

I thought about them all the time, my parents. Every minute, I felt oppressed by them, like their shadows were hanging over me, following me around, preventing me from sleeping at night and eating during the day. Their legacy haunted me. Tormented me. Challenged me. I wanted to stand up, look them in the eye and tell them how much I hated my secret last name. But, of course, I'd never have the opportunity to talk to them. I was forever condemned to live with all this unresolved anger bottled inside.

Now, I lay in bed, watching the night slip away, toying with my father's Silver Triangle. I could see it clearly, in the dark. The ribbon was rough and coarse, the medal scratched and dirty.

Ichthyosis first.

ENCE LECHATELIERITE

I arrived home from school to find Nurtic in his Frost's Delivery Service flightsuit, tossing a helmet at me. Catching it, I looked up at him, questioningly.

"Rettis cancelled, last minute," he said through tight lips. Rettis Hah was my babysitter. She was a black-belt in three different forms of martial arts. An interesting choice for a sitter, indeed. "I put a child-sized flightsuit on your bed. Strap up and meet me outside, asap." And, with that, he turned and disappeared down the stairs.

I couldn't believe it. Nurtic was taking me up! Not because he wanted to, of course, but because he had to. He sounded real mad about it. Grinning, I ran to my room. This was my chance to learn to fly. Finally!

Nurtic left me to figure out the suit on my own. He knew I'd be able to. He knew my skillset so damn well.

Five minutes later, I was on the tarmac, ready to go. In this day and age, most neighborhoods had runways and aircraft parking-lots. Though, Nurtic was the only tenant in this particular building to have his own wings.

"I already loaded everything in the cargo bay, last night. This'll be a direct flight," he said as we climbed aboard. "Don't touch anything," he added fiercely, as he helped me with my harness. "You are to sit still the entire time without touching a thing, unless I specifically instruct otherwise. Understood?"

"Yes," I retorted, eyes rolling.

"If we're about to crash, I'll tell you to eject." He pointed to a button. "But, that's it. Otherwise, keep your hands to yourself. Got it?"

"I said *yes*."

He could forbid me from touching, but he sure couldn't stop me from seeing. As he got situated in the seat before me, I drank in my incredible surroundings, instantly memorizing every detail. Things looked a bit different than in the manuals in Nurtic's closet.

Forgotten on the floor by my feet was a white contraption that looked like an old-fashioned cell phone. Leaning forward, I picked it up. Engraved on the back was an acronym: 'P.A.V.L.A.K.' That didn't ring any bells. It certainly wasn't mentioned in any of Nurtic's pilotry books. I removed the covering and, immediately, a vast holographic grid sprang forth. The menu seemed to be written in another language, like a scrambled version of Nurian with lots of extra accents and consonants. Staring intently at the first option, I played with the letters in my mind… and, somehow, after only a couple minutes, could tell that it said, 'Historical Maps of First and Second Earth.' I wanted to select the feature to see if I was right. Instinctively, I reached up and tapped the floating phrase. Sure enough, the long list got instantly replaced by a giant world map, captioned by a string of numbers: '01/01/01/01 - 02.' January first of the first age of the first era of Second Earth.

"What are you doing?" Nurtic's voice jolted me from my mesmerized stupor. He glared over his shoulder. "I told you not to touch anything!" With that, he reached over and snatched the device from my hand.

"What *is* that thing?" I breathed.

He didn't answer.

"Where did it come from? What language is it in? What else can it do, besides show maps?"

We began taxiing down the runway.

"Why do you have it? Where did it come from?" I insisted. "Nurtic?"

"I'm busy, Ence," he said, tersely.

I pictured the menu in my mind and found that, when I concentrated hard enough, I could figure out what most of the words meant. They just... made sense to me, after a while. The first four options had to do with mapping and navigation. But, the fifth and sixth were what really intrigued me: 'Recorded Battles' and 'Strategy Planner.' So, this was a piece of *military* technology. Ichthyothian military technology. A relic from Nurtic's soldier days.

"Why don't you use your Ichthyothian Diving Fleet PAV-LAK system, Nurtic?" I asked, grinning behind my mask.

He shifted about, visibly alarmed that I was able to figure out what the gadget was, so quickly.

"It's really not that difficult to decipher the display, you know," I chuckled. "Ichthyothian is like Nurian, but wordier and with extra syllables and stuff."

Nurtic said nothing.

"So, anyway, can I ask you some things about flying?"

Silence.

"I'm just curious about 'Instrument Landing Systems and Range,'" I went on. "Pilots can use RADAR to determine distance while doing an instrument landing, right? Well, how exactly does that work? Is it as simple as receiving ranges from ATC? Is the assistance of an ATSU necessary?"

"Tell me, right now, where that question came from," Nurtic demanded, anger and alarm punctuating his usually-mellow tone.

"What, don't all seventh-graders wonder about ILS?"

"Ence!"

"Alright, alright. I looked at the books in your closet."

"Looked?"

"Okay, I read them."

"You *read* them?"

"Well, not the two on aviation management, just the ones on pilotry."

He exhaled loudly into the intercom. "For your information, those resources are really outdated. I've had most of them since I went to civilian flight school, before you were born. Some of the planes they cover aren't even manufactured, anymore. Not to mention, commercial and military aviation are far from identical."

"Yeah, but, the general principals of flight are timeless and adaptable, aren't they? Why else did you start out with getting a private pilot's license, flying prop planes and such, before you went onto the Diving Academy?"

Nurtic's left hand actually shook on the joystick. It was incredible to see him so tense. He rarely ever lost his cool. I probably could've thrown a million tantrums and he wouldn't have gotten as furious as he was, right now.

"Are you going to answer my question?" I pressed.

"No."

"I'm gonna find out no matter what, you know. You're just pushing me to do more research. Why not spare me the trouble?"

His breathing got louder and faster.

"Please? I'll shut up after, I promise."

"The outer marker is the primary range indicator during an ILS," he snapped. "That's what's used to distinguish the final descent point. You have to identify a known range and correlate it with an altitude, or else you might wind up getting a fake glideslope indication."

"So, you don't use RADAR fix?"

"I've never seen it used for that purpose, no."

"But, *could* you use it? Like, in case of emergency?"

"Well… I guess so, if all other options became unavailable, for some reason. But, it's definitely not the best choice."

"What *are* the other options, anyway? I know about VOR radial, but what else is there?"

"Range position can be designated by VOR radial, DME fix or GPS fix. I suppose, if there was an outage, a controller could provide the pilot with the fix by using the ATC radar."

"What about an onboard weather radar?"

"No. That can't clearly mark ground positions."

"Can cross-radial ranging be used to detect a final descent point?"

"It *could*, but you're supposed to use OM for that. Cross-radial ranging is really meant for distinguishing initial descent fixes and intermediate fixes, or to differentiate traffic."

"But, you still *can* use it for final descent if you want to, right? If OM isn't working for some reason?"

"Yes."

There was a pause.

"Resourceful, aren't you?" Nurtic grunted.

"I don't like the idea of being dependent on any one thing," I said. "At any time, something can break or malfunction. I'd want to have options. You never know what might happen."

"Yes, you never know," he breathed, sadly.

NURTIC LEAVESLEFT

Ence would be home from school, any minute now. Rettis, his babysitter, was on her way over. I fastened the collar of my flightsuit, snatched my helmet from the kitchen table, and went to fetch my keys from my nightstand drawer.

They were missing.

Suspicions piqued, I opened the coat closet and, sure enough, Ence's flightsuit was also gone.

I threw open the front door and bolted downstairs, blowing past Xis Robyan, an elderly neighbor.

"Nurtic?" she croaked after me, arms full of groceries. "What are you doing, here? I mean, I swear I just saw you taxi down the runway..."

I made it onto the tarmac in time to see my own plane lift off.

"Good day," said Ze Beda, a resident of the third floor, dog leash in hand. He did a double take. "Wait a minute, if you're here, then who—what—?"

I plunked on my helmet, visor up, and yelled into the intercom, "Ence!"

"Don't worry, I'm not running away," he calmly replied, retracting the landing gear. "I'm just testing out what I learned from you, yesterday. So far, so good. I'll come back when I'm done."

"What he's *learned* from you?" Ze echoed, overhearing Ence's transmission. "You're teaching your *kid* to *fly*, Mr. Leavesleft?"

I ignored Ze. "Ence, you need to get back here, right now. I'm going to give you landing instructions, okay? Listen closely and follow *everything* I say. Got it?"

"I can't believe you." Ze was incredulous. "You should go to jail for this!"

"I already know how to land," Ence retorted. "I saw you do it yesterday and I've read your manuals. I don't need help." He began to circle, widely and neatly.

"I don't care what you think you know!" I boomed.

"I'm calling the police," Ze declared, though without making any movement toward the cell phone bulging in his pocket.

"Alright, the first thing you need to do is configure the gear down. The flap setting you need is—"

"I already know the right flap setting and how to set it," Ence interrupted.

I watched as the gear slowly unfolded. I gave him a target landing speed and demanded that he report his current descent rate.

He relayed it to me. "And, it's pretty constant, too," he added, proudly. "No need for power corrections."

"None, at all?" Usually, even when all was dandy, *some* degree of power correction was required.

"That's right."

"Are you sure?"

"Yes!"

The wind suddenly picked up, causing Ence to approach the runway at a slight angle.

"You're weathervaning," I warned. "Crosswind correction, now. Use the rudder to align the nose of the plane with the runway centerline. Use the ailerons to adjust your left wing." The wing dropped. "Too low—scale it back a few degrees!" The wing elevated. "Good. Now, because you're crosswind-correcting, you're going to touch down with your upwind main gear first, then—"

"Then, the secondary main gear, and the nosegear last, I know. Quit lecturing me," Ence shot.

"Alright, you're in the flare, now. Reduce your power to idle." I told him his target pitch angle. "And, pull the nose up, quick; your pitch isn't flat enough."

"Okay."

I held my breath as Ence touched down.

"You may've hit tarmac, but you need to maintain the crosswind correction," I warned as the plane veered a little.

Once Ence slowed to a stop, I ran across the lot, jumped onto the hull and bodily pulled him from the cockpit. He made it. He was safe. My craft wasn't going to become his coffin, after all. I couldn't believe it.

On the sidewalk, Ze was still immobilized.

"Nurtic," Ence whined, squirming in my arms. "Nurtic, I can't breathe."

"Don't you *ever* do that again!"

"Why not? You've done way worse; you've been to war."

"Not when I was six!"

"I'm almost seven. Moreover, my father was already actively training for combat at my age." He pulled away from me. "Even as a kid, his life had real purpose. He got to put his talents to use."

"Going to school and having fun is all the purpose someone your age needs. You'll have plenty of time to bear adult burdens when you're an adult."

His head shook. "What if I'm ready, now? What if I don't want to wait?"

"The fact that you think you're ready now is proof enough that you aren't. Not to mention, even your father believed in waiting. He fought hard to tear down the Childhood Program." Yeah, too bad the Trilateral Committee overturned that decision about ten minutes after his death. "And, like I said before, your mother made it very clear to me that she wanted to keep you away from—"

"Yeah, well, neither of them are around to tell me what to do, now are they?" Ence growled.

"But, *I* am. Your legal guardian. And, I happened to respect their wishes."

He angrily threw my keys at me and jumped down onto the tarmac. "I'll meet Rettis inside," he muttered, stomping away.

"Ence," I called after him. "Ence!"

He skidded to a stop. "Yeah?"

"I'm glad you're okay."

He didn't respond. He just stood there and regarded me for a while, face deadpan. I wondered what was going on behind those glassy grey-green eyes.

I forced myself to turn and climb aboard. Time for my daylong roundtrip to Notser City.

"Nurtic," Ence piped, before I could shut the cockpit.

I poked my head out. "Yes?"

"It was... beautiful," he breathed, face still stoic, though ruddier than usual. "Piloting, I mean. Even for just a few minutes." He swallowed. "I understand why you love it so much."

And, before I could answer, he crisply wheeled around, marched past our still-gaping neighbor and disappeared upstairs.

I prepped for takeoff, a strange sensation building in my chest. Ence's reaction to flying reminded me so much of my own, roughly a decade ago when I went up solo for the first time. I remembered everything about that day. It was the fall of my senior age of high school. The second

Saturday in November. Light wind, partly cloudy. Fifty degrees. The plane was a 'NurroJet 25' with a 'TFE731' on its left side. I remembered the thrill of jetting off without an instructor in the copilot's seat. It was just me and the open sky. Pure joy.

That was how Ence felt, today.

Ence wanted to join the ROTC so that, someday, he could also become a military pilot. Was it right to deprive him from what he truly loved? My parents weren't exactly thrilled about my decision to enlist, but they let me do it anyway because it was what I really wanted.

No. It was what I *thought* I wanted. What my naïve, sheltered teenage self thought I wanted. I had no idea what awaited me long after the military world chewed and spat me out: a lifetime of heart-wrenching grief and psychological turmoil.

I exhaled into my flight-mask, resolve burning. I was going to do something right for a change and make sure Scarlet's wishes were honored.

ENCE LECHATELIERITE

I loitered at the foot of the stairs until Nurtic's plane disappeared into the horizon. Then, I shed my flightsuit, revealing the ratty t-shirt and jeans underneath—all I planned on taking with me. Everything else, I'd manage to get when needed, later on.

Rettis awaited me, in Nurtic's apartment. But, soon enough, she'd realize that I wasn't coming up. Let her look for me. Let her panic and call the police. Let Nurtic freak and cry and traverse the hemisphere in search of me. Because they weren't going to find me. No one would. For I didn't want to be seen. It was as simple as that.

For the past few weeks, I'd monitored the schedules of the trade ships. Yesterday, I chose my ride: today's 'NS 725,' bound for Aventurine City, Ichthyosis.

Vanishing from sight, I headed for the ports.

* * *

Overall, being a stowaway was fairly easy. I never required much food to begin with, and whatever I did want, I invisibly stole from the kitchens. When not creeping around to snag essentials or use restrooms, I saved my spectrum and hid out the good old-fashioned way: by squeezing amongst stuff in the cargo bay.

That was the difficult part for me. Not because I couldn't fit—for once, being small came in handy for something—

but, because it was tough to sit still for so many consecutive hours a day. I became restless. I wanted to kick something. Punch something. Knock something over. Make something bleed. But, no, I couldn't mess with the crew, here. This wasn't the street. I couldn't just break these people's faces then go home and forget about it. I was a passenger on *their* ship. I needed them. If I hurt them, I'd be shooting myself in the foot.

I couldn't wait to get to Ichthyosis. I wasn't running away, I was setting myself free. I was going somewhere I'd belong.

NURTIC LEAVESLEFT

When I touched down on the tarmac in front of my apartment complex, I was greeted by a congregation of policemen and neighbors. At the center of it all stood a rather pink-faced Rettis.

My stomach flipped.

I clambered out of the cockpit, tossing my helmet aside. "What's going on?" I demanded. "Rettis, where's Ence?"

An officer strode forward, carrying a large plastic bag… containing a child-sized flightsuit and helmet.

"Mr. Leavesleft," he began, voice grave.

"What's going on?" I repeated.

"Nurtic, I'm so sorry," Rettis sobbed, grabbing my left sleeve. "I couldn't call you while you were in transit—"

"What's going on?" I repeated, though I already had a strong hunch. I just couldn't accept it. I refused to.

"Ence… never came home, this afternoon," she whispered, confirming my worst fears.

"He did," I objected, dumbly. "Before I left, he went upstairs. I saw him."

"He never actually came inside your place. He left his gear on the steps," Rettis said.

"We have search and rescue crews, scouring the city as we speak," the officer added.

"The city?" I snorted. "Ence isn't going to stay in the city. Hell, he isn't even going to stay in the *country*. He's probably aboard a ship to Ichthyosis, right now."

The policeman was definitely taken aback by that. "Ichthyosis?" He blinked. "Mr. Leavelseft, trade ships have tight security."

"You don't know Ence," I retorted, hollowly. "Ence can sneak anywhere he wants, without being seen. *Anywhere.*"

He rolled his eyes. My six-age-old was missing, and this guy actually had the nerve to *roll his eyes* at me. It took my every ounce of self-control not to shatter his nose-bridge with my fist and wind up in cuffs.

"Why would he even want to go to that frozen wasteland?"

I wasn't going to waste another second talking to him. Wordlessly, I turned on my heel and ran back to my plane, snatching my helmet from the pavement along the way, ignoring every cry of, "Mr. Leavesleft?"

NURTIC LEAVESLEFT

After spending every waking minute of the past fortnight scouring the southern Ichthyothian coastline to no avail, I returned home to recoup for a bit while the authorities continued combing Alcove City. With neither spectrometers nor diffusion technology—tools entirely out of civilian reach—I doubted any of us stood a real chance at tracking down an eye mage. We needed military intervention. But, alas, Inexor Buird refused to mobilize his fleet for the hunt.

"The cops don't even know what they're looking for," I'd told Inexor over the phone, earlier this week. "And, even if they did, it wouldn't matter—they don't have the right resources. We need your spectrometers and your soldiers' knowledge of the magical."

"I'm sorry, but I'm afraid that the steep economic recession makes your wild-scabrous-chase cost-prohibitive," he responded, tiredly.

Excuse me? "I'm talking about rescuing your dead best friend's six-age-old son, and you have the nerve to whine about *cost?*" I snarled.

Inexor sighed. "Leavesleft, you and I are the only ones who even know that Ence is a mage, aside from a couple members of the Icicle medical team who've been sworn to secrecy at penalty of their lives. Do you realize that you're asking me to blow his cover?"

"You can't trust your own men to have some discretion? Don't they still care about Ence's parents?"

"They sure do, but you know full-well that they aren't the ones we need to beware of. The Trilateral Committee monitors my every move, trying to limit government spending. If I authorize the use of military resources and manpower on something like this..."

"When Cease Lechatelierite was in charge, he always did whatever needed to be done, no matter the risk," I growled. "He didn't fear the Trilateral Committee."

"Yeah, well, he should have," Inexor gave a sour chuckle, "because whenever he put a single toe out of line, he *always* got caught and *always* paid the price—him and his entire fleet. You of all people should remember that he never got away with a damn thing. If I sanction this mission, the Trilateral Committee *will* uncover everything and they *will* see to it themselves that Ence gets thoroughly screwed."

Forget 'screwed,' I was afraid that Ence wouldn't even live to see his seventh age. "Sir," I pleaded, throat tightening, "how can you turn a blind eye to the fact that my little boy is out there on the streets, fighting to survive?"

"That's the thing, Leavesleft; if everything you've told me about him is true, he's not a little boy, and he'll win whatever fight he encounters. I trust him with his own future a hell of a lot more than I do the Trilateral Committee."

Inexor really was going to sit on his hands, hanging Ence and me out to dry. I couldn't believe it. "Your kind may think nothing of child-abuse or neglect," I spat, "but, normal people would be appalled by the words leaving your mouth."

"Leavesleft—"

"In your world, it may be typical for young kids to have to fend for themselves," I half-shouted, "but, in *my* world—

Ence's world—it's unthinkable. Criminal. I can't rest until I know he's safe!"

Inexor exhaled, loudly. "I'm sorry, I really am. But, I can't get the fleet involved. That's my final answer."

"Sir!"

"You're a better man than me, Leavesleft. I admire everything you've done and are trying to do for Ence. He's lucky to have you, even if he can't see it. For his sake, I do hope that you find him. But, if you don't... just have a little faith in him, okay?"

And, before I could say anything more, Inexor hung up.

NURTIC LEAVESLEFT

Exhausted beyond belief, I yanked my door open and stumbled inside without bothering to turn on any lights. I threw off my helmet; it hit the tile with a resonating bang and rolled underneath the kitchen table. I went to Ence's room and lay on his floor, amidst his laundry and books and papers.

I never should've made that stupid promise to Scarlet. If I hadn't forcibly imposed myself on Ence's life, he would've still been here, in Alcove City. He would've been ignorant and miserable, but safe. I buried my burning face in Ence's swim-team jacket, inhaling his strange salt-smoke scent.

When would I learn? Everything and everyone I ever tried to help or save always wound up failing, dying, ending, getting hurt or falling apart. Commence July Lechatelierite now joined the lengthy list of lives I'd inadvertently ruined, in my effort to do what I thought was right.

ENCE LECHATELIERITE

Whiteness surrounded me. From the snow-covered mountains to the wool-woven sky to the sterile high-rises, all I saw was white, stretching endlessly in every direction except that of the cobalt-blue shore. I was in a land made of glass.

And, I was cold. Bitterly cold. I wasn't expecting that. In Alcove City, I thrived in so-called 'inclement weather.' But, apparently, Aventurine defined 'inclemency' rather differently. Here, snowfall was measured in feet, not inches. Here, a 'chilly breeze' meant winds strong enough to knock a full-grown man to his ass. Here, ice didn't flutter from the sky and gently glaze the pavement, it pierced your face like needles and smacked the ground hard enough to make a sound.

Apparently, being of Ichthyothian descent wasn't enough to be comfortable in an Ichthyothian environment. People around here didn't show a sliver of skin while outside; they wore coats, scarves, hats, hoods, gloves and visors. In my t-shirt and jeans, I definitely stood out, totally looking the part of a street urchin.

I didn't plan on being one for long, though. I was going to join the military. But, first, I had to figure a few things out.

As days passed, I settled into a routine. I cloaked myself with magic to steal food and sneak into places to sleep. I prowled the streets and fought for supremacy among the other urchins—not for fun, this time. I taught myself to read and write Ichthyothian almost overnight; Isolationist Laws long forgotten, it wasn't difficult to find the tools I needed to do so.

It helped that Aventurine City had become a 'nocturna-town' in recent ages. I always had somewhere to go. Places were always open. Though, whenever I did enter a public facility, like a library, my reddish hair and permanently-sunburnt skin attracted a lot of attention. It seemed like everyone on this island had dark hair and pale complexions. One day, a nervy little kid actually asked me if I were a Conflagrian terrorist. It took a lot of self-control not to show him with my eyes just how Conflagrian I really was.

My coloring wasn't the only reason I was a magnet for stupid inquiries and suspicious stares. Looking like a starving vagabond certainly made life interesting. In various facilities, staff would actually order me to leave because 'homeless aren't welcome.' I always obeyed—I didn't want to add the Aventurine City Police Department to my list of concerns—but, I made sure to secretly return at some point to even the score via ransacking or vandalism. Retaliating gave me a sense of relief. I had so much rage inside of me, all the time. So much. My constant mistreatment served as a continual reminder of how messed up the world was. What was so detrimental about a homeless person sitting quietly at a library, minding his own business and *reading?* Was my very presence so offensive that others couldn't even stand to be in the same building as me? It made no sense. If a poor unemployed guy didn't study, how'd he better himself? The world system kept down those who were already down and elevated those who already had it all.

That wouldn't be the case if I were the ruler of everybody.

When I wasn't getting kicked out of public places, I was being asked dumb questions like: where's your mommy?

Why aren't you dressed properly? Are you cold? Would you like me to find you a book more *suitable* for your age?

Sometimes, I was confronted by people like Nurtic. People who thought that their purpose in life was to make themselves as miserable as possible for the supposed benefit of everyone else. People who wouldn't let themselves enjoy a damn thing, as long as there were others out there suffering. Why couldn't anyone understand that problems weren't solved by a meager 'one person at a time' approach? Second Earth didn't need neighborhood missionaries humbly reaching out to one or two souls a day; it needed forced large-scale reconstruction. Purging. Rebuilding. By a leader who ruled with an iron fist.

One thing I noticed about all the 'Nurtics' I came across was that they were never particularly well-off, themselves. Why did it always work that way? Only the poor wanted to give to the poor, while the rich went on hoarding their riches. I decided I'd only ever take from the wealthy. Of course, the wealthy never willingly *offered* anything to me, which meant I wasn't accepting donations, I was stealing.

Fall slowly crystallized into winter. Today was December twenty-second, my seventh birthday. The seventh anniversary of my mother's death. The day my father would've turned twenty-six.

I was ready.

AUTOERO AUSTERE, JR.

Unlike dear old dad, I didn't enjoy being a 'student seeker' one bit. Whether taking newborns from the arms of weeping mothers or seducing stupid seventeen-age-old civilians in high school cafeterias, recruiting was dull and dirty work.

Today, my job was to haunt the cafeteria of Aventurine City High, enticing impressionable juniors and seniors with glossy brochures full of lies. Many thought that it was pointless to enlist Ichthyothian adults because we already snagged all the good candidates in infancy. The Trilateral Committee experimented with acquiring adult Ichthyothians in the past and my father didn't particularly like the outcome. Well, I supposed that the TC didn't learn from its mistakes after all, because here we were again, giving it yet another shot, at least for a couple months.

A few minutes before the end of today's lunch-period, I was approached by a kid who obviously didn't belong to the student body of Aventurine City High. Filthy, emaciated and dressed in a holey t-shirt and jeans, he carried neither backpack nor meal-trey. He had a cold, coarse look about him despite appearing only about five or six ages old. The wildcat expression on his flushed face instantly told me that he was bad news.

"I want to join the Diving Fleet," he announced, grey-green eyes scowling from beneath a mop of vivid vermilion hair.

I blinked. "You're too young."

The walking turd actually cocked his jaw. "I'm seven," he declared, as if that changed anything.

"Come back in a decade, then."

"No, I'm ready, now."

I sighed. "You're too young for adult enlistment and too old to enter the Childhood Program. So, why don't you just run along home to mommy and daddy?"

Spindly arms folded across his hollow chest, he staunchly repeated, "I want to join the Diving Fleet." There was something oddly... *compelling* about his voice. Something convicting. Something that made me want to hear him out, though I knew he was a total waste of time. "You'll want me on your side, believe me."

"Yeah?" I asked, raising a brow. "And, why's that?"

"Because I know how to end the war," he answered, "and I'm going to do it with your help... or *theirs*."

Even as a slight chill plucked my spine, I went ahead and laughed openly.

"What's your name, boy?" I asked, just so I'd know what to call him when retelling this hilarious story to my comrades, back at base.

"It's Commence July Lechatelierite," he calmly replied, "but, you can call me Ence."

It was as though the room temperature instantly dropped a dozen degrees.

"Excuse me?"

He blinked. It was his first blink, since the start of our conversation. "I'm the son of your former commanders. You know, Cease Lechatelierite and Scarlet July."

I dropped my clipboard on the table, stricken by the poor taste of this twerp's joke. How *dare* he!

"Get out of my sight now, you disrespectful bastard," I barked.

“I’m not a bastard; my parents were married, you know. And, if you don’t believe that I’m who I say I am, why not take a blood sample?” He drew a shard of broken glass from his pocket and started to slice open his palm.

“Stop that!” I snatched the fragment from him. Was he crazy?

He grabbed a napkin from beside my lunch-bag and blotted his wound. “How about you go and get that tested,” he suggested jovially, tossing the scarlet wad at me, “and I’ll make sure to hang around this part of town for a couple more days?”

And, right before my eyes, his cut scabbed over. I stared, astonished. He was self-healing… like a hair mage.

With that, he stowed his hands in his pockets, flashed me a mischievous smile, and stalked away.

ENCE LECHATELIERITE

They came back for me, the following afternoon. I knew they would.

They took me to Icicle where they fed me, dressed me, strung me through a rather invasive series of medical tests and treatments, and subjected me to an extensive battery of physical and mental exams. I was kept isolated throughout the entire process, only ever interacting with a small handful of doctors and academy administrators.

Amongst the numerous evaluations, I was given a four-part pilotry diagnostic. The first phase, 'Two Hand Coordination,' involved keeping a crosshair on a moving target, at all times. The target rotated along a fixed oval; its varying rate was the only element of surprise. What a joke.

The second part, 'Complex Coordination,' entailed using one joystick to control the vertical movement of a cursor while using a second to simultaneously guide the horizontal motion of a rudder bar. The objective? To keep the cursor centered on the large cross bobbing up and down the screen while chasing the rudder-bar target from side to side. I almost laughed out loud.

The third section was very different than the first two. It was even easier: 'Item Recognition,' designed to assess short-term memory. A series of seven digits flashed on the screen for a couple seconds, then got replaced by a single figure after a hilariously-brief pause. My job was to determine whether the new number was part of the original sequence.

The fourth segment, 'Activities Interest Inventory,' was meant to evaluate attitude toward risk-taking. The problem with this test was that it wasn't practical. I was simply given multiple-choice questions about what I *would* do, *if* faced with various difficult situations.

I emerged from the series feeling disgusted. Was *this* all that the Diving Fleet required of its pilots?

I found out soon enough that the answer was: hell no. That test sequence was actually designed for four-age-old Childhood Program trainees. As the days wore on, I found myself facing challenges that were actually... well, *challenging*. And, today, January seventh of the second age of the eighth era, I was finally going to fly a vitreous silica simulator for the very first time.

By now, all military crafts and sims had built-in PAVLAKs whose features and graphics far outstripped that of Nurtic's old handheld unit. Settling in the sim cockpit now, I excitedly flicked it on. But, after less than ten minutes in flight, I realized that I hadn't glanced at the hologram once. It just... wasn't helping. On the contrary: I found it annoying to have this big glowing cube sharing my cramped cabin, partially obstructing my windshield. I was better off just using my eyes and instincts. So, I terminated the projection.

When signing out of my session, the test administrator, a diving officer with bored brown eyes whom I'd never met before, asked me how many ages of flying lessons I'd had back home.

I stared. "I'm only seven."

"So, what?" he snapped.

Huh? "What flight school in southern Nuria would take a kid?" I breathed.

"I can recognize experience when I see it." His arms folded. "So, how about you answer my question truthfully?"

"I did, sir. I swear."

He marched over to the console, logged in with his own username, *IlliaFrappe*, then loaded my flight record from today.

"It says here," he pointed, "that you turned off your PAVLAK seven minutes and twenty-five seconds after takeoff. Why would you do that?"

I shrugged. "It bothered me."

Illia Frappe leaned forward. "It *bothered* you?"

"It blocked my view. And, I can always see everything on my own, anyway."

"I'm going to ask you, one last time," he growled, "how old were you when your adoptive father began teaching you to fly?"

So, he knew about Nurtic. Though I didn't mention Nurtic's name once since leaving Alcove City, Frappe knew about the adoption. Obviously, though, he didn't have a clue how short that little arrangement lasted.

"He's not my father," I retorted, acidly.

"Answer the question, soldier."

I sighed. "Sir, I read some old manuals in his closet and I watched him run *one* delivery, but he never let me touch an arcade game, let alone take a real flying lesson."

Frappe goggled at me. "The man lives and breathes for aviation. And, you're telling me that he kept his own son away from that world?"

"With all due respect, sir, I sure as hell am not his son."

INEXOR BUIRD

Illia Frappe entered the conference hall where Autoero Austere, Jr., Krustallos Finire VII and I were waiting.

"Here you are, sir." Illia passed a binder to me. "The records from Ence's first vitreous silica sim." Since Ence arrived at Icicle a couple weeks ago, Illia had been monitoring and evaluating his progress from afar, helping to plot the next step of his training. Today was Illia's first time meeting the boy, face-to-face. "As you can see, he continues to function at the level of a trainee on the cusp of graduation."

"He doesn't even have a formal education beyond the seventh grade," Autoero commented in wonder. "He's self-taught."

"Like his mother," I chimed, flipping through the packet.

"Except without half the magic," Seven murmured, under his breath.

"Must we keep him in isolation much longer, sir?" Illia inquired. "He needs to learn to function in a chain-of-command."

My head shook. "At the very least, I'd wait until spring or summer before allowing him to attempt the graduation testing sequence."

"But, sir," Illia objected, "I daresay that he can already fight and fly better than most of our Nurian comrades."

"He also has a chronic insubordination problem and the worst temper of any soldier to pass through these doors," I said, flatly.

"Not to mention," Seven added, "he revises commands without approval because he thinks he knows better."

"To be honest, he usually does," Illia chirped. "He doesn't like to follow stupid orders. Who can blame him?"

Seven's crystal-blue eyes narrowed. "Must *I* really be the one to remind you all how dangerous and deadly that kind of attitude can be?"

"Which brings us back to my initial conclusion: Ence still has some growing up to do, before he can join our ranks," I said.

"No kidding," Seven snorted. "If he got any smaller, he'd vanish out of existence."

"I don't think the Commander was talking about *physical* growth," Illia retorted. "If I remember correctly, Cease Lechatelierite was about four feet tall when he graduated."

"Which *did* cause problems," I recalled. "For ages, there were places he couldn't reach, equipment he couldn't carry, people he couldn't support in formation... the list goes on."

"Scarlet July was also small, but it never seemed to hold her back," Illia argued.

"Because of her powerful spectrum, which Ence doesn't have," Seven grumbled.

Illia's temples pulsed. "If we're going to wait for Ence to grow big and tall, we shouldn't hold our breaths. I mean, look his parents. I doubt *they* ever made two-hundred pounds, put together."

"Maybe, because neither of them ever ate nor slept," Seven muttered.

"I never said that Ence needs to be *big and tall,*" I echoed, irritably. "But, temperament issues aside, I agree that a few more months of carefully-monitored exercise and nutrition would do him some good."

"But, must we keep him in solitary confinement for the duration, sir?" Illia pressed. "When spring or summer rolls around, are we really going to yank him from complete isolation and immediately throw him into battle alongside hundreds of comrades he's never met?"

No. Ence needed to learn teamwork as much as anybody else, and I preferred if he didn't begin that portion of his education in my fleet, with lives at stake. "I suppose we could send him to an academy, until then."

Illia nodded. "Which one—the Childhood Program or Icicle's newly-reopened adult school?"

I shook my head. "Neither. He spent most of his life in Nuria and, whether he admits it or not, he's a lot more like them than us, culturally. He should go to the Nurian Academy."

"You mean you want to stick him with a bunch of mindless hormonal Nurian teenagers?" snorted Autoero, who'd been spending way too much time in high-school cafeterias lately.

Illia ignored that remark. "He'll be glad to hear it, sir."

Turning to the back of the binder, I found Ence's PAVLAK log curiously barren. I looked up at Illia, questioningly.

"Sir, he terminated the hologram, a few minutes after takeoff. Said he's able to 'see everything anyway,' on his own."

An odd mix of anger and awe pricked my chest. "Is that so?"

"Well, sir, he *did* complete the operation without a hitch."

"That's incredible," Autoero breathed.

"But, the PAVLAK isn't a bonus accessory anymore, it's foundational. It's replaced every radar, entirely," Seven shot, fiercely. He was a fairly heavy user of the system, wielding it like a scalpel, catching things that evaded the eyes and crosshairs of even the most experienced pilots. "Going into battle without *any* sort of radar isn't commendable, it's reckless and foolish."

Illia shrugged. "The academy will teach him to use it properly. At least, we don't have to worry if it'll become a crutch for him, as it is for so many of our other top pilots, these days." Did Illia just take a jab at Seven? "Anyway, I still can't believe that Ence lived with *Nurtic Leavesleft* and never had any real exposure to the world of flight, before coming here. I thought Leavesleft's name was synonymous with aviation."

It was Seven's turn to shrug. "It's been ages since you've interacted with him. People change."

"Plus, Nurians are prone to making random bad decisions for no apparent reason," Autoero said.

Autoero was right about Nurians in general, but not about Leavesleft in particular. Leavesleft was one of the wiser and more level-headed Nurians I knew. Despite his faith in the invisible and tendency toward touchy-feely sentimentality, he had a logical mind and didn't make serious decisions willy-nilly. I knew the *real* reason he wanted to keep Ence away from his plane, not to mention anything else that could remotely spark an interest in military life: his word to Scarlet.

Well, I'd never say this to Leavesleft's face, but I was happy that he failed at keeping Ence from us. Likewise, I was glad that my officers and I were in complete agreement that Leavesleft needed to stay in the dark about Ence's current whereabouts. Because, he and Scarlet were wrong: the Diving Fleet was obviously the only place a Lechatelierite could belong.

NURTIC LEAVESLEFT

It'd been six months since Ence pulled his disappearing act. It was all a blur to me. Four of those months, I spent scouring the northwestern hemisphere, occasionally pausing to complete a delivery run or a NurroAir flight, so I wouldn't go totally broke. But, by the time winter melted into spring, something inside me snapped. I just… lost hope. Like bullet in the gut, it finally dawned on me that Ence was gone for good. I suddenly started hating the plane in which I'd spent almost every waking minute from November through March. Without explanation, I suddenly quit all my flying jobs, no longer willing to approach an aircraft. I could care less if I never set foot outside of Alcove City again. I was through with being a globetrotter.

Now, it was five o'clock on May twenty-fourth. Feverish and sweaty, I crawled to the bathroom and hunched over the sink to splash my hollow cheeks with cold water, hardly recognizing the dead-eyed man in the mirror. Even my blonde hair already had premature grey flecks. I slid to the floor, back against the vanity, names and faces flashing through my mind. Ecivon Wen. Tnerruc Ruetama. My parents. Arrhyth and Dither weren't dead, but they were gone indefinitely. Cease Lechatelierite. Scarlet July. And, now, Ence. Ence was the final tip of the scale. The grain of sand that broke the scabrous's back. I hinged my last hope on him and, just as Selepoh predicted, he let me down.

* * *

At dawn, I inexplicably found myself meandering to the train-station, where I boarded a direct line to Seaview City. Three hours later, I found myself at Linkeree Link's doorstep. She let me into her apartment without hesitation, made me a cup of hot chocolate—my first sugar in nearly a decade—and allowed me to cry myself dry on her living-room couch, all morning.

Linkeree had the news on, humming in the background. Headache pounding and eyes bleary, I glanced at the screen and saw the big letters at the bottom: 'LIVE AT THE NURIAN DIVING ACADEMY GRADUATION.' And, in the middle of the procession, there stood a soldier far shorter and smaller than the rest, auburn hair shining amidst a sea of blonde and light-brown. Instantly, my stomach disappeared.

It was Ence.

ENCE LECHATELIERITE

May twenty-fourth. Icicle Base Diving Fleet barracks. Twenty-five o'clock.

"Welcome, Nurian Academy grads. My name is Comat Acci," my new unit-leader introduced himself. He sure looked a lot younger than the rest of the veterans. "I'd present my sub-leader, but the System quite literally roasted him at sea, yesterday," he added in a rather matter-of-fact tone. I couldn't be more thrilled. I'd only just arrived at base and an officer position was already up for grabs! "Locker-room, now. Practice commences in fifteen."

Acci headed for the showers along with us, chatting up a storm. I was surprised and a little disgusted. If I were in his place, I'd maintain some professional distance from my subordinates.

"Hey, there," he called, finding his way to me, much too quickly. "You've been quiet. Nice to meet you."

I returned his salute, closely watching his face. He was right; I'd been silent since setting foot at Icicle, but only because I was too busy studying all the vets. As quickly as possible, I needed to have everyone's psyches mapped out so I could put my plan into action. My plan to get on top, molding this fleet into exactly what I needed to end this stupid war, once and for all.

Acci was certainly an interesting subject, himself. I figured that his civilian-esque friendliness was likely nothing but strategy. Because no one attained rank by being an amicable buffoon.

"Got a name?" he asked.

"Ence." He didn't need to know that I was a Lechatelierite. Not yet.

"Ah, so *you're* Cease Lechatelierite's son. Frappe told me you were coming."

Great.

"Thought you'd withhold your surname to evade the burden of filling daddy's boots, did you?" he asked, smile growing edgy.

I was stunned by his sudden malice. I hadn't even said two words to him, and things between us were already going south?

I opened my mouth to reply, but he shocked me yet again by hooting, "Gotcha!"

I didn't laugh.

"I've seen your test scores, Ence Lechatelierite," he plowed on. "I know you don't have a thing to worry about. You've got your father's legacy in the bag. Am I right?"

Now, how could I respond to *that?* If I agreed, I'd sound cocky. If I disagreed, I'd sound self-deprecating or falsely humble. So, no matter my answer, I'd look bad. He was laying out a trap before me.

But, instead of waiting for me to fall into that trap, he went right on talking: "So, Frappe told me that you were raised by Nurtic Leavesleft." His eyes burned with interest. Now, I was really starting to boil. Acci—and, who knew, maybe all the officers—had all kinds of intel on me while I didn't know a damn thing about them. Not to mention that Nurtic Leavesleft wasn't exactly my favorite topic. I didn't want my very first conversation with my unit leader to be about *him*.

"I only spent a few months with him, sir," I answered. "He didn't raise me."

Acci blazed on: "How's he doing?"

I shrugged. "How should I know? I haven't seen him since November." My vocal control was slipping.

"Yeah, well, I haven't seen him in over seven ages, so you've got me beat. Spill!"

"He's fine," I stiffly replied, refraining from adding: *Well, sir, the last time I saw Nurtic, he was working three jobs, trying to offset thousands in crippling debt. Yeah, overall, sir, he's struggling to the point that it shouldn't have been legal for him to adopt a child in the first place, even for just a few months. Not to mention, he's probably sick to death with grief, right about now, from losing me.* "He's found a way to market his piloting skills." I forced some cheer into my tone. "He flies for a delivery service and a passenger-liner."

"Commander Buird said he works at an orphanage," Acci commented.

"Well, he does that too, when he's in-between assignments from the aviation ministry that he's in—"

"Wait, he has four jobs?" Worry struck Acci's face. "Is he doing alright?"

Ugh, did *everyone* care about Nurtic? Was there a single human being on Second Earth who *wasn't* totally smitten with him?

I was silent.

"Well, is he?" Acci pressed.

I'd had enough. "Yes, sir, he's alright, I guess. But, I'm curious how you even know him? You seem a bit young to have served with him."

Acci's head shook. "I was never his comrade-in-arms. I was his student, back in public school."

What? "I didn't know Nurtic was a teacher."

"Teacher's aide. When he was a college freshman, he volunteered for the second-grade class I was in, at Vitaville's 'K-12.'"

"You're Nurian?" He sure didn't look it. He had the classic Ichthyothian dark-haired-fair-skinned-pale-eyed combo.

"No. I was raised in the Childhood Program, until it was dismantled in the ninety-fourth age. I lived in Aventurine City with my parents for barely a week before the Spectral Hurricane hit, forcing us to relocate to Vitaville. As you can imagine, it was a lot of change to swallow, all at once. I didn't handle it too well. In fact, I probably would've self-destructed, if Nurtic didn't come along. He really helped me recoup." Acci smiled, and I fought to keep my irritation under wraps. So, once upon a time, my own unit leader was a fellow Nurtic 'community service project.' One of the poor lost souls whom Nurtic heroically rescued. Lovely. "I sped through civilian public school pretty fast, went to the Nurian Diving Academy, and now, here I am in the fleet. But, it's by choice, this time."

"Does Nurtic know," I asked, "where you ended up?"

"Probably not. He only worked at the grade-school for about a month before he left for the Tri-Nation Campaign."

"Off to save the world," I muttered.

Acci's hands clasped. "So, tell me, Ence, why *do* you hate Nurtic so much?"

"What, no, sir, I-I never said that," I sputtered, taken aback.

"You've been pissed off, this entire conversation." Acci glowered at me. "If this isn't about Nurtic, what's going on? Why are you so strung-up?"

"I'm not."

"Really? Because you just bit off your officer's head. Again." His arms folded. "I'm going to ask you one last time, soldier: what the hell's wrong with you?"

This was going from bad to worse. So much for first impressions.

"Nothing, sir, I swear," I breathed. "The past is in the past, okay? I'm over it."

"Is that so?" he snorted. "Ence *Lechatelierite* put the past in the past?"

What did my last name have to do with any of this? "Sir, I don't think—"

"I can smell baggage from a mile away," he cut across me. "Believe me, I used to have enough cargo to fill a crystalline, myself. But, you, my dear subordinate, have got enough to stock an entire fleet of vitreous silicas for eras."

"Sir," I protested.

"I wasn't finished," he snapped. "You better find a way to dump your dung fast, before you blow your future in this fleet straight to hell. Got it?" I could feel a few photons flicker through my eyes. That son of a—"After surface-riding practice, you will report to the south field behind the hospital wing, so you can deal with your crap, once and for all," he ordered, crisply. What in the world was in the south field behind the hospital wing? "Understood?" he barked.

I glared at him for a moment longer, then hissed, "Sir, yes, sir."

"Now, take your shower and meet everyone at the shore in five," he growled, stalking away.

Gnawing my lip until it bled, I shed my clothes, stepped beneath a spout and scrubbed myself raw. Acci sure knew how to get under my skin. I hastily dried off, threw on my diving suit and stormed outside, into the snow. The water in my hair quickly froze into tiny ice crystals. A *real* hair mage could've made all the moisture instantly evaporate.

I lifted my chin to the sky and exhaled, breath condensing into white puffs that reminded me of the cigarettes smoked by the stupid people in the Alcove City streets.

Some of them were so poor, they couldn't eat, yet they let themselves develop an expensive, unnecessary, unhealthy addiction. Stupid. Didn't they know that total independence was the ultimate life-hack? That the key to success was to need nothing and no one? Dependence on anything was akin to slavery. As was attachment and association.

I needed to be free of Cease Lechatelierite's shadow. But, by coming here, I couldn't help but wonder if I'd walked right into it.

* * *

After practice, I trudged to the south field, the Septentrion Sea rippling in the near-distance, reflecting the silver-black of the night sky. I perused the vast white expanse, wondering what exactly I was supposed to find here. What did Acci want me to see? Or, was this some sort of trick?

And, then, I noticed a slight rectangular elevation in the snow. Of course. My eyes pulsated in their sockets. I ran over to it and started kicking off the accumulations, agitation growing by the second. How did Acci think that *this* would help me cope with my past? Moreover, why in the world would the Trilateral Committee determine that a flat perpetually-buried plaque was a suitable monument for whom they called the greatest military leader to walk Second Earth?

At last, the engravement became visible:

In Memory of:

Cease Terminus Lechatelierite
Diving Fleet Commander
Leader of the Ichthyothian Resistance
December 22nd of the 75th Age — May 25th of the 94th Age (7th Era)

And, that was it. No quotes, poems nor praises. Nothing but his name, rank and the span of his much-too-short life.

May twenty-fifth of the ninety fourth age. Damn, he really was only eighteen when he died. Only eighteen when he married a sixteen-age-old mage and sired me. Blood churning in my ears, I dropped to my knees before the plaque, already lightly dusted with fresh snowfall.

"So, here I am," I said to the cold concrete, underneath which no body lay. My voice came out dead. Killed by the wind. I breathed out through clenched teeth, feeling stupid already. "Here I am, at Icicle," I continued, nonetheless. "Are you happy? Have I made you proud, *father?*"

At that moment, as though in response to my question, a particularly-sharp sleet pellet hit my left cheek; I could feel my skin break, blood freezing on my face. Seconds later, the cut scabbed over and I felt the pull of fatigue from my meager spectral exertion.

"But, you know what, father? I'm not here to fill your boots. I don't want to be like you. I don't care if everyone in this hemisphere worships you—I sure as hell don't." Fists balled, my veins budged through my translucent skin. "One day, I'll have control... complete control... over everything. And, when I do, I'll be sure to punish people like you. All the negligent fools who left others to clean up their messes." Shaking with rage, the edges of my hair suddenly ignited—but, only for a moment. Overcome with acute exhaustion, I involuntarily face-planted in the snow.

"Ence?" a voice called from behind, sometime later. I recognized it as Ouy Pleh, a fellow member of my graduating class. He was nineteen and also in unit two. "It's after lights' out; Acci sent me to look for you," he said. "Are you alright?"

Ouy was a little bit like Nurtic, always 'caring' and trying to 'help out.' In other words, he constantly stuck his nose in others' personal business, oblivious to the possibility that might drive people up the wall. He took hold of my shoulders now, hoisting me upright. I was embarrassed that anyone should see me like this, but grateful that the witness was no one of consequence.

"I'm sorry," he murmured, looking at the stone. "I didn't know what you were doing. I didn't even know this thing was out here."

"No one does, do they?" I muttered, darkly.

Ouy's eyes were wide and worried. "I can talk to Acci for you. I'm sure he'll let you stay out here as long as you'd like, once he knows what—"

"He knows," I interrupted, quietly. "He ordered me to come out here, and now he's using you to snoop on how it's going."

Ouy's forehead wrinkled. "Oh." There was a pause. No doubt, he was wondering what sort of military leader would command his subordinate to visit the grave of his dead parent, especially considering the Laws of Emotional Protection and all. "Well, I guess I'll leave you alone with your dad." He stood.

"Don't call him that," I hissed.

Ouy froze in mid-step, confused.

Without bothering to clarify, I got to my feet, pushed right past him and trudged back to the building, my footprints rapidly vanishing beneath fresh flurries.

COMAT ACCI

He sure was interesting, that Ence character. I think the best descriptor would be: 'screwed-up.' Like most Nurians I knew, he had little self-control, but *unlike* the majority of his fellow new grads, his lack of discipline was compounded by serious daddy issues, a god complex and a boatload of unresolved angst and anger. Brilliant as he may've been on the battlefield, his emotional maturity seemed on par with my old peers from Mrs. Termag's second grade.

Second grade. Those were rough days. I probably wouldn't have made it through Vitaville's 'K-12' with my sanity if it weren't for Nurtic. Though Nurtic was never a child-soldier, he still saw right through my mask and understood my unique pain. He was a veteran, after all; he knew what it was like to live a life of total physical and psychological sacrifice. He knew the sorts of scars and callouses that kind of life could leave. Even the little things about Icicle and Ichthyosis—like the bland food and the perpetual lack of sunlight—he was no stranger to. So, at Vitaville's 'K-12,' he knew to provide special sugarless snacks for me, whenever Mrs. Termag passed out cookies or candy. He knew to bring sunscreen for me to use at recess, even on cloudy days. He paid attention to the small stuff.

His patience with me set an example. It taught me to tolerate my comrades at the Nurian Diving Academy. It wasn't easy. For seven full months, my temper was continually tried and tested by hundreds of crazy teenagers who seemed rather incapable of abstinent, decorous, sugar-free military life. Many of those same buffoons still served alongside me today, but at least they no longer comprised the totality of my human contact.

Anyway, graduation weekend was definitely the most memorable part of my time at the academy. The eve of the ceremony, my eighteen-to-twenty-age-old peers threw a little celebration in the barracks, complete with smuggled junk-food and alcohol. I admit that I was excited by the party atmosphere, though I didn't really intend to partake in any of the illegal goods. It was enough of a thrill to simply be in the same *room* as the contraband; there was no need to spoil the fun by actually making myself sick with it. But, I soon learned that my classmates weren't content to let me merely watch them throw down. They wanted me to participate. They insisted. They wouldn't let up. And, I slowly realized that after seven months of excruciating ostracism for my age and nationality, this was my chance to finally become 'one of the guys.'

I was handed a cupcake and a beer. While everyone watched, I nervously took a bite. My tongue flattened the soggy crumbs against the roof of my mouth, afraid to chew or swallow. It was the strangest tingling sensation, the taste of refined sugar. I didn't know what to make of it. It was unlike anything I'd eaten before. Tangy, but not sour. Sharp, but not salty. And, the cake's texture reminded me of bread, but moister and gooier. I swallowed the chunk whole.

Beer tasted the way I imagined urine would: bitter and burning. I spat out my first sip, immediately countered by a chorus of 'boos.'

"Ladies and gentlemen, Ichthyosis's finest!" jeered Yllub, a nineteen-age-old from Alcove City. "Can't even take a sip of beer without puking!"

"I didn't puke," I said, acutely aware of how childish I sounded.

The laughter intensified.

Anger pricked my chest. "Sorry, Yllub," I blazed on, sounding a lot braver than I felt, "but, I can't drink something that tastes like the runs you still get before every practice battle. Don't worry, you're not the only one who has blowouts before fights; my comrades in the Childhood Program did, too—well, at least, when they were toddlers, anyway."

Hoots and cheers surrounded me. "Oooh, the little boy's got a mouth!"

Yllub's eyes narrowed. "Coward," he growled. "A pesky little anemic coward—that's all you are and ever will be. You only pretend to be one of us."

There it was: my greatest fear, vocalized for all to hear. I also knew that, thanks to my age, it wouldn't be much easier winning over the Ichthyothian vets we'd meet the following afternoon, shared nationality or not. Basically, I belonged nowhere. I didn't fit in with anyone. Unless, of course, I won over my Nurian peers, right now. Everything came down to this moment.

The room watched in silence as I slowly lifted the beer to my lips. Tipping my head back, I took a long draught. Acid singed my throat. At last, I plunked the empty can down on the table, suppressing my gag reflex.

The barracks burst into applause.

"Now, for dessert," Yllub grunted, giving me a thin-lipped smile.

Without breaking eye-contact, I finished the whole cupcake, one methodic bite at a time.

* * *

I pooped myself in my sleep. The next morning, I awoke with soiled sheets, a raging bellyache and a crippling headache.

And, I threw up all over Admiral Sive's boots, during my walk across the graduation stage.

ENCE LECHATELIERITE

Breakfast.

I sat alone at the end of a long table, brooding over a plate of white rice and cold salmon paste, when I was suddenly assaulted by two unit-leaders who looked to be in their late twenties. So, I sprang from my seat, drop-kicking them both. They landed hard, on their asses.

"Whoa there, little guy!" called the man with puffy brown curls. He spoke Ichthyothian with a slight Nurian accent.

"We just wanted to sit with you!" chimed the one with the platinum crew-cut.

My arms crossed. "Then, why did you attack me?"

They looked at each other, faces all scrunched and sentimental.

"Aw, just listen to him, asking us to explain our normal behaviors like he's a robot or something," cooed the swirly-haired guy, getting to his feet. "Just like his father."

The blonde also stood and smiled. "And, he looks like him, too! But, his eyes—they're more like Scarlet's."

If there was anything I hated more than being talked about in the third-person directly to my face, it was being talked about in the third-person directly to my face *while* getting fussed over like some cuddly kid. I was a soldier here like everybody else, not their baby brother.

"We weren't *attacking* you," buzz-cut laughed. "You're not base-raised; you should understand a friendly thump on the back!"

"Yeah, you're the one who escalated things." Corkscrew-head offered his hand. "Arrhyth Link, officer of unit seven. Nice to meet you—well, sort of, anyway."

Of course, that's why they looked familiar: they were in one of the dusty photos on Nurtic's mantle. Except that they both looked a lot leaner and scruffier now, their smiles dimmer and weaker. I supposed that nearly a decade of combat took its toll.

Before the blonde could introduce himself, I said, "Dither Maine."

Dither beamed. "Been doing some database hacking already, li'l Lechat?"

I hadn't, but I wasn't inclined to share the real reason I recognized him. I stayed silent.

Arrhyth winked. "No worries; your secret's safe with us."

"What's your unit?" I asked Dither briskly, eyeing the stripes on his sleeves.

"Eight," he answered. "But, mark my words," he shook his fist at Arrhyth, "I will surpass you again, sooner or later!"

Arrhyth's eyes rolled. "In your dreams, man." He regarded me. "Once upon a time, Dither was one rank above me. But, those days have long passed. I got promoted *way* earlier."

"Only because your predecessor died before mine!"

"Ikil was impaled, but Doric didn't die; he just got injured."

"Whatever. Same thing!"

"Dying and breaking your back is *not* the same thing!"

"Well, career-wise, it kinda is. Dude isn't going sailing anytime soon, is he?"

Arrhyth grinned at me. "As you can see here, Ence ol' boy, we've been neck-in-neck since day one."

"And, we wouldn't have it any other way."

I stared at them, alarmed. *These* flippant goons were officers? A couple of the finest tactical minds in the northwestern hemisphere?

"So, li'l Lechat, mind if we dine with you?" Arrhyth asked.

"It's dawn, Arrhyth," Dither said. "Nobody's *dining*. I believe this meal is called 'breakfast.'"

"Breakfast, lunch, dinner, midnight snack—how am I to tell?" Arrhyth peeked at the serving line. "There's nothing breakfast-like about any of the food, here. And, at this latitude, it's not like its necessarily dark at night or light during the day. In the summer, we have, what, thirty hours of daylight? And, in the winter, it's the other way around—in other words, the definition of total misery. Nothing about our lives here actually distinguishes morning from night."

Dither nodded. "The only way I can tell time is by using my watch." He stared down at his empty wrist. "Oh, wait, I don't have one, anymore… because *you* destroyed it during ice-surface practice, last week!"

"Ugh, you're still on about that? What do we even need watches for, when we have PAVLAKs?"

"Uh, yeah, I'm 'still on about it'—your skis almost sliced off my hand!"

"I never understood what you were doing on the ground, in the first place. If you don't want to get run over, don't recline in the middle of combat."

"I wasn't *reclining;* I was dodging Frappe's fire. Maybe, when you ski, you should look where you're going!"

"Let it go, man! I've apologized, like, a gazillion times."

"Arrhyth, I almost *lost a hand!*"

"You guys should probably get something to eat," I interrupted loudly, desperate to stop their endless babble. These two certainly made a lot of noise—talking and talking and talking—without ever actually *saying* anything.

They heeded my advice... then, unfortunately, came right back. While we ate, they occasionally cast me curious sidelong glances, especially when they thought that I wasn't paying attention. The hunger in their eyes betrayed exactly what was going on in their heads. I hated the fact that whenever anyone around here looked at me, all they saw was my parents.

"I know it's been a while," Arrhyth asked, delicately, "but, um, how's your dad doing?"

I froze in mid-chew. What sort of twisted joke was that? Cease Lechatelierite died before I was born. Everybody knew that.

"My... dad?" I asked, slowly.

"You know," Arrhyth said, "Nurtic Leavesleft."

My scalp heated. "Nurtic isn't my *dad*. I was only with him for a few months."

"I really do miss him," Dither breathed, mournfully. "You know what? I think I'm starting to forget what his face looks like. Sounds crazy, but the harder I try to picture it, the more I think I'm screwing it up."

"Linkeree," Arrhyth moaned. "She must've graduated from college and grad-school, by now. Might even be married with kids, for all I know." His fork chased the lumpy paste around his plate. "There's a lot about home that I can't properly remember anymore, you know? Like, what temperature does it normally reach in, say, July? Seventy-five? Ninety? I forgot what those numbers even mean, what they feel like."

"Rain," Dither murmured. "I can kinda recall rain. Like snow, but... wetter."

"You know what I really want to experience, again?" Dither asked, peeking out the tiny window on the far wall.

"A sky without clouds. A sky that's actually blue. And, the feeling of sunlight against skin."

"Four distinct seasons," Arrhyth mused. "And, darkness only at night and light only during the day. Colors besides white, grey and black."

"A body of water that's warm enough to swim in, *without* a scuba-suit."

"So, yeah, Ence, if you couldn't tell by now, we've been here a long time."

"A long, long time."

"So, how *is* Nurtic doing now, anyway? You never told us."

Ugh, for crying out loud. "I don't know. It's been six months since I've seen him."

Arrhyth's brows lowered. "Six months, huh? Try seven ages."

"Yeah, so, quit being a selfish bastard already and answer the damn question," Dither spat.

I was taken aback, but far from intimidated. Dropping my utensils, I flashed them a nasty smile. "Alright, then," I began in a sour-honey voice, "last I saw Nurtic, he was living alone in a miserable sewer-hole of an apartment that he could barely afford, eating plain yogurt for dinner, and working four jobs to put a dent in the mountain of medical debt left by his dead parents."

"Oh, my gosh," Arrhyth gasped. "John-Paul and Mary-Esther *died?* What? When? How?"

Dither actually reached across the table to grab my collar. "You son-of-a—"

I wrenched myself from his grip. "You're the ones who insisted on asking about Nurtic's miserable life; all I did was give an honest response. Now, if you'll excuse me, this topic has killed my appetite."

Abandoning my trey, I stalked out of the mess hall.

ENCE LECHATELIERITE

The Second-in-Command, Krustallos Finire VII—whom everyone called 'Seven' for some reason—was a heavy PAVLAK user. Well, everyone here was, but Seven especially. After only about a week in the fleet, I noticed how the man wouldn't even perform a fair-weather landing without practically sticking his head inside the hologram. He always kept his projection at full magnification, whenever he flew. I was frightened by his total reliance on the thing. Yes, no one could deny that the PAVLAK was indeed a fine piece of technology—even I'd come to find worthwhile uses for it, by now. But, to me, it was an asset, an advantage. Not a crutch.

So, after practice one afternoon, I confronted Seven about it. I told him how dangerous I thought it was for our pilots to be helpless without the aid of some software that might go down at any moment.

"Nobody's *helpless*," Seven sneered. "And, the system hasn't malfunctioned since it was first introduced in the ninety-fourth age."

"With all due respect, sir, that doesn't mean it *can't*."

"The PAVLAK has replaced all radars. You want everybody to start flying around without *any* radars? You think *that'll* make us safer?"

"No, sir," I replied, keeping the irritation in my voice to a bare minimum. "But, I just don't feel comfortable setting sail with a bunch of lazy unobservant pilots, knowing we're all totally screwed if some computer blips."

"Hey," Seven barked, "watch your tongue; you're talking to an officer!"

My jaw clenched. "Sorry, sir."

"And, *I'm* sorry that our methods here make you 'uncomfortable,' little kid, but here's a newsflash for you: war isn't supposed to be comfy and cozy, so either grow up now or get the hell out of my fleet," he snarled.

Blood pounded in my ears like a machine-gun. Seven was smarter than this, he had to be! I was unwilling to believe that our Second Commander was stupid enough to half-heartedly dismiss the risk of extreme mass dependency on a single piece of tech.

I trudged away, gnashing my teeth. He was going to pay for ignoring my warning, one day. Him and the entire fleet.

* * *

A couple hours after sunset, Acci called me to his quarters.

"You have a terrible attitude," he greeted me in a matter-of-fact tone, without so much as a 'good evening.' "You've got a big mouth and an enormous heated lance up your ass. But, you're also the smartest dragon turd to walk these corridors in quite a while, and I need to replace my sub-leader whom the System so kindly toasted for us last week, so I guess that's that."

I stared. "Sir?"

"You need me to break it down further for you? Alright, then." He inhaled. "I'd take a competent loudmouth over a subservient idiot, and since those are the only two choices I've got around here, you'll have to do."

Heat rushed to my scalp. Only Acci could manage to bury a promotion beneath layers of scathing insults. I was obviously the most brilliant and capable soldier in this fleet—sharper than Commander Inexor Buird, himself—yet, Acci dared to claim that he was choosing me with reluctance? I scrunched my eyes shut for just a moment, afraid of accidentally setting the man ablaze.

Wait… was that a hint of amusement in his stoic stare? Of course. He was testing me, baiting me to blow up and prove that I wasn't disciplined enough for leadership, after all.

Biting my tongue, I stiffly saluted.

"Thank you… sir," I mumbled, upper lip twitching.

He gave me a maddening smile. "For someone who grew up with the most patient person I know, you sure are a hotheaded little bastard. Dismissed." And, with that, he shoved some rank-bands in my fist, pushed me out the door and slammed it in my face.

ENCE LECHATELIERITE

October twenty-fourth, seventeen o'clock.

The crystalline to my left—piloted by Seven, who was in charge of our primary offensive today—dove sharply, to catch my unit. Too sharply. All eight surface-riders missed him entirely and disappeared with the current.

"Seven!" I cried. "What the hell?"

"I… I couldn't see them," he panted.

How was that possible? "They were making a clear shot from, what, ten yards away?"

"They were… in my blind spot."

Blind spot! "What are you, a flivver-cab driver?" What was wrong with him?

"My… my PAVLAK blew out," he finally admitted.

I was seeing red. Unit two was the fulcrum of our strike. Seven was supposed to deliver them to the hull of the Conflagrian mothership. They'd trained endlessly for the infiltration. They carried special equipment for the penetration and raid.

And, now, they were hurtling aimlessly through the sea at hundreds of miles per hour.

Seven, crippled without his holographic crutch, made yet another sloppy swerve, narrowly evading a stream of fire. I had a sense that his successful dodge had more to do with the enemy's incompetence than his own skill.

"Is *your* PAVLAK working?" he asked me, voice pained.

Mine wasn't even on, yet. I hastily flicked the switch, but nothing happened. "No."

"Lookout at seven-two-five!" Illia's voice boomed in our helmets.

Three crystallines turned tightly to avoid colliding with an oncoming dragon ship, wings scraping together, surface-riders sandwiched like salami. When the shuttles separated, four of the surface-riders fell off, broken limbs flapping.

"Attention!" Inexor boomed, universally. "The PAVLAK navigation system is out of service. Please use crosstalk to coordinate maneuvers. Over."

"Acci," I called to the vitreous silica, where he and Inexor were currently stationed, "we lost our unit. Requesting permission to send out unit one, instead?" They weren't fully outfitted for the job, but they were far better than nothing.

"The Commander and I are fine with that, but you need to ask Seven if you want to use his men," Acci replied.

"Roger, sir." I bit my mouthpiece. "Seven, can you spare your unit for the infiltration?"

Silence.

"Sir, where are your men?" I insisted.

"I'm… not sure."

My pupils heated. I gnawed my mouthpiece, again. "Unit one, report to my hull, immediately. You're our new infiltration task force. On my mark, we'll—"

"Hey, I never authorized that!" Seven interjected.

"My apologies, sir," I said through gritted teeth, "but, I assumed that since you weren't even aware of your men's positions, you hadn't given them anything important to do, and since you totally lost *my* unit, whom we were supposed to use—"

"Ence, now isn't the time to run your mouth!" Seven screeched. "Unit one, report to *my* hull; we're going in.

Frappe, Austere, Link, pass any surface-riders you may have to Maine and cover my tail. You too, Ence."

"Sir, yes, sir!" the officers cried.

As I begrudgingly got into position, I noticed something flicker in my peripheral vision. "SEVEN, TO YOUR RIGHT!"

Seven—now hauling unit one—swerved to the left, narrowly avoiding a smoldering ball of Underwater Fire.

I'd had enough. "Second, I'm taking over." I pulled up beside him, so his divers could hop aboard.

"Get back in line, Ence," he coldly answered. "Behind me."

"But, sir—"

"Just do what he says, li'l Lechat." Dither sounded simultaneously tired and wired. His hull was positively swarming with all the surface-riders the other pilots dumped on him.

The hairs on the back of my neck stood at attention—not from spectrum. "Maine, drop at least twenty feet, now," I spouted.

"What, why?"

"NOW!"

Dither descended, but not quickly enough. His dorsal fin got whisked off by a swooping Conflagrian craft, sending his crystalline into a wild spiral. His surface-riders sprayed off like fireworks, flailing and screaming. Dither himself ejected.

Immediately, I circumnavigated the scene, deploying my cable net and scooping the stray men like a school of salmon. The full sack trailed after me like a balloon—a ridiculously easy target. Dragon ships instantly converged upon me, so I rolled and darted and spun and did everything I could to keep my disoriented passengers safe. But, I knew that I couldn't keep up the evasive maneuvers indefinitely.

"Commanders," I told the vitreous silica, "I have a delivery for you."

The manta ray hovered above me, ventral gate open.

"Toss 'em up, Ence," Inexor ordered.

I positioned the butt of my shuttle directly beneath the opening, lurched forward, and released the net. It flew upward, heading straight for the hole. So far, so good.

And, then, without warning, the vitreous silica bobbed, causing the sack to splat like a pancake against its belly.

"Commander!" I shrieked.

"I-I'm sorry," Inexor sputtered. "I thought I saw something, but it was a false alarm."

I bit my lip until it bled. Even Inexor couldn't hold his own without the PAVLAK?

Arms and legs started poking through the weave of wires as the poor, shaken-up, probably-injured soldiers within desperately attempted to grab hold of something, anything. One of them snagged the edge of the opening and tried to haul the entire load in. Of course, he wasn't strong enough. I ascended, nudging them to safety with my nose. The shaft slid shut. I exhaled.

Now to find Seven and cover his tail like I was supposed to.

"I'm here, sir," I breathed to him, pulling up at the rear of his chain.

"Took you long enough," he grumbled. "Ready, soldiers?" The mage mothership loomed before us. "Three… two… one… go!"

We dove.

In seconds, the System carrier nicked Illia's right wing. He spun out and ejected, heading for my hull.

Moments later, it also took out Arrhyth's left engine. He followed Illia's lead.

Then, it demolished Autoero's dorsal fin. He joined the other two, on my back.

And, last but not least, it struck Seven's right wing. He and his surface-riders fled, coming at me all at once, my intercom relaying a blaring mishmash of shouts. With a spectacular thump, a white suit smacked into my windshield, right arm flopping like a boneless sack of flesh.

It was Seven.

"Lechat," Arrhyth cried, "you have an unbounded soldier!"

"I can see that quite clearly," I said, dryly. "Will someone grab him, already? He's totally obstructing my view."

"Attention!" Inexor called, universally. "Abort mission! I repeat, abort mission! All units report to the manta ray!"

Maneuvering like a circus trapeze-artist, I slowly made my way back to the vitreous silica, where we all collided spectacularly with the internal 'resonance screen'—a sort of force-field engineered exactly for this purpose. It was a new invention, and it was about time, if you asked me; far too many surface-riders survived brutal battles only to die upon the impact of arrival inside the carrier. My craft—along with several divers—now bounced off the gelatin-like surface and onto the spongy floor. Traditionally, after a battle, all survivors would remove their helmets and toss them at the screen, in celebration. But, today, not a single helmet flew. The atmosphere inside the manta ray was strained and subdued.

Today's casualties were staggering. As we congregated, it was impossible to ignore how many of us were missing. Pale eyes dropped to flippers. Cheeks bore pink twinges. Shame fueled the tension. Shame of knowing that we were nothing without a computer system.

Seven squirmed on the floor like a worm, battered and broken-armed. He peeled off his helmet, turned his head and vomited on his own shoulder. Twice.

I heard the sound of boots stomping down a metal ladder. In came Acci as I'd never seen him before—flushed, sweaty and literally shaking with rage. He stormed over to Seven and kicked him in the head, chest and gut, screaming,

"You lost me my unit! You shot this battle to hell, you son-of-a—!"

"STOP!" I screamed.

Instinctively, my hair lashed out, seizing Acci's neck from behind and forcibly pulling him off of Seven… whose face was no longer recognizable, so much it was bloodied.

The room went dead silent. It was the first time that any of my fellow divers saw me use offensive magic. In my comrades' eyes now, I saw shock, awe, fear and disgust.

Without warning, a wave of exhaustion washed over me, causing me to drop Acci like a sack of potatoes. I teetered on the balls of my feet as shapes and colors spun all around me. Sprawled at my feet, Acci gasped with an open mouth, clawing his collar.

"Damn, Lechat," Arrhyth breathed. "Scarlet never used her powers against *us*."

The vitreous silica jolted as it docked. We were home.

No longer at the helm, Inexor barged in, jaw clenched and temples pulsing. He glared at Seven. "Get up."

Seven moaned.

"I said, *get up!*" Spit flew from Inexor's mouth.

Seven only managed to hobble to his knees. "I'm s-sorry, sir," he heaved, "I… I just—"

"I didn't give you permission to speak!" Inexor roared, tearing the stripes right off his sleeves with superhuman strength. Then, he turned and addressed the entire fleet—or, what was left of it, anyway: "I hope you're all as sorry as this heap of dragon dung." He pointed at Seven. "Every pilot in this room has as much to apologize for as him. Cease Lechatelierite is rolling over in his grave, right now." He began to shake. "Thank heavens that Ambrek Coppertus spared him from seeing what'd become of his fleet!"

Not a single soul dared to breathe.

"Ence," Inexor suddenly addressed me, "you're my new Second-in-Command." He tossed the rank bands at my boots and stormed out into the hangar.

Slowly, everyone began to follow Inexor's lead, until finally there was no one left inside the carrier but Seven and me.

When I knelt to help him up, he recoiled.

"Seven?" I croaked.

"I didn't need you to defend me from Acci or Buird. I can fight my own battles."

Well, clearly, he couldn't fight worth a damn. I exhaled through my nostrils. "You're welcome," I grunted, turning to go.

"Ence," his voice caught me. "Ence… you almost killed Acci."

I froze. "No, I didn't."

"You couldn't see his face." Seven shook his head, swallowing. "It was blue. You were strangling him, Ence. Give it a couple more seconds, and he would've suffocated to death."

My heart drummed against my ribcage. "Well, I *didn't* give it a couple more seconds." Because I ran out of spectrum. "Because I have control over my powers."

"Do you?"

His heated words hung in the frigid air.

ENCE LECHATELIERITE

It was nearly midnight. I entered my new quarters—Seven's old room—and was greeted by four white walls, a bed, desk and laptop. Tossing my new rank bands aside, I sat in the rigid chair and logged into the computer, startled to discover that I wasn't connected to the internet. What the hell? I was supposed to be the right hand of the Leader of the Nurro-Ichthyothian Resistance. Why on earth would the Trilateral Committee cuff me like this? Since joining the fleet, I'd done nothing but perform excellently. I never gave anyone a single reason to distrust me.

That's when it clicked. Of course, the TC's wariness had nothing to do with my own actions, but everything to do with whose blood ran through my veins. With *their* net access, my parents wreaked serious havoc. They wrote angry letters to higher-ups, conducted research to dismantle the Childhood Program, found a means to expunge Cease's criminal record, requested a conference with the Second Earth Order, published revolutionary articles… I probably didn't even know the half of it. I was the son of Second Earth's biggest cyber-troublemakers.

No, 'troublemakers' was too mild a word. My parents went down in history as hardcore rebels. And, a handful of resources didn't portray their insurgency in a totally positive light. By some, they were considered radicals. Extremists.

I crossed my legs, flustered. Understanding *why* the TC shackled me didn't make me alright with it. If I was supposed to co-lead this resistance, I damned better have every possible asset at my disposition. They had no right to blindfold me—to rob my arsenal—while making me fight their war. Didn't they realize that shutting me out did nothing but solidify my resolve to get in?

Well, I was too tired to get started on that, *now*. I closed the laptop, threw off my uniform and sprawled naked in bed, muscles aching.

Less than a decade ago, these quarters belonged to my mother. She once lay on this mattress, stared at this ceiling, perched at this desk, padded across this cold metal floor. I leaned my head against the wall, listening to the pitter-patter of Inexor's keys. Then, I rolled over on my belly and inhaled, as though expecting to find Scarlet's scent still in the sheets.

There came a knock at the door.

"I'm not dressed," I murmured, sleepily. Around here, that didn't mean much. Even the showers were communal. I wondered how teenage Scarlet coped with all that. "The door's unlocked."

Seven opened up, regarding me unflinchingly. His arm was bound in a cast and sling, with countless bandages adorning his face and neck. "Sir, I left my notebook in the second desk drawer."

Wordlessly, I got up, grabbed the strangely-warm handle and yanked. It didn't budge.

"I meant the second from the *top*, sir. The one you're pulling, now—don't bother. It's always been stuck."

Was that so? "Here you go." I tossed the pad at him. "Dismissed."

"Thanks." Tucking it under his arm, Seven saluted awkwardly and toddled away.

I closed the door behind him and swiveled back around, pulse hammering. I approached the desk slowly, as though about to ambush an enemy. Kneeling, I carefully fingered the jammed drawer, once again. It was warm.

With spectrum.

Scarlet's spectrum.

Hyperventilating a little, I scooted away. Then, I closed my eyes and allowed all my magic to surge into my hair, enabling me to lasso the bar.

Apparently, I'd underestimated my strength, because the drawer didn't just open up, it flew out. Literally. The metal box soared across the room and smacked loudly into the opposite wall—Inexor's. Paper fluttered everywhere.

"Ence?" came Inexor's voice. "What was that?"

"N-nothing... sir," I panted, fatigue nearly knocking me out. I plopped onto my bed, noticing a sheet settling inches from my head. I reached for it.

It was a portrait of my father, realistic as a photograph.

Instantly, I sat bolt upright, exhaustion instantly eradicated by adrenaline. My greedy unblinking eyes memorized every pencil stroke... including two curious words scrawled at the bottom: '*If only*.' I frowned. If only, what? I stared intently at Cease's face. Crisp, sharp edges. An angular jaw. Pale, glassy eyes. A pinched nose.

Smiling.

That was it, wasn't it? I swallowed. *If only*. If only Cease Lechatelierite really smiled like that.

I circumnavigated the room, finding several sketches on lined paper, one crumpled scrap of cardstock... and a graphite pencil, almost ground to the eraser. I stared. It was the first non-mechanical writing utensil I'd seen since coming to Ichthyosis. It was wooden, coated in shiny orange paint. Its vivid color contrasted with the stock-white floor, ceiling, walls and furniture. It seemed downright obscene in this sterile room. I pocketed it.

Curled in bed, I flipped through each of Scarlet's illustrations. Some of them looked like they were meant to be battle diagrams, but they were too beautiful. Everything was drawn to-scale and labeled—the crystallines, dragon ships, vitreous silicas, even the individual divers. I squinted; apparently, Scarlet's sight was even better than mine.

The next image was of Arrhyth Link and Dither Maine, roughly a decade younger. Their cheeks were fuller, eyes brighter. They were shorter and plumper and had a sort of naïveté to their smiles.

Nurtic Leavesleft. I almost didn't recognize him. How he'd aged since this portrait was done! His grin was radiant, his cheeks were dimpled and his fair hair was thick and windswept. I'd never seen him look so healthy and joyful.

Some people, I didn't know. Conflagrians, from their dress. They wore scruffy robes and carried primitive torches, bows and arrows. Stringy hair hung from hoods, warrior-paint streaked cheeks and sandals were laced to knees. One mage was tall, had a dark complexion and wore a flowing gown with a sword hitched to her belt. Her colorless hair reached all the way to her hips. She stood beside a wiry man with a grandfatherly countenance and a deep-set stare that told of a thousand trials.

And, then I hit the jackpot: pictures of my mother and father… together. I got to see how their faces looked from different angles. Cease almost always wore the same stern scowl. Scarlet's expression almost always reflected a paradoxical mix of ferocity and fear. And, the two of them were *always* depicted working—performing the spin-toss maneuver, poring over battle plans, surface-riding, diving, typing. There were no casual nor romantic poses, none with just the two of them 'smiling at the camera' or leaning against one another. They were working, always working.

The very last sketch was a close-up of a guy I'd never seen before. A man who didn't show up in any of the other drawings. His face and neck filled the whole page, so I couldn't tell if he were mage or Nordic. He had a square jaw, a muscular neck, spiky hair that stood every which way and a rather menacing gaze. Something kept drawing me back to those eerie eyes. They were oddly familiar.

Of course. My dream! I bit my lip. A thousand times, I'd dreamt of a pair of wide golden eyes, regarding me with awe and dread. Nurtic Leavesleft asked me about that dream. He was very interested in it. He thought that it was a real memory. He said that it helped him research my origins. But, he never wound up revealing the man's relation to me.

The longer I peered at him, the more anxious I became. Acid smoldered in my abdomen. There was something wrong. It was as though my body were trying to warn me about him. I didn't like the look of him. Something told me that he was a bad man.

I swallowed. Why should I hate or fear him? I had no logical reason to. He was a total stranger. I was being stupid. After all, if Scarlet cared to immortalize him in art, he couldn't possibly be wretched, right?

I wondered why he was depicted alone, rather than in the presence of Scarlet's other friends or comrades.

I went to the bathroom—my bellyache was worsening by the minute—and sat on a cold metal toilet seat. Yes, even the toilets here were metal. A shiver ran all the way from my pelvic bone to my throat. No matter what, I couldn't get my bowels to loosen. I strained forward, cheeks cupped in my palms. I stared at the floor, examining the bits of dust and dirt caught in the grout. I tried to run my fingers through my tangled hair. That's when I noticed that my scalp was warm, surging with spectrum as though I were gearing up for a fight. No, not warm. Hot. Like a stovetop. But, weirdly enough, I wasn't drained by the magical exertion. Why? How?

I returned to my room, unrelieved. The mystery man seemed to watch me from the page on my desk. So, I flipped it over. Now, he couldn't see me.

I lay on my stomach in bed, feeling Scarlet's pencil stab my thigh and Cease's medal pierce my chest. Slowly, the scent of burnt fabric filled my nostrils… there were flames leaping from my pillow! I tossed it to the floor and hair-whacked it until it turned to ash.

I crawled back under my blanket and tried fruitlessly not to see through my scrunched lids, since that always made falling asleep harder.

And, even though the paper was overturned, I swore those amber eyes still followed me.

INEXOR BUIRD

Ence reminded me more of his father, every day—small, young, furiously ambitious, unbelievably brilliant. Ence's blatant emotional volatility was the one attribute that distinguished him from Cease. Cease may've been a total fliver-wreck on the inside, but on the outside, he typically kept his crap together. Though Cease had a mean temper, he usually knew when to keep his bottle corked. Ence, on the other hand, consistently wore his heart on his sleeve, reacting passionately to everything and anything. And, his face always betrayed his feelings—well, if his loud mouth didn't already.

I tossed in bed, remembering what Cease was like when he was Ence's age. Seven. I was eleven. At the time, I was yet to violate the Laws of Emotional Protection. Sure, I had plenty of acquaintances, but no real friends. And, I had to admit, it got lonely sometimes. Outside of class or practice, I hardly opened my mouth. My thoughts had no choice but to percolate endlessly inside my own skull. The more time passed, the more frustrated I became with the isolation of it all. I needed an outlet. Desperately.

That's when the dangerous idea occurred to me: maybe, I could pursue a friendship. Just one. Trusting more than one person would compound the risk too much.

Of course, I had no idea how to go about surreptitiously convincing someone to break the law for me. So, I spent my scant free time furtively researching social anthropology, carefully strategizing a plan of attack to accomplish my mission objective. Ultimately, I boiled my findings down to a simple five-step process.

Step one: choose a target. Step two: show interest in said target by asking him questions about himself, with the natural expectation of reciprocity, thereby giving him the opportunity to learn about me as well. Step three: using my newly-acquired intel about the subject's personality and background, offer praise where appropriate, to generate gratitude and other such positive feelings. Step four: using my newly-acquired intel about the subject's personality and background, offer aid where appropriate, allowing him to perceive an incentive (self-advancement) to perpetuating our interactions. Step five: repeat steps two through four, as often as necessary.

Step one was a huge hurdle, in itself. I had to be very careful with my selection. My target had to be someone wise, discrete and disciplined. Someone with the stamina to bear another's burdens, atop his own. And, above all, my new friend had to be smart and driven. Interacting with him had to be intellectually stimulating. I didn't want to attach myself to a deadweight who'd become an obstacle to my education or career. Rather, I wanted someone who'd challenge and motivate me.

Excitement was thick in the air at Icicle Academy, the day my class heard that Cease Lechatelierite—the grandson of the great Captain Terminus Lechatelierite—would be joining our grade-level. Outstanding reputation far preceding him, everyone hoped to get a course or two with the seven-age-old wonder, to see his nimble mind in action and learn the secrets to his success.

As for me, I couldn't think of a better candidate for my inaugural friendship. After all, if Cease was going to be some great commander one day, there was nothing to lose and everything to gain from getting on his good side now, while he was still small.

No pun intended. Cease was so small, I almost didn't spot him, the first time he entered my physics seminar. True to the rumors, he was barely over three feet tall and looked lighter than my knapsack. Angular and thin, he resembled a walking piece of vector math.

As he marched down the aisle, the room fell silent. Though clearly aware of the attention he was drawing, Cease fixed his gaze straight ahead, refusing to utter so much as a 'hello' to those who greeted him. The thought of pursuing emotional closeness with the likes of him was seeming more far-fetched, by the minute. The kid didn't even speak when spoken to. How was I ever going to progress to step two?

Then, our teacher came in and uttered a miracle: my lab-partner broke his neck during diving practice yesterday night, so Cease Lechatelierite would replace him as my counterpart. I couldn't believe it; I had an official excuse to talk to Cease, at least every other day.

He settled beside me now without glancing my way.

I cleared my throat. Here went nothing. "Inexor Buird," I said firmly, holding out my hand. "Nice to meet you."

He didn't take my hand. He just looked at me. The others weren't kidding when they said that his eyes were silver. They were like pools of water or chips of ice—near-colorless and mirrorlike. It was unbelievably disorienting.

At long last, he curtly replied, "Cease Lechatelierite," as if everyone didn't already know.

Time for step two: ask questions. Show interest. Get him talking about himself.

"So, um... how... how are you liking your new grade-level, so far?" I blurted clumsily, resisting the urge to shove my own boot down my throat.

Did he ever blink those chilling eyes? "It's fine." His tone was curt, almost accusatory.

"So, uh, what's your favorite subject?"

"Irrelevant," he snapped, clasping his hands. "All are necessary to adequately prep for combat."

Well, of course, they were. I wasn't asking which were *needed*, I was asking which he *liked*. I wanted his opinion.

"Okay... but what do you personally enjoy the most?"

"Why does it matter?" he asked, facing front.

So, when holding a conversation, he either stared daggers at you, or he didn't look at you at all? How awkward and disconcerting. So far, this entire exchange was totally stilted and off-putting.

I shrugged. "Just curious."

"Diving," he crisply answered. "That's my favorite."

More silence.

Sheesh, he sure was making me work for it; I anticipated that my questions would motivate *some* degree of mutuality, but apparently, Cease didn't have the faintest desire to learn a damn thing about his new lab-partner.

"Mine is computer science," I volunteered. "I love programming and hacking."

He didn't speak.

"Well, anyway, I'm looking forward to working with you, this age," I painfully pushed onto stage three: praise and butter up. "You're definitely ahead of the pack, that's for sure. The academy admins must've known you were leadership material ever since you took on Colonel Austere in strategy class, last summer." I'd heard all about that incident. The whole academy *still* buzzed about it. Cease actually had the nerve to disrupt a lesson to defend the Conflagrian enemy to his teacher. And, not just *any* teacher, but the esteemed Colonel Autoero Austere.

"I was a fool," Cease spat. "Those fire-savages don't deserve anyone's sympathy."

"Of course, they don't," I said, taken aback. "But, it was still brave of you to stand up for your beliefs, like that. Very revolutionary."

"Rebels don't make good soldiers," he declared frostily, unaware that he'd become one of the most revolutionary figures in Second Earth history, a mere decade later. "Military service requires discipline and obedience—qualities you clearly lack." His voice was no longer just condescending and patronizing, it was downright scathing.

Anger flared in my chest. Our exchange was barely underway, and I'd already had enough. Cease was pissing all over my dignity. He obviously wasn't the right person to befriend. I'd never trust him, and he'd never respect me. I needed to go back to square one and pick someone who wasn't such a mouthy pompous bastard.

"You know what, Cease? You have an enormous heated lance up your ass," I said sourly, no longer giving a dragon turd what he thought of me. "Everybody's expecting you to command the fleet one day, yet you can't even converse with your lab-partner for two minutes without giving him a few reasons to want to break your anemic face. I can hardly stand to sit beside you; who the hell will be willing to follow you into battle?"

Cease tore his gaze from the front of the room and regarded me, again. But, this time, the caliber of his stare was different. There was something new there. A spark. A flicker of interest. His face was deadpan, yet his curious eyes conveyed that I'd opened his door a crack. I guessed that no peer of his ever had the courage to give him a taste of his own medicine, before.

Leave it to Cease Lechatelierite to turn step three on its head.

* * *

It turned out, Cease and I had all our classes together except Nurian; I was in level four while he was in level one.

"It's strange that they'd let you speed through all the other subjects, but make you wait until you're in my grade before permitting you to *start* Nurian," I commented one evening, as we sat in the barracks.

"I didn't just start," Cease said quietly, poring over his workbook. "I took level one, last age."

I froze, hardly daring to breathe. Cease Lechatelierite, Icicle Academy's finest, flunked a course? Moreover, he flunked a course and was willing to openly admit that failure to someone else who probably would've never found out otherwise: me.

My pursuit was working. I couldn't believe it. Cease was starting to trust me. He was being vulnerable with me.

"You did?" I breathed, delicately.

He nodded.

"Oh." I swallowed. Did I dare attempt step four? Offer aid where needed, so he'd perceive some tangible value to perpetuating our interactions. I didn't think I'd ever get the chance to try that with Cease, because he was supposed to be amazing at everything already. "I'm pretty decent at Nurian. If you'd like, I could give you a hand," I feebly suggested.

There was a pregnant pause during which I could almost see the gears turn in Cease's brain, behind his glassy gaze. Come on, I thought. Accept my offer. Need me.

"Sure," he finally replied, to my profound disbelief. And, with that, he actually handed me his half-finished assignment, to look over.

I stayed silent for a couple minutes while I read, trying not to let the horror I was feeling creep across my face. Cease jumbled the simplest words and fouled up the most basic conjugations. The majority of his sentences were fragments with missing articles, misspellings, words in the wrong order and verbs still in the infinitive. Sometimes, his spelling was so bad, it was impossible to tell what he was even shooting for, in the first place.

I looked up at his snow-pale face. The super soldier had a serious weakness. A tragic flaw. And, he was counting on me to save the day. But, could I help him when he was so far gone? Would I wind up letting him down, botching our budding friendship in the process?

* * *

As the night wore on, Cease's speaking ability proved even worse than his writing—a feat I hadn't thought possible. Cloaked in a heavy Ichthyothian accent, his sentences sounded like slushy strings of consonants.

"Almost everything in Nurian is pronounced phonetically," I explained for the umpteenth time. "So, quit skipping over the vowels and smearing everything together, okay? Take things one syllable at a time."

He nodded.

"Now, repeat after me: *I would like a drink of water.*"

"Iwldlkadrkawatr," he mumbled.

"Slower," I instructed. "Draw out the vowels more."

"Iyyyawuddliiikaaadriiiowwaataa."

"Better," I said, though it was still atrocious. "Pause a little, between words."

"Iyyy wud liyk ay drrinkk offf…" he hesitated.

"Yes, keep going," I urged.

His face fell. "I forgot how to say 'water.'"

Seriously? "What do you mean, you forgot? You *just* said it, a second ago!"

"I know, but I can't remember it anymore."

My teeth gnashed. I was on the brink of drowning his books in the sea and telling him to go learn Nurian in hell.

"You're getting frustrated with me," he observed.

"Yes," I admitted, through tight lips.

He immediately began packing up his stuff.

"Wait, no, what are you doing?" Great. Some friend I was turning out to be. Step four was going south fast. "I'll be more patient from now on, I swear."

"You've already been remarkably patient," he countered, and suddenly the whole situation didn't seem so bad anymore. "But, I can recognize a waste of time when I see it."

Those words made my chest ache, and not just because I was worried that Cease's hopelessness and failure could derail my friendship plan. No, I was concerned because... well, because I actually felt bad *for him*. It hurt me to see him so discouraged. I genuinely wanted him to succeed, not just so I'd accomplish my mission objective, but because... I actually cared for his wellbeing. Holy crystallines, I was starting to attach to him. To break the Laws of Emotional Protection for real. I couldn't believe it. In my belly, I felt a flurry of excitement punctuated by fear.

"Cease, if you don't make some serious progress fast, you'll wind up tanking level one, again," I said. "I don't want that to happen."

He stiffened. "Why?"

Uh oh. I hesitated. "What?"

"What's it to you, if I bomb Nurian?"

I was silent. After a few intense seconds, he looked away, brows furrowed. So, he knew. He figured me out. He saw what I was up to. Of course. Now, the question was: what would he do with this realization? Wall off? Lash out? Tattle?

Reciprocate?

He slung his knapsack over his shoulder. "Well, I don't understand why we even need to learn Nurian, in the first place," he breezed on. So, for now, he chose to pursue casual talk. That was a good sign. A *friendly* sign. "We live in an isolationist world. Why are we busying ourselves with foreign languages?"

I shrugged. "Nurian is the closest thing that Second Earth has to an international tongue. I guess fluency would be a useful skill for a traveling soldier. And, Ichthyosis isn't in the Order, anyway. Legally speaking, *we* don't have to be isolationist."

"Inexor," his tone was dry, "the whole world practices isolationism. What do you think that makes us?"

Hm. "...Isolated."

And, I thought I saw tiny smile dimples briefly touch Cease's cheeks.

* * *

Only a couple days later, during physics lab, Cease asked if we could give language tutoring another shot, sometime.

"Sure," I breathed, enthused. "What made you change your mind?"

He stayed quiet for a long while. Then, he finally said, "I've got to know Nurian really well, if I want to go there someday to ask them to ally with us."

KRUSTALLOS FINIRE VII

Ence was behaving oddly. Well, he always behaved oddly, but *this* little tirade seemed particularly strange, even for him. Sitting across from him at the breakfast table now, I could tell that his 'rant' wasn't really a rant—it was far too detailed. Too thought-out. Well-calculated. He scrambled his grammar and spoke quickly as to make his speech *sound* like a disorganized stream-of-consciousness, but I had a hunch that he pre-planned every word.

"Come on, everyone knows that our defensive strategy isn't accomplishing a damn thing," he declared, leaning over his plate. His hair seemed to slither and squirm like a heap of snakes. Though I'd seen Scarlet's hair do that plenty of times, I still found the gesture extremely creepy. "All our pansy method's doing is dragging out the war for eras, while the economy plummets. It won't be long before we hit a full-scale depression. When's it supposed to strike, the twelfth age?"

Of course, Ence already knew the precise prediction—we all did. He was playing dumb, to bolster his faux spontaneity.

"The eleventh," Maine answered.

When Ence's eyes went wide, I fought the urge to scoff. I found the kid's facial expressions and body language far less believable than his tone. He was a masterful voice-actor, but everything else about him was almost caricature-like.

"That's in less than a decade!" he cried, hands wringing.

Although this was news to no one, people still looked jarred. The economy's abysmal fate wasn't something discussed very often around the breakfast table. So, exclaiming loudly about it, the morning after a particularly long and exhausting battle, was a quick way to make everyone intensely uncomfortable.

"So, what exactly do you want us to do about it?" Link griped, as Ence popped a heavily-salmon-smeared cracker into his mouth. "Invade Conflagria or something?"

Ence's cheeks were packed. The table waited in suspense as he methodically chewed, swallowed and wiped his mouth.

"Well, yeah." He shrugged. "Why not?"

Not a single morsel touched a pair of lips.

"What?" Maine croaked.

"That'd wrap things up a lot faster than if we continued doing what we've been doing since the Second Infiltration in ninety-four—basically, sitting on our hands." Ence's words seemed to echo off the metal walls. Sometimes, it seemed like the boy's tone could pierce the soul. Like his father.

Inexor shifted in his seat, right hand clenched so tightly around his fork, his veins protruded like bootlaces. Ence was insulting his strategy, in front of everybody.

"So, yesterday, when we raided a System carrier—and actually made it in, this time—we grabbed a handful of magic books and some other indiscernible spectral gismos. Now what?" Ence went on—much too loudly, of course. "What are we going to do with all that stuff? Does anyone around here actually understand a lick of spectroscopy?"

"Ence," Inexor growled, "that material could be vital to our comprehension of Conflagria's magical fighting methods—"

"How so, sir?" Ence dared to interrupt.

"That cannot possibly be determined within the next few minutes, over breakfast," Inexor shot. "Now, sit down."

Wait, when exactly did Ence get to his feet, in the first place?

"Has anyone even cracked open a single one of those books, yet?" Ence blared, arms folded across his bony chest.

"We've had them for one night," Comat chimed.

"So, what? What are we waiting for? The depression is going to hit by the *eleventh age*, people! If that doesn't motivate us to hurry up and *do* something, what will?"

Inexor slowly blinked his cool blue eyes. "Did *you* look at them yet, Ence? Since you're being so belligerent about it, I assume you did."

Ence tossed his head back. "You would assume correctly, sir."

Dozens of brows raised. I wasn't sure I believed him, myself.

"Really? What did you learn, then? Please, enlighten us," the Commander jeered.

"I'd love to." Ence gestured to the room. "Soldiers, report to the lecture hall at eight o'clock for a presentation."

"Hey," Inexor barked, "you can't plug up everyone's schedules without *my* permission!"

"My apologies, sir," Ence bowed to Inexor in a very mage-like manner. "May I inform the fleet of my findings today at eight, in the lecture hall?"

"Yes," he grumbled, "but, at seven-forty-five. We've got a busy day to get to, afterward."

Ence, brimming with smug satisfaction, left the cafeteria in the instant. Appetite shot to hell, I abandoned my trey to tail him… all the way to hangar, where the manta ray's cargo bay bore three unopened bags of spectroscopy books and 'gismos.'

I gawked at Ence. "You lied to the Commander," I breathed. "To all of us."

Ence got to work, sheering the sacks with his razor. "So, what are you going to do about it?" he grunted, whipping out his PAVLAK and loading the translator app. He opened a book at random and started scanning pages.

"How do you even know that you're going find something worthwhile to talk about?" I was stunned. This kid really was something else. "And, before seven-forty-five?"

"Easy. All I need is for you to get the hell out of here and let me concentrate."

"Good luck," I snorted. "After your whiny mutinous display at breakfast, everyone's expecting a real revelation from you, in about twenty minutes."

Ence grabbed my broken arm, enough ice in his gaze to freeze the entire Fire Pit in an instant. There was something really strange about his iridescent lime-slice stare. Something that struck the core of my being. What could possibly make his eyes scintillate like that? Perhaps it was... spectrum?

Holy crystallines. Was Ence a multi-sourced enchant?

When Ence released me, I scuttled like System mages were hot on my tail.

* * *

"Nurtic Leavesleft once told me that Scarlet July's eye-fire inspired the System's Underwater Fire," Link said. "The two basically share all the same properties."

Ence shook his head. "No, they don't," he replied, confidently. "Eye-fire is far more versatile."

"How so?"

"For one, it can catch onto small masses while UF can't."

"Really?" Link yanked a curl. "It's obviously been quite a while since I've seen Scarlet in action, so I don't necessarily remember what she could or couldn't do. I mean, she hardly ever used offensive magic around us, to begin with."

"I know what I'm saying," Ence insisted. "UF is way more limited, believe me."

"Why should we?" Inexor cut in.

Ence's acidic gaze gouged his face. "Excuse me?"

"I said, why should we believe you?" Inexor jumped up. "How do you know what eye-fire's like? The only eye mage in history died the day you were born. Being her son doesn't make you an authority on her—not when you've never actually interacted."

Ence spoke with a sort of quiet intensity that captivated the whole room: "Actually, my mother *isn't* the only eye mage in history."

There was a heavy pause.

"Whoa, hold the phone," Link breathed. "You're a multi-sourced enchant?"

Ence smiled. "I am."

Inexor cleared his throat. "I don't believe you."

"Sir, the idea isn't *that* crazy," Maine said. "I mean, Scarlet could've passed on the gene."

The Commander rounded on Ence, barking, "Prove it. Set something on fire with your eyes, right now."

Ence hesitated. "In... in here?"

"Why not?"

For once, Ence's vocal control faltered: "Because... well... that's dangerous; we're in a tight space..."

"Scarlet was able to produce 'safe flames,'" Inexor countered. "I once saw her overturn a jar of fire on a mattress, and the sheets didn't even catch."

"Well, sir, my eye-magic isn't *quite* as refined—"

"Is it unrefined or nonexistent?" Inexor blared, facing us. "He can't do it. His BSC is a *point*-seven—hardly enough for a single source, let alone two." He whipped out his PAVLAK, loaded the spectrometer app and advanced on Ence, holding the little device right up to the boy's sweaty forehead. "See? He's infrared, like the rest of us. No aura."

Inexor's torso was ablaze! Crying out, he dropped to the floor and rolled, but the flames didn't die… until Ence tossed his hair forward to smother them.

Inexor's lay still on his back, shirt blackened and smoking.

"Sir," Ence gasped, dropping to his knees.

Inexor sat up, unbuttoning his uniform. I expected to see horrible burns all over his chest, but to my profound disbelief, his skin remained unblemished. Everyone stared at Ence, in shock and awe.

"See? Safe-flames," Ence said, numbly. "Could catch onto cloth, but not skin."

"You *are* a multi-sourced enchant," Link gasped.

"And, eye-fire *is* more diverse than UF," Illia added.

"That was amazing," Maine chimed.

"Warn me before you do that next time, okay?" Inexor asked, too relieved to be angry anymore. He stood.

Ence stayed put, complexion as white as the walls. His expression was self-satisfied, exhausted, surprised and panicked, all at once. I had a hunch that his little demonstration wasn't intentional. Inexor didn't realize how close he just came to death.

"I'm going to change. Excuse me." Inexor ducked out, leaving Ence alone with his men—all of whom were now ogling him like a mythological deity.

Taking advantage of his enraptured audience, Ence continued with his presentation—sitting, this time. And, within minutes, he swiftly and masterfully changed the subject from spectroscopy to the alliance's next step in the grand scheme of the war. Over and over, in that hypnotic voice of his, he hammered us with his mantra: *What we're doing now isn't working. We need to take more drastic action to finish off this war, once and for all, before the economy crumbles. I know what to do. I know how to do it. Want to defeat Conflagria? Want to end the conflict for good? Follow my lead. You're in safe hands. Just trust me. I can do this. We can. Together.*

Ence sure had some nerve, saying things like that behind Inexor's back. And, to make matters all the more outrageous, everyone seemed to be listening to him. I mean, really listening, hanging onto his every word, intermittently vocalizing universal agreement. We were playing right into his hands, legitimizing his stolen authority. I wanted to scream: stop going along with him—he's manipulating us! But, I didn't. Why? Because, slowly, he was even starting to get to me. The war really was dragging on, for no legit reason. The economy really was on the brink of collapse. The eleventh age really was a tight deadline. I was as anxious as the next man to see things change. If nothing we'd attempted thus far did the trick, why not try something new?

I liked many of Ence's ideas. But, what I *didn't* like was the mutinous manner in which he presented them. Not to mention that he acted like he knew the enemy far better than any of us, though he hadn't even been involved in the war for very long. He kept saying things like, 'If we try *this*, the Conflagrians will probably do *that*.' Why was everyone so quick to accept his analysis of the mage mind, when he grew up in Nuria? Of course. Because he was a mage, himself. A multi-sourced enchant, no less. He was the son of the beloved Scarlet July.

Once upon a time, Cease Lechatelierite leaned heavily on Scarlet, running all his concepts by her and making practical use of every last one of her incredible talents and insane brain-children. But, all the while, we were still *his* fleet. Not Scarlet's. Scarlet never vied for our allegiance nor tried to go over our Commander's head. She always deferred to him, content to be a weapon in his hands. But,

Ence? Ence was no one's gun. He clearly wanted to be the one aiming the crosshairs.

Ence dismissed us before Inexor could return—a strategic move, no doubt. I sauntered out of the lecture hall behind Link and Maine, who were chattering excitedly.

I sighed.

Link turned at the sound. "Hey, Seven. Some presentation, huh?"

I scowled. "The boy's got vision, I'll give him that. But, I don't like his attitude. He's acting like he's Scarlet-incarnate, or something."

Link yanked a curl. "Well…"

"Scarlet and Ence aren't one and the same, Link. Ence is—"

"A multi-sourced enchant. Quite possibly, *the* Multi-Source Enchant. Have you considered that? The prophet might be with us, right here, right now. What if he truly can end the war?"

"I don't get it," I grumbled. "What does the prophecy have to do with the war?"

Link shrugged. "Scarlet always used to think the two were connected, in some way."

I scowled. "Scarlet *also* thought the prophecy concerned the Crystal's end and the spectral diffusion and the Red Revolution and the Tri-Nation Campaign and world isolationism and about a gazillion other things."

"So?"

"*So*, that means that Scarlet clearly didn't have the slightest clue what the prophecy meant."

"Yeah, well, maybe because it wasn't written for her, but for Ence. That's probably why he's so fired up and anxious to get things moving."

How could Link be so blind? "Link, do you really think that Ence said all that stuff right now because he actually cares what some old manuscript says? Do you really think that he's filled with noble desires to save the world? Hell no. He's just trying to stir the pot so he can ultimately overthrow Commander Buird. His motives are selfish."

"What? Says who?" Link's brows scrunched together.

"Says everything he's ever done, since setting foot on base. The kid has no shame. He doesn't even try to hide the fact that he's a power-hungry, ruthless, manipulative bastard who only cares for himself and his own agenda."

Link's jaw literally dropped. "I can't believe you'd say something so awful about Cease and Scarlet's own flesh and blood!"

"What does it matter, whose DNA he shares? Ence is a *very* different person than his parents; he's got none of their discipline nor decency, and he's clearly out for Buird's head!"

"Ence is a dedicated soldier who, at a very young age, decided to give up middle-class civilian life in a great man's home to consecrate himself to the alliance," Link retorted. "He left Nurtic and Alcove City, *for us*."

"He hated Leavesleft and your polluted swamp-city. Leaving his civilian life behind was no *sacrifice* to him—he couldn't wait to get out."

"And, since when have you been so dedicated to Buird, anyway? He embarrassed the piss out of you."

"Mutiny is a serious matter."

He chortled. "Look who's talking. If my memory serves me right, you once tried to overthrow Scarlet."

"Yeah, and it was the biggest mistake of my life. I owned up to that fact ages ago, paying a heavy price. I've learned my lesson and my place."

Link snorted.

"Ence is following in the footsteps of my eleven-age-old self," I insisted, "except that he's doing it with seductive words and fancy magical displays, rather than brute force. Are we just going to sit back and let him tear this fleet apart?"

"Look, Seven," Link said, dryly, "I know Ence took your rank, but there's no need to let your personal junk obscure your opinion of him and everything he's trying to do for us."

Personal junk? "This isn't about me!"

Link's arms folded. "How can I put this to you?" He inhaled. "When Scarlet died, she left behind a lot of incomplete work—work that many believed only she could've done. But, now, we have Ence. And, when I look at him and listen to his words… I don't know… I just…don't feel so hopeless, anymore. I think, 'hey, here's a guy who may be able to do it, to finally finish what Scarlet started.' So, I'm going to stand by him, and so is the rest of this fleet. If you don't want to join us, it's *your* loss." And, with that, Link jogged to catch up with Maine and the rest.

I trudged to the barracks, far behind the pack, thinking of the logs that I read when I was first promoted to Second—the ones about Cease Lechatelierite and Ecrof Ecreoc. Cease usurped Ecreoc. I, myself, tried to usurp Scarlet. And, now, Scarlet's son was hot on Inexor's trail. Gnawing my lip, I curled the fingers of my broken arm around my cast's cuff. No matter how much we studied history, it always inevitably repeated.

NURTIC LEAVESLEFT

I stayed in Linkeree's guest room for two weeks. And, I realized by the end of the fortnight that the only reason I ever got out of bed in the morning was to see her face.

When I returned home, I found the strength to talk to my old boss at Frost's Delivery Service to ask for my job back. The next day, I finally flew again. I took Linkeree for a visit to UVA.

We eloped two ages later.

"Linkeree Leavesleft," she murmured, on our wedding night. "Though still annoyingly alliterative, at least it's no longer blatantly redundant."

"I'm family, now. Which means, from this day forward, I'll never call you 'Ree' again," I teased.

Her nose wrinkled. "You know what? I'm actually okay with that. I never thought I'd see the day that I'd find my real first name beautiful."

I smiled. "I always thought it was beautiful."

We had a child of our own, several ages later. We named him Ehud, after the lefty leader of Israel from the Book of Judges. I liked to sit Ehud on my lap and tell him stories of the Ichthyo-Conflagrian War, the World Revolt, and all the amazing people thrown in my path along the way—Cease Lechatelierite, Scarlet July, Krustallos Finire VII, Inexor Buird, Arrhyth Link, Dither Maine, Ecivon Wen, Tnerruc Ruetama and the long-lost Commence July Lechatelierite, the son of two of the most incredible human beings I ever had the privilege to know and love. These names became legends to little Ehud.

"Some of them, you'll never get to meet, like Cease, Scarlet, Ecivon and Tnerruc," I told Ehud, sadly. "But, though they're gone, they must never be forgotten. We must keep them alive in spirit by retelling their stories, throughout the generations." Squirming in my lap and yanking his light-brown curls, Ehud watched me intently with those enormous hazel eyes of his. "Others, like Dither and Uncle Arrhyth, you will get to see in a few ages, when they return from Ichthyosis. By then, you'll be a big boy. But, don't resent them for their absence, honor them for their service. It's the sacrifice of people like them that gives the rest of us the freedom to live."

As soon as Ehud could speak full sentences, he asked me why he'd never get to meet 'Scawlet' and 'Ceee.'

"Why'd they haveta go?" he piped, the words instantly breaking my heart into a thousand pieces. "I wanna meet 'em, 'specially Ceee—he's cool."

I didn't joke around or evade his question or tell him pretty lies. I simply said, "This is the nature of war: it tears friends and families apart. War destroyed First Earth and continues to plague our world. Perhaps, one day, humanity will find a way to end the violence, once and for all."

At that moment, Ehud dropped the bombshell I knew was coming, all along: he asked me if Commence could visit.

"Maybe, someday," I said, stroking his swirly hair. "If he's willing. I can't promise anything. I can only hope and pray for time to heal his emotional wounds. You see, Ehud, sometimes people refuse to face their past pains because they're afraid. Sometimes, people like to pretend that things never happened at all because they erroneously think that'd make life easier."

“What about right now?” Ehud asked. “Do you think he’s happy, right now?”

I was silent. *Was* Ence happy as a diver? Did his six-age-old desires breed true?

I thought about my own tumultuous past, about how I wouldn’t trade any of it for the world, despite how many scars I still bore from the horrors I’d endured. Often, through it all, I found myself at the right place and time to affect positive change. Who knew how things would’ve turned out if I never left Scarlet boxes of cereal and packages of beef jerky by the Alcove City Train Station. If I never busted Cease Lechatelierite out of his trial and reinstated his command. If I never helped my prison captor, Fair Gabardine, break through the System’s mental shackles to go into hiding with me. If I wasn’t around to pull Scarlet, unknowingly pregnant with Ence, from the Fire Pit after Ambrek Coppertus killed Lechatelierite. If I never found Ence at the orphanage and uncovered the truth about his origins. I couldn’t deny that, though anything but easy, the choices I made and the challenges I faced literally altered the course of history.

I always knew that Ence was meant for great things. Maybe, *this* was it—what Ence was supposed to do with his life. Maybe, his purpose on Second Earth was to be the next secret magical weapon of the Nordic Diving Fleet. The next game-changer in this war and in this world. The next Scarlet July.

I looked down at my lap and saw that Ehud had fallen asleep before I could answer his last question.

I carried him to his room, tucked him in and kissed his round cheek, thinking about how I no longer needed rigor in my life to be content, as I did in my teens and twenties. All I needed now was my family.

Ehud wasn't a replacement for Ence; I didn't believe that one person could ever really take the place of another, in the human heart. But, he and Linkeree constituted a completely new chapter. The happiest of my life.

EHUD LEAVESLEFT

Deer ~~Ence~~, ~~Comence~~, Ence ~~Leshatleeairight~~ Leshatleairite,

~~Hi how are you? Im fine.~~ I dont reelly no how to begin this. You dont no me but I think I no you becaus daddy told me alot about yuou. ~~I miss you.~~ If your tierd of diving any time yuou can all ways come back home hear. We dont stay in Alcove City for ~~much~~ verry long at one time becaus we go on alot of mishions ~~alot~~ but yuou ar welcom to come with us on them some time to. They ar alot of fun and we meat alot of cool peepol. Daddy would even let yuou fly his plain if yuou want too. I all ways wanted to no what it woud be like too have a big brother and I think yuou woud make a verry good 1. You coud tell me storys about the diving fleat in ~~Ikhosis~~ ~~Ikthosys~~ ~~ICkthosis~~ the Iland of Ice and I coud play my viola for you (daddy is teeching me already).

~~Sinseerly~~,

~~Lov~~,

~~Yuour brother~~,

Lov,

EHUD LEAVESLEFT

INEXOR BUIRD

December twentieth of the tenth age, eighth era. The eve of the depression.

Ence's strategy didn't win the war. Invading Conflagria only added civilian deaths to our consciences. Despite his brilliance, Commander Ence Lechatelierite was unable to deliver what he promised to his men, nine ages ago when he usurped me. Could we really blame him, though? Could *anyone* end this war? By now, I'd all but lost hope.

Ence no longer reminded me of Cease. And, he was certainly nothing like Scarlet. He had all of their talent but none of their self-control nor sense of right and wrong. He was vicious, tyrannical, sadistic. While Cease's authority was grounded in mutual trust and respect, Ence relied on instilling fear. Over the ages, his spectrum gradually strengthened, enabling him further to use physical force as a disciplinary tool. He'd whip us with his hair, burn us with his eyes, deafen us with his voice. He'd play malicious life-threatening tricks on us for his own amusement, like magically cloaking crystalline handlebars from sight during surface-riding practice. Ence's favorite target was Krustallos Finire VII. Hmm, come to think of it, I hadn't seen Seven in a few days...

Ence was a lot like Commander Ecrof Ecreoc—Cease's predecessor. Ecreoc also had a scapegoat, a favorite soldier to torture. Ironically enough, that soldier was Ence's father.

Whenever Cease put a toe out of line, Ecreoc would order him to his quarters that evening where he'd set his stun-gun on low to temporarily immobilize his limbs, then beat him senseless with his glacier-thawing lance. Cease would return to the barracks in the middle of the night, polka-dotted with bruises and burns. And, everyone would pretend not to hear when he moaned in his sleep.

History sure had a way of repeating itself. I was just glad that Cease was spared the agony of watching his own son press rewind.

ENCE LECHATELIERITE

December twenty-first of the tenth age, eighth era.

I practiced my magic almost every night for the past nine ages, but my endurance was the only thing that seemed to substantially improve. I was still mediocre at wielding my spectrum, though somewhat better at hiding the fatigue that followed.

One evening last week, I ordered Seven to my quarters to face the repercussions of mouthing off during practice earlier that afternoon. When he came in, he noticed that Scarlet's drawer was open a crack, so he blindly reached in, grabbed a fistful of her drawings and tore them right down the middle.

I lost all control. Screaming, I hair-whipped him across the face—crimson erupted from his nose with explosive force—then, pushed him backward into my desk. His head hit the metal edge with an audible thump; he instantly collapsed to the floor in a heap, unconscious. Angry and exhausted, I abruptly went to bed. I awoke a few hours later to the sight of Seven in the exact same position. So, I begrudgingly dragged him to the hospital. Until today, he was yet to return to service.

And, his bloodstains still adorned my wall, no matter how much I scrubbed. That was the problem with the color scheme, around here. White got dirty too easily.

ENCE LECHATELIERITE

December twenty-second, seven o'clock. The morning of my sixteenth birthday.

I often used my location in the mess hall as a weapon. If, for any reason, there was a specific soldier I wanted to wear down, I would sit by him at every meal for days on end, depriving him of his unwinding time. Today, however, there was no one in particular I needed to intimidate, so I chose my victims at random.

Breakfast was usually the quietest meal of all, as everyone still felt somewhat subdued by the madness of the previous day. But, Arrhyth Link and Dither Maine could always be counted on to buzz like twin vacuum-cleaners, no matter the hour. They chattered animatedly with Comat Acci… until they noticed my approach.

"Sir," Arrhyth breathed, freezing in mid-chew.

Anxiously, Dither peered up from his plate.

Comat's gaze went deadpan. "Good morning, sir," he calmly said.

"Morning." I settled beside Comat, directly across from Arrhyth and Dither.

"So, where were we?" Arrhyth's fork stroked his salmon paste.

Comat shrugged. "I was talking about my brief stint in civilian public school, but we can move onto something else."

I cleared my throat. "Please, don't let me interrupt. Say whatever you were going to say." I lifted my water to my lips.

The three of them exchanged concerned looks.

"Oh, no, that's alright." Comat's hand waved.

I took a sip. "Why? What don't you want me to hear?"

"N-nothing."

"Then, speak," I demanded.

"Well... um... I was just reminiscing about my time in Mrs. Termag's class... where N-Nurtic Leavesleft used to work..."

I plunked my glass down on the table, causing Arrhyth and Dither to jump like preteen civilian girls who just spotted a spider. Comat stayed still as a stone.

"Go on," I prompted, tone low.

Comat's elbow accidentally rested on the handle of his spoon. It snapped up, propelling a wad of fishy goo in my face.

"Sir!" He grabbed his napkin. "I'm so sorry! Here, let me—"

"Don't touch me." My fingers pawed the slime off my cheek. I may've been strict about most protocol, but I didn't mind getting messy while in ceremonial uniform and I didn't tend to punish soldiers for unpolished boots or stained garments. Since childhood, filth never bothered me. Nurtic, Ce and Selepoh could attest to that. "I believe I ordered you to finish your thought," I grunted.

"A-alright, then," Comat choked. "So, um, after maybe a month or two in second grade, I tested into the twelfth and got abruptly thrown into the college-application madness. I considered a lot of schools, but wound up picking the Nurian Diving Academy so I could eventually find my way back here."

"I'm amazed that you'd *want* to return to service," Arrhyth breathed. "I mean, wasn't the Childhood Program traumatizing?"

Comat nodded. "Nurtic dressed some of my wounds, I won't deny that. But, still, an experience like the CP never really *leaves* you, you know? It sits in your chest like an ice block, all the time, no matter what. It never fully dissolves. It's like… even while I lived in warm suburban Vitaville, a part of me still felt trapped between Icicle's cold sterile walls. I couldn't even glimpse at the ocean without getting combat flashbacks. I couldn't smell or eat seafood without my stomach turning. For a time, I was even afraid of the color white, because it reminded me of the uniforms, walls, furniture, weather and, well, pretty much everything else around here."

"I don't get it," Dither interjected, "after all that, why'd you voluntarily return?"

Comat nibbled a cracker. "I figured that if I finally faced my fears, maybe I'd get over them for good. I didn't want to live the rest of my life hiding from snow and water and white fabric. And, to be honest, I was also very worried about my future. I didn't think there was any other career I *could* do. I didn't think I could ever develop the cultural awareness to function normally in civilian society. Nurtic *helped*, but he didn't cure me. I don't know if anything really could. That's what the Childhood Program does to you; it rewires your brain and leaves a permanent mark. All the therapy in the world couldn't erase an experience like that—not entirely."

"Wow," Dither murmured. "And, here I thought we Nurians had it bad, being stuck on base for a couple decades or so. At least, we *volunteered* to enlist—long after getting potty-trained and learning to walk and talk."

Arrhyth frowned into his oatmeal. "And, to think, the Trilateral Committee didn't even wait until Cease Lechatelierite's corpse cooled before reinstating the program that he and Scarlet fought so hard to dismantle." He glanced at me, suddenly realizing just whose death he was making cavalier comments about. "Um, no offense, sir."

I gnawed the inside of my cheek, grasping my knife until my knuckles turned translucent. I felt offended alright, but not by Arrhyth. He was right; the Trilateral Committee really didn't give a damn about any of us, did they? They handed out fancy titles to make us foot-soldiers *feel* like we were the ones at the helm of this war, but in all honesty, they still always did whatever they wanted, whenever they wanted, no matter what any of us pawns thought. The TC only ever cared about their own agenda, to the hell with whoever got in their way.

"Sir," Arrhyth piped, leaning forward, "are you alright?"

Not even my father—the best of the best, the Resistance Leader who literally gave his life for the alliance—warranted an ounce of the TC's respect. They didn't even wait an age before betraying their word to him. Not one! And, in the sixteen ages that followed, did a single diver lift a finger against the TC to try to restore their fallen Commander's legacy? Everyone here claimed to love and admire Cease—everyone was so quick to profess their undying devotion to him—but when push came to shove, did anyone actually put their money where their mouths were? Did anyone fight for him, when he could no longer fend for himself? No. Cease's former comrades, sitting all around me now, chose not to do a damn thing in over a decade and a half, bowing in submission to a corrupt committee of old, expiring, out-of-touch, ingrate sons of—

The table was on fire! Flames raced to either end at an alarming rate, metal melting like ice. Shouts and screams surrounded me. Lacking the energy and willpower to snuff out such a sizeable conflagration, I let it burn. Abandoning the mess hall, I ran all the way back to my quarters, blood churning in my ears.

I couldn't do this, anymore. I'd been discontent at Icicle for quite some time now, but *this* felt like the last straw. The final push out the door. I didn't want to give another minute of my life to this godforsaken fleet that existed to do the bidding of an organization of selfish bureaucratic bastards who remorselessly betrayed one of their own. One of their own who did more for the Nurro-Ichthyothian Resistance than any man in Second Earth history.

ENCE LECHATELIERITE

With the sub on autopilot, I spent a good chunk of my trip sewing. Unfortunately, the only fabric color I could find at Icicle was white. Shocker. Mage robes were supposed to match auras—that was the stupid tradition, in Conflagria—which was problematic for me now because my wavelength definitely wasn't white. Actually, I still didn't have a clue what color I was supposed to be at all; I couldn't see my aura, nor 'sense my place in the web,' nor any of that spectrally-self-aware stuff that was supposed to be instinctive for magic-folk. Normally, that'd mean I were infrared, but I knew *that* couldn't be the case either, because I had usable sources. Three of them: hair, eyes and throat. How on Second Earth could I have three functional sources but no visible frequency? I was a spectral anomaly, alright. A half-blood covalent freak.

All I owned now was a homemade robe and my father's Silver Triangle. Even the scout I was fleeing in, I wouldn't keep—I couldn't, under any circumstances, reveal who I was or where I came from to anyone in Conflagria, at least not for a while. I needed to lie low until the time was right. Showing up in a big Nordic submarine would sure draw a whole lot of unwanted attention.

So, when I came within about seven miles of land, I abandoned ship and swam to shore. Exhausted from battling the current without a diving suit for four hours, I slept for the rest of the day and straight through the night, right there on the beach, in my wet robe. Some way to spend the remainder of my sixteenth birthday.

Anyway, morning came, and I awoke feeling like a vacuum-cleaner had sucked out my insides. For crying out loud, I'd gone, what, eighteen hours without nourishment? How was I already *this* famished? Ugh, we were so pampered at Icicle. I'd grown so soft, over the last nine ages.

I wobbled to my feet, seeking energy from the blazing sunlight. It was revitalizing. Empowering. I stared at the sun as I walked. The heat was only thing keeping me going.

No, it wasn't. There was also something *else* holding onto me, something touching the core of my being, feeding my colorless frequency, illuminating my senses. It took me a while to discern what it was: the spectral web. I knew that the web stretched all across the world—Nordics and mages alike had their places in it—but, the network's presence became all the more perceptible to a mage when in closer proximity to the Core Crystal. This was the nearest I'd ever been.

As Diving Commander, I'd conducted a few Conflagrian air-raids but, until now, never actually tread upon these shores with my own two feet. Without a PAVLAK, I wandered without a clue where I was going. There were no street signs, landmarks, buildings, nothing. Nothing but great lumps of sand. So, this must've been the 'Dunes.' The nearly-deserted region. Supposedly, the only people I'd come across out here were the gypsies.

I meandered for hours, heading nowhere. All the while, something prodded my mind and plucked my invisible wavelength, as though vying for my attention.

"Where am I?" I asked it—whatever *it* even was.

Where do you want to be?

"Well, that's what I'm trying to figure out," I grumbled. "If you could point me toward some civilization, that'd be a start."

So, the great Commence July Lechatelierite, Ex-Leader of the Nurro-Ichthyothian Resistance... admits that he needs help.

What? "How do you know my name?"

Is 'Commence' your name?

Anger pricked my scalp. "As a matter of fact, no. I never let anyone call me that. I'm 'Ence.'"

Ah, then, I must be speaking to the wrong person. Goodbye.

"No, wait! Don't go."

Why not?

"Because... I..."

Yes?

"I... need help. I'm hungry and thirsty and tired and lost."

What did you expect, Ence? You came here with no plan, no support system, no resources. This is a dangerous, war-torn, third-world nation; you can't just wash up on the beach one day and expect things to magically work out for you. Benevolence is hard to find on Second Earth, here more than anywhere. You've been lucky so far, stumbling across people like Nurtic Leavesleft and Inexor Buird, who willingly opened doors for you and gave you everything they had. But, that's not how life typically works.

"Excuse me? *I'm* lucky? How dare you. I'm an abandoned child of war. I have no family. No friends. I have nothing."

Only because you consistently and deliberately alienate yourself from everyone who tries to get close to you. There are people out there who care for you. Deeply. But, you turned your back on them all. You can't help the fact that you were orphaned at birth, Ence, but you must take responsibility for consciously choosing to walk away from everything you've been handed since.

"Shut up; I was never 'handed' a damn thing! I made a life for myself, against all odds. Who the hell are you to lecture me anyway, my mother?"

You made a rash decision to come here like this, and now you're going to deal with the consequences. Your military training should've taught you better than to leap before looking.

"Shut up!"

Do you really want me to? Do you realize that if I shut up, you'd be even more alone than you already are? For someone who claims to despise the isolationist world system as much as me, you sure keep finding ways to isolate yourself, day after day.

"Either help me for real, or go away."

I can't rescue you from this mess, my child. You put yourself in a tight spot, and now you've got to figure your own way out. That's how you like to do things anyway, right—on your own?

"Some guide you are."

Who said I'm a guide?

"Well, you probably know this place better than I do."

I am this place.

"What's that supposed to mean?"

My dear, who do you think you're talking to?

"I don't know… the spectral web?"

The spectral web has no voice. It's not a sovereign being. It's an entanglement of magical energy.

"Then, what the hell are you?"

I trust you mean 'who.' I live in the spectral web. I hold it together and protect it from those who hate freedom.

"That seems like a lot of work."

It's what I was born for.

"How were you 'born' when you're not even a person?"

Who said I'm not a person?

"What?"

Quit talking to yourself, silly boy, especially if you're going to do so out loud and in Ichthyothian. The others will think you're either a Nordic spy, or that you've lost your mind. Or, perhaps, both. Personally, when it comes to you, I can't rule out the latter.

"Others? What others? Who's here?"

"Who're you talking to?" came an obscure vowelesque mishmash.

I turned and saw a young child in a dirty dark-green robe, clutching a hunk of blackened meat on a stake.

"You make funny noises," he said incomprehensibly, head cocking. "Is that a Dune dialect? Are you a gypsy?"

This kid was clearly a leg mage, as his thighs were easily the most muscular part of his scrawny body. I lifted my gaze and saw that, behind him, sprawled an entire village—wooden cabins, fire-fields, bustling crowds and all. In the near-distance, curls of smoke undulated from an immense blue-white inferno, around which a line of hundreds snaked. The Fire Pit.

This was Ardor Village.

Holy crystallines. How did I manage to stroll into the *nation's capital* without even noticing? I was supposed to see everything.

Just how many hours had I been walking?

The boy repeated the same string of unintelligible garble. I pressed my lips together, afraid that more Ichthyothian would slip out. He gnawed his meat, face smeared with brown juice.

The sight of food was painful. I salivated. Grunting, I held out my hand.

He didn't give me his lunch. Instead, he took off, motioning for me to follow him. Though weak and dizzy, I tailed him like my life depended on it. We tore through the town and skidded to a stop before a stone well where a lot of shabbily-dressed, bucket-toting, sweaty-faced adults were huddled. He started talking to a middle-aged woman with enormous ears, gesturing at me with his stake while hopping animatedly on the balls of his bare feet. The woman replied in a raspy voice, casting me sideways glances. I assumed that her filthy beige robe was once yellow at some point, in solidarity with her canary aura. Even my own clothes, not a day old, were no longer a blinding Ichthyothian-white. The dusty, sticky air had already darkened it.

While the two of them spoke, I drank in the depressing sight of my surroundings. About a block away, a young girl squatted on the ground, back against a shack… giving birth. A few teens nearby caught sight of her and spontaneously decided that the half-born infant's head would make a suitable kickball for their games.

Something touched my shoulder and I jumped.

"Relax. 'S only me," the green boy said. I actually sort of understood him. How? "Mamma says we're not able to host no travelers, right now. Food's too scarce, and we don't got no extra tarps. But," he pulled off a chunk from his skewer, "you can have some o' my dragon, if you wanna."

He was still speaking Conflagrian, I was sure of it. But, somehow, his words now made a little bit of sense to me. I couldn't believe it. True, I'd absorbed Ichthyothian rather easily and rapidly, but I expected to have a much harder time with Conflagrian since it bore no similarities to either Nordic tongue.

"Deaf Man." The kid tugged my sleeve.

Jolting from my stupor, I took the food from him, bowing. In that moment, I realized that I didn't know how to say 'thanks.' It wasn't one of the words I'd overheard, yet. He returned the bow and ran away.

I lay low for several days, scavenging, people-watching, eavesdropping and sleeping amongst the ruins of battle-torn cabins. Word on the street was that Principal Tincture's administration was about as stable as a three-legged scabrous. Conflagria was essentially an anarchy, ripe for the taking.

I could hardly wait.

* * *

Well, all too soon, I learned that waiting was inevitable. 'Enemy Life and Culture' class at the Nurian Diving Academy hardly scratched the surface of the way things *really* worked—or didn't work—around here. I was as ignorant as ignorant got. Even after two weeks on the island, I still felt like a snowflake in a sandstorm.

At first, everyone I came across thought that I was hard of hearing. But, once I gathered the courage to open my mouth, my nickname instantly evolved from 'Deaf Man' to 'Deaf Man Who Speaks.'

"But, I can hear, just fine," I now objected for the umpteenth time.

"You're always studying our lips," piped a random old man. "Your gaze is so big, so wide. Only those with weak ears watch the world like that."

"Then, blindfold me," I dryly said, "and stick me in a room, alone. Then, speak to me. I guarantee that I'll be able to reply without a problem."

To my profound shock, they followed my sarcastic suggestion to the letter, wrapping my face with several yards of smelly swathe and shutting me in an outhouse. Great. Barely a fortnight in this loony country, and I'd already managed to submit myself to a shackled interrogation. Brilliant.

"Let's begin, Deaf Man Who Speaks," the elderly bloke shouted through the door.

"I'm not deaf!"

"Firstly, what is your name?"

I swallowed. I had to say something, before the silence got suspiciously long.

"Ence."

My answer was met with confused mumbles. 'Ence' wasn't Conflagrian, they said. It didn't imply any colors nor powers.

"Ants?"

"*Ence.*"

"What does it mean?"

The hairs on the back of my neck stood at attention, and not from spectrum. "Why does it have to mean anything?"

"Who exactly are you?" someone else demanded.

That was just a tad ambiguous. "I'm... lost."

"Where did you come from?"

I hesitated.

"I told you, he's a Dune gypsy," came the voice of the green boy, whom I now knew was called 'Neerg Egl.'

At once, I seized the story: "Yes. I lost track of my tribe, by the northern shore." I was suddenly glad to be hidden; despite nearly a decade of military service, I never mastered the art of facial stoicism.

"How?"

My mind raced. "I... overslept... and they left without me."

Skeptical murmurs resounded.

"I struggle with insomnia," I babbled on, "so, I always had trouble rising with my tribe at dawn. For ages, it didn't matter; they consistently waited for me, however begrudgingly. Until one day last week, the chief gave me an ultimatum. He said that, the following morning, if I was even a second late, they'd leave me behind. Well, turns out, they weren't kidding."

Ugh, seriously, Ence? Was that the best I could come up with? That was the stupidest story ever told. Well, now, I was stuck with it.

More murmuring.

"How did you wind up in Ardor Village?"

"I walked," I answered, honestly.

"You walked all the way from the outskirts?"

"Yes."

"Have you served as Dune Messenger, before?"

Say what? "No."

"So, you've never been to Ardor Village until recently."

"Correct."

"How did you find your way, then?"

All lies I uttered, I'd have to keep track of. "You'll think I'm crazy if I tell you."

"Try us. We're difficult to surprise."

I smiled to myself. That was exactly the type of response I'd hoped for. Unlike in Nuria and Ichthyosis, nothing was 'weird' around here. In mage country, strangeness was the expectation. Nordics had much a narrower perception of 'normalcy.' And, so, I brazenly told them about the mysterious voice who led me as I wandered. The nameless entity who claimed to 'live in the spectral web.'

At once, the door to the outhouse opened and my blindfold got removed. All around me, jaws hung.

"He speaks of the voice of the Red One!"

What in the world? Wait, wasn't 'Red One' a reverential name for my mother?

"She communed with you directly?"

"With *words?*"

Holy crystallines, did I really chat with Scarlet July's aura!?

I nodded. "Um, yeah. I heard her pretty clearly, in my head at least."

The buzz grew louder. I was intensely relieved that this particular group of mages thought of dear old mommy as a savior rather than a dangerous radical. Imagine if I'd told this story to System supporters!

"Amazing!"

"Most mages go their entire lives without gleaning a single whisper of hers!"

"And, those who do only hear from her once."

Of course, 'entire life' had to be taken with a grain of salt, here—Scarlet's 'voice' couldn't have been in the web for more than sixteen ages. But, I got the point, nonetheless: she probably wouldn't converse with me again.

I silently screamed at myself. I got *one* shot to speak to my mother and I wasted it with whining like a prepubescent brat about my empty stomach!

"No wonder you were stricken deaf for a few days; you heard the voice of the Crystal's Protector!"

Hands reached out, pulling me into the crowd.

"Tell us your color, Enlightened One."

My color. Crap. What was my color? "Y-you can't detect it?" I asked, feebly.

Heads shook.

"Perhaps, because it's quite weak," someone said.

Heat rushed to my cheeks.

"Are you Useless?"

Uselesses were the low-lives, the despised deadweights of the island. The ones killed for sport, in the arenas. The ones executed in the Pit, when times got rough.

That was no way to start building my empire.

"No, I'm not. I'm a mage."

"If your frequency's infrared, you're not a mage."

"Yeah, color gives a mage his identity."

"Oh, so, now, I don't have an identity?" I snarled.

"What's your magic?"

"Hair." To prove it, I let mine squirm. There was no way I'd reveal that I was multi-sourced. Not yet.

"An auraless hair mage!"

"Infrared Ence, you are a mystery indeed."

They had no idea.

ASH ARGENT

January seventh of the eleventh age.

If there was one place where flying came in handy, it was Ardor Village. Crowds in the markets? No sweat. Wagon jam on the paths? No prob. Anxious mobs clambering for fire rations? No worries. Oh, Tincture, I loved being a wing mage.

Sometimes, I flew for no good reason at all, just to get away. To lift my feet from this coarse sand, putting some distance between myself and this cesspool of a village. Up in the air, there was no war, no System, no Reds. Just me and the sun.

Don't get me wrong; the Reds were my friends and allies. I wouldn't be alive today, if it weren't for them. They took me in when I was a helpless, abandoned child. Though a son of late System warriors, they raised me like their own. But, to be perfectly honest, sometimes they were the ones I flew away from. Because, I was tired of politics and taking sides and fighting. I was tired of all the crazy, dangerous stuff they did. I knew they only did what they had to. I just wished they didn't have to, all the time. I wished there was another way to initiate change than to resort to violence.

It was evening. I circled my cabin now, prepping for landing. My door was on the roof. No point in having it on the ground, where anybody could reach. I was about to touch down when I caught sight of a spindly figure curled beneath my deck, twiggy legs poking out. What on Tincture's island? I didn't think that a human body could fit under there, not even a child's. Anyone *that* thin had to have been on the brink of starvation.

Holy Tincture.

I landed in the sand. Unlike most folks these dreary days, I wasn't cold-blooded enough to leave a man to perish on my own property for no good reason, not when there was something I could do about it. My own life got saved by the compassion of strangers, after all. What better way to repay the universe? I could use the company, anyway.

I cautiously approached the young mage. He was breathing, thank Tincture. Though, the fact that I could neither see nor feel his aura meant that he was likely already too close to death to be saved. Either that or he was a Useless infrared.

"Hey, there," I lightly tapped his shoulder. He leapt up with the reflexes of a warrior, lassoing my neck with his hair. If I didn't know any better, I'd say his iridescent eyes scintillated with spectrum.

I gagged. Well, he definitely wasn't Useless, that much was now certain. The edges of my sight slowly blackened. But, a moment before I would've passed out, he released me. I dropped to my knees, panting like an old scabrous.

And, to my surprise, so did he, gasping and moaning as his diamond-emerald eyes scoured the orange sky. His gaze looked particularly eerie in the direct sunlight, set off by his ruddy complexion, pinched nose, sharp jaw and red-black hair.

After a few more suspenseful seconds, the man—just a boy, really—slowly rose to his feet, stirring clouds of dust.

"Who are you?" he barked at me.

"I was gonna ask yeh th'same thing," I replied, also getting up. "Yeh were sleepin' on meh prop'rty." My wings unfurled.

He smirked. "Property. Right. People in this country still pretend that they actually own things." His hand swept his hair back—a strange gesture for a hair mage with autonomous control over his locks. "If I wanted to take that from you," he pointed at my cabin, "all I'd need to do is go to the square, stir up a mob and get them to follow me over here. Everybody in this village is so pissed all the time—so ready to ignite at the first sign of a spark—that I could probably get enough of them to commit whatever atrocities I wanted." There was something striking about his voice. Something compelling. Capturing. Convicting. If I didn't already know that his source was his hair, I would've thought it was his throat.

My arms folded. "If I were yeh, I wouldn't dare try anythin' 'gainst meh."

"Oh, yeah? And, why's that?"

"'Cuz, then, yeh'd have t'answer teh th'Reds."

Something in his face changed. "You're with the Red Revolution?" he breathed, relief imbuing his powerful tone.

I nodded, glad to see that this was good news to him. "Do I know yeh?" I swore I'd seen those uncanny eyes, before.

"I don't really know anybody, around here," he murmured, turning away.

"Hey, where yeh goin'?" I called.

"To find another crappy shack to nap under," he muttered.

"Yeh can stay wi'me," I blurted.

He froze.

"I've got room," I said, "'n' you 'pparently got nowhere t'go."

He revolved, slowly. "You're inviting me in? I just attacked you."

I shrugged. "Self-defense, I figured. I'm a warrior; I know how it works 'n these parts."

He was silent.

"What's yer name?"

He didn't reply.

"C'me on," I urged. "I just welc'med yeh 'nto m'home. Least y'could do's gimme that much."

He blinked—it was the first blink I'd seen from him, yet. "Ence."

"Ants? What kind o' name's Ants?"

"It's *Ence*," he repeated, furiously.

"What's it mean?"

"Why does everyone keep asking me that? It doesn't have to mean anything!"

I shrugged, again. "Alright, then. I'm Ash Argent, by th'way." I offered him a bow that he didn't return. "Don't happen t'have no last name, do yeh?"

"No, I don't."

Silence.

I gave Ence a boost to help him climb onto my roof. He was so light, I could've easily carried him all the way to safety, but I had a hunch he wouldn't have liked that very much—I could already tell that he was a rather prideful fellow. Then, I opened the skylight and flew on in. Standing in my living-room now, I looked up at him, peeking uneasily through the opening.

"'S a bit o' a drop," I warned him.

"I can see that."

"Just use yer hair t'lower y'rself down."

He ignored my suggestion, choosing instead to jump like a cat. He sure didn't land like one, though. He smacked into the hardwood floor with a thud, rolling onto his side. He groaned.

"Why didn't yeh use yer hair?" I gasped.

He slowly sat up, arranging his colorless robe.

Colorless. Of course.

"Ah, I know who y'are," I said.

"You do?"

I nodded. "News gets 'round fast. Lost trav'ler from th'Dunes?"

"Uh, yeah," he answered, eyeing the pot of stew that was hanging over my fireplace. "My tribe left me one morning, when I overslept. I walked here, guided—"

"By th'voice o' th'Red One," I finished, eagerly.

"Yeah," he repeated. His tone was perfectly placid, but his eyes were sad. Tincture, was this child's face readable.

"Why so glum? Communin' wit' her aura's a great blessin'."

"So, I've heard," he murmured.

"Y'know, I used t'know th'Red One pers'nally, back when she was alive 'n' well 'n' leadin' th'Red Rev'lution."

Ence's auburn brows constricted. "You can't possibly be old enough."

I chuckled. "I'm twenty. So, that'd make me 'bout four when th'Red One found meh. Don't rememb'r too much 'bout 'er 'xcept that she was balloonin' wit' 'er mystery baby at th'time."

Ence's eyes grew hungry, and not just for food. "What?"

And so, as I handed him a bowl of scabrous-stew, I gave him a glimpse into my peculiar past. "I'm a child o' war," I began. "Th'son o' a pair o' System warriors."

The boy immediately tensed, fingers tightening around his wooden spoon.

"They were killed at sea, b'fore I could make no memories o' 'em," I went on, taking a gulp directly from my pot. "I was a kid o' th'paths for a couple o' ages; Tincture only knows how I s'rvived. I was lit'rally on th'brink o' starvin' t'death when, one day—I think it was 'n th'summer o' ninety-four—I snuck 'nto a storage closet at Red 'eadquarters 'n' stayed there fer days, eatin' dust 'n' bugs 'n' trash 'n' crappin' myself 'n th'dark. I sucked my own piss from m'robe, so much I was th'rsty."

"Drinking urine would just dehydrate you more," Ence said in a matter-of-fact manner.

"Try tellin' that t'a desp'rate toddler. So, anyway, I stayed there fer days, cov'red 'n meh own waste, wings too weak t'unfold. Until, th'door op'ned… and there she was. I thought she 'n' th'others were gonna kill meh. I cowered 'n' cried—cried w'thout tears, mind yeh, as there wasn't a drop o' water left 'n meh. But, to meh s'rprise, Scarlet fed 'n' bathed 'n' clothed meh. Saved m'life. Ages passed 'n' I got passed from stronghold t'sronghold, under th'care o' diff'rent folks ev'ry couple o' days, 'til I turned sixteen 'n' decided to go out on m'own."

Ence's shocked expression took on an inexplicable irritated edge. Why?

"My mem'ry o' Scarlet ain't much, but I hold ont'it," I continued, smiling. "If there's one thing 'bout 'er that I'll nev'r f'rget, aside from 'er bulgin' pregn'nt belly, its 'er eyes. Great green all-seein' eyes." I gave Ence a curious glance. "Kind o' like yers. Yers got th'same sort o' fire, but a bit cooler."

He looked away, temples pulsing.

"Don't be upset, now." I took another sip. "I just paid yeh a mighty compl'ment."

"I'd like to go to bed, now," Ence declared, putting down his bowl, though it was still mostly full. "Can you show me where I'll be sleeping?"

ASH ARGENT

It was late May, not sure of the exact date. It was mighty hard to keep track these days, since every minute that passed was pretty much the same as the last. The constant danger associated with living in a warzone sure got tedious and repetitive, sometimes.

In January, I found Ence wasting away under my porch, and I invited him in. Now, four months later, he was still here, living and hunting and going about the craziness of everyday life with me and the Reds. We were friends. Sort of.

Everything about Ence's behavior and attitude told me that he wasn't used to being close with anybody. He claimed to have no family—no ties to a single soul anywhere, except for 'those Dune mongrels' he no longer wished to associate with—yet, he never showed an ounce of interest in filling what must've been a rather painful lonely void with new substantial relationships. He and I were constantly together, yet he never seemed to lower his guard. He would've been dead if it weren't for me, but he didn't seem the least bit grateful, either. It was like I was something he had to *cope* with, to get by. I wasn't his companion, I was merely an annoyance he had to tolerate, to survive. If he ever opened his mouth around me, it wasn't to engage on a deeper level, but to say something snide, or to ask questions. Oh, Tincture, did he ask a lot of questions.

For someone so sharp and clever, Ence was remarkably ignorant about, well, everything. He didn't even know how to read or write. No joke. One brisk day in February, when we were visiting Seventh Cabin, the truth about his illiteracy came out. Here's what happened:

The folks we came to see wanted to research something about bending light. So, I tossed a spectroscopy book at Ence and asked him to open up to the chapter on reflectors and refractors. For five whole minutes, he sat there, mumbling under his breath and turning pages this way and that, until he finally declared, "I can't find it."

I glanced over his shoulder. "What're yeh talkin' 'bout, Ants? Yeh're on th'right page."

There it was, in all caps, for the world to see: 'REFLECTORS & REFRACTORS.' Ence always said that he could 'see everything,' and though no one on Tincture's island knew what that actually meant, I assumed that it included the ability to notice the obvious.

"Of course. I was kidding," he laughed hollowly, face matching the red highlights in his hair.

"No, yeh w'ren't," I breathed.

Busted, he *then* claimed that Dune tribes didn't always teach you to read and write 'if you're poor.' I said that definitely sounded odd to me, and wasn't *everyone* 'poor' these days? The Reds immediately arranged for Ence to get some tutoring. Within a week, he outstripped his teachers. Everyone was thoroughly shocked by his rapid progress. So, *then*, Ence started claiming that he was literate, all along; he just needed a refresher since it'd been a while since he exercised the skill. Everyone seemed to accept that story. Except me. I knew Ence better than all of them; I knew that he never forgot a thing. Once he learned something, he remembered it, forever. So, something fishy was up.

One March night, over dinner, Ence got all riled up about something political and started ranting in consonant gibberish. I asked him about it the next morning, after he'd cooled off, and he shrugged and claimed it was a Dune dialect. So, I said, no, it didn't sound like *any* form of Conflagrian, at all—our alphabet didn't even have letters for harsh syllables like that. I told him that his words reminded me more of those strange Nordic tongues.

Ence was very startled by that. He got all restless and anxious, like I'd made some horrible accusation. He asked me, when on earth was I ever exposed to Nordic languages? I told him that, when I was little, I'd heard it from the mouths of World Revolters who came by on business, like Nurtic Leavesleft and Inexor Buird. For some reason, those names made him totally clam up and wall off.

But, the weirdness didn't end there. Ence was supposed to be a hair mage, but all he could really do with his hair was swish it around like an elastic whip for a moment or two. So, I got a few folks from Fifth Cabin to give him some introductory training. During his lessons, Ence seemed to understand the *science* of spectroscopy, well enough—far better than me, actually—but, he was wholly inept at putting those concepts into practice. Sometimes, after his lessons, he got real sick. He'd writhe on the floor, gasping for breath, scratching his scalp until it bled. Then, he'd sleep for hours upon hours.

"What, they don't teach yeh t'use yer spectrum 'n th'Dunes, either?" I dryly commented, one day. "How d'y'all survive, out there?"

He didn't answer.

The more time passed, the more suspicious I became of his backstory. I wanted to know which gypsy tribe he was from, why his name had no meaning, why his powers were not only weak but unschooled, why he had a source but no visible aura, why he wasn't literate at sixteen, why he knew some Nordic words. And, most of all, I wanted to know why he was so ignorant about the basics of life on the island. It was like he'd been living in a scabrous cage, until I found him. Even Dune gypsies weren't that clueless. Even Uselesses weren't that helpless. I welcomed him into my life and provided everything he needed to survive—I opened my *home* to him—yet, he shared absolutely nothing in return.

So, tonight, I decided to confront him. I decided that it was time to put an end to his secret-keeping once and for all, because I was through with sharing a cabin with a total stranger.

At dinner, I struck up some conversation. And, instead of just letting him change the subject whenever he wanted, I became insistent.

"But, *which* tribe?" I asked for the umpteenth time, this evening.

"Ash, you know that I don't like talking about my nomadic days." He rubbed his eyes. "It's all bad memories that I want to forget. I'm an Ardor-Villager now, like you. A Red. My past isn't important."

"'Tis t'meh," I argued. "What could've poss'bly happ'ned t'yeh 'n th'Dunes that's *so* bad, it'd make yeh wanna try an' f'rget ev'rythin' yeh've ev'r known?"

"I said I don't want to get into it."

"Why not? What did yer tribe do t'yeh, b'fore they left yeh behind?"

His fists balled. "Sheesh, just get off my case, will you?"

I'd had enough. "No, I won't!" I shouted. "I gave yeh ev'rythin'—shelt'r, food, trainin', education, friendsh'p—'n' all I ev'r wanted 'n return's t'know *who* I've been givin' it all teh!"

His lips pressed together. The silence instantly shredded up my insides.

"Yeh're no friend o' mine," I half-whispered, getting to my feet. "Yeh're just a user, like th'System."

He also stood. "Ash, no," he began, throat-mage-like voice dripping with deceptive earnestness. "I never meant to—"

I held out my hand and, to my surprise, he actually shut up.

"Yeah, yeh did, Ants. If that's ev'n yer real name. Yeh've been lyin' t'meh, since day one. Yeh're not a lost gypsy. F'rget *who*—I don't ev'n know *what* yeh are."

And, with that, I spread my wings, jumped up through the skylight and disappeared into the deep-brown night sky.

ENCE LECHATELIERITE

Ash unfolded his metallic wings and rocketed straight up through the skylight, vanishing into the murky night. That's what Ash always did whenever he got mad or stressed: he flew away, and not to anywhere in particular. If possible, he'd probably live out the rest of his days just gliding aimlessly amongst the clouds.

This time, he took off because of me. Because he was bothered by my secrets.

Since January, I'd spent a lot of time and energy feeling furious at Ash for his privilege. Technically, we were both orphaned children of war, yet he still managed to grow up surrounded by people who cared for him. People who loved him like family. People who nurtured him and opened doors for him. Even my own mother looked after him for a time, while she was pregnant with me. The unfairness of it all stabbed me in the chest.

But, alas, at the end of the day, I knew that it wasn't Ash's fault that he was a luckier war-child than me. The screwed-up world system was to blame for the fact there even *were* any war-children on this earth, to begin with. I had no right to begrudge Ash for the advantages that circumstance offered to him, since those were beyond his control. I did have every right, however, to resent him for what he did with everything he'd been given. Or rather, what he *didn't* do. The man had no ambition. It seemed to me like he was just waiting around, hoping to grow old and die before Conflagria got wholly inhospitable. I got the impression that he cooperated with the Reds not because he was particularly passionate about their platform, but because that was how the chips fell in his life. Here he was, a wing mage with a blazing aura, extraordinary powers, a huge support network… and no drive, whatsoever. We couldn't have been more different.

And, yet, he had compassion for me. Despite all the risks involved, he invited a total stranger into his home and his world. Since then, he continually concerned himself with my wellbeing. He was troubled by my spectral setbacks and earnestly longed to see me strengthen and prosper. Why? What did he want from me? What did he hope to gain from my own advancement? The answer was only too obvious: nothing. Because Ash was another Nurtic. Another generous lunatic who just didn't understand that personal assets should be a private arsenal.

His generosity, because it made no sense to me, always sort of repulsed me, the way Nurtic's did. I only accepted his help because I was desperate. I *needed* him. Oh, how I hated that word. There was nothing I despised more than being dependant on anyone or anything.

This wasn't the first time Ash walked—or, flew—out on me, since we became roommates. But, it *was* the first time it seemed to personally impact me. I was shocked to realize that I wasn't just frustrated by the potential inconveniences posed by his momentary departure, but rather… my feelings were actually hurt. It stung, to watch him go. Why? I swallowed. Was it possible that I was genuinely starting to care for him? Did I actually feel guilty for upsetting him with my lies?

Yes.

Holy crystallines.

If Ash's mere words and actions could wound me, that meant he had some measure of power over me. Not physical power, but something even more dangerous: he could get under my skin. In my head. He didn't have to strike me to draw blood.

I rubbed my temples. I wasn't in a position to voluntarily give anyone power over me. It was insane, illogical. It could drag me down, interfere with my goals. I couldn't have a *friendship* holding me back.

But, if friendships only tended to generate pain and problems, why did so many people bother with them? Why did everyone outside the Ichthyothian military seem to think that friends were important to have? There had to be a plus-side.

Of course. Since January, I'd already been reaping plenty from my one-sided friendship with Ash. Perhaps, making it a two-way street would compound those benefits. Giving Ash reasons to *want* to help me (well, reasons beyond his own inexplicable Nurtic-esque altruism) could only ever propel me toward greater success in his world—the magical world, which still felt foreign to me, even after all these months. It could stock my arsenal with more ammunition.

So, what to do now, with this discovery? I didn't know how to conduct a mutual friendship. I'd never done it before. And, by now, Ash clearly believed that I wasn't interested in having one with him. So, I supposed the first step would be to rectify that and make my intentions clear. How? I personally favored bluntness, but I had a hunch that people didn't just brazenly declare to one another, 'I'd like to befriend you, now.' There had to be a subtler, more proper way to go about it. Well, what did Ash do, to pursue me? He wasn't very articulate; he mostly conveyed his feelings and attitudes through his actions. He gave me shelter, food and access to education. Hmm. Well, I certainly couldn't do anything like that for him. And, he didn't need those things, anyway; he already had them, in spades. So, what else *could* I do? What on Second Earth did I have that Ash could possibly need or want?

His words echoed through my mind: *I gave yeh ev'rythin'—shelt'r, food, trainin', education, friendsh'p—'n' all I ev'r wanted 'n return's t'know who I've been givin' it teh!* That was it. I needed to tell him who I really was.

I cupped my head in my hands. That was a big step. But, honestly, I'd long since grown tired of hiding. I'd been hankering to move forward with my plan to topple Tincture anyway, upon which my identity would *have* to become public knowledge. Why not let Ash be the first to know? Besides, that way, I could possibly garner his help with carrying out my plan—I could sure use his connections and resources. That's what friends were for, right?

I couldn't wait for Ash to come home.

* * *

I wound up having to wait two full days. That's how mad I apparently made him. He didn't return until the night of May twenty-fourth.

"I want to be honest with you," I blurted, as soon as he swept in.

He gave me a strange look. "'N' who made yeh 'nto a saint ov'rnight?"

"It's been over forty-eight hours."

"Had 'nough time t'think up o' s'me mo' clev'r lies?" His wings folded.

"I'm done lying to you," I said, battling a swell of rage already building in my scalp—a swell of rage that told me that friendship with a bumpkin like him wasn't worth the humiliation I was feeling now.

Ash watched my readable face contort. "Uh huh. Sure, y'are."

I took a deep breath. He'd been back for all of thirty seconds and my fuse was already on the brink of blowing. Great.

"Ash," I began, as calmly as possible, "my real name is Commence July Lechatelierite. I'm the son of the Red One and Crystal's End," I used the reverential names that the Reds called my mother and father. "I have three sources—hair, eyes and throat—but, my powers are weakened by covalence. The reason I didn't know the first thing about Conflagrian life when you found me in January… is because I'd just come from Ichthyosis, where I served in the Diving Fleet for almost a decade. Before that, I grew up in an orphanage, in the Nurian capital."

Ash kept a straight face, the entire time I spoke. For a few seconds after I finished, he stayed quiet and contemplative.

Then, without warning, he erupted into laughter.

My eyes grew hot. "Ash?"

"'S that th'best y'could come up wit'?" he howled. "I'm th'coval'nt son o' th'prophet!?"

My invisible aura stung my lashes. "Ash, I'm telling the truth."

His hoots only intensified. He even slapped his thigh with an open palm, like a Nurian cartoon character. "Hey, guess what, Ants? I've got somethin' teh tell yeh, too… I'm really Tincture 'n disguise!"

Pain struck my face as my pupils acutely heated.

Oh, no.

I scrunched my lids and bowed my head, but it was too late: the front of Ash's robe was already ablaze. Screaming, he dropped to the floor, rolling like a riptide. But, my spectral flames proved too stubborn to extinguish that easily. I had no choice but to beat out the fire with my hair. Then, exhausted beyond belief, I collapsed onto the floor.

Ash's grey gaze was wide and terrified. "Wh-wh-what-d-did-y-yeh—?" he sputtered.

"Ash," I breathed, "you're okay. Everything's fine. Please, calm down."

"Yeh… yeh set me on fire!"

"It was an accident; I'm sorry. And, you're alright now, so there's nothing to—"

"Yeh set meh on fire *wit' yer eyes!*" His whole body shook. "You're tellin' the truth. Holy Tincture, yeh're really 'im. The Multi-Source Ench'nt. The Red One's son. Holy Tincture! I've been hidin' th'prophet o' Conflagria in meh *house*, all age!"

ASH ARGENT

"C'mmence," I called, knuckles rapping against the wall between our rooms. "Yeh've got 'ny idea where I might'o misplaced meh huntin' spear?"

Door swinging open, Ence advanced on me, grabbing my silver swathe with ferocity. Apparently, that aggressive gesture was a residual habit from his diver days. Last night, he told me that he used to seize soldiers by the belt when he wanted to 'get all up in their faces.'

"Why belts?" I'd asked. "Why not… I dunno… coll'rs 'r somethin'?"

He grinned. "So, their necks can stay free for my hair, of course."

I suppressed a shudder. I knew that he had a dark side—that much was glaringly obvious since the moment I met him—but, I honestly didn't have a clue just *how* dark it really got behind those iridescent eyes.

"Don't you *ever* call me that, again," he now breathed.

Inhale, exhale. Inhale, exhale. Got to stay calm. "Call yeh what, C'mmence? Last night, y'told meh that's yer real name. Th'name th'Red One gave yeh."

He released me and folded his arms, floppy sleeves swinging almost comically. By saying his real name, I'd unintentionally struck a nerve. It was a trigger of sorts. Why?

"It's… it's just…" he sputtered like a scared kid. It was incredible how quickly he snapped between the two personas—that of the terrif*ied* child and that of the terrif*ying* drill sergeant. "It's just… not me, okay?"

I blinked. "Huh?"

He sighed. "Like you said, it's the name that *she* gave me. The name of the mage whom the Red One's son's supposed to be, by now. While, the reality is… I'm… I'm not… I don't know." He exhaled through his nostrils. "Just forget it, okay? I go by 'Ence'—always have—and there's no reason to suddenly change that. Alright?"

"Th'mage whom 'er son's *s'pposed* t'be?" I echoed, confused.

"Yeah." He gestured, wildly. "You know… like… grand, or something."

Grand? "Well, yer moth'r was real tiny h'rself. Not ev'n five feet at sev'nteen ages ol'—"

"No, no," he shook his head, "I don't mean *physically*. I mean—"

"What, int'llectu'lly? 'Cuz yeh def'nitely got that goin' fer yeh, bigtime. I mean, yeh're as ign'rant as a scabrous 'bout lots o' things, but still th'sharpest arrow I ever—"

"Ash," he cut across me, voice low and dry, "I know we're friends and all, but please don't ever finish my sentences again, okay?"

I shut my mouth.

"What I meant was," he plowed on, "I'm almost the age my mother was, when she died. By my age, Scarlet had already lived a full life: she mastered her magic, co-commanded the Diving Fleet, attacked the Crystal, and started a domestic and world rebellion. And, well… I'm sure she never expected her own son to grow up to be an aura-less military dropout who can hardly light a candle without kneeling over. The Red One's son is supposed to be some mighty multi-sourced enchant who—"

"But, yeh *are* a multi-sourced ench'nt, Ants; not ev'n yer moth'r had *three* sources—"

"ASH!" Ence barked.

I looked down at my sandals. "Sorry."

He turned away, hands in his pockets. "Just forget it. All I'm saying is that I'm not where I need to be yet, but I'll get there. Soon. I've got a plan."

"'S that so?" I chuckled. "Whatchou got 'n mind?"

And, with that, he went off like a firecracker about some crazy cock-and-bull coup scheme he concocted. Uh huh. Overthrowing the System wasn't exactly the most unusual idea, around here.

"Ants," I chortled, eyes rolling, "what d'yeh think th'Reds've been tryin' t'do since before yeh're born?"

"Not what *I'm* talking about," he answered, tie-dye eyes alight. "The Reds are fighting a civil war with the goal of establishing a constitutional democracy. What *I* want is to overthrow the System... so, I can become it."

My stomach flipped. "What d'yeh mean, *b'come* it?"

"I mean, replace it. Build a government in its image, but without its corrupt platform. My platform would be more like that of the Reds."

I was no poli-sci whiz, but even I could tell that made zero sense. "Ants, th'entire Red platform's based on th'idea o' d'mocracy. If yeh built a gov'rnment 'n th'image o' th'System, it'd have teh be—"

"A dictatorship." He swallowed. "I know."

There was a tense silence.

"Um, how'd that be any bett'r than what we've got, right now? What's th'point o' replacin' T'ncture wit'a repl'ca o''im?

"No one ever said I'd become Tincture's replica. I have a different leadership style in mind. I'd be going off a totally different model."

My wingtips curled. "Whose? Scarlet July's? 'Cuz, yeh know, yer nothin' like 'er."

He snorted. "Good. Conflagria doesn't need another Scarlet July. It doesn't need another soft, benevolent, people-pleasing bleeding-heart. It needs someone who isn't afraid to forcibly mold the nation into what it *needs* to be, regardless of whatever or whoever tries to get in the way. Someone who'll *make* this country safe and secure, for good. But, not right away, of course. You see, to really get people under your thumb, you've got to dangle the prize before them, for a little while. Make them really pine for it. Make them beg you for it, at your feet. Make them *want* to bow before you and eat from the palm of your hand."

Ence always had a crazy streak. He was always somewhat of a troublemaker. A 'bad boy,' if you will. But, I just thought that meant he was merely rough around the edges. I didn't know it meant that he was actually secretly pure evil, through-and-through.

"Yer *sixteen*, fer cryin' out loud," I piped.

"So was Scarlet when she started the Red Revolution. And, like I said, I've got a strategy, all worked out. I'll have this island wrapped around my little finger by July, if all goes well." *July?* Was he serious? "So, are you with me?" he demanded, voice piercing my brain like a needle, drugging me, paralyzing me, compelling me to obediently open my mouth and say:

"O' course."

He grunted, "I'm counting on you, friend."

I looked away, disgusted with both of us. I was *with him* alright, but only because I never wanted to know what it'd be like to stand against him.

ASH ARGENT

As spring boiled over into summer, I watched as Ence continued to lay the groundwork for his plan. Turned out, it wasn't all that hard for him to gather support, not when he was a dangerously-gifted-throat-mage-slash-ex-military-commander-slash-son-of-the-legendary-Scarlet-July-and-Cease-Lechatelierite. He knew exactly what to say—with the perfect vocal inflections, of course—to convince folks that he was their only ticket out of hell. As for finding enough people—and the right people—to lure and incite, that was where I came in. My connections throughout the Red Revolution ran deep. Unfortunately, however, the Reds whom Ence seduced had no idea that his platform secretly bore zero resemblance to that of our beloved Scarlet.

So, July rolled around and Ence went on rallying the masses, training his ever-growing guerilla army, using his invisibility to spy on the System, and exercising his multi-sources under the direction of various Red tutors I'd hooked him up with. All the while, I followed him around like an obedient scabrous, helping where I could and staying out of the way when I couldn't.

Ence scheduled his big showdown for today, the twenty-fifth of the month. It was the day of the largest annual Fire Pit execution, attended by thousands of villagers and several key members of the System administration, including Principal Tiki Tincture himself. Ence's warriors were now strategically planted in the crowd, awaiting his signal. I stood amongst them, sweaty and nervous. Here went nothing.

The first slaughter on the agenda was an old purple lady. She dangled from a rope over the Pit, flames licking the hem of her tattered robe and the soles of her gnarled feet. I fought hard to keep a straight face as I watched her struggle to flap her shackled wings.

"The termination of Violet Ari Pennon, for the crime of inadequate contribution to society due to advanced age, will commence on this twenty-fifth day of July of the eleventh age of the eighth era, by order of System Principal Tiki Tincture," a man at the gate read from a scroll. Nearby, the Principal, donning an emerald crown and a velvet robe, sat in his golden chair, flanked by two burly arm mages.

"Kill the deadweight!" the crowd chanted, waving their torches.

Tincture nodded. "Let her fall."

On cue, Ence squinted at Tincture's chest. The guards, accustomed to handling attempts at their boss's life, immediately drew their water-guns and shot at the fireballs... but, to everyone's shock, the stream itself ignited, engulfing both Tincture and his security personnel. Violet Pennon tumbled, but I swooped over and caught her, right in the nick of time.

All hell broke loose, in the square. People screamed, cried, cowered and ran, dropping their fire rations and grabbing their children. Within a single minute, Ence's inferno swallowed the entire System delegation on the platform... unfortunately, along with the rest of the tied-up Uselesses.

Reinforcements from the Mage Castle rapidly arrived at the scene. But, Ence's expertly-trained army and water-catching eye-fire overcame them all, almost too easily.

Ence now clambered onto the Pit's stone gate, white robes stained with the blood of his enemies, a great conflagration smoldering on his scalp. Lime eyes alight, he raised his hands at the vast panicking crowd.

"Behold, citizens of Ardor," he boomed, voice both unbelievably loud and irresistibly enticing, "the Multi-Source Enchant is here!"

The vacuum-like sound of a thousand gasps filled the air.

On cue, ten of Ence's guerillas—including Pha Rynx and Ette Brun, seasoned Red vets from Scarlet's day—joined him on the stone, raising stakes bearing the decapitated heads of various System administrators.

"I am Ence July Lechatelierite," his magically-amplified voice continued, "the son of the Red One and of Crystal's End, here to announce that the rein of the System is over! I, the one with *three* sources—eyes, hair and throat—will serve as Principal in Tiki Tincture's place, bringing safety and security to the Island of Fire, once and for all!"

Spellbound, the square broke into wild cheers and applause. Oh, how easily the desperate masses swayed!

Ence didn't have a crown with which to coronate himself; Tincture's had totally melted. Instead, Ence shed his colorless robe in favor of his mother's red one—a relic from Red Headquarters. Everyone understood what the gesture meant: Ence Lechatelierite was hereby replacing Scarlet July as the most powerful and influential mage in Conflagrian history.

"Principal Ence! Principal Ence!" the people cried.

Ence called me by name, demanding that I join him onstage, and the next thing I knew, I was being pushed up by dozens of hands. I now stood beside my new ruler, trembling openly.

"Ash Argent, you will serve as my primary advisor," he thundered. I felt Pha's fists press down on my back, forcing me to my knees. Ence placed his bloody sword on my shoulder, like I was a First-Earth knight or something.

I blinked at the countless colorful faces swimming before me, raucous chants buzzing in my ears. And, when Principal Ence commanded me to rise, I doubled over and vomited on his sandals.

ASH ARGENT

December twenty-second of the eleventh age. Principal Ence's seventeenth birthday.

I lacked the stomach to describe in much detail what Ence's reign entailed, thus far. I supposed that one could just think of some of the most terrifying rulers of First Earth—Adolf Hitler, Joseph Stalin, Genghis Khan and Moulay Ismaïl—fused with System's worst—Clement Tange, Penn Pekoe and Tiki Tincture. Ence was like a nightmarish mishmash of them all.

Unlike most historical dictators, however, Ence never used his power for sexual abuse. He never raped nor had concubines nor seduced young naïve girls. Women threw themselves at him all the time, but Ence always spat on them (often, literally) and pushed them away.

Ence also mercilessly tortured rapists, prostitutes, child-abusers, neglectful parents, unmarried couples 'caught in the act' and even destitute wedded pairs who continued to reproduce despite their poverty. Additionally, Ence rapidly established a number of institutions for orphans and 'street kids.' And so, it became clear to me that Ence's own abstinence wasn't just about self-preservation or being a one-man island.

Yesterday morning, Ence asked me if I'd like to attend a private execution, that evening. Well, of course I didn't *want* to, but somehow, I found myself there anyway, watching a woman burn alive on a stake, but not like Tincture and his guards who disappeared in a flash. No, this lady baked slowly, flesh peeling off her bones and dropping like ribbons to the ground, legs twitching and kicking and thrashing. I screamed and cried like I was the one being slaughtered, while Ence chuckled heartily and told me to 'toughen up, already.' I vomited three times in a row, right there in the sand, then fled the scene, the Principal's laughter echoing in my ears and the smell of roasted human flesh staining my nostrils. This morning, I asked Ence what that woman could've possibly done to deserve any of that. He said that she was a single mother who recently abandoned her toddler.

He also said that he would soon 'deal' with Fair Gabardine, the spectroscoper allegedly leading the System's endeavor to diffuse Scarlet's aura.

I dreaded every moment I spent with the Principal and my fellow throne advisors, Ette Brun and Pha Rynx, who sincerely egged Ence on. Often, after our conferences at the Mage Castle, I'd disappear into the sky for a bit, flutily attempting to clear my head. I only wished that I could fly backward in time, before the reign of the Multi-Source Enchant, when there was only the Red Revolution and Tincture's System and the monotony of endless civil war. Back when the line between good and evil was clear and I knew which side I was on. Back when I could live with myself and fall asleep at night.

These days, I kept my flights fairly short, because I couldn't take pit-stops. I couldn't take pit-stops because I didn't dare to land in the village. I didn't dare to land in the village because I couldn't bear to face the townsfolk who hated and feared everything I appeared to stand for.

There was no doubt in my mind by now that Ence was worse than the System. I was rescued from the System at a very young age and raised by Reds only to wind up serving the worst of them all, in adulthood. Not that Ence was a *real* Red, by any stretch of the imagination. The true Reds—like Prunus Persica and Gel Kylarks—publicly denounced the new Principal, deeply grieved to see what became of Scarlet's son.

One evening a couple months ago, I asked Ence without preamble, "D'yeh sleep at night, Princ'pal?" Gone were the days in which I called him 'Ants.' He was just 'Principal' or 'sir' to me, now.

His face was deadpan. "Yes," he solemnly replied.

Looking at my sandals, I simply murmured, "Sorry t'hear that."

ENCE LECHATELIERITE

I dragged my feet through the Mage Castle, exhausted from the day's stresses and spectral exertions. All I wanted now was some food and rest. A massage would've been nice, considering how badly my muscles ached, but I refused to call for one. I didn't like to pamper myself. I wasn't one of those rulers who reveled in luxury, like Pekoe or Tincture. I may've held the title of 'Principal,' but I knew that I'd always consider myself a soldier, first and foremost. Even the finery of the System Castle disturbed me. Upon moving in—something that I unfortunately had to do, to reaffirm to the masses that I was their new leader—I stripped the place down, as much as possible. Unfortunately, a lot of the carvings and decorations were built into the structure of the building itself and couldn't be easily dismantled.

By the time I trudged up seven flights of stone steps, I decided to skip dinner and head straight for bed. I opened the door to my quarters—not Tincture's vast fancy chamber, but a modest room that once housed a servant—without bothering to light a single candle or torch.

To my surprise, I found Ette Brun sprawled on my sheets, swathe untied, chestnut hair cascading around her voluptuous curves.

"Rough day?" she asked in a sultry tone, patting the spot beside her.

Weary, I sat at the bed's edge, looking away. "Leave," I coldly ordered.

She slinked over to me, robe falling open, fully revealing her tanned body. "You worked hard today, Principal Lechatelierite," she said, and each syllable of my Ichthyothian last name seemed to roll off her tongue, sounding unusually elegant and seductive. No one ever called me by my Nordic surname—I was always just 'Principal Ence.' "How about a little reward?" she cooed.

Her hands squeezed my shoulders… and, the next thing I knew, she was untying my swathe and clawing off my robe. Then, rubbing my chest, she leaned in and gave me my first kiss. I clung to her and followed my instincts, enjoying the taste of her lips and the smoothness of her skin. She pushed me onto my back, straddled me and—

I sat up, throwing her off of me with violent force; her body made an audible thud upon impact with the stone floor. Pulling my clothes back on, I leapt to my feet and kicked her in the gut, several times. Then, I dragged her downstairs by the hair and threw her, naked, into the night, shouting at the top of my lungs that people like her were the reason there were so many godforsaken orphans in this world.

She screamed and cried and tried to cover herself. "But, Principal, I don't understand! Any child of yours wouldn't be an orphan, he'd be an heir!"

"No," my voice boomed, "I'm a soldier, not a king. Any offspring of mine would be a child of war."

Shuddering with rage, desire and, most of all, disgust with both Ette and myself, I stormed back inside, wadded up her filthy brown robe and my defiled bedsheets, scurried across the square and hurled them into the Fire Pit. I trembled as I watched them parachute into the flames. Panting, I ran my hands through my smoldering hair, frightened by my own weakness and terrified that I almost let myself get seduced by one of my own advisors. Forget the System, I thought darkly, the real enemy dwelled under my own roof.

* * *

I wasn't going to let Ette get off that easy. She deserved formal punishment like any other criminal. At dawn, I had her taken into custody. I decided to deal with her alongside Fair Gabardine, a System spectroscoper bent on dissipating my mother's aura. They both deserved a fate worse than death: they deserved to be tortured mercilessly, then left alive to contend with the resulting physical and emotional scars.

Entering their cell now, I found them bound up with diffusion rope, tied to a boulder.

"Stuck me in here with your *whore*, did you?" Fair screamed. "Rape them then beat them—is that your routine, Your Majesty? Thank Tincture that Scarlet July got slaughtered before having to see what's become of her spawn!"

Anger welled in my scalp. "How dare you even speak her name!"

My stove-hot hair struck Fair's face. Blood erupted from her nose, dribbling down the front of her white robe.

"I've been sabotaging the System's project, for ages!" she tearfully cried. "Why do you think there hasn't been any *real* progress in a decade?"

"Liar!" I shouted, whipping her over and over and over, until my spectrum ran dry.

ENCE LECHATELIERITE

Face planted in my pillow, I felt the nagging sensation that I was being watched.

"Go away," I murmured. "It's already hard enough to relax."

"So, Ash was right, then; you *do* have trouble sleeping at night," said a strangely-familiar female voice. It was young, though I could somehow tell that it belonged to a person whose life-experience far outstripped her ages. It was a girl's voice, really—not a woman's—but, I oddly recognized it as one who commanded men into battle, gave compelling speeches to large audiences, spoke dozens of different languages, wept over the deaths of loved ones—

"Who are you?" I demanded, twisting in my damp sheets, frightened by the foreign memories forcibly invading my mind. "What are you doing to me?"

The fog before my eyes slowly cleared, replaced by the minuscule figure of my mother, a perfect reflection of her own pencil drawings. The colors of her features were even brighter than I'd imagined—far more intense than my own. Her fiery hair made my red-black locks look like mud, and the emerald saturation of her irises made my own gaze appear as though diluted with dirty water. Moreover, her aura glowed brighter than a dozen mages; her sheer redness positively filled the space between us. Now, *this* was a spectral presence to be reckoned with. This was a true multi-sourced enchant.

Slowly, as I peered into her striking stare, anger bubbled to the forefront of my internal emotional hurricane, like molten lava. She was like the rest of them—the selfish, careless women who bore children without paying any mind to their inability to raise or provide for them. My teeth gnashed. While a military leader, fully aware of her tremendous societal burdens, she brought me to this earth… then, abandoned me.

"Take off my robe," she commanded, harsh voice clashing with her sweet childlike face.

I didn't budge.

"I said, take off my robe," she repeated. "You're defiling it."

I gave her a nasty smile. "Don't you see, mother?" I held out my hands. "I did all this for you. To finish what you started."

"No." Scarlet July's head shook. "Everything you've ever done is for yourself. You destroyed my legacy. You're no Red, and you're certainly no son of mine, *Ence*," she spat the name she never gave me. The name that was now synonymous with fear and terror and absolute power, across the island.

"You lost your right to have any expectations of me, the day you left me to fend for myself," I growled.

Her flushed face twisted. "I didn't *leave*, you fool. I was assassinated."

Unable to move my feet, I settled for leaning in. "Is he still alive," the question almost involuntarily erupted from my lips, "your assassin?" No one had seen nor heard from him in seventeen ages—it was widely assumed that he was dead.

Scarlet stayed silent and stoic, impervious to my throat magic. But, she didn't say no. My stomach abruptly jumped up into my esophagus.

"Where is he?" I raised my voice. "If you live in the spectral web, then you know—you can track his lifeline. Tell me where he is!"

Scarlet still didn't speak.

My scalp burned. "ANSWER!" I screamed.

Her upper lip twitched, ever so slightly. "Why do you want to know?"

"Why else? To take back what he stole." I surveyed her tiny frame, forever seventeen. "You were so young," I croaked, rage heating my hair. "You had your whole life ahead of you. Your *whole life*."

For a moment, her mask slipped and she looked, for all the world, like a concerned mom who wanted nothing more than to embrace her little boy and tell him that everything was going to be alright. But, alas, she stood her ground and spoke without a trace of tenderness in her tone:

"Taking his life won't bring back mine."

I was hyperventilating, now; all I could see in my mind's eye was a striking yellow gaze. That sour, amber stare from my visions.

"Don't harm him," Scarlet begged. "If you find him, promise you'll leave him be."

Her words jammed every gear in my brain. "How can you stand there, *defending* him?" I seethed. "How could you plead for his life when he took everything from you? From *me?*"

Scarlet put her face in her hands, like a scared teenage girl. "Please, my son, listen to me. He's already paid dearly for his actions. And, I forgave him on my own deathbed; that's why he spared your life."

Flames broke out, on my head. She *forgave* him? How could she? How dare she? As for him 'sparing' me—what a joke. Willingly endangering someone then saving that person from your own snares was hardly a sacrificial or benevolent act.

Scarlet got down on her knees—a sight so jarring, it electrified every last photon in my invisible aura. "Please, I beg you, don't hurt him, don't do anything you'll regret—"

"Look who's talking!" I roared. "*Your* impulsiveness ruined my life!"

Scarlet looked confused.

"Nurtic Leavesleft told me himself," I went on, "that I was a mistake."

At this, she gave a sharp cry, like a baby scabrous. "Nurtic Leavesleft told you that?"

"Not in so many words. I know the truth; you can't deny it, *mother*," I spat. "You never wanted me."

"My son, my dear son, a life with you and your father was all I ever wanted." She bowed, again. "Please, Commence, this is the only thing I'll ever ask of you: do not avenge my death or Cease's. What's done is done and there's nothing you can do now to change it. All vengeance *would* do is put yet another man's blood on your hands."

"I'm sorry, Scarlet," I whispered, "but, what I do with my hands was, is and always will be out of yours."

ENCE LECHATELIERITE

It was what filled the hours between waking and sleeping. It became the reason I lived and breathed, an obsession as I'd never had before. I toiled, day and night, researching the whereabouts of the amber-eyed man.

"But, Your Grace," Pha piped, "no one has seen nor heard from him in nearly two decades. He's long since been presumed dead."

"He's alive, I know it."

"How, sir?"

I didn't answer.

Pha's brows lowered. "Well, if he is, he'd have no shortage of enemies. He's done extensive damage to both the Reds and the System—he doesn't have a place on this island, anymore. Where could he possibly hide when there's politics in every town?"

I shook my head. "Not *every* town." My arms folded. "Pha, I want a wavelength-sweep of the Dunes. Get the spectroscopers to figure a way to pluck lifelines without him sensing that he's being hunted for."

"Principal," Pha breathed, "I told you, it's been nearly two deca—"

"I don't care!" I blared. "I want Ambrek Coppertus… alive," I swallowed, "so, I can kill him myself."

ENCE LECHATELIERITE

January first of the twelfth age.

Just as I'd presumed, Ambrek Coppertus was living out his days by the northern shore, amongst the nomads who claimed to neither agree nor disagree with the current political atmosphere. He was traveling with the Mauler Tribe, a gypsy clan primarily consisting of hand-mages who, quite literally, did all their plowing and farming by hand, without the aid of 'inorganic tools.' Consequently, their forearms were all permanently stained, their fingernails torn and blackened. Rather than sporting robes of their distinct colors like everyone else, they wore dark brown, in solidarity with the earth.

The Mauler Tribe was a perfect community for a man in hiding.

For a principal, I sure didn't mind doing dirty work. In general, I avoided delegating whenever possible, choosing instead to take matters into my own hands. I preferred to be the one in control. So, once my spectroscopers located Ambrek Coppertus in the Dunes, instead of sending bounty-hunters after him, I decided to head for the hills myself. Alone.

Magically concealing a scabrous for days on end would've been an enormous spectral exertion, so I chose to hike to the shore on foot, saving most of my spectrum for the showdown itself. I set out with nothing but a couple water-canteens, a few strips of dragon jerky and my magically-fortified wooden sword.

And, by the morning of January seventh, I found the Mauler camp.

I'd done quite a bit of research on Ambrek Coppertus since I'd spoken to my mother's aura and learned that, aside from espionage, pilotry was once his specialty in the System Water Forces. Generally, that wasn't an uncommon profession for hand mages, considering their superior dexterity. But, even when compared to others of his kind, Ambrek was considered above the curve. He had a reputation for being the best navigator in Conflagrian history. Rumor had it that he could give Nurtic Leavesleft a run for his money. High praise indeed.

Anyway, after about ten hours of furtive eavesdropping, I learned that, apparently, Ambrek's fellow gypsies were well aware of his astounding talent for flight, giving him the one duty that could possibly require it: Town Messenger. Every two weeks, he was responsible for traveling to Ardor Village on pine-dragonback, to collect fire rations for the entire tribe. It was obvious that the Maulers didn't have a clue who Ambrek really was; if they did, they surely wouldn't have chosen to send him, of all people, to the nation's capital on a regular basis.

I now watched as he prepped for takeoff, concealing every inch of his enormous self with layers of dark cloth, leaving a mere slit for his eyes. At last, he mounted his pine dragon and galloped away from camp. This was my chance. In minutes, he'd be soaring the open sky, traversing a vast expanse of desert. There'd be little to no witnesses around for miles.

Invisible, I ran as fast as I could and leapt onto the beast's back, behind Ambrek. The dragon was young—there wasn't much room for two—so, as I clung for dear life, I hardly dared to breathe. Mere moments later, Ambrek yanked the reins and took off, at a steep angle. That's when I learned that flying a pine-dragon—something I'd never done before—was absolutely nothing like toting around on scabrouses. With an unexpected tail thrash, I found myself inadvertently thrown onto my back, only holding on with my legs. When I tried to pull myself upright, my hood snagged a scale. Gagging, I clawed my throat and, after several agonizing seconds, finally managed to undo the fastening, sending my robe into the wind like a flailing scarlet ghost. I struggled to sit up, wind whipping my bare chest. My father's medal, bouncing on my collarbone, quickly grew hot as a smelter's iron in the blazing sunlight, burning my exposed skin. For crying out loud, I didn't even need Ambrek to hand my ass to me; my parents' relics were doing that for him!

Roughly a half-hour later, I determined that we were far enough from camp to get this show on the road, already. Sword in hand, I clambered to my feet, balancing on the rear of the saddle like a Nurian surfer. Then, I jumped up into a flip, right over Ambrek's head, and landed before him, catlike.

And, that's when I lifted my invisibility.

A military strategist may wonder why on earth I'd blow my own cover before the deed was done. Why not just strike from behind while still cloaked? It would've been so easy. Well, I didn't want to slay Ambrek quietly and anonymously. I wanted him to spend his last fleeting moments beholding his assassin's face.

Ambrek gasped audibly at the sight of me. In his gold eyes, I saw the very fear and terror that I'd witnessed in my recurring dream. It was beautiful. Smiling, I lunged at him, but—with a single lightning-quick motion—his bulky right hand caught my blade.

And, he waited.

Shock rippled through my hair. He didn't want to hurt me. I couldn't believe it. He was only interested in defending himself. He wasn't going to fight back.

My job just got so much easier.

Grinning broadly, I looked him in the eye and squinted… but, nothing happened. Apparently, my extensive spectral cloaking had depleted my aura until not a single disposable photon remained.

But, of course, my arsenal wasn't empty, quite yet.

Wrenching my sword from Ambrek's grasp, I wedged it into the dragon's mouth, deep enough to make it gag a little. When I withdrew my weapon from its jaws, the blade itself was ablaze. Swiveling back around, I plunged it into Ambrek's stomach.

The world stood still, for just a few seconds. Then, he softly uttered a single phrase:

"J-just know that I'm s-sorry, Lechatelierite."

And, with that, the flames devoured his burly body whole.

ENCE LECHATELIERITE

"Princ'pal?" Ash Argent's grey gaze brimmed with concern. I pushed past him, stomping up the stone stairs. He tailed me, all the way to my room. "Princ'pal, yeh a'right?"

"Yes," I croaked. "Goodnight."

"Want somethin' t'eat, sir?"

Food was just about the last thing on my mind. "No, I don't. Dismissed."

He bowed deeply, but didn't leave. "Sir, where've yeh been, all week? 'N' what happ'ned t'yer robe?"

Unhitching my bloody sword from my belt, I tossed it to the floor with a clatter.

He recoiled, face green. "Yeh went teh th'Dunes, dinchou?"

"You're dismissed, Ash," I repeated.

Bowing again, he finally obeyed, wings twitching.

I collapsed into bed, every muscle in my body throbbing like a broken heartbeat. I rubbed my hands—covered in blood and grime—in my sheets, but nothing made the scarlet go away.

"It's useless," came a female voice, from nowhere. "They won't get clean that easily."

Without warning, blackness swallowed my peripheral vision so that all I could see was her. I tucked my chin, staring instead at my own dirty bare feet.

"I told you not to do it," she scolded.

I didn't answer.

"It was the only thing I ever asked of you."

I unstuck my throat, daring to meet her paralyzing gaze. "I owe you nothing."

Her eyes were pure ice. "I'm your mother."

"In flesh alone."

Abruptly, she collapsed to the floor, bawling like a little girl who scraped her knee. I stared, stricken. I always imagined Scarlet as impossibly strong and fearless. The ultimate embodiment of spectral strength. The epitome of warrior. But, the person I saw now was helpless. Terrified. Defeated. Her sobs were unfiltered, shameless. With neither restraint nor dignity. The very sight of her ugly-crying like this struck the root of my being as never before. Why? I never knew Scarlet, never really loved her nor saw her as true family. Since the day Nurtic uncovered my past, I mostly just harbored resentment toward her. So, why did her pain disturb me so much, now? If anything, the fact that I had *this* much power over someone like her should've invigorated me. Because power was all I ever wanted. Well, here was the proof, right before my eyes, that I had it, in spades. Not a soul on this island didn't fear me. Even the aura of the Red One could no longer hold her ground before me. Satisfied, Principal Ence?

No, I answered myself. Because, it turned out that absolute power wasn't all that it was cracked up to be. There was no fight in it. Nothing to work for. Nothing to win. Everything just collapsed, all around me. So, what if I was the last one standing? What was the point in walking upright amongst ashes? What good did that do anybody? What good did it do *me?*

And, quite suddenly, I felt very alone. I shivered, as though whipped by Ichthyothian wind.

"Stop it," I told her. "Please, just get up, just stop; I can't take much more of this."

"How do you think I felt," she gasped, "watching you today?"

"You… *watched* me?" I breathed, vocal control faltering.

"How could I not?" she roared. "The spectral web is my home. I dwell in the auras of every individual. It's not an easy existence. Every time a mage dies, a part of me goes with them," she swallowed, "like Ambrek Coppertus."

Outrageous. "But, he murdered you!"

"No." Her hair crinkled and curled. "The man who killed Scarlet July also died on December twenty-second of the ninety-fourth age of the seventh era. The Ambrek Coppertus I've come to know since then is someone different. Someone absolved. Clean. Faithful. Pure. He was my friend."

"Impossible!" I shouted. "No one can just… *change*, like that!"

"But, they can," she objected, "through forgiveness."

My head turned sharply, as though slapped. "No. *No one* deserves forgiveness after… after all he's done."

Scarlet's stare was like an emerald dagger. "There's no act he's committed that you haven't."

At this, my mind shrieked, *that's not true!* I'd destroyed and killed, but I never turned on anyone the way Ambrek turned on Scarlet and everything she stood for. I never hid hatred beneath false love. Back in Alcove City, I could've easily made Nurtic believe I loved him; that would've made both our lives a whole lot easier. Likewise, when Ash first took me in, I could've duped him into thinking that I wanted to be his friend long before I actually did. But, I didn't trick either of them because I knew I could never wear a mask like that. I was a lot of despicable things, but a liar wasn't one of them.

"Is that so?" Scarlet asked.

What? "Get out of my head!" I growled.

"What about Inexor Buird and the Diving Fleet?" she plowed on. "What about your Conflagrian constituency? Have you always been forthright with all of them? When you convinced them to put their lives in your hands, did you give them any indication of what kind of leader you were going to be? What kind of *person* you were going to be?"

At this, the hairs on the back of my head stood at attention—not from spectrum.

"You say that *this* is all you've ever wanted." She gestured to our surroundings. "But, if that were the case, why are you still so upset? Why do your so-called victories bring you nothing but more discontentment? Can you confidently say that you're happy with your accomplishments? With who and what you've become?"

"I know what you're trying to get me to do, and it's not going to work," I countered loudly, even as I felt my heart gun against my ribcage like a semi. "By now, I've accepted that there's no point in fighting who I am. There's no way I can ever depart from the path I've set myself on. People don't change. I've made my tarp and, now, I've got no choice but to lie in it, for the rest of my life."

"Ambrek Coppertus changed, in his twenties and thirties. You're saying that you can't, in your teens?"

"I've gone so far," I argued, "so far down." I swallowed. "What if I'm…" I trembled in my sandals, already intensely humiliated by the words about to escape my lips, "what if I'm beyond help? What if I can't be redeemed?"

The silence that ensued felt like it lasted a thousand eras.

"No one is, my child," Scarlet finally declared. "Not even you."

I stowed my bloody hands in my pockets. "Then, tell me what I need to do, to make it so."

Her mouth hardened. "I'm not sure that I can. And, I'm not sure that you're really willing. Because the question you just asked now betrays the desperate laziness of your soul. Lasting change is long, hard work, and you're already trying to find an easy out. A shortcut. There's no instant magical remedy that I can hand you. No simple twelve-stage plan that I could dictate to you."

Typical. "So, you're not going to help me," I snorted. "Shocker."

"I can't lay out your whole path, Ence, but I do have one small step in mind. A starting point, if you will."

"What's that?"

"You can forgive me. And, your father."

Yet another excruciating pause.

My temples pulsed. "I... can't do that."

"Why not?"

My jaw clenched. "Because, you two are the reason I'm in this mess, in the first place."

She sighed. "Always making excuses, aren't you? Always trying to find a backdoor, a way out. Nothing's ever your fault. The mighty Conflagrian Principal, the former Leader of the Ichthyothian Resistance... is a helpless product of his circumstances?"

I didn't like her malicious tone. "Stop it," I barked. "Quit patronizing me."

"*Stop it*," she echoed, pitch high and whiny. "Oh, grow up."

"How can I," I growled, "when I was never properly raised—"

My voice abruptly died as my mind got overwhelmed by a cascade of foreign images and emotions. Clear as life, I could see my mother and father now, embracing on a balcony in the dead of night, wintry wind beating their backs as he handed her his Silver Triangle. I could feel the anguished joy that overcame Scarlet's heart as that little medal hung from her neck, for the first time. I could see Scarlet kneeling by Cease's flat gravestone, mere weeks later, weeping as her hair melted the ice from his last name. I could see Scarlet sitting in Red Headquarters with Nurtic Leavesleft, laughing as he touched her belly, feeling my kicks. I could see Scarlet curling up in her tarp at night, clinging to the thought of her lost beloved for solace, singing happy birthday to him under her breath, dreaming of raising her son in his likeness. And, then, came the real bomb: I saw Scarlet sprawled on her back on her bedroom floor, Ambrek Coppertus standing over her with a sword, carving a premature fetus from her flesh… but, not to kill him, but to save his ethereal life, because Scarlet turned her assassin's heart with a single expression of love and forgiveness. I watched as Ambrek held an impossibly-tiny baby to Scarlet's flushed cheek. Words couldn't describe the look on her face as she beheld her child for the first time. Despite myself, I broke down into sobs. How she loved me! It was impossible to comprehend the magnitude of her adoration. I never loved anyone or anything like that. Not even myself. Not even power. The greatest emotions of my life positively paled in comparison.

You did want me, I silently cried to her, you wanted me and loved me and had no desire to ever leave my side. Death was the only thing that could've possibly kept you from me. You were willing to go any length, for my sake. I took precedence over everything. What happened to both of us in the end was completely out of your hands. You went above and beyond to give me the life I had now, the life I squandered. The life I used to kill and destroy.

I forgive you, mother, I thought. And, I'm so sorry for victimizing everyone around me, in the throes of misguided rage.

Scarlet smiled a sweet smile full of love and understanding. *It's okay,* her eyes seemed to say, *the past is in the past, and I'm with you now as you pursue your future.* Eagerly, I reached forward to take her tiny hands in mine, but at that moment, she vanished; my fingers grasped nothing but cold air.

And, I woke up—alone, as I'd always been.

PART II

COMMENCE: SON OF NATIONS

"I think one of the most devastating things about war is the children left behind."

—J.K. Rowling

"The war is over for me.
But, I'm sure it will still be there
for the rest of my days."

—From Platoon

"I would like you to give a message.
Please do your best to tell the world what is happening to us,
the children, so that other children don't have
to pass through this violence."

—15-age-old girl abducted into the
'Lord's Resistance Army' in Uganda
as told to Amnesty International

COMMENCE JULY LECHATELIERITE

Feverish and restless, I rose from my tarp, dawn sunlight filtering through my thin curtains. Blinking sweat from my eyes, I sifted through my nightstand drawer for a thermometer. Holding the glass tube in my mouth for a couple minutes, I wondered how my old Diving Fleet comrades would react to the sight of *this* primitive artifact. I sure missed Nordic technology, sometimes.

'106°F.'

I stared at the marker for several seconds. Then, I hastily threw on my old colorless robe—I lost my mother's in the Dunes, yesterday—and ran out into the hall, calling for Ash.

He scurried over. "What is it, Princ'pal?"

"Ash, something weird is going on. I just checked my—SON OF A SCABROUS!" My hand sharply withdrew from my stove-hot hair. What the hell? Channeling photons into my scalp wasn't something I just accidentally or subconsciously did. Any spectral activity—even heating a single lock by a few degrees—took concentration.

"Did yeh just burn yerself, sir?" Ash gaped.

"What do you think?" I snapped, staring at the red marks on my fingers. In a flash, they disappeared. Effortlessly.

Fear struck Ash's face. He took several steps back, straightening his posture.

"What's *your* problem?" I growled.

"Nuthin', sir," he answered, bowing. "It's just that... yeh usually don't smolder up like that 'nless yeh're furious 'bout somethin'... or when yeh're 'bout teh... um... yeh know... beat someone real good."

I swallowed. "Yeah, well, you can cool your gliders, because I'm not going to do stuff like that, anymore. Well, at least, nothing too over-the-top, anyway." Criminals deserved punishment, of course, but maybe I could scale things back a bit, as far as the severity of the torture I dished out. Maybe, I set the bar too high when I decided on hair-whipping as a baseline for minor misdemeanors.

Ash blinked. "Do what, Princ'pal?"

"I also don't want to be called *that* anymore," I demanded, realizing only after the words escaped my lips how harsh my tone still was. Using throat magic to continually scare the dragon dung out of my subordinates was sure going to be a hard habit to break.

He stared. "Sir?"

"Not that, either," I shot. "Please," I added, feebly.

"W-what should I call yeh then, s-sir? Just 'Ants'?"

Ence. I chewed my lip. No. Too many monstrosities were committed under that name.

"How about 'Commence'?" I suggested, forcing myself to smile, so he'd calm down. That's what nice people did to put those around them at ease, right? Smile and act happy?

Ash didn't relax, not one bit. "I thought yeh said yeh nev'r want t'hear that name 'gain."

"Well, I changed my mind."

"Um... 'kay... C'mmence," he said, uneasily. "Now, what was it yeh wanted teh talk teh meh 'bout?"

I ushered him into my quarters, where I handed him the thermometer. He gave it an impassive glance.

"What's wrong, si—C'mmence?"

"What's wrong? That's *my* fever!" I exploded. Whoops. Damn, this patience thing was tough.

"So?"

"*So*, why am I not having a heatstroke?" I shouted. Ugh, I did it, yet again! I'd been awake for barely ten minutes and was already failing miserably at benevolence.

His hands wrung. "I-I'm sorry, sir."

It took everything in me to meet his terrified gaze and gently say, "No, I'm the one who should apologize. I shouldn't have yelled at you."

He gawked at me as though I'd spontaneously spouted my own set of wings. After a lengthy pause, he finally passed the tube back and said, "Yeh don't got no fever. One-oh-six's 'ealthy as a 'obnail."

"I got a bad flu once, at the orphanage," I recalled. "I was two ages old and developed a temperature of one-oh-five. The staff went nuts."

"Why?"

Ash was never the sharpest arrow in my quiver—far from it—but, was he always *this* thick? "That's seven degrees higher than normal."

"No, 's not. Ninety-eight'd be hypoth'rmia. Yeh're a mage, now, Prin—C'mmence."

A mage, *now?* "I've always been a mage, Ash. Growing up overseas didn't change my DNA."

There came a knock at the door. "Good morning, Principal." Pha strolled in, carrying a scroll. "Today's first order of business is—" He stopped dead. "Is something the matter, sir?"

I threw my hands up. "Why does everyone think I'm upset?" Aside from the fact that I just yelled, now. Again.

Pha squirmed. "You're… well, you're *glowing*, sir. Why else would you be giving off so much spectrum?"

"Everyone here uses magic, all the time! Just because *I'm* also doing it doesn't mean I'm about to kill someone!"

My words seemed to echo off the stone walls.

"Yeh know," Ash breathed, "I always thought yeh're freq'ncy's infr'red, but now, I sense a sort o'... m'roon col'r."

"Ash is right." Pha squinted. "But, it's too reddish to be maroon. It's more... auburn."

"No, def'nitely m'roon. It's got a lot o' black 'n it."

"It's auburn. That's his hair-color, and he's a *hair mage*, so it'd make sense if—"

"His hair's not aub'rn, Pha. It's red 'n' black, mixed togeth'r."

Two jaws dropped.

"Wait... 're you an Ir'descent?" Ash choked.

"But, how can anyone's wavelength go from infrared to iridescent, overnight?" Pha wondered.

"How should I know?" I snarled. "I only—"

Quite suddenly, my eyes spontaneously and uncontrollably rolled to the back of my head, blackness engulfing my sight. Panting with an open mouth, I blindly groped my surroundings. Fighting panic, I dropped to my knees, moaning.

And, then, there it was. For the first time, I could really *see* the spectral web, clear as day itself. All around me, countless wavelengths wove together, forming a dense network of electromagnetism. From the farthest reaches of the earth to the scintillating Crystal itself, individual lines stretched and coiled, braided and looped, spun and bowled. The mass moved like a den of multicolored snakes, new lines blossoming and old ones severing. And, somehow, amidst the shimmering chaos, I found a couple familiar frequencies—black and red, blending into a vibrant pulsating auburn. It wasn't two distinct entwined threads, but rather a single strand with two tones. So, it belonged to one mage. An Iridescent.

Me.

No, it couldn't be. Since birth, covalence had sentenced my aura to a weak infrared existence. My line was supposed to be colorless and frail. There was no way that I possessed not one but two powerful tones in the visible range of the electromagnetic spectrum.

"Principal Ence? Sir?"

"C'mmence, 're yeh 'kay?"

"*What* did you just call him?"

"C'mmence. It's 'is name."

"I know, but he's made it very clear that he is to be called 'Principal Ence' and nothing else. Are you *trying* to get yourself whipped?"

"Pha, C'mmence just told meh that 'e don't want to be called 'sir' or 'Princ'pal' no more."

"What?"

"Nev'r mind that, now—'e needs 'elp!"

"Principal Ence?"

There was only one way to be sure that beautiful iridescent wavelength was indeed mine. I willed a lock of my hair to move. And, as it swung, I watched as the red-black cord vibrated faster, like a plucked harp string.

"Maybe, 'e's 'n a coma? Call Olea fer 'elp!"

"A *coma?* He's upright!"

"But, 'e's unr'sponsive!"

"Perhaps, he's having a vision or communing with the Red One?"

Something bumped my shoulder.

"No, Ash! What are you doing? Don't you dare disturb his vigil!"

I let go—of what, I couldn't be sure. Accordingly, the spectral web receded from the forefront of my mind. But, it was still present, in the back of my consciousness. Accessible like never before. On a whim, I could dance upon it, feeling its diverse energy course freely through my aura. How and why did I have dominion over the web, all of a sudden? More importantly, how could I use this to my advantage?

No, no, no. I shuddered. The right question was: how could I use this to *Conflagria's* advantage? Power wasn't just a tool for personal gain anymore, it was a responsibility. A means to serve my people.

"Principal Ence? Sir?"

"C'mmence? Olea's on 'is way."

I cracked my lids to the sight of Pha and Ash, bending over me with wide eyes.

"Don't have a cow, you two," I retorted. "I'm fine."

"A cow? What's that?"

"'S that some kind o' Ichthyothian an'mal?"

I got to my feet. "No, it's Nurian. Cows eat grass—something that's in rather short supply, in an ice land."

"Why di'chou tell us not teh have one, then?" Ash scratched his head. "Where'd we get it?"

Ugh, seriously? "I said I'm okay, alright? I was just… exploring the spectral web. I wasn't having a vision, or talking to my mom, or anything like that."

"Told yeh," Ash murmured to Pha.

Heil Olea appeared in the doorframe.

I rounded on my advisors. "I shut my eyes for a minute and you call for a *medicine man?*"

"Yeh were 'n an unr'sponsive trance, on yer knees! What were we s'pposed t'think?"

Olea cleared his throat. "Is everything alright, Principal?"

I grunted, "Yes," at the same time Ash cried, "No!"

The old man stared.

Well, I figured that as long as I had a medical professional barging into my bedroom, I might as well make use of him. Maybe, he could shed some light on why and how my spectrum spontaneously strengthened overnight.

"I have an aura," I told him. "It's iridescent. Red and black."

Olea blinked. "Yes, I can see that quite clearly, Mr. Principal."

"No, I mean, I didn't have one before, but when I woke up this morning, I did. Do."

He stroked his chin. "How's that possible?"

"You're the expert," I grumbled. "You tell me!"

"I'm afraid that this falls outside my area of practice, sir. I'm a healer, not a spectroscoper."

Great. "So, you have no idea, whatsoever?"

He stood still for a moment, frown pensive, before finally saying, "Well, sir, Nordics have been known to develop semblances of auras before, but certainly not overnight."

Nordic*s*, plural? There was someone else, aside from my father? "Who?"

"I've only met one of them personally, but his name now escapes me… He was one of the leaders of the World Revolt, many ages ago. A pilot."

"Nurtic Leavesleft?" I blurted.

His fingers snapped. "Yes. That's the one. He twined to your mother, gradually generating a sort of yellowish haze."

Hmm. I sure didn't remember Nurtic having any sort of perceptible glow when *I* knew him.

"He never got any training," Olea answered my thoughts. "And, if you don't use it, you lose it. He slipped back into the infrared range shortly after the Red One passed away." His hands clasped. "Now, the very *first* Nordic to modify his wavelength, Crystal's End, used his budding black aura to—"

"To end the Crystal, yes, I know," I interjected. "It still baffles me that visible frequencies can be honed by those with no blood-spectrum-content whatsoever."

"True magical potential can't be exclusively measured in parts-per-milligram. That's something the Red One taught me."

"My BSC is a point-seven," I quietly admitted. It was a shameful fact that I'd only dared to tell Ash, until now; I knew that abysmal number could jeopardize my authority in the eyes of my constituency. Conflagria, behold your mighty ruler whose entire body bore less spectrum than a typical foot-mage's pinky toe.

Olea's bushy brows shot to his hairline. "*Point*-seven, sir?"

I nodded. "But, now, it feels more like a seven-point-oh. I can use my sources easily. Too easily. And, I can see and feel the spectral web, quite clearly."

"Like the Red One," Pha spoke up. "She was always able to access the web like no other. She could even picture it, in her mind."

We all looked back at Olea.

His shoulders squared. "Like I said, I'm a medicine man, not a spectroscoper."

"Ash." I turned. "Get me Fair Gabardine." No doubt, this mystery was too great for the average spectroscoper. I needed Conflagria's finest scientific mind on the case. "She somehow managed to escape bondage shortly after her torture session—I need her back, asap."

His wings drooped. "I'll prep a prison cell."

My head shook. "No, no, that won't be necessary. I'm not planning on capturing her again; I'll just convince her to help me voluntarily, as a free woman."

Ash halted in mid-step. "Uhm, sir?"

My hand waved. "I'll have her on my side, soon enough. Once I make my public apology and propose my new project..."

"Apology?" All three men stiffened in their sandals. "Project?"

I only smiled.

ASH ARGENT

"And, then, she told me, 'There's no act he's committed that you haven't.'"

Flanked by Pha and me, he stood upon the Fire Pit's stone platform where, not too long ago, he spilled Tincture's blood. His colorless robe—wholly unsuitable, now that he had a rather vivid iridescent aura—flapped noisily in the dusty wind as the townsfolk stared up at him in a confused mix of fear, wariness and awe. Not that there was anything particularly frightening about what Ence—um, Commence—was saying. But, every citizen on this island knew, all too well, what kind of leader he'd been, thus far—ruthless, sadistic, power-hungry—so, they were, understandably, struggling to swallow the idea of such a rapid, dramatic, self-proclaimed turnaround. As was I. Did the Red One truly say these things to Commence in a vision, as he claimed? If so, was he actually convicted and transformed by her words or did he just want us to think so, for some conniving reason? Was he really turning over a new page of parchment, or was he only using that slippery voice of his to cleverly manipulate us to some twisted end?

Every photon in my aura desperately hoped for the former.

"Principal Ence is dead," he proclaimed. "I am Commence July Lechatelierite, and I'm just like all of you." He got to his knees and bowed his head. We watched with baited breath as he added, "I hereby forfeit the throne."

A galvanizing wave swept through the square. Mages gasped and gawked and whispered to one another.

Pha visibly jolted, as though electrocuted. "Principal!" he hissed, grasping the boy's slight shoulder. "Principal, what are you *doing?*"

Commence looked up at him. "I'm not your Principal anymore, my friend."

"Hey, you can't do that!" a voice called from the crowd. I slowly located its owner—a random teenage boy with a pronounced scar on his left cheek.

"Yeah, what if we don't accept your resignation?" someone else shouted. "You can't just leave us high and dry like that!"

That statement was met by a general murmur of agreement. Despite Principal Ence's terrorism, no one could deny that Conflagria experienced more stability during his reign than at any point since the Crystal ended.

Commence rose to his feet. "I may not be your *principal* anymore, but I have no intention to abandon you outright. I wish to become your president, just for a short while, until we find someone more suitable. Not your dictator."

"President," the teenager echoed. "What does that even mean?"

Commence smiled. "Normally, that would mean I'm voted into office. But, Conflagria isn't ready for a formal election, yet. When it is, and a new leader gets chosen, I'll gladly scoot out of the way. Until then, I'll only be your *interim* president."

"I don't get the difference," the scarred boy insisted. Brave kid.

"The difference is that my authority is no longer absolute—the public will have a say in every decision I make. It means that from now on, I'll use my power to reform the nation into a democratic-republic, finally ending the civil war between the Reds and the System, as well as the greater conflict between Conflagria and the Nordic alliance."

"System? What System?" cheered a random middle-aged throat mage I didn't recognize. "You crushed it!" Well, technically, that wasn't true; the System was only endangered, not extinct.

"Hurrah for Principle Ence! Hurrah for Principle Ence!" a chant began.

"But, isn't the international war already over?" interjected a purple mage with a basket on her head. "If the System's dead, who're the Nordics fighting?"

"*Hurrah for Principle Ence!*"

"For a war to end, there needs to be more than just a *lack of fighting*," Commence answered, sounding a little too agitated with his audience's ignorance. Easy there, changed man. "There needs to be collaboration and formal resolution between the two sides." He inhaled. "Ultimately, there needs to be a treaty. I want to be the one to draft that treaty. But, before we can get there, *this* nation needs to be united. For Ichthyosis and Nuria to trust us, they need to know exactly who they're dealing with, what we stand for. So, we can't make peace on the world stage until we do so on the home-front."

"And, how the hell do we do that?" basket-lady bellowed, as if on cue.

"It won't be easy; I'm not going to lie. I won't be able to take care of everything myself, either. I'm going to need everyone's cooperation. And, I mean *everyone*, not just those who call yourselves throne loyalists."

It was only too obvious who he was *really* addressing, here. Commence's eyes scanned the square, seeking out those who didn't participate in the chant of 'Principal Ence' today or any day. The Reds. The *true* Reds—those who adhered to Scarlet July's noble vision long after Principal

Ence corrupted it. Not the spineless mercenaries who rallied to Ence the moment he slaughtered Tincture, like Pha and Ette. I swallowed. And, me.

"Why should we help you?" cried Gel Kylarks. He was in a wheelchair, feet severed nearly two decades ago by System warriors. Once upon a time, he was the fastest leg mage in the land and the Red Revolution's primary messenger.

Standing right beside him was none other than Fair Gabardine, arm laced through Prunus Persica's.

I did a double take. What was the System's most prized spectroscoper doing amongst Reds? And, not just any Reds, but diehards. Leaders of the movement. If Commence noticed Fair there—which he probably did, considering that he saw everything—he gave no indication.

"You have every reason to doubt me," Commence's words sliced through the dense silence, "as I've been anything but trustworthy, since my reign began. When I first usurped Tincture, I genuinely believed that I was fulfilling the Red Revolution's goal. But, by now, I've come to realize that, despite my intentions, I've been the Reds' enemy, all along. I'm not trying to excuse my behavior; I know nothing ever could. But, I am asking you to forgive me. Scarlet July did. And, if she can, anybody can. She's the one I've wronged the most, in all of this. I perverted her work, mutilated her legacy and essentially turned my back on the country she died for." Lids scrunched for a moment, he inhaled. "Reds, I'm laying down my sword and holding out an olive branch. In the months and ages to come, I'll be working on reforming Conflagria and ending the international war, no matter what. So, we might as well do it together, right?" His voice was so captivating. Compelling. Convicting. "But, even if you choose not to forgive and join forces with me, always bear in mind that you—that is to say, *your platform*—still won, all the same.

Even if you're not the ones physically occupying the Mage Castle, your platform is still what my administration will be pursuing, from here on out. I'm effectively under your influence. Game over."

Thoughtful chatter consumed the crowd. Commence began pacing, letting his declaration sink in for a few moments before raising his arms for attention. Every man, woman and child instantly fell silent, once more.

"To elaborate further on a prior point I made," he said, "a key difference between presidency and dictatorship is that presidents actually have boundaries. You may wonder where those boundaries come from. Who makes them up? Who puts them down on parchment? More specifically, who'll write a constitution that governors and citizens alike would willingly follow? I obviously can't do it—at least, not all by myself—because a constitution must limit the executive office, and I have a hunch that no one will truly trust limits that I put on *myself.* A constitutional monarchy isn't what I'm going for, here. I want republican democracy. You might be wondering what that is. You've read First Earth history; you've seen the term a dozen times before. But, how does republican democracy actually play out, on a daily basis? On a practical level? I think, to gain the depth of understanding we'd need to make it happen for ourselves, we should take a good look at some real-live examples. We need to see something with our own two eyes—something we'd want to imitate. Unfortunately, in this isolationist world, most of us won't get the chance to witness another democracy in action. I'm one of the lucky few who have. I've lived in each Nuria and Ichthyosis, before coming here—two countries full of political theorists and legislators who could possibly help us out. If we ask nicely, I'm sure *someone* out there will be willing to assist us with authoring a suitable constitution—one that'll bestow rights, not rules. That's a mistake my mother made when she spearheaded the First Red Revolution: she didn't seek outside assistance."

"Yes, she did!" Kylarks cried so loudly and suddenly, everyone within a multi-yard radius of him quite literally jumped. "She made several appeals to the alliance, and those high-brow arrogant Nordics rejected every single one!"

"Only because she asked for a specific kind of help that they couldn't afford," Commence delicately replied, clearly wanting to avoid a public hostile shouting-match with a respected wounded veteran of Scarlet's Red Revolution. "That is to say, financial and military help. I don't know if you all are aware of this, but the alliance is entering a severe depression, as we speak. The Nordic economy has been declining sharply for the past couple decades. So, how could they possibly spare us any ships, weapons or currency? They've got their own war to pay for. A war with *us*."

"No, their war's with the System, not us!" scarface growled.

Commence didn't miss a beat: "The System is all but dead, but *we're* not—and that makes us the only ones around, to clean up their mess. It's not fair, I know, but we still must do it. How do we do it? We help the alliance by helping ourselves; if our country is their problem, then that's the first thing we need to fix. But, we can't fix ourselves *by* ourselves—that's something that Scarlet July already tried, without success. We need help. And, the kind of help that I'm talking about won't cost the Nordics a thing."

"This all sounds rather fine and dandy," basket-lady interjected, "but, how the hell will we get those infrareds to lift a finger for us, regardless of what it does or doesn't cost them?"

As Commence grinned at her, I found myself wondering if basket-woman and teenage-scarface were audience-plants.

They sure seemed to raise a lot of crucial points at exactly the right times.

"We'll begin by writing a letter to the Nurian heads-of-state," Commence answered, "asking if we could send over a small delegation to study their governmental structure, collaborating with a couple of their legislators on a Conflagrian constitution."

There was yet another murmur—this time, of consent. Oh, how quickly the masses blew with the breeze! Clearly, the same fearful anxiety that made everyone rapidly bow to Principal Ence last July urged us now to follow President Commence into yet another unknown.

It was either that or collectively stand against the Multi-Source Enchant and his terrifying guerilla army.

We were crazy, sure, but not suicidal.

PRUNUS PERSICA

"We'd be fools to pass up this golden opportunity," I said to Gel Kylarks. A couple hours had passed since the Principal-turned-President delivered his bizarre speech. "Ence—or *Comm*ence, or whatever he calls himself, now—is essentially waving a white flag before us. He's actually asking the Reds to step into government. This is the big break we've been waiting for, since the civil war began. We've got to take it. Let's send one of our own to be an ambassador to Nuria, alongside the President."

Gel's arms folded across his chest. "*President*, my amputated foot," he spat. "He can call himself whatever the hell he likes; I still won't trust him. Moreover, working with the likes of him would be an outward expression of approval. Do we really want the Reds to openly condone a power-hungry madman who's proved himself capable of unspeakable monstrosities?"

"Gel, his case is no different than my wife's. We took Fair back, after she communed with the Red One's aura and consequently had a change of heart, didn't we?" Since her one and only vision of Scarlet, Fair started sabotaging the System's diffusion mission. She kept at it for about a decade... until Principal Ence effectively blew her cover by publicly denouncing her and flaying her within an inch of her life. It was a miracle that she escaped, after her torture session. I had a hunch that Scarlet's aura had something to do with that. "If anyone can awaken consciences, it's Scarlet July. I say, let's give Commence a chance the way we did Fair, all those ages ago."

"Like we really have a choice?" Gel snarled, dryly. "The boy deals in absolutes. If we don't take his phony olive branch, he'll use it to beat us to death." Sighing, he wheeled himself to the door. "Just don't count on me to spread the word to all our strongholds."

ASH ARGENT

The 'Son of Nations' was what folks started calling Commence, since his apologetic speech in the square. I wasn't sure what it meant, but it certainly sounded a whole lot better than some of the other names I'd heard people use behind his back since he took over.

"White isn't my color," Commence greeted me, first thing this morning. Since he lost his mother's robe in the Dunes, he'd taken to wearing the old colorless one he brought from Ichthyosis. "I'm an Iridescent and I should dress like one. That's the custom around here, to don your color. Why shouldn't the president do it, too?"

I told him that I didn't think it mattered what he wore; no matter what, he'd always stick out like a snowflake in a sandstorm, around here. Some people were just born to, regardless of how much they tried to fit in.

"But, I don't want to stand out, anymore," he replied. "I don't want to be different."

I grinned. "Yeh're a half-blood, coval'nt, iridesc'nt, triple-sourc'd ench'nt. Yeh're diff'rent whether 'r not yeh want teh be 'n' whether 'r not yeh dress like it."

Commence didn't smile back. For a moment, I saw a familiar dangerous spark in his citrus stare. I held my breath.

"Well... I won't give up that easily," he mustered, a little too cheerily. "I'll dye my robe auburn and blend in with everyone else, you'll see!"

I exhaled, gnawing the inside of my cheek. Tincture, I needed to be more careful. Just because the boy was playing the role of 'changed man' didn't mean that I should lower my guard and actually treat him like one. After all, his 'transformation' was mere days old.

The war between Ence and Commence had likely just begun.

FAIR GABARDINE

He was once place ahead of me, in line. It took me a moment to recognize him because, from behind, he looked like any other auburn kid, sent by his parents to fetch his family's daily ration. I held my breath as fear pricked my scalp. Why on Second Earth would the most powerful mage in Conflagrian history come out here *himself* for a scoop of fire? He owned the whole damn Pit, for Tincture's sake. I was about to quietly slip away, forfeiting my place, when the burly mage at my heels accidentally bumped into me, propelling me forward. As if in slow motion, Ence whirled on the balls of his feet, dropped his empty torch and caught me in his arms. His post rolled away, vanishing beneath countless pairs of trampling sandals.

"Hmm, I guess I should've used my hair instead, huh?" he laughed, face immediately taking on a (more) startling likeness to Scarlet. "Nordic habits die hard, I suppose. I'm not used to using *this* for everything." He rumpled his messy two-tone hair.

Wordlessly, I wrenched myself from his grasp.

"Good to see you, Fair Gabardine," he went on, sticking out his right hand like the Nordic he was.

Oh, hell no. Mr. Faux President wasn't about to pretend that everything between us was smooth as coconut milk. Without so much as a nod, I turned and fled. Heading nowhere fast, I ran until I was literally out of breath, skidding to a stop in a random alleyway. Back to a splintered wall, I slid to the ground, panting and quivering.

"Wait," his voice called from somewhere, "I need to talk to you!"

Holy Tincture, he followed me! I jumped back up, frantically glancing around for an escape-route.

"Fair Gabardine!" He appeared at the end of the chasm. "Please, wait!" He scurried toward me.

Instinctively, I drew my sword. His stopped dead in his tracks, the tip of my blade a mere inch from his right pupil. I held my breath, waiting for him to unleash a literal firestorm.

But, alas, several seconds passed… and nothing happened. He didn't even flinch or step back. Why?

"I saved your mother's aura," I dared to whisper, chest trembling. "I saved her from diffusion and you repaid me with my own blood. I'm a *Red*, you bastard." My arm shook, blade brushing his long red-black lashes. "I'm a Red like you'll never be. I don't care if you wear Scarlet's face and change your name and pretend to rally to us. I can see behind your phony façade; I know you stand for everything that Scarlet July gave her life to fight against!"

He still didn't move nor speak. He just continued to stand there, tormenting me with his gentle greenish gaze.

"Well, what did you want to tell me?" I raised my voice.

"Fair, please, calm down," he breathed. "Let's go sit somewhere and figure things out, okay?"

Was he insane? "I'm not going anywhere with you!"

"Okay, that's fine, we don't have to. We can talk, right here."

Right here, in this secluded alley. Great.

"So, talk," I hissed through clenched teeth. There was only one thing preventing me from thrusting my sword straight through his head, right now—when I peered into his lime-slice eyes, all I saw was Scarlet, staring back at me.

"First, would you put that thing down?" He blinked. "It's a bit distracting."

"*I said talk!*" I screamed. "First, Cease and now you! What did I do to deserve the Lechatelierite curse on my life?"

"Wait, what about Cease?" he asked.

I snorted. "Don't play dumb with me!"

His brows scrunched with what I might've construed as concern, if I didn't already know that he was the devil incarnate. "Fair, what did my father do to you?"

Seriously? "Typical Nordic mind-games," I spat, rage heating my hair. "You're just like him!"

He let out a grieved chuckle. "No, I'm not. Cease Lechatelierite was a far better man than me. He never took a moment's pleasure in the blood on his hands. Everything he did was for his country."

How dare he! "You have no idea what you're talking about," I seethed, terrible memories percolating my mind. "You have no idea what Cease was capable of!"

"Maybe, I don't," he sighed. "But, he still couldn't have been worse than me." His heartbroken words seemed to eradicate all the warmth from the sweltering air.

But, before I could respond, his hair whipped forth like a maroon snake, seizing my blade. Alarmed, I pulled the hilt with all my might, but his grip was impervious. To my great shock, he guided the sharp tip from his eye to his chest, burying it deeper and deeper into the folds of his robe until it struck flesh. He grunted as a patch of scarlet seeped through his clothes.

Horrified, I released the sword entirely. He let go too, the weapon falling noiselessly to the sand.

He looked down at the growing stain on his chest, almost impassively. "It'll heal," he whispered. Of course, it would—he was a hair mage. But, hair mages still felt pain, like the next man. Anyone else in his sandals would've been screaming and crying, right about now. "And, as this wound will heal," his chin lifted, "so will all of yours. Inside." With that, he stooped down, retrieved my sword and gently placed it in my hands. Then, he turned and walked away, slowly and without looking back.

I noticed a tiny scrap of parchment, impaled on the dirty blade, scrawled with, *21:00, Mage Castle.* I crumpled it up, furious. Who was he, to tell me what to do?

The question lingered in my brain for the rest of the day and well into the evening. Even as I found myself lacing up my sandals and hiking back across town, Prunus at my heels.

* * *

He opened up before I could even knock. A ruler who answered his own front door?

"Glad you decided to come," he greeted me, face looking particularly gaunt and eerie in the shadows.

I gave him a cold stare. "I don't forgive you," I said, voice hard.

He smiled. "Ah, but you're here, nonetheless."

"I'm not coming in." My arms folded. "If we're going to talk, come outside."

"Brought some backup?" He eyed the bushes behind me, where Prunus was indeed hidden.

I was silent.

"You do know that I can see in the dark, right?" He stepped out onto the porch. "And, that my primary advisor is a wing mage who just *might* be circling overhead, as we speak?"

"Ash Argent wouldn't raise a feather against me," I said.

"Ash Argent is *my* aide."

"Only because he's afraid of you. That's the sole reason you have any followers, to begin with." I began walking at a brisk pace. "So, why did you call me here?" I demanded, over my shoulder.

He tailed me, silver-jade eyes reflecting Alpha and Omega's melancholy glow.

"Why didn't you kill me today, Fair?" he asked, hands in his pockets. "We were concealed and alone. No one would've seen nor interfered." His voice dropped an octave as he added, "I wouldn't have resisted."

I looked away. "I know."

"So, why didn't you do it?"

"I-I don't know."

"Do you hate me, Fair?"

"I don't know," I repeated.

His gaze grazed the mud-brown sky. "Hate is a very strong word. Very definite. There's no 'maybe' in it. No grey area."

"Stop it," I interjected. "I'm not in the mood for your twisted military mind-games. Either tell me, right now, why you summoned me, or let me go."

He breezed on, undeterred: "If you have to wonder if you hate me, then you probably don't. If you did, you wouldn't have any doubts about it. You'd just know. Hate is decisive."

"Okay, fine." I threw my hands up. "I don't hate you. But, don't get too happy, because I sure as hell don't like you, either."

"Fair enough. By showing up tonight, you've already given me a chance that I don't deserve. Now, I want to know why."

"Why what?"

"Why don't you hate me?"

That impossible son-of-a—"Do you *want* me to?"

"Of course not. I just want to understand what's going on in that wise white-haired head of yours."

"So, you're psycho-analyzing me."

He shrugged. "I analyze everyone I deal with, all the time. So, do you. So, does everybody, really. That's what social consciousness is. Synthesizing information. Discriminating. Making judgments." He swallowed. "How are you judging me, right now?"

My lips pressed together.

"Come on, tell me: what do you think I am?"

What. Not who. There was a long pause. "Confused," I finally answered.

Another deafening silence.

"You call yourself a Red, correct?" he asked.

"I don't just *call* myself one, I *am* one," I replied, hotly. "As you'll—"

"As I'll never be. So, you've said. But, you were a System supporter for quite some time before you came back, am I right?"

In the instant, my stomach flipped. I was talking to the man who assassinated Principal Tincture with his own spectrum, after all. Commence may've been an evil bastard in his own right, but he still loathed the System with his every photon, which meant that he'd naturally be unsettled by my less-than-spotless record. But, his tone didn't sound particularly accusatory, now. He was simply stating a fact.

A fact I couldn't deny.

"I was," I admitted.

"Why?"

My head shook. "You're still a relatively new arrival on these shores, Commence. You didn't live through the ages upon ages of chaos that the rest of us did; you have no idea what we've been through. We were desperate, all of us. Desperate to end the madness. Without Scarlet, the Red Revolution fell apart faster than a crystalline immersed in a million gallons of UF. I couldn't fill her sandals—not without her spectral prowess nor perfect memory nor charisma nor overblown sense of sacrifice. So, like most people, I started to panic. I began to long for the way things were before the Crystal ended, before the civil war. Life was peaceful. We were happy. I started to see the mind-suppression as a sort of anesthetic, rather than a poison. I thought that maybe, our kind *needed* to be tamed by external forces. Maybe, mage society really *didn't* possess the self-control to live freely." My hair shuddered. "It wasn't long before the Tincture administration approached me, demanding that I find a way to diffuse Scarlet's aura. They already had a task force assembled—a task force they wanted me to lead. I figured that if the System was going to attack Scarlet's frequency no matter what, I might as well get involved, so I could find a way to achieve their ends while harming her the least. So, I cooperated with them. For ages. Then, one day, I had a vision. I spoke with Scarlet's aura, face-to-face. She neither screamed nor cursed at me, as I deserved. Instead, she humbled herself and begged, on her knees, for me to stop aiding and abetting the System. That was about a decade ago. She hasn't appeared to me since, and I don't expect her to. She told me she wouldn't. 'I'm sorry it has to end like this,' were her last words to me." I wiped my face in my sleeve. "Anyway," I swallowed the hobnail-egg growing in my throat, "for some time after that, Scarlet's words slowly burned in my heart, eroding my resolve. Then, late one night as I was alone in a System lab, I really did figure out how to diffuse her aura, completely. I sat there for hours, stricken, unsure what to do with the information. The next morning, I decided to take it to the Reds. I went to Prunus Persica and Gel Kylarks, the Red Leaders. I told them everything I knew. I told them that I wanted to go undercover for the Red Revolution from then on, sabotaging the System's work, purposefully leading their spectroscopers away from the answer I'd found. After some deliberation, they decided to trust me. I served as a double-agent from then on… until you came along and blew everything up. So, now, I openly live and work with the Reds."

Commence took in my crazy story without so much as a blink. "So, it was your encounter with my mother's aura that changed everything for you."

I nodded.

He gave me another freakishly-Scarlet-esque smile. "Like me."

I bit my lip.

"Your crimes aren't nearly as bad as mine, of course," he went on, "but, maybe, since you've experienced a similar transformation, you can find it in your heart to forgive me, one day."

Not as bad? Was he kidding? "Commence, I nearly restored the mind-suppression of the System," I breathed.

He grinned, wanly. "And, I *became* the System. I win."

I felt the words rise uncontrollably from my throat, like vomit: "But, I'm the reason Scarlet got killed in the first place, on December twenty-second of the ninety-fourth age."

He stopped walking. "No, you aren't." I could practically hear his heart pound. "Ambrek Coppertus assassinated her."

I hesitated.

"Ambrek Coppertus is responsible for her death," he repeated, more forcefully. "That's why I hunted him down. That's why his blood is on my hands."

"Y-yes, Ambrek Coppertus was the one who b-broke into Red Headquarters and took a sword to Scarlet's belly," I finally babbled. "But, I-I was the one who left her alone in our cabin that evening, in the first place—magicless, helpless and seven-months pregnant." My whole body quaked. "I didn't leave for work-related reasons, either… but, because I wanted to visit my then-boyfriend." Tears of guilt and shame dotted my lashes. "I c-could've protected Scarlet if I stayed home, that night. But, I didn't stay home. Because I put my personal life before her, before the entire revolution." I scrunched my lids, hiding my face behind my palms. "You have every right to hate me, Commence. The reason you're so screwed up is because you weren't raised properly. Because you never had Scarlet. Because of me."

I felt something warm touch my wrists. Gently, like a child. It was Commence. He slowly pulled my hands down.

"I don't hold anything against you," he whispered, face mere inches from mine. "You didn't know that Ambrek Coppertus was coming, that day. There was no way you could've guessed."

"I-I shouldn't have left Scarlet's side, no matter what." I hiccupped. "It was irresponsible of me. I wasn't doing my duty."

"It's hard to be on duty, nonstop, for eras," he said. "Believe me, I know. Sometimes, you slip up. Sometimes, you just need to take a break from it all. You're hardly a villain for wanting to spend a little down-time with a loved one." He regarded the black clouds, hanging overhead like sludge in a muddy stream. "Ash goes on a lot of random flights. I never stop him, even when he's got piles of unfinished work waiting. I understand why he does it. Sometimes, I wish I were a wing mage too, so I could also fly away like that. When I was a kid, I lived in Alcove City with… a pilot… for a short while, and whenever he started strapping up unannounced, loading nothing in the cargo bay, hastily calling my babysitter, I knew that he didn't have a delivery to run, he just needed to escape for a bit." Commence ran a finger along the edge of his sharp Cease-like jaw. "Sometimes, I wish I could take off this face and be normal for a while. Sometimes, I wish I were never born a multi-sourced enchant, bearing the burdens of history's two biggest troublemakers." He sighed through closed lips. "But, like my pilot friend often quoted from Scripture, 'to whom much is given, much is required.' I used to get angry when he said that, claiming that I *wasn't* given anything. It took me ages to realize that isn't true. My parents are gone, but they didn't leave me with nothing. I have more gifts than most, and I'm meant to use them to help people."

I stared at him for a long while. "You really have changed."

His grin returned, but this time, it had a dangerous edge. A little too much Cease in it. "It's tough, but yeah, these days, I'm trying hard not to be *so screwed up*."

He both bowed and held out his hand like the confused covalent half-blood he was. And, this time, I took it.

* * *

"I'd like to send two ambassadors to Alcove City," Commence said, getting down to business.

"Only two?" I asked.

He nodded. "As Ursula Le Guin—a famous First Earth writer—once said, 'Two is a delegation. Three is an invasion.' We mustn't forget that Conflagria doesn't exactly have a pretty track-record, when it comes to international relations."

"The *System* doesn't, you mean. We aren't the System."

"Try telling that to the Nordics. Not to mention, increasing the number of cooks in the kitchen would compound the potential for disagreement." Cooks in the kitchen? What a weird expression. Must've been a Nurian idiom or something. "The document we draw up will have to be revised and ratified by many hands, of course, but we can't have a huge crew working on the initial draft. In American history, the entire convention at Philadelphia signed the Declaration that only Thomas Jefferson wrote."

Tincture, he sure loved spouting First Earth references. Showoff. "Who should we send over?"

"Well, me, of course," his hand waved, "because I know the language and am already fairly familiar with how a democracy functions, since I spent most of my life in one—or, two, actually."

"But, you're the Princi—President. Conflagria can crumble if left unsupervised for a second. Who'll take the reins, while you're gone? You don't have a vice-president."

He smirked. "That's because I'm not really a president. I'm still a dictator, only under a different title. That's what we're working to change." Aha, so, he was aware that he still had absolute power; he only pretended otherwise. Interesting. "I'd like to appoint your husband, Prunus Persica, in my place, while I'm away. Of course, I'd want to leave the Reds in charge."

Of course? "I'll let him know," I agreed, simply. "So, who else will go with you to Nuria?"

"Another Red, of course." There was that 'of course,' again. He certainly didn't want me to doubt his new loyalties, not for a moment. "How about you?"

"Me?"

"Why not?"

"Well, for starters, I don't speak Nurian."

"Does anyone, around here? You're one of the rare few who speaks Ichthyothian. Nurian isn't so different—I can teach you."

"Whoa, hold the torch! I'm not Scarlet; I can't just drink in a new language overnight."

"Nobody said anything about overnight. I'll give you a couple weeks."

"A couple *weeks?*"

"If you don't learn it in time, I'll just translate for you at the meetings."

We were getting way ahead of ourselves. "Okay, language thing aside, why do you want *me?* Why don't you take someone you're more accustomed to working with?"

"Like who?"

I shrugged. "I don't know. Your primary advisor."

"Ash?" Commence's enormous eyes rolled. "I can't take Ash."

"Why not?"

His upper lip twitched, as though holding in a laugh. "It'd give him a nervous breakdown, that's why. He doesn't have the mind for this sort of thing. I only made him my advisor in the first place because I owe him... and I felt sorry for him."

Ouch! "Um, isn't Ash flying cover for us, right now?" I hissed.

"Yeah, so?"

"*So*, you just insulted him!"

It was his turn to shrug. "He's high up; he can't hear us."

"Are you sure?"

"No, but what does it matter? He already *knows* that he's not a suitable candidate, so—"

"Just stop!" For Tincture's sake! "Quit rubbing salt in the wound, will you?"

"Could we just forget about Ash for a moment, please?" Commence cut across me. "Are you or aren't you interested in coming with me to Nuria?"

I gnawed the inside of my cheek. "Don't you have other advisors? I mean, ones who actually *like* politics?"

He snorted. "Pha Rynx likes politics, alright. A little too much. I think he's still in denial about my decision to forfeit the throne and try for democracy. And, as for my third advisor, I dismissed *her* a while ago, when she tried to seduce me."

A bumpkin, a power-hungry lackey and a whore. "You've surrounded yourself with fine mages," I muttered.

"Now, you see why I came to you?"

"Way to make me feel like a last resort."

"You're not my last resort, you're the first one I asked. So, are you in?" he demanded, throat magic like a hot sword in the ear.

"Yes, I'm in," I found myself saying. "Just don't ask me to be your vice-president, come election season."

"Don't worry; I have no intention to run, in the first place."

ASH ARGENT

Commence was struggling. It wasn't super obvious to onlookers or anything, but I knew him well enough to tell that something was seriously wrong, pretty much all the time. Something on the inside. Like his new self hadn't settled in, quite yet. Like his old self was still lurking in the shadows, waiting to ambush him the moment he let his guard down. He constantly told everyone to treat him like an equal, but when folks actually went ahead and *did* it—interrupting his sentences, disagreeing with his opinions, helping themselves to food or fire before he had his fill, and so forth—he got all anxious and broody. While he didn't totally flip-out in public anymore, he still tended to get a bit surly and snappish. And, even with a smile on his face, he was still liable to utter little underhanded remarks that subtlety and maliciously hurt you like a parchment-cut. Take last week, for example: when he got Fair Gabardine to agree to go with him to Nuria and I asked if there was anything I could do to help them prep, he laughed and patted my wings and said something along the lines of, 'Oh, Ash, I wouldn't want to make you crazy with all this political mumbo-jumbo.' It was true that I didn't have a single political feather in my wingspan, but those gestures and words still rubbed me the wrong way, maybe because I didn't like being petted like a baby scabrous or talked-down-to like a weak-minded simpleton.

Lots of times, Commence didn't respond when people called to him. I stood right in front of him yesterday and yelled, 'C'mmence!' yet he didn't even glance my way. So, then, I muttered, 'Oh, Ants,' under my breath and he looked up and chirped, 'Yes?' Later that same night, when I called him 'Ence'—deliberately, that time—he got all mad and went off about how he'd moved on from 'that devil' and was somebody else, now. I personally believed that he was still on the border between good and bad, and I sure didn't want to be the one to poke the sleeping hobnail. After thinking about it for a while, I figured that maybe he was having difficulty responding to 'Commence' because he wasn't used to *being* Commence. After all, if everyone suddenly started calling me 'Aqua' or something, I probably wouldn't instinctively react, either. Ash was my name and silver was my identity and nothing could ever change that. I knew who I was—my strengths and weaknesses and preferences and fears—which was a whole lot more than Commander-slash-Principal-slash-President Ence-slash-Commence could say about himself, any day.

This morning, out of nowhere, Pha suggested that we give Commence a nickname that indicated his newly-emerged colors. "Why should the President of *Conflagria* have a *Nordic* name?" he said, incredulously. "It's demeaning." So, I asked him why he thought foreign names were disgraceful and he couldn't really come up with a good answer, so that was the end of that.

FAIR GABARDINE

It was nerve-wracking, to work so closely with Commence, every day for hours on end. I couldn't bring myself to meet his eye for more than a few seconds at a time. But, if he noticed my flinches, which I'm sure he did, he didn't say anything about it.

Anyway, he and I wrote to the Nurian congress, asking if we could send over a couple ambassadors to study their democratic structure and get help with drafting a Conflagrian constitution. Commence brazenly signed it with '*President Commence July Lechatelierite*,' which turned out to be everything he needed to get their attention and, ultimately, their invitation.

Commence was boyishly excited by the good news, flailing his arms and bouncing like a little kid who just got the toy he'd always wanted for Summer Solstice Day. In their reply, the Nurians alerted us of a very useful bit of new exorbitantly-expensive technology: ear-implant translators. The entire government only owned three of them, one of which they were willing to lend to me, during our stay. While that meant Commence would still have to verbally translate everything *I* said, it was a huge leg-up nonetheless. I was tremendously relieved that I wouldn't have to swallow a new language by our departure date, January seventeenth.

We were scheduled to begin drafting on January twenty-fifth. Until then, Commence and I would spend eight full days auditing various governmental proceedings, like senate meetings, to 'observe a democracy in action' and gain a more practical sense of what we'd be instituting, back home.

So, the week came and went, and Commence and I got a sense, alright. A sense that the Nordics didn't have a clue how to run their own country. It was a miracle that anything ever got accomplished. I found it hard to believe that Nuria was supposed to be the superpower of the world. I initially thought that issues raised in senatorial sessions would get resolved in hours or days, but soon came to see that deliberations on a single topic could literally last ages. Not to mention, congress wasted loads of time on procedural formalities, and pomp and circumstance. And, bickering. Lots and lots of petty bickering. Dozens of bills—ranging from ridiculous to reasonable—were proposed but hardly any of them were allowed to proceed to stage two. It was a vicious cycle—potential legislation got introduced, mutilated, argued, mutilated some more, argued again, then ultimately killed.

"Well, *that* was about as productive as trying to extinguish the entire Fire Pit with a stream of piss," I muttered to Commence as the two of us left our gazillionth meeting about an idiotic water-rationing bill that wasn't worth the breath it took the senator to suggest. "Promise me that our democracy will be more efficient."

At this, I expected Commence to get fired up, bellowing something like, 'Of course, *my* government will be a hell of a lot swifter! That rep from Seaview was so pig-headed, I was rearing to set his speech ablaze, literally!' But, instead, he surprised me with, "I can promise no such thing, Fair."

I stopped dead. "What?"

His palms pressed against his tired eyes. "Their methods may seem slow and cumbersome, but in the end, they work."

"But, what about that dumb rationing bill?"

"Exactly. What didn't deserve to pass... didn't pass. What needed to happen, happened."

"Yeah, but, if it took *that* long to dismiss an idea *that* bad..."

"Well, I'd expect pretty much everything to take forever in Nurian congress because of their size. Conflagria wouldn't need half as many regional reps, so things should move along a little quicker for us. But, only a little."

"Seems to me that their system is designed to zap absolutely everything. How many bills actually become law?"

"There needs to be a tight filter; you see how much trash crops up."

"No kidding. I mean, Nuria isn't a desert or anything, so why restrict water usage? Why would any primate with a brain—let alone a scholar with a fancy degree—suggest anything so absurd?"

"Easy. Someone paid him to." What? Was he pulling my leg? "No, I'm not joking," he answered my blank stare.

"Someone *paid* him to?" I gaped. "That's not against the law?" If *that* was permissible in a democracy, maybe I really didn't have a clue what democracy was.

Commence shrugged. "Democracies may seem impeccable, compared to anything Conflagria has experienced. But, in truth, they are far from perfect. Corruption and grey areas exist in every political environment. It's unavoidable."

"So, anybody can just pay a legislator to say whatever they want?" I breathed.

"*Technically*, it's illegal to bribe your bill into congress. But, there are loopholes."

"Like what?"

"Like giving a generous *donation* to a political party, then making it clear to them what you *wish* their reps would pursue."

My jaw dropped. "You're not serious."

"I am."

"But, isn't that the same thing as bribery?"

"Sure is."

"And, no one's realized that? No one's trying to put an end to it?"

"Well, what could anyone really do? Make it illegal to donate? That's how parties get a crucial chunk of their funds. If donations weren't allowed, the whole structure would collapse."

"Well, we'll definitely ban it in Conflagria!" I cried, hotly.

"We most certainly will not. Conflagrian political parties are going to need resources as much as Nuria's do."

I rounded on him. "What?"

"Come on, Fair, there's no real way around it. Without contributions, parties would have to rely *entirely* on the wealth of their members and candidates, which isn't exactly fair, either."

I looked away, suddenly consumed with disgust for everything and anything related to politics. "It's like I've always told Scarlet: I'm a spectroscoper and a warrior, not a politician. Politicians are the leeches of the earth. Nothing but liars and hypocrites, all of them."

"You're speaking to a national leader, thank you very much," Commence muttered.

I smirked. "I meant no offense to you, Mr. Dictator-Who-Pretends-To-Be-President."

"None taken, Mrs. Political-Ambassador-On-Assignment-As-We-Speak."

Oh, how I wanted to whip a lock of hair across his smarmy face. "I'm only here because you dragged me."

"Your husband is a politician too, you know."

"No, Prunus is the Red Leader. He's military."

"Well, I used a military coup to take the throne, and I'm certainly not the first person in history to do so. Almost all the dictators to walk First Earth were warriors, at some point in time."

"So, what? Are you really trying to equate slimy, selfish politicians with soldiers who're willing to die for their country?"

"No, I'm just saying that the two jobs can be tightly intertwined. The Red Revolution is far from being a purely-militaristic operation, anyway. Your goals are political. And, what's your dear husband up to, right this minute? Filling my sandals. Governing. That's what the Reds wanted all along, isn't it?"

My arms folded. "Prunus is *nothing* like the slippery suits we've been watching, all week."

Commence's eyes glinted with Cease-like ice that chilled my every photon. "Well, we came here to learn from those *slippery suits*, because you sure as hell don't see *this* nation using supernatural inhumane means to forcibly restrain the minds of its masses while systematically executing the weak and elderly in a giant pit of fire. The Nurians may not be flawless, but we obviously still have a lot to learn from them, so you better drop that self-righteous, all-Nordics-are-scum attitude before I discharge you as my partner and send you back to Conflagria on your ass."

My eyes narrowed. "You wouldn't."

"If you think I wouldn't, then you're giving my new self way too much credit," he chuckled. "I'm a filthy dictator who won't hesitate to use every last weapon in my arsenal to beat you into submission, the moment you quit cooperating with my agenda."

He said this laughingly, but I had a hunch that he wasn't joking. Not entirely.

"You only pretend to be a changed mage, but you're really the same son-of-a-scabrous who washed up on Conflagria's shores last age, you know."

"Believe me, I know," he growled. "But, do you realize that whenever you call me things like that, you're also insulting your dead best friend?"

"Excuse me, sir," an over-dressed Nurian congressman interjected in his language, "but, are you President Commence July Lechatelierite?" He gave us a great, big, gooey politician's grin, sticking out his right hand.

Immediately, all surliness vanished from Commence's countenance as he smiled a smile as bogus and vomit-inducing as the senator's. "Yes, I am, Representative Ekaf Sugob, sir," he answered, undoubtedly dazzling the man with his instant name-recollection. Sugob likely had no idea that Commence's memory was perfect, so he must've felt flattered by the attention that the Conflagrian President apparently paid him during the sessions, one man out of a hundred. Oh, how I hated Commence at that moment, hated how he could just willingly turn on his artificial charisma, instantly concealing his true inner vileness. What an actor he was. What a *politician*.

As Commence and I walked with Sugob, I tried hard not to let my face betray how peeved I was by their phony pleasantries and white-toothed vote-for-me grins.

While Sugob busied himself for a moment with his handkerchief, Commence turned to me and whispered in Conflagrian, "What the hell's wrong with you? Quit *glaring* for heaven's sake; you're making the guy uncomfortable!"

"I'm not *glaring*; I just don't see any reason to smile like a used wagon salesman," I answered, acidly.

Commence looked like he wanted to toss me out the window with his hair. "Well, if you don't find a reason to smile *right* now, I'll give you a couple reasons to cry, when we get back home. And, yes, Fair, I *do* mean every word I'm saying. Literally."

"Bastard," I hissed.

His glassy eyes rolled. "My parents were married, you know. So, technically, I'm not a—"

"My apologies for the holdup, sir, ma'am." Sugob was apparently done blowing his nose. "I'll be meeting with you on the twenty-fifth, to begin drafting your constitution. We'll be in room seven-two-five," my translator buzzed.

"Wait a minute, *you're* the one who volunteered to help us?" I blurted in Conflagrian, horrified.

Sugob looked at me, then at Commence. "Excuse me, but what did your partner just ask me?"

"Oh, nothing," Commence quickly replied, smile unwavering despite the intense discomfort in his citrus stare. "She was talking to me."

"No, Commence, I was addressing the senator," I declared—in Ichthyothian this time, so the language's similarity to Nurian would enable Sugob to gather some semblance of my meaning.

"Could you excuse us for a moment?" Commence pulled me aside. "Fair, what's gotten into you? Conflagria's future literally depends on this man!"

"If that's the case, we might as well pack up and head out now, because we're doomed."

"What do you have against him?"

"I don't know... I just... don't feel right, about him. Something's off."

Commence exhaled through his nostrils. "Will you get over the fact that he's a politician, already? We're all politicians, here. Even you."

"No, it's not that. It's... I don't know... I can't quite put my finger on it."

Commence scowled. "So, he's obnoxiously cheery and has a strange accent. So, what?"

Dependent on my translator implant, I wasn't aware that Sugob had an accent. How strange. "Why does he have an accent?"

Commence shrugged. "I don't know, maybe it's regional or something. Some Conflagrians have different accents than *us*, after all. Ash talks like a country boy because he spent most of his upbringing in Red strongholds south of Ardor Village. And, Nuria's way bigger than Conflagria—there's even more room for variation."

"Regional? He represents Alcove Province. His Nurian shouldn't sound any different than yours."

Commence chewed his lip. "Maybe, he was raised in a different province, before moving here?"

Why on earth was Commence so ignorant about the linguistic diversity of his own homeland? He spent the first several ages of his life, right here. Did he pass that time locked in scabrous cage, or what? "If that's the case, then I want to know *which* province he's originally from," I insisted.

Commence nodded.

We returned to Sugob. After about fifteen more minutes of fluffy chatter, Commence managed to slip in a question about his accent.

Sugob's plastic grin grew wider—a feat I hadn't thought possible. "I grew up in northern Nuria, in Pola Province. Pola's a beautiful area—cold and snowy—not to mention, heavily influenced by Ichthyothian culture since the sudden burst of immigration in the nineties, following the Spectral Hurricane."

"Really? Your accent doesn't sound very Ichthyothian," Commence commented.

"You know how Ichthyothian sounds?" the senator inquired.

Commence blinked. "Of course. I served in the Diving Fleet for almost a decade."

Shock flashed across Sugob's wrinkled face, though only for a moment. "Oh, yes, of course. I knew that."

"Being a high political figure, I sure hope you did." Commence's tone was playful, but I could tell from the flicker in his silver-jade eyes that he was starting to grow irritated and suspicious. "On the other hand, the Trilateral Committee made sure that the Conflagrian System stayed in the dark about my command, for security reasons. After my father's service and all the attention it drew, the Nordic alliance made a concentrated effort to conceal from the enemy the identities of all its high-ranking combat-active officers."

"Yes, of course," Sugob squeaked.

"So, as I was saying, your accent doesn't sound very Ichthyothian."

The man's eyes tracked about. "Well, of course, it wouldn't be *purely* Ichthyothian; the cultural blend throughout the area created something new."

"Huh, I wasn't aware that Ichthyothian presence was still so prevalent, up there," Commence smoothly countered. "I thought the boom only lasted through the mid-nineties, before the onset of mass reverse-migration. I lived in Pola when I attended the Nurian Diving Academy, roughly a decade ago; I didn't perceive much lingering Ichthyothian influence, even back then."

"Oh, well," Sugob's hand waved, "of course a *military academy* would be isolated from the regional culture. Men from all over the country go to that school. How many northerners were actually part of the student body?"

"Actually, the vast majority of the student body was, and still is, made up of northerners," Commence answered, placidly. "Those from colder climates are more likely to pass the entrance exams."

"Yes, of course, of course," Sugob mumbled.

"So, when did you move down here? I imagine that congress enforces certain residency requirements."

"Yes, they do indeed require a five-age minimum, which is exactly how long I've been here. I was elected, just last term."

Commence glanced around. "Where's your partner?" Every Nurian province had two reps.

"He's on vacation."

Commence looked concerned. "I was told that Mrs. Gabardine and I would be working with two senators, not one."

"You will. Mr. Dink Innoc of Vita Province will be joining us for the drafting. He's newly elected, as well."

I was disgusted. We asked Nuria for help with something as serious as creating our nation's first democratic constitution, and they gave us two *rookies?*

Typical Nordic elitist bastards.

COMMENCE JULY LECHATELIERITE

"President Lechatelierite, sir, it's an honor! The Conflagrian Multi-Source Enchant, himself!" Senator Dink Innoc greeted me, this morning—the twenty-fifth. Unlike Sugob, his cheeriness and enthusiasm didn't seem forced. He was genuinely glad to meet me. But, he was a bit *too* awestruck for my liking. *The* Multi-Source Enchant, he called me. Not *a* multi-sourced enchant. He attributed me the prophetic title.

"It's not all that great or glamorous, believe me," I said, honestly.

I found that, on a day-to-day basis, having a boatload of magic at my disposition actually wasn't all that advantageous. I hardly needed to access the full measure of my powers, especially since I was no longer engaging in regular combat nor torturing people for sport. During my days as Diving Commander and Conflagrian Principal, I pined for spectral prowess, dreaming of all the terrible things I'd do with it. But, now that I finally had it, there was no real use for it.

After another minute or so of pleasantries, we all settled down, Fair and I on one side of the table, Innoc and Sugob on the other. A holographic computer terminal sat between us. Time to begin.

Immediately, Innoc began clicking away, looking up Nuria's own constitution as well as that of Ichthyosis and a few democratic First Earth nations, like the United States of America.

"Examples to emulate are a-plenty," he said, getting right down to business. "But, Conflagrian culture is quite distinct, so a carbon-copy approach obviously won't work. While using these documents as springboards, we need to focus on a couple key questions like: what does *magekind*, in particular, need to thrive? What would the nation of Conflagria require that these other constitutions wouldn't already provide? How can we alter and tweak these examples to satisfy those specific demands?" I was liking Innoc more by the minute. He was sharp and to the point. Things would likely go fairly smoothly with him, if only we didn't also have to deal with—"Mr. Sugob," Innoc innocently appealed to his fellow senator, "what have you observed, in regards to the unique requisites of mage society? I think the two of us should give our guests some outside perspectives before we dive into their own ideas and perceptions."

Sugob, as overdressed as he was yesterday, bowed his head and cleared his throat. Sure, it was wintertime and all, but I thought that three dress-shirts and a woolen suit-jacket was a little extreme.

"It's clear to me that Conflagria has always had a serious issue with control," he spoke up.

No duh. "Right you are, sir," I agreed, resisting the urge to roll my eyes. What a relief it was, that the man could see the obvious. What profound legislative expertise he was already bestowing upon us all. "The island has a lengthy dictatorial history, my own reign included—"

"No, that's not what I meant, Mr. President," Sugob cut me off. "I meant that magefolk strike me to be… well, let's just say, in need of some containment."

Oh, boy.

"Sir?" Fair croaked.

"Correct me if I'm wrong, sir, ma'am," Sugob went on, "but, since the onset of rebellion nearly two decades ago, your country has experienced continuous chaos, has it not?"

Fair whispered to me in Conflagrian, "So, this guy's a bigot *and* a racist? A Nordic-supremacist who thinks that anyone with a visible aura is a feral hobnail in need of whipping?"

Sugob's gaze flickered for a moment, perhaps angered by Fair's tone, since he obviously couldn't understand her meaning. He peered at me, questioningly.

"My partner would like you to elaborate," I pretended to translate.

Sugob's stare scoured Fair's face. "It's simple. There was order until *they* disrupted it."

"They?"

"The violent rabble-rousers who call themselves the Red Revolution."

Fair's hair twitched.

Sugob reached for the terminal and pulled up the System Syllabus, transcribed into Nurian. "As long as we're looking for examples to imitate, I think we should consider this one, as well. Especially since it has already proved operable in your society and culture."

"I'm sorry, sir, but I don't think that's a very good idea," I replied, tone ever-so-patient. I wished I could control my facial expressions as well as I could my voice. I wondered if I looked as angry as I felt. My scalp certainly was hot. "There never was true order, under the System. What they provided was only an illusion." Laying a hand on the keyboard, the hovering document vanished.

"I concur with Mr. Lechatelierite," Innoc said. "The System never actually achieved peace in their homeland, it only appeared to."

Undeterred, Sugob flicked the projection back on. "Well, if it walks like a scabrous and squawks like a scabrous…"

Wait, did the Nurian senator just use a Conflagrian idiom?

"Appearance and reality aren't the same thing," Fair breathed, incredulous.

I was halfway through with translating when Sugob erupted, "But, if something *appears* a certain way, *feels* a certain way and *functions* a certain way, then by all means, is it not so?"

I stared. "Senator, I wasn't done relaying Mrs. Gabardine's statement."

"You didn't need to; it was obvious, what she was about to say! You're so predictable, all of you!"

"You racist bastard," Fair spat.

Innoc—appearing rather intensely embarrassed by his compatriot's pigheadedness—held his coffee mug with trembling hands as he spouted, "Sirs, ma'am, please, let's just—"

"No, Fair, this man isn't a racist," I suddenly declared. "Or, should I say, this *mage*."

Innoc's mug abandoned its trek to his lips.

I reached across the table, right through the hologram, and seized the imposter's collar with both hands, forgetting to use my hair, whose grip far out-muscled my fingers, any day. "Northern accent, huh?" I roared, shaking him by his many layers. "You did a fine job concealing your aura, *System mage*," I seethed. "You may've fooled us longer, if only it weren't for your complete and utter ignorance of the needs of our kind."

* * *

In the end, Fair and I worked only with Innoc. Things went remarkably smoothly; the young senator's rookie detachment from the political system made him an invaluable asset. Yet to be (too) corrupted by the political game, he had his own ideas to share, rather than just parroting 'the way things always were.'

Which was why I made sure our draft included strict term-limits for all political offices. As Ash would say, gotta keep 'em fresh.

COMMENCE JULY LECHATELIERITE

February arrived by the time we finished drafting. Finally, the Conflagrian Constitution—and, two rather exhausted ambassadors—was ready to go home and face the masses. The night before our departure on February seventh, I decided to take Fair sightseeing around the city. Since arriving at the Bay River Hotel last month, we hadn't managed to snag a single second of free time; it was all work, work, work. Until now.

It was astonishing, how the capital of the democratic world regressed since I was last here. There were less shops, less shoppers, less merchandise, less flivvers and more homeless on the street, not to mention more dirt and grime covering everything like a grisly grey film. Worst of all, though, were the faces of the passerby. Hungry. Tired. Sick. Desperate for the exile to end.

Hold on, everyone, I thought. Isolationism was my next target. I just needed to finish scaling *this* mountain before I could drum up the strength for another.

I guided Fair all around, carefully avoiding the side of town where I grew up. I didn't want to face those familiar sights, again—the orphanage I loathed, the grade-schools I briefly attended, the little complex where Nurtic lived... Nurtic himself. I swallowed. Nurtic's face, a decade older, scarred by my warpath.

"Hey," Fair touched my arm, "you okay?"

Damn my readable face. "Yep," I croaked. My former Ichthyothian comrades knew about the adoption, but I hadn't told any mage but Ash about it, and I wanted to keep things that way. Fair once spent several months hiding out with Nurtic, day-in and day-out. Fair respected him and would hate me if she knew how I'd treated him. Pretty much *everybody* who got to know Nurtic wound up caring about him. And, until recently, I never understood why. Blinded by rage and self-pity, I never appreciated the fact that I had one of the most decent human beings on the planet looking after me, loving me like his own son.

"Are you sure?" Fair insisted.

It would be so easy. I was already here, in Alcove City. I could just go up to his apartment right now, ring his doorbell and apologize for all the hell I'd put him through. And, I could finally thank him for finding me at age six and uncovering the truth about my identity. And, I could fill him in about my current endeavor to reform Conflagria, doing everything in my power to honor my mother's legacy. He'd be so proud.

No, I was being stupid. Nurtic probably didn't even live around here, anymore. That miserable apartment probably belonged to someone else, by now. Who knew, maybe Nurtic moved out of town, entirely. Or, at least, that's what I found myself hoping, because I sure didn't want to run into him on accident. Alcove City was enormous and crowded, so the chances of that were obviously quite slim, but I still found myself cautiously scanning every corner, chest tight with paranoia.

"Commence, you're acting really strange," Fair commented.

Shrugging, I grunted.

"Do you want to go back to the hotel?"

"Yeah, sure. I'm getting tired."

In truth, I was far too wired for rest. But, I liked the idea of staying inside, right now. I was relieved that our departure was scheduled for the crack of dawn, tomorrow. I couldn't wait to get out of here.

That's right, Commence, I thought. Run away.

* * *

It was morning, and Fair and I were waiting in the hotel lobby for our pilot to arrive. I had the couch while she had the armchair.

"It was very kind of the Nurian government to sponsor our stay," I commented, "since they hardly have funds to spare."

The inn, which was far from nice, was nearly void of guests; domestic tourism was at an all-time low, due to the economic depression. It was a miracle that this place—dirty, smoky, dimly lit—wasn't out-of-business, by now.

Fair snorted, eyes closed. "What they call depression on these shores would count as luxury, back home. Nobody here has the right to complain about a damn thing."

I shrugged, silently disagreeing with the absoluteness of her statement. By now, I'd learned that argument with Fair was an extreme sport—only attempt if you had endless patience and free time.

"I guess the Nordics think that we're a worthy investment, since *our* reform will hopefully help solve many of *their* problems, in the long run," I said.

"Hopefully," she echoed, inspecting her sandals, "in the long run. Nice optimism."

"I'm being realistic."

"I know. I actually like that, about you. You never set your expectations too high. Scarlet, on the other hand..." Fair sighed. "Scarlet always divided her attention a dozen ways, trying to solve every problem in the world, all at once. But, you? You prioritize, and you're in no hurry."

"Hey, I'm young."

"So was she." There was a pause. Then, still studying her toes, Fair surprised me by chuckling, "The funny thing is, you're plowing through your to-do's a lot faster than her, though you're not as hung-up on a tight timeline."

I shrugged, again. "I wasn't always this patient, believe me. After several ages of agitated haste, I've finally come to see that unrealistic deadlines generate nothing but stress and waste. So, nowadays, I just set some reasonable objectives and let things run their natural course. A good goal is worth all the time it takes to get there, as long as we get there. Right?"

Fair smiled sadly, at the floor. "Oh, Commence, if only you were born a couple decades earlier. How much grief you could've spared us all."

For some reason, it cut me deeply, to hear her say that. Her words were meant to be complimentary, but I wasn't encouraged by them. Maybe, because it almost sounded like she was saying that she wished Scarlet never existed, that Second Earth would've been better off if I took her place in history. It was like she believed that all Scarlet ever did was leave me a mess to clean. Nothing could be further from the truth. When I arrived in Conflagria, eager to instill change, I found a revolution already in place, complete with a well-formulated ideology and thousands of willing minds. I didn't have to go through the tremendous effort of *organizing* all of that in the first place, because Scarlet already did. And, in doing so, she paved the way for my current work.

I wanted to tell this to Fair—tell her that she had no right to dismiss the labors of Scarlet's hands, because Scarlet's shoulders were what I now stood upon. But, I didn't have the energy to engage in a debate with her. Not now.

Fair sifted her fingers through her long hair, gaze shifting from her ankles to mine. "Since the nineties, the whole world's been spinning backwards. It feels weird when something *positive* actually happens. I almost don't know how to process it."

I nodded. "Like the sudden emergence of my aura. It literally surfaced overnight. One day, I just woke up with full access to my three sources."

"So, I've heard," Fair murmured, still staring at our feet, which was strange considering that neither of us were foot mages.

"You're a genius spectroscoper," I piped. "I've been meaning to ask you about that, for a while. How's it possible, to go from infrared to iridescent, so quickly?"

Her head shook. "I honestly have no idea. As far as I know, your case is unique. A couple Nordics have changed their wavelengths before—your father and Nurtic Leavesleft—but, neither of them did it overnight."

She fell quiet then, concerning herself with hands-free hair-braiding. Her locks autonomously parted into three thick white ropes that wove together like writhing snakes. It was oddly mesmerizing to watch, like a ritualistic dance performed by a pale octopus. Octopuses dancing. What an odd image; I stifled a laugh. Fair gave me a confused glance, clearly wondering what on earth was going on in my head. I thought of telling her, but decided against it because I didn't know how she'd react. She was always so sensitive, so quick to misunderstand and extend her claws. Especially around me. She seemed to tolerate me well enough by now, but something about my presence definitely still disturbed her. She hardly ever looked me in the face. Not even during important work-related conversations. I was a very visual person—I liked solid eye-contact, whenever I spoke with someone. So, Fair's evasiveness always bothered me.

"I can't wait to go home," she now breathed, laying her cheek on the puffy armrest.

Home. I curled up on the couch, folding my legs to my chest. Fair wanted to go home. Where was home, for me? I grew up here in Alcove City, but it never felt like home, even when it was the only place I knew. Likewise, Icicle Base wasn't my home; I hated it there, hated how every man I'd dealt with was a mindless tool of the Trilateral Committee. Civilian Aventurine City certainly didn't welcome me with open arms, either. The entire Ichthyothian culture felt so cold, so inhospitable. Conflagrian society was diverse and quick to accept any quirk, but I doubted I could ever walk those sandy shores again without feeling haunted by my past mistakes. Did I belong nowhere, then? I supposed. Because, I believed, for somewhere to be 'home,' it had to be more than just familiar. It had to be a place of comfort. Shelter. Refuge. A stronghold where you could unwind and momentarily forget about the scars on your heart and the weight of the world on your shoulders. All my life, I was never able to relax, even before I knew whose legacy I bore. I was always on my guard, always fighting. Always watching. What I really needed was a place to shut my eyes and actually *not* see anything, if only for a moment.

The revolving doors spun. Our pilot was here, to take us 'home.'

ASH ARGENT

The masses gathered at the Pit to witness the homecoming of the President and his fellow ambassador, bearing the Conflagrian Constitution. The people were so eager, *so* enthusiastic, I had a hunch that Commence could probably bring back a scrap of parchment covered in scribbles and the document would *still* pass with flying colors.

But, alas, that wasn't what Commence delivered. For once, he wound up actually keeping his word to his constituency. Upon arrival, he recited the whole thing aloud, right there in the square, while Fair handed out copies printed on smooth white Nordic paper. I was no politician, but everything the boy said sure sounded good to me—like something that might've come from Scarlet's own mouth. When he was done, the crowd erupted into cheers and applause that literally lasted for hours.

* * *

The Red Revolution was no longer necessary. There was nothing to rebel against, anymore. But, the Reds still had plenty to do. Soon, they would nominate a candidate for the upcoming presidential election—a candidate other than Commence because, as far as the kid was concerned, he was reaching the end of his first and last 'term.' The opposition to the Red Party—there had to be one because, as Commence explained, democracies had to achieve 'majority rule with minority rights'—became known by the complimentary color.

And so, as the Red and Green parties gathered support and reached for the nation's reigns, Commence was free to slowly recede from the domestic stage in favor of world affairs. It was noted by many how he worked to fix Conflagria first *before* attempting to dabble in the international arena, unlike Scarlet July.

Commence also differed from his mother in another profound way: he paid no mind to the prophecy. He didn't seem to care about figuring out what it meant; he just did things for Conflagria and for Second Earth because he had the means and he wanted to. But, why did he want to, so badly? What was his motivation, if not the prophecy? Everyone murmured amongst themselves, wondering and speculating, but no one gathered the courage to actually ask Commence. So, Commence never answered.

COMMENCE JULY LECHATELIERITE

February twenty-fifth, seven o'clock.

"You know, I think the Constitution was good practice," I greeted Ash.

"Practice f'r what, C'mmence?" He carried a pot of porridge from the fireplace to the table.

Yawning, I shrugged. "For a peace treaty between Conflagria and the Nordic alliance."

The corners of Ash's lips twitched as he poured some slop into my bowl. "Oh, 's that all?" He slid me a spoon. I tossed the utensil aside, lifting the clay pot to my lips and drinking the hot sludge straight-up, lumps and all. I hated porridge because it reminded me of the orphanage's soup. So, when I had to eat it these days, I preferred to get it over with as quickly as possible.

After breakfast, I hopped aboard an old System sub—now, property of the Lechatelierite administration. By midday, I approached the southern Ichthyothian shore, cloaking my craft from sight and spectrometer. I abandoned the ship upon arrival, literally leaving it to drown in the depths of the sea. Still invisible, I marched up to Icicle's main gate and stood off to the side, anticipating an eventual opportunity to slip in. I wound up waiting for four and a half hours, until a shipment of Nurian foodstuffs arrived. Those two-hundred-seventy minutes were brutal, not spectrally but emotionally. How I wished I were truly as patient as I pretended to be, these days.

Anyway, by now, it was dinnertime for the divers. As I crept toward the mess hall, I retrieved a length of diffusion cord from my robe pocket and wound it several times around my head, at my hairline, fully suppressing my aura. And, wholly visible, I yanked the cafeteria doors wide open.

Instantly, every man in the vicinity leapt up, weapons drawn.

"I'm unarmed," I announced in Ichthyothian, hands raised. "No spectrum, no tech. I'm completely at your mercy."

I scanned the room. Inexor Buird was nowhere to be found. Krustallos Finire VII advanced on me, sidearm leveled at my head. Was he the commander, now? Great. I'd counted on putting my life primarily in *Inexor's* hands, today. Not in the hands of the one Nordic who hated me more than anyone.

"Well, if it isn't our infamous absconder, Principal Ence," Seven hissed, only halting when his muzzle was but an inch from my face.

No, he wasn't the commander; his sleeves only bore two stripes each. Where was Inexor?

As if on cue, I felt something forcibly seize my wrists from behind, tying them tightly… with more diffusion cord. All this aura-scrambling gear made my body feel as though submerged in the frigid Septentrion Sea, naked. I wasn't expecting to come in contact with quite *so* much of it, today. The pain it caused was far greater than I anticipated. I could imagine Ash, if he were here, whispering in horror, "Um, C'mmence, are yeh *sure* y'know what yeh're doin'?"

The honest answer was: hell no.

"Since I've been g-gone, I overthrew the S-system," I choked, focus already faltering. My eyes watered like a river; I could hardly see through the burning tears. "And,

I r-reformed Conflagria into a d-democracy. I'm their t-temporary president, n-now."

Silence.

"Are you n-not aware?" I breathed. "I've been working w-with Nuria on a c-constitution—"

"We heard that you met with some Nurian senators," Inexor retorted to my back. "But, we sure as hell have no idea what went down, upon your return to your island. Conflagria is far from transparent." He walked around me, weapon digging into my cheek. "Dictatorships never are."

"We're n-not a dictatorship, anymore. We're in t-transition; there's a d-democratic election, in the w-works. The Red Party and th-the Green Party are c-campaigning, as we s-speak." Holy crystallines, these ropes were freaking unbearable!

"For all we know, your little stunt in Alcove City was all an act, a façade, to lull the alliance into a false sense of security," Inexor snorted. "You'll understand if no one here is inclined to put a lick of faith in what you or your savage race are up to."

When exactly did I drop to my knees? "I'm telling the t-truth, s-sir, I swear. W-why do y-you think n-no one's attacked you at s-sea, all age?" Without throat magic to conceal the excruciating agony, my voice came out embarrassingly thin and high. "B-because there's no more S-system. I crushed y-your enemy, c-completely. I'm the interim P-president of the South C-conflagrablaze Republic. R-republic, n-not Captive. M-my nation isn't a th-threat to you or a-anyone, anymore. The n-northwestern h-hemisphere is n-no longer in d-danger of imperialism."

"Why should we trust a single word from your lips, *Ence?*" Inexor roared. There was something different about his tone, now—the shift was subtle, but I could still hear it over the blood churning in my ears. He sounded enraged, yet… hungry. Anxious. Like he desperately wanted to believe me.

"I'm n-not that m-man, anymore—the m-man you s-served under," I gagged, "o-or the m-mage who s-slaughtered T-tincture. Believe m-me, if I-I were y-you, I w-wouldn't t-trust C-commander E-ence o-of the D-diving Fleet or P-principle Ence of th-the S-south C-conflagrablaze C-captive, either. B-but, since th-those d-days, I've s-seen things… seen *s-someone…*" My whole body shook, prickly-numb and saturated with cold sweat. Stripped of spectrum, I felt so vulnerable, so exposed. Helpless. But, wasn't that the whole point? Wasn't this the most genuine I'd ever been, with these men? "I-I killed the m-mage who assassinated m-my p-parents, even a-after my m-mother's a-aura begged m-me n-not to. I had a v-vision of her, that n-night. The s-sight of her f-filled me with so m-much guilt and fear, I w-wanted n-nothing m-more in that m-moment th-than to d-draw my sword and t-take m-my own l-life. The d-desperation and s-self-loathing I experienced—i-it was b-beyond c-compare. That's when s-something in m-me s-snapped. I h-hit m-my breaking p-point. S-scarlet July f-finally m-made me s-see that I'd b-been u-using my p-power w-wrongly, a-all along. She m-made me see that p-power is a tool, a r-responsibility, n-not a t-toy nor a w-weapon. She e-essentially c-convinced me that I n-needed to t-take my c-country in a d-different d-direction. To w-work with the Red R-revolution instead of f-fighting against it. To r-replace my d-dictatorship with d-democracy. M-magekind is w-well on its w-way to f-freedom, now. I'm o-only their p-president until the f-formal election, l-later this a-age." I dared to raise my chin and declare, "S-scarlet July's p-platform has f-finally won. W-which means, *you* w-won."

There was a long, loud silence. I could no longer tell if the tears in my eyes were just from the caustic rope, or if I was starting to panic. Son of a scabrous, I was starting to panic! No. I couldn't. Not now. Everything hinged on this confrontation. I tried to take a deep breath but wound up gagging and coughing blood onto my knees, instead.

"C-commander B-buird, s-sir, I've c-come and p-put myself completely at y-your m-mercy. C-commence July Lech-chatelierite, the M-multi-Source Enchant—l-lays himself at y-your f-feet. D-do w-with me wh-what y-you will."

At last, Inexor lowered his weapon and signaled his men to do the same. They obeyed, some more reluctantly than others. And, at long last, Seven and Illia pulled off all my diffusive shackles. Still trembling, I slowly got to my unsteady feet. And, I thanked Inexor wordlessly, with a deep bow.

He regarded me, almost impassively. It was shocking how dead his eyes were, how lethargic his motions. Seven and Illia still fingered their sidearms.

Spectral sight steadily returning, I surveyed the room. Every gaze I met was glazed with exhaustion and icy suspicion.

"Commence," Inexor tried out my real name for the first time, almost sadly. "What do you want from us? Why did you come here?"

Inhaling, I spoke slowly, "Sir, I'm the President of Conflagria and you're the Leader of the Nurro-Ichthyothian Resistance." I put as much compelling thrust into my voice as possible as I added, "I want us to agree to end this thirty-five-age war, once and for all."

"The Leader of the Nurro-Ichthyothian Resistance," Inexor sighed, "is an empty title. We, here at Icicle, don't have the power to agree to squat. We're only foot-soldiers.

Pawns of the Trigon Center. Go there, if you want to make peace."

"The Trilateral Committee would never listen to a single word I say, if I say it alone. Any letter I send would be ignored… unless it also bears your signature, Commander. Your title isn't empty—that's only what they want you to believe, to keep you down. The truth is that, if you shout, they'll have no choice but to pay some mind."

"What do you want me to do?" Inexor asked.

"Write a treaty with me. One we can present to the Trilateral and Alliance Committees."

Murmurs swept the hall.

"The System isn't attacking, anytime soon," I said, smiling the first genuine smile my former comrades ever saw on my face. "Got anything better to do?"

* * *

Turned out, Inexor and I didn't have anything better to do for two months. Which wound up feeling more like two *eras*, since my co-author seemed fully committed to making my life difficult, every step of the way. I didn't anticipate him being so combative and disagreeable. He resisted the vast majority of my propositions and insisted on changing practically every other word I typed.

"Quit asking for so much, will you?" he spat for the umpteenth time today. "We just want to end the damn war, not restructure the entire Ichthyothian military. What does all this junk about abolishing the Childhood Program have to do with anything?"

What the hell was his problem? "Sir, don't you *want* to see Ichthyosis quit systematically abusing minors?"

"Of course, I do, but that doesn't mean I should actually pursue it," he growled, as though it were outrageous to work toward something he—gasp—*wanted*, not needed. "I cared deeply for your father, Commence, I really did. So, believe me when I say that I hated watching his work come undone, more than anybody. But, I don't think this is worth the risk, right now. What you're suggesting would seriously tick off the Trilateral Committee. Why give them a glaring reason to reject our entire proposal?"

"I don't think they'll throw away the whole document, over one tiny request," I insisted. "I mean, we're just asking them to use some common sense. If there's no active war, why should Ichthyosis maintain a youth training program?"

"Countries on First Earth kept militaries all the time, not just during war. It's a matter of national security."

"Of course, Ichthyosis can keep a military, age-round. But, the Childhood Program isn't a normal military operation; it was initially instated as a sort of draft, a last resort. If there's no ongoing conflict, why keep up the drastic measures?"

"Don't ask me where the TC gets its policies; that's a mystery not even a mind like Cease's could crack." Inexor rubbed his tired eyes. "We've got so much ground left to cover in writing this thing, but we can't even *get* to it because you've been hung up on this stupid provision for forever. Is there any way that I can get you to move on *without* adding it?"

"No," I said, flatly.

Inexor threw his hands up. "Fine. Make your ridiculous demands. But, if the Trilateral Committee refuses to get onboard unless we take it out, we're taking it out!"

Triumphant, I pounded away at the keyboard.

"Stubborn bastard," Inexor muttered.

I smirked. "I never understood why that's everyone's favorite insult for me—I mean, my parents *were* married. And, every time you say that, do you realize that you're also insulting your dead best friend?"

"Allow me to correct myself, then," Inexor said, coolly, "you stubborn accidental spawn of an eighteen-hour 'marriage' that wasn't even legal until months after it already ended." Folding his arms, his brows raised. "Was that better?"

I stopped typing in mid-word. "What?"

Inexor blinked. "What, you didn't know that Cease died mere hours after eloping with Scarlet? Their 'marriage' lasted for, like, half a day, if that."

I knew *that*. What was news to me was—"What's this about legality?"

He shrugged. "It's a long story, but the short version is: your parents tried to 'tie the knot,' as the Nurians would say, in the spring of the ninety-fourth age, but their union wasn't formally recognized by the state until sometime that autumn, months after Cease already passed away."

I felt like I swallowed a hunk of raw scabrous meat. "Give me the long version," I demanded.

He shrugged, again. "Well, out of ignorance or denial or whatever temporary insanity they were both simultaneously afflicted with at the time, the two of them honestly and idiotically believed that all they needed to do to marry was sign a form. No judge, no stamps, no filing, nothing official—Cease and Scarlet just signed a piece of paper, and that's it. I wish I were kidding. Well, unfortunately for them, that paper promptly got lost. So, Scarlet had no choice but to head home to Conflagria after the Second Infiltration, pregnant with a fatherless child and lacking so much as a scrap of proof that she was a so-called 'widow.' But, then, that fall, I actually found the original document, buried in Cease's stuff. Immediately, I knew what I had to do, and I got my officers to help out. We fought long and hard to force the Trilateral Committee to legitimize the contract. Then, when the World Revolt began, I had

Arrhyth Link and Nurtic Leavesleft deliver the stamped form to Scarlet, in Conflagria. Leavesleft said that the very sight of it made her break down into tears. Practically-speaking, that slip of paper didn't change a damn thing about her daily life. But, I guess it still… I don't know… made a difference to her. Emotionally. I knew it would for someone like her, which was why I pushed so hard to make it happen, in the first place. And, my men didn't hesitate to rally behind me, though news of such a serious violation of the LEP should've seriously pissed everyone off. Because, in the end, we decided that we loved Cease and Scarlet far more than we ever cared for the letter of the law."

I sat there, speechless. I didn't often find myself literally unable to utter a single word.

Inexor watched me, closely. "Commence, you okay?"

There was something in my left eye, something that felt suspiciously like a tear. I blinked it away, nodding. And, silently, I got back to work, revising the peace treaty to include a section demanding the dissolution of the Childhood Program. Inexor tactfully left me alone for the rest of the afternoon.

Just before lights' out, I went to show him my edits. On my way from his quarters, after extracting his begrudged agreement, I met his gaze and softly breathed, "Sir… thank you."

I wasn't thanking him for accepting the new provision, and somehow, he instantly understood that. Because, with a sad smile, he solemnly said, "It was the least I could do for my best friend and the woman he loved even more than the country he died for."

COMMENCE JULY LECHATELIERITE

April 25th of the 12th Age, 8th Era

Inexor Ghuot Buird,
Leader of the Nurro-Ichthyothian Resistance

Commence July Lechatelierite,
President of the South Conflagrablaze Republic

"I never thought I'd see the day," Inexor breathed, beholding the shining ink of our signatures on the finished peace treaty.

"Don't celebrate, yet," I murmured.

His dark-ringed eyes rolled. "Looks like you inherited your father's chronic pessimism."

"My colleague, Fair Gabardine, calls it realism, thank you very much," I replied. Inexor always seemed to stagger at the sound of Fair's name, and I could only wonder why. "After all, if I never set my expectations too high, I'll never be disappointed."

He cocked a brow. "Sounds to me like you've had a hell of a lot of disappointment in your short life."

Oh, he didn't know the half of it.

* * *

The Alliance Committee may've been stuffy and traditional to the point of reactionary pigheadedness and the Trilateral Committee may've been rusty and out-of-touch with the rest of the military world, but the leaders of either organization weren't *complete* idiots, so they could recognize their salvation when it stared them in the face. They accepted our document almost instantly, Childhood Program provision and all.

"Anything to end this war," Admiral Sive said, seconds before placing his signature below mine. With the Trilateral and Alliance Committees onboard, the executive offices of the Ichthyothian and Nurian governments followed suit without question.

And, that was how the Second War finally ended. Not a moment too soon. And, maybe, thirty-five ages too late.

For you, father.

ASH ARGENT

Conflagria was pretty much standing on its own two feet now, so Commence figured that it was time for the world to stand up, too—against isolationism. But, with the three-and-a-half-decade war freshly over, the nations who were supposed to lead this 'Second Tri-Nation Campaign'—Conflagria, Nuria and Ichthyosis—just wanted to take some time to enjoy the moment, for Tincture's sake; to the hell with the rest of the planet, at least for a little while.

But, Commence refused to let anybody 'waste' a second in celebration. Without so much as a pause to catch his breath or bask in his victory, he forcibly pushed all three nations into a full-scale rebellion against the Second Earth Order. Sure, the boy *called* himself patient—he liked to tell everyone that he paid no mind to schedules and deadlines—but, sometimes, he was far more like his mother in that respect than he cared to admit.

Anyway, with both the Ichthyo-Conflagrian War and the Red Revolution out of the way, conditions for this World Revolt were far better than that of the first, no doubt. For one, we could actually afford to focus all our time and energy on the task at hand. Secondly, Commence had a pre-prepared platform at his disposition: Scarlet's. He had access to entire databases of ready-made propaganda—everything from essays to videos to brochures, transcribed into hundreds of languages. And, last but not least, it helped that the planet was already familiar with the ideologies championed by Scarlet and her staff in the ninety-fourth age. Scarlet already broke the ice for us. All we had to do now was remind everyone of what she'd already said. In every possible way, the Red One had laid the foundation for our present work. We were simply picking up where she left off.

Time passed in a blur; I could hardly keep up. Progress was insane. As rhetoric circumnavigated the globe, public opinion swayed this way and that, prompting more successions from the Order. Every day, our shores got flooded with new reps and our staff swelled like the sea. At the center of it all was Commence, running nonstop like the Core Crystal itself—or, as Arrhyth Link would say, 'the Energizer Bunny.' According to Arrhyth, the Energizer Bunny was a mascot for a First Earth company whose ideas and slogans somehow found their way into modern Nurian advertising. It was astounding, how much influence the First Earthlings still had over all of us. Humanity was a race of copycats, that much was certain.

As such, I wasn't surprised one bit by the amount of time and energy that Commence put into researching the fall of First Earth, applying what he learned to our current endeavors.

"We're so quick to condemn them," he said in a widely-broadcasted speech, last week. "We're so critical of their every move, claiming that we know better. But, do we? Second Earth turned to isolationism to try to avoid First Earth's mistakes, and look where that got us. Manned space programs, outlawed. Wars, condemned but not prevented. Poverty, shunned but not combatted. I say, instead of blindly snubbing the First Earthlings, we should study their motives, gaining a better understanding of the logic *behind* their decisions and actions. And, maybe, in the end, we'll come to see that not *everything* they believed was foolish. Maybe, we'll discover that they actually had several good ideas, just blown out of proportion. Maybe, we'll realize that their greatest crime is something we're guilty of ourselves: extremism. Extremism, *in any form*, is toxic to the survival and progress of mankind. Globalization didn't end First Earth, *extreme* globalization—that is to say, militarism and imperialism—is what did. Likewise, *radical absolute* isolationism is what's harming our world, today.

"My goal in this Tri-Nation Campaign isn't to swap militant isolationism for militant globalism. I have no intention to turn Second Earth into a copy of First Earth. I have no desire to swing the pendulum to the complete opposite end. What I want is to find a balance. The world-system I hope to establish will incorporate elements of both the Isolationist Laws *and* the foreign policies of some of First Earth's most meddlesome superpowers, like the United States of America. Because *moderation*," he breathed, magical eyes alight, "is the answer."

I chuckled to myself as I listened to Commence's presentation. Yes, a covalent, iridescent Ichthyo-Conflagrian would know a little something about balance and blending, wouldn't he?

* * *

One afternoon, as Commence, Fair and I were having lunch at my old cabin, I randomly wondered aloud where the name 'Tri-Nation Campaign' came from, in the first place.

"'W'rld R'volt' is a pr'tty obvious thing t'call a... well, a w'rld r'volt," I said, chewing a stringy bite of dragon meat. "But, 'Tri-Nati'n Campaign'? *Campaign?* That's a... I dunno... very p'litically-c'rrect term. A whad'yehcallit—yoopamism?"

"Euphemism," Commence corrected.

"Right. That."

"Well, it is," Fair chimed thoughtfully, grabbing her goblet. "'Revolt' sounds violent and militaristic, while 'campaign' sounds brighter, nobler and more positive. Word-choice here *is* important, since we want to appeal to the everyday civilian family." Her eyes rolled as she laughingly added, "Personally, I think that squeaky-clean twenty-age-old Nurtic Leavesleft came up with it just so he wouldn't have to put anything too blatantly inflammatory on his resume."

Commence started angrily sawing away at his over-cooked scabrous steak with an enormous knife.

"*Speaking* of Nurtic Leavesleft," Fair obliviously blazed on, taking a sip of berry-wine, "Commence, why don't we contact him to get him involved in the World Revolt?"

Uh oh.

"No," Commence grunted, intense eyes on his plate. I was beginning to grow genuinely worried that he'd set his food ablaze... followed shortly thereafter by my table, floor, walls and the rest of my cabin.

"Why not? He used to be one of our admins."

"Yeah, like, eighteen ages ago."

"So, what? We could use his experience."

"We've already got the help of people with *real* political experience, from all over the world—presidents, prime ministers, senators, congressmen. Nurtic Leavesleft's credentials are nothing special."

"Nothing special? He used to lead the Nurro-Ichthyothian Resistance—"

"So did I, and for a hell of a lot longer than him!"

It seemed as though Commence and Fair could hardly coexist in the same space for more than thirty seconds without spitting venom at each other. Why, oh why, did I invite them over? My house wasn't big enough for both of their egos.

"He's the most amazing pilot I've ever met," Fair insisted, long hair autonomously leaping over her shoulders. "He's a stealthy smuggler *and* a gifted manager. We could use him. He's one of those bleeding-heart types, which I personally find annoying as hell, but Scarlet loved that about him and even found ways to use it to our advantage. I mean, once you adapt to his impossible cheeriness, you'll see that he's actually—"

Commence threw down his butcher's blade. "I said, NO!"

Silence.

"What do you have against him?" Fair finally squeaked. "Do you even *know* him?"

The boy's temples pulsed. "We've met."

Her white brows jumped. "When? How?"

He didn't answer.

"Well, if you really *have* met, you'd know that I'm right," she continued, fiercely. "You'd know that he's decent and brilliant and could serve our cause well."

Lids scrunched, Commence slowly inhaled. I could practically hear Principal Ence screaming and punching and kicking, inside his skull.

"Last I saw him," he broke the ice, tone tense and low, "he was a mess—depressed, tired, scarred and totally done with being a soldier. I just don't think that we should drag him into this, okay?"

From what I'd heard of Nurtic, I was sure that the man would drop everything to run to his long-lost son's side, within seconds of being summoned. But, apparently, Commence was through with asking his adoptive father for sacrifices.

"Depressed?" Fair's jaw unhinged. "*Nurtic Leavesleft,* depressed? He was always so obnoxiously happy, I wanted to smack him."

"Well, the Nurtic *I* knew was a miserable paranoid who thought little of himself and his ability to help others."

"We've got to be talking about different people," Fair blankly objected. "Nurtic isn't any of those things. Like Scarlet, he only ever saw the good in people, even those who really *were* just plain evil."

"Yes," Commence murmured, gaze downcast, "I know."

"Well, if that doesn't make him an optimist, then I don't know what an optimist is."

"Nurtic was a depressed optimist. It's a combination I hadn't thought possible, until I met him."

"Whenever *did* you meet him?"

Commence aimlessly pushed his food around. "Let's just say, once upon a time, he was willing to believe in *me*, when everyone else in my life had long since written me off as a psychopath." He stabbed his steak. "He really wanted to help me. But, I didn't let him."

Fair looked more than a little confused. "What?"

"Look, I don't want to get into it now, okay? The bottom line is: I'm not calling him. Ten ages ago, he told me that he's finished with military life and, for once, I'm going to respect his wishes."

Fair tossed her handkerchief onto the table. "Nurtic once told Scarlet the same thing, back when he was first discharged from the Diving Fleet in the spring of ninety-four. Not even half an age later, he swallowed his words and joined the World Revolt—as an admin, to boot. So, basically, no matter what Nurtic says, he doesn't give up on stuff. Period. So, I still think we should—"

"I wouldn't go against my wishes, if I were you," Commence whispered menacingly, casting Fair the same scathing glower that Principal Ence used to give his torture-victims.

We ate in silence for several more minutes. Well, Fair and I did, anyway. Commence just continued to sit there, staring daggers at his lunch.

"What about someone else, then," Fair mumbled through a full mouth. "I'm trying to remember her name… hmm. She used to write propaganda. Tincture, how could I forget her name?"

"Well, maybe, 'cuz it's been n'rly two decades," I chuckled. "Not all o' us got a mem'ry like C'mmence, 'ere."

"But, her name's so funny, I *should* remember it." Her fingers snapped. "Linkeree! That's it. Linkeree Link. Great journalist. Very prolific. Wrote a ton for us in a very short space of time. I think we've already recycled half of her old articles—published under a pseudonym, of course."

"*Linkeree Link?* Seriously?" Commence snorted. "And, here I thought the System was bad at 'christening.'" He blinked. "Is she, by any chance, related to Arnold and Arrhyth Link?"

"Yeah, she's Arrhyth's little sister."

Commence nodded. "It makes sense that the Link kids would get involved in international affairs."

"Well, actually, Linkeree got hooked up with us via her friendship with Nurtic. They grew up together in Alcove City and wound up at the same college. The two of them would come over from UVA sometimes, in Nurtic's plane." She giggled into her goblet. "For Tincture's sake, little Ree was always giving Nurtic googly-eyes, but at the time, he was way too smitten with Scarlet to notice. I wonder if anything's happened between them, since then…"

Commence's arms crossed.

"Oh, come on," Fair growled, "most of the Diving Fleet—in other words, many of our current campaign colleagues—were all close with Nurtic, at some point. Does that mean we should fire the whole lot?"

His fingers drummed the table. "Where does this Linkeree Link live, these days?"

"How would I know? Like I said, the Links are originally from Alcove City, but I suppose that Ree could be anywhere, by now. But, we can always find—"

He held up his hand. "No. We're leaving her alone. She *and* Nurtic. And, if anyone tries to contact either of them behind my back, I'll know."

Fair's jaw hung. "There's no need make threats, *Ence*."

"It wasn't a threat," he replied in a rather threatening tone. "It's a warning."

"Coming from you, is there a difference?" With that, she got to her feet, tossed her empty plate into my washing-pail and stormed out.

A long, uncomfortable pause ensued. Commence resumed eating, methodically and mechanically. I sat still, unable to chew the bite lodged in my cheek. Being alone in a room with an angry Commence was enough to make even the strongest of stomachs turn.

"So, uh," I blurted, stupidly, "where'd Fair get so much loy'lty teh Nurtic, anyway?"

He shrugged. "People always have extreme reactions to bleeding hearts. You either love them for their complete altruism or hate them for that very same trait. Nothing in-between."

"Why'd anyone hate someone fer altruism?" I wondered. "I s'spect it'd feel real good teh be 'n th'comp'ny o' someone like that."

"It can also thoroughly piss you off," Commence sleeve-wiped his greasy lips, "because you know that no one can possibly be *that* good. It's abnormal."

"Ah, so, it makes yeh jealous. It makes yeh feel bad 'bout yerself 'n c'mpar'son."

Another pause. "Well... yeah," he said, slowly, "I guess so."

Huh. "Well, then, sounds t'meh like it's not Nurtic who's got a probl'm, but th'pe'ple *'round'*im who do."

Commence had nothing to say to that. Tincture, did I just push the envelope?

"I guess Fair's one o' th'ones who love 'im?" I rambled.

"She didn't always, I think." He took a long draught of berry-wine. "But, if you haven't noticed by now, Fair's a bit of a flighty hot-tempered hag."

I froze, startled. Thus far, I'd assumed that Commence thought highly of Fair since he chose her, of all people, to accompany him to Nuria.

"She's always looking for a new cause to throw herself behind," he raged on. "A Red one day, a System supporter the next—whichever happens to sound right to her, at the moment. Just look at how she argues. She makes it sound like she's always been a hundred-percent sure of her opinion. But, in reality, she probably only decided yesterday that's what she believes. And, she acts like it'd be totally *outrageous* to disagree. She argues and whines like a five-age-old."

And, you argued and whined back like a three-age-old.

"She's got a missionary zeal about everything and anything," he continued, "which'd be fine if she actually shut up and kept her opinions to herself, once in blue moon."

"A mish'nary zeal," I repeated the curious phrase, without comprehension. Why would a 'missionary zeal' bother anyone? From what I gathered, missionaries were good people who helped others. Then again, Nurtic was a missionary and Commence despised *him*. "So, yeh don't like mish'naries?" I asked.

Commence gave me a cold look. "Huh? What the hell are you talking about?"

I shrugged. "Yeh said yeh don't like that Fair has a mish'nary zeal, so I was wonderin' if that's 'cuz yeh don't like mish'naries, like Nurtic?"

He blinked. "What?"

I shrugged, again. "Nuthin'." By now, I'd learned that it was safer to dismiss myself whenever I said something that apparently made no sense to smart people like Commence.

The boy promptly returned to his rant: "Fair worked for *ages* to diffuse Scarlet's aura for the System, before suddenly chickening out and jumping ship. That woman flows with the tide, I swear."

At this, my cheeks grew hot. Fair's homecoming wasn't based on a whim. She returned to the Reds because her conscience got stirred by none other than Scarlet July.

"She got turned by a vision o' th'Red One, not a tide. Jus' like yeh."

Commence's gaze pieced my face like a sword ablaze. "I made *one* big change in my life, at my mother's word. I didn't make five or six switches, prior to that. Ence was an ass, but at least he was a consistent ass. He stood his ground until he had a solid reason not to. I didn't just blow wherever my passions and emotions took me."

Really? I felt like asking him: what brought you from Alcove City to Aventurine City to Ardor Village, if not your passions? What made you forbid us, just now, from contacting Nurtic, if not your emotions?

Why could Commence see everything clearly but himself?

INEXOR BUIRD

Today, I'd travel to Conflagria to meet with the leaders of the Red Party, Prunus Persica and Gel Kylarks, who were running for executive office.

"The commander of a Spartan military isn't really one to ask for advice on how to manage a democracy," was my initial response to their call for help, a few days ago. "The Diving Fleet is dictatorial."

With the permission of the Trilateral Committee, we'd recently issued PAVLAKs to a few key admins of the World Revolt, including the Red Leaders. Persica's peach face hovered over my projector, garbling in vowelly Conflagrian.

On the contrary, sir, read the scrolling translation. *Your system is far more democratic than you think.*

I cocked a brow. "Is that so?"

Your soldiers cooperate with you because they want to. Because they believe in the same things that you do. If they did not, you would have no way to control them.

"What you're describing isn't exactly groundbreaking anthropology," I grunted. "Basically, to get someone to cooperate with you, you have to appeal to their will. You have to convince them that's what they truly *want* to do."

Persica nodded. *To force compliance despite differing opinions is dictatorship. To care about others' perspectives, incorporating them into your own designs, is democracy. Diving Fleet Commander Ence was like a dictator. He derived power from fear and physical force, unwilling to take anyone's perspectives into consideration but his own. But, your authority is different. Your troops follow you because they genuinely desire to. Because they have a say in what you do. You are like a democratic leader.*

He was making me very tired. "Well, then, it looks like you've got it all figured out," I grumbled. "You understand government far better than I do. Guess you don't need me." My finger hovered over the 'END' option, on the projected grid.

Persica chuckled. *If not your advice, we need your endorsements. It is difficult to campaign in a country full of people who are not used to having a choice in anything. It would help us very much to show Conflagria that the Leader of the Nurro-Ichthyothian Resistance—a fellow World Revolt administrator—supports our party. Come. And bring your Second.*

"My Second can't really leave his post right now, not even for a moment," I objected. "He's our chief computer-hacker, and the Order comes up with new barriers, every day." Every day? Try, every minute.

Then, bring any officer from your fleet who is willing.

"Fine," I gave in. "But, overseas PAVLAK use is insanely expensive and I don't have an ear-implant—"

My wife is fluent in both our tongues. She will translate for us.

"Alright. When do you want us?"

* * *

Arrhyth Link was the first of my men to volunteer.

"Can I come, too?" Dither Maine asked. It was no secret that he and Link were best friends. It was a blatant violation of the Laws of Emotional Protection. But, I wasn't one to point fingers.

"I'm sorry, Maine, but the Reds are only making room for two." Frankly, I was relieved that Maine couldn't join us. Independent from one another, he and Link were actually capable of functioning with moderate intelligence. But, when put together, they spontaneously morphed into total imbeciles who continually exhibited everything I hated about civilian Nurian culture.

Persica asked us to arrive on June twenty-first. A day of joyful celebration, he called it. The summer solstice was a national holiday, in mage country.

So, Link insisted that the two of us learn to say 'Happy Summer Solstice Day' in Conflagrian, so we could 'greet our hosts appropriately' upon arrival. I said, sure, fine, long as he did the research and taught it to me. Link, already trilingual, actually enjoyed the tedious world of phonics.

Mere hours later, Link had successfully constructed the Conflagrian phrase, transposed it into phonetic Ichthyothian and proudly shared it with me. It was such a mishmash of vowels, I didn't even want to try echoing it. I may not have been as bad at language as Cease—no one was, except perhaps mentally-retarded gelids—but, I wasn't exactly a Scarlet July, either.

"Just say it for me, okay?" I told Link, tiredly. His face fell, but he didn't object.

* * *

Link was embarrassing me. The moment we stepped off our plane to the sight of a colossal Red welcoming party, he started repeatedly bowing and bellowing, "Happy Summer Solstice Day!"

"Will you cut that out?" I hissed. "You're making fools of us!"

"The Nurro-Ichthyothian military has a reputation for being ridiculously uptight, sir," Link pleasantly replied. "I'm helping to fix that."

"How? By showing everyone that we're dimwits, instead?"

"When in Conflagria, do as the mages do," he insisted, waving at the crowd. "Come on, it's a holiday! Lighten up, have some fun."

I exhaled through my nostrils.

The crowd parted to let Prunus Persica and Gel Kylarks though, both of whom were grinning broadly like the politicians they were. As they approached, Link enthusiastically bowed to them. I reluctantly followed suit, feeling silly. The two of them returned the gesture rather than reaching for our hands. (Gel Kylarks, confined to a wheelchair, simply ducked his head.) Facing the masses, Persica then put his arm around my shoulders and spurted a rapid string of vowelly Conflagrian, to the sound of roaring applause. Link stood to my left, beside Kylarks, beaming buoyantly. He was clearly enjoying the attention. I tried to imitate his ease and smile, lest I come across as hostile. All my life, I'd been taught to keep my face deadpan regardless of how I felt. But, since the Nurians came along, I'd begun to understand that absence of expression was interpreted negatively by non-base-raised people. For some reason, they assumed that if you *weren't* smiling, it was because you were upset.

Accompanied by continuous cheers and chants, Persica and Kylarks led Link and I from our landing site to a nearby cabin, inside which a certain white-haired girl awaited.

Fair Gabardine.

My breath caught in my chest.

"Happy Summer Solstice Day!" Link shouted at her with a bow.

Fair bowed back, amused mockery in her oil-black eyes. That was something I always loved about Fair—she was rough around the edges. There was nothing easy about her. She was sarcastic, tough, argumentative. Not easily conquered. A force to be reckoned with. Like Scarlet, but sassier and brassier. Scarlet's internal strength was probably a major attraction to Cease. Despite her physical littleness and tendency toward gooey sentimentality, Scarlet was fiery, passionate and sharp. A warrior, like him. Cease never could've loved a weak soul—he would've crushed someone like that. A weak soul would've lost herself in Cease's dominance. When the Nurians talked about their old girlfriends, they often mentioned stuff like 'delicate' or 'meek,' as though those were desirable attributes. But, I'd never want a glass girl whom I'd have to handle with care. I wanted someone who'd hit back. A battle. A hunt. A struggle. Like Fair Gabardine.

"Hey, Inexor," she said in Ichthyothian, taking my hand.

"Hey," I echoed, noticing how very smooth her skin was, despite her warrior's lifestyle. "So, uh… why are you here?" I added, dumbly.

"To translate, of course," she chortled, prying her hand from mine. "My husband and his running-mate don't speak Ichthyothian, you know. On this island, only former System soldiers do, like yours truly."

Husband? I froze. *Prunus Persica?*

"Sit down, please." She gestured to the cluttered floor. "Everyone, come on."

Link, Persica, Fair and I sat in a circle, atop heaps of indiscernible junk. I could hardly bear to glance at Persica, who was still wearing his insufferable politician's smile.

"Inexor, Arrhyth, would either of you like something to drink?" Fair asked.

In Conflagria, 'something to drink' meant one of three equally-awful things: chalky coconut-water, bitter sludge made from fermented berries, or bacteria-ridden well-water.

"No, thanks," I answered for both of us. We knew to bring our own canteens.

There was an awkward silence.

"So," I felt the word-vomit creep up my throat, "do you and Persica have any kids?"

Fair paused for several seconds, clearly taken aback, before wildly shaking her head and croaking, "Oh, no, none, at all," as though the very concept of starting a family with her husband by her mid-thirties was totally outrageous.

"Well, speaking of kids," Link interjected, cheerily, "you'll be glad to know that all the students in the Ichthyothian Childhood Program have been sent home."

"That's wonderful," Fair breathed. "Scarlet would've been so happy to hear that."

"It's a provision that Commence included in the Peace Treaty."

"I was about to ask you," she spouted, eyeing Link's diving suit, "how come you're still in the fleet? The war's over; why don't all the Nurians go home?"

Link grimaced. "We decided to keep serving until we're totally certain that the World Revolt will pull through—as you know, we're all fairly entrenched in facilitating the information-exchange, using Icicle's resources and tech."

"Wow," Fair gaped, "you guys must have the sacrifice gene. I can't believe you'd be willing to stay on base any longer than absolutely necessary, considering how many ages you already gave up."

And, now, I was beginning to grow seriously annoyed. For goodness' sakes, why did everyone seem to think that living at Icicle was some form of horrendous torture or inhumane imprisonment? Fair couldn't *believe* that Link would *sacrifice* more ages to the fleet. Did that make my whole life a never-ending sacrifice, then? Because, it sure didn't feel like one, to me. To me, my life was just… life. The only life I'd ever known.

Well, no, maybe, that wasn't entirely accurate. Deep down, I did feel discontent, sometimes. After all, didn't I envy Cease for his relationship with Scarlet? Didn't I wish for the opportunity to connect with a woman like that? Me and my fellow base-raised comrades wouldn't get to leave Icicle until we were old and useless. And, perhaps, not even then; there were always those like Autoero Austere, Sr. who tried to stomach the outside world upon retirement, only to rapidly divorce his wife and quit his desk-job in favor of Icicle's sterile white walls, dragging his newborn son along with him. Was I destined to follow in the Colonel's miserable footsteps?

My morbid thoughts got interrupted by the official commencement of the meeting.

"Conflagria's already held elections for every political office besides the presidency," Persica began, and Fair translated. Already, she seemed a bit stressed by the task—which was understandable, considering that she wasn't exactly a professional linguist.

"The Reds currently hold a majority," Kylarks added.

"Nice," Link commented—which Fair didn't bother to relay.

"Why's the presidency being left for last?" I asked. That was odd.

"Because Commence needs to be in office for a little while longer." Persica winked. "The people aren't ready to give him up, yet."

"He'd be a hard act to follow, I imagine," Link murmured. "But, since he endorses you, Mr. Persica, I'd say that you're a shoe-in."

Fair glared at Link. "Could you at least *try* to avoid weird idioms and metaphors?"

He nodded sheepishly, curls bouncing. "Sorry. What I meant to say is: I think Mr. Persica's chances at the presidency are very good because Commence supports him, and everybody loves Commence. Is that better, Fair?"

Fair answered Link with an eye-roll, then conveyed his words to her husband.

Persica smiled. "I'm glad you have such faith in me, Officer Link. But, I'm well aware that, if I win, it won't be because the masses necessarily know and like *me*, but because I'm from the Red Party—the party of Scarlet July and her Iridescent son who overthrew the System and ended the international war. My success would be entirely thanks to heuristics, which isn't ideal for a political leader interested in a long-term career."

Link shrugged. "Hey, whatever floats your boat, right? If heuristics will get you where you want to go, what difference does it make? As long as you stick to the platform that folks seem so hung-up on, they'll adore you like you're their favorite uncle or something."

If Fair were an eye mage, Link would be crispy, right now.

"Uh, what I meant was," he quickly revised, "it doesn't really matter if they know you personally, as long as you commit to carry on Commence's work. If that's what everyone cares about, why not just give it to them? Let *that* be your identity, in their eyes."

Persica's head shook. "Of course, I'm devoted to Commence's vision. But, if that's *all* I ever show of myself, people may wonder if I've got something to hide. They need to know that I don't have a single skeleton in my closet."

"Hey, that's an idiomatic expression," Link grumbled, under his breath.

"A reasonable concern," I commented.

"So, you want us to help you rebrand your campaign," Link slowly clarified, "to focus more on who you are and less on the legacy of Scarlet and Commence?"

"Yes, exactly."

"No offense," Link chirped, "but, Commander Buird and I don't really know the first thing about either of you, Mr. Persica, Mr. Kylarks. You'd be better off asking your friends, family and comrades. Like, get your warriors to share why they followed you into battle. I'm sure you'll find some powerful stories."

"You think we haven't thought of that?" Fair delivered Persica's reply. "We've compiled dozens of testimonies from Reds across the island. But, that's the problem—it's all from *Reds*. Members of our own party. We need input from outsiders—preferably, outsiders who are highly esteemed and respected in their world. Men with institutionalized authority, on their turf."

"Us," I said.

"Precisely. The Leader of the Nurro-Ichthyothian Resistance and his Second."

"I'm not his Second," Link piped.

"That's right, my apologies. We initially asked Commander Buird to bring his Second, but we were told that he's indisposed."

"Sorry you got stuck with me," Link grumbled, which Fair had the brains not to relay.

"But, what a pleasant surprise it was, to receive the son of the noble Mr. Arnold Link, instead!" Persica continued, enthusiastically. "Such honor and fame that'll bring us!"

"Oh. Eh." Link blushed, yanking a curl.

"You two are exactly what our campaign needs," Kylarks agreed. "So, let's get started with the interview, shall we?"

"Interview?" Link looked alarmed. "I thought you already decided that you want to use us?"

Chortling, Fair answered him directly: "No, silly. *You're* going to interview *them*. You need to get to know them a little better, so you can say good stuff about them, remember?"

* * *

Once the sun set, our hosts decided that it was time to lay aside our work for the day and join in on some of the public holiday festivities. We stepped outside to the sight of children dancing and scurrying about, flying kites and waving ribbons. The auburn sky was alight with firecrackers and the air was thick with the smell of roasting dragon meat. Though I never liked the stringy texture or pungent taste of scabrous steak, there was something oddly satisfying about the smell.

As we mingled with the singing, chattering and feasting masses, it slowly dawned on me that the people here were actually… happy. The last time I set foot on these shores, everyone I came across seemed totally miserable. But, now, we were positively surrounded by excitement and laughter.

Even I had to admit, the exhilaration was infectious.

FAIR GABARDINE

July sixth.

Inexor and Arrhyth, by their mere presence, were doing wonders for Prunus's political image. As we predicted, whatever they said was taken at face value, because they were 'outsiders'—and prestigious ones, to boot. The average mage had long since learned to distrust his or her next-door neighbor. But, these reputable Nordics from thousands of miles away? Now, *their* views were pure and fresh.

Oh, Tincture, people were so freaking stupid.

"I can't believe that anybody would consider *me* a neutral voice," Arrhyth echoed my own thoughts, last night. "Of course, I'm going to be biased like hell—every single aspect of my life has been impacted by the state of your nation. Otherwise, I'd probably be in Alcove City right now, married and with six children."

Like the presidential campaign, the World Revolt was also gaining momentum, every day. We had so many countries onboard now, many hands made light work. Well, maybe not *light*, but certainly light*er* than the First Revolt, whose burdens rested inordinately on Scarlet, Nurtic, Inexor and me.

There was just one tiny thing making my job a whole lot harder than it needed to be: the constant presence of the son of my dead best friend and my old prison captor.

Even after all this time, I still couldn't get over how much Commence's wild eyes and smoldering passion reminded me of Scarlet, or how his sharp jaw and short fuse reminded me of Cease. I was bothered by these likenesses, now more than ever, because the World Revolt seemed well on its way to success… and his parents would never know it. Worse yet, they were missing it by only a handful of ages. The unfairness of it all made me want to scream.

Unfortunately, Commence was deeply involved in my husband's political career, so it seemed like he was always coming around to see Prunus, for one reason or another. He practically lived at our cabin.

As if on cue, the kid materialized on my porch, right now. But, before he could let himself in, I babbled, "Prunus isn't here at the moment; sorry." And, I gave the door a shove.

Commence stopped it with a single strand of hair. "Actually, I'm not here for Prunus," he said, smoothly, "but, for you."

I hastily grabbed my quiver and bow, slinging them over my shoulder. "Oh, um, well, I was actually on my way out, to hunt. Barely have a scrap of food left in the house." With that, I slipped past him, scurrying down the rickety wooden steps.

"Fair!" he called after me. "Fair, come on; where are you going?"

"Hunting," I croaked. "I just told you."

Suddenly, something grabbed my shoulders. I cried out.

"Fair?" Commence breathed, letting go. "Fair, what's wrong? Talk to me. I thought we got over our junk, months ago."

I didn't speak.

"I'm not going to harm you, you know," he said, quietly. "I'm not going to harm anybody ever again, if I can help it. At least, not in the way you're thinking. I'm committed to that."

"I know," I said to my sandals.

"Then, why are you avoiding me?"

There was a long silence.

"Because it hurts just to be around me, doesn't it?" he continued, softly and sadly. "Because of who I remind you of."

I realized then that I was crying. Enormous tears rolled down my cheeks like marbles. Great. I always wanted to weep in front of the President of Conflagria, the Son of Nations, the Multi-Source Enchant, the soon-to-be liberator of Second Earth.

My dead best friend's child.

"I'm not Scarlet, Fair," Commence said, which just made me sob harder, "and I don't want to taint your memory of her. You two had a good friendship. A great one. You saw each other through unspeakable circumstances. The time you had with her was cut short and can never come back. So, please, do yourself a favor: guard her memory by keeping me out of it."

Nodding, I sleeve-wiped my nose.

"I'm not Cease, either," he went on, brazenly. "I'm sorry that he gave you reasons to hate and fear him, Fair, I really am. But, I refuse to inherit your hostility toward him. I can't help who my parents are any more than you can help the fact that yours remain System supporters, until this very day." He inhaled. "Fair, look at me."

I still wouldn't. Instead, I stared at his slight collarbone, poking sharply through his robe like Scarlet's always did. He was so thin, so delicate. Like her.

He sighed. "Seems to me that, until you've been reconciled with my parents, we won't be able to have a real relationship."

I blinked, slowly finding my voice: "*Reconciled* with them? They're dead, Commence. There's no one for me to make amends with."

"I'm not talking about shaking hands with their ghosts. You need to be reconciled with them in *here*." He touched his chest. "And, you can start by forgiving Cease for whatever happened between you two, eighteen ages ago."

As if. "I'll forgive him for that when Conflagria freezes over," I spat.

For just a moment, I raised my chin and met Commence's metallic stare, expecting to see corrosive anger. But, instead, all I saw was sorrow. Disappointment. Heartbreak.

"Why are you begging on his behalf, anyway?" I asked, coldly. "Why do you care what I think of him?"

"I actually don't care, not personally," Commence declared, to my surprise. "After all, his reputation differs in every region of the world, and you're just one person. Just one voice in an endless chorus of judgements. His ashes certainly don't give a damn what you think, either. As for the way your bitterness has stifled our working relationship—to the hell with that too, because the World Revolt now has so much support and momentum, it'll definitely survive even if our friendship doesn't. It doesn't need you and neither do I."

I gritted my teeth. "You son of a—"

"I don't want you to forgive him for my sake or his," he cut me off, "but, yours. So, you can be free of hatred's heavy burden. It's a tremendous load that you've been carrying for nearly two decades."

I snorted. How very noble of him. "Why do you care what burdens I bear?"

"Because, believe it or not, I actually care about *you*. Just because I *can* run this thing without you doesn't mean I want to. I like having you around. And, I think other people would be more inclined to as well, if you stopped being so argumentative and unpleasant, all the time. I'm not the only one you constantly spit fire at, you know, not by a longshot. Even Arrhyth and Inexor have complained to me about it." They have? What on Tincture's island! Inexor always seemed so happy to work with me. "I think I get what's going on with you, though. Your tough-girl act is a guise, fueled by anxiety. You're overcompensating for your internal insecurities. Believe me, Fair, I know how it feels to live that way." As he took a deep breath, I noticed how very tired he looked. There were dark circles around his eyes and premature lines streaking his thin face. Scarlet looked like that at his age, too. "I think fifteen-age-old Fair Gabardine was a very different person than sixteen-age-old Fair Gabardine," he went on. "Since you met Cease Lechatelierite and got poisoned by your own vitriol, you began transforming into the bitter, sarcastic, paranoid person you are, now. And, until you find the courage to let go of the past, you'll likely stay that way forever."

Every gear in my mind abruptly jammed. How *dare* he! Was I harmed by my own choices or by the trauma that *Cease* inflicted on me? This dragon turd was young enough to be my son—how dare he psychoanalyze me! How dare he pretend to know my heart or what'd make me feel better! How dare he belittle Cease's role, in all this! Heat rushed to my scalp. I wanted to tell him to go throw himself in the Fire Pit but, before the words could leave my lips, I realized that mouthing off would just reinforce his point that I was a volatile person.

"You've had a vision of Cease, before." Commence took my stunned silence as an invitation to go right ahead, ripping me to shreds. "Kneeling, his aura begged for absolution."

What? I started at him. "How do you know that?"

He breezed on: "Fair, you'd be hard-pressed to find a soul, living *or* dead, who'd be willing to bow like that to *anyone*. He was doing something extraordinary—swallowing his pride and practically handing you your liberation. But, you didn't take it. And, now, you may never get an opportunity like that again—to see his face and hear his voice and get direct reassurance from his aura that everything is good between you two. Now, you're just going to have to manage to forgive him, all by yourself. It's much harder, that way. But, that's okay—the Fair I know never shies away from a challenge, right?"

With that, he briskly turned and left.

* * *

At night, I had a vision of Cease. My first one in seventeen ages. He didn't speak a word, just looked me in the eye and smiled. No bows, no pleading, no overblown apologies, no tears. Nothing dramatic. Just a small, simple smile on his thin lips. So, I silently met his silvery gaze and nodded.

And, with that, I was finally alright.

FAIR GABARDINE

Hot wind struck my face like a whip as I journeyed across the Dunes on scabrousback. I arrived at the graveyard by early evening. The sun was crimson on the horizon, sliding down the orange-brown sky like a dragon egg on a skillet.

I went to the right corner of the last row, to the smallest wooden slab in the field. The only mark it bore was a diagonal red slash. I dismounted, tied down my beast, and stood before the board. Smiling.

"These are good times." What a strange thing to say in a graveyard. People usually came here to weep or mope—if they came at all. "But, I'll talk more about that later. That's not why I wanted to see you."

I settled in the sand, studying the texture of the red paint dashed across the splintered plank. So, that was all my people gave to commemorate the greatest political and military leader to have walked the island?

"Your son and I," I inhaled, "we're not exactly friends, but we're comrades." No, that word wasn't right, either. Because the war was over. For the first time in three and a half decades, Conflagria was at peace with itself and with the world. What did that make of Commence and I? "We're… colleagues."

What an odd term. Since my teen ages, warriorhood comprised the bedrock of my identity. For the past couple of decades, I had neither peers nor coworkers, only comrades.

Whether I was designing weapons or wielding them, I'd always only lived for war. Who was I, without a battle to fight? What was life like, free of the constant danger of killing or being killed? The question electrified my entire body with fearful excitement.

"Commence and I are coworkers, Scarlet. We work together, day and night, rebuilding Conflagria and combating isolationism. And, though I have no right to complain about this to *you*, I'll admit that being around him has been... tough, for me." I frowned. "The toughest challenge I've faced, since losing you. He's the one who figured out why. He said that I'm projecting my issues with you and Cease, on him. He said, until I sort stuff out with each of you, he and I stand no chance at peaceful coexistence. He's right." I grabbed a fistful of coarse sand and let it filter through my fingers. "Which brings me to the first big thing I came here to tell you, Scarlet." I took a deep breath. "I've forgiven Cease!" I laughed. "Can you believe that? After eighteen ages, I've decided to close that chapter for good. I know that, to some extent, I'll probably always hurt over what went down between us. I know that the emotional scar-tissue may always linger, no matter what. But, even as I nurse my wounds, I've realized that I don't have to live the rest of my life angry and hungry for vengeance. That gets me nowhere—but, in more pain." My voice went small as I added, "It really helped that I could see his face. His aura visited me, last night. He didn't say a thing, only stood there and gave me a small smile. And, just like that, I knew. I knew that he and I were finally okay. I'm not his prisoner, anymore. I'm free." I blinked a few times, trying to dispel the sand that *must've* blown into my eyes, making them sting and blur. "But, I don't expect you to ever come back to me, in a vision. You said that you wouldn't, and you always keep your word." I chewed my lip. "And, you know what? I'm alright with that. I'm not going to wait for you, anymore. I'm readjusting my expectations, sparing myself further suspenseful agony. I'm going to choose to enjoy your memory and let you go, rather than tormenting myself by holding onto foolish fantasies. Remember when I told you not to wait around for Cease's aura to visit you because, in doing so, you were likely setting yourself up for disappointment? Well, I was correct, and it's about time that I take my own advice. I can love and miss you while neither wanting nor expecting anything from you. Because, as you know all too well, nothing hurts more than a hopeless hope."

My teary eyes perused the sky—the sky that sheltered a world of war for over three decades. It was thick with the pollution of a thousand battles. I lowered my chin and gazed at the shore, at the crashing sea that housed many a soldier's corpse.

Those gristly days were over, and not a moment too soon.

I swallowed. "What I really came here to say is... I'm sorry. To you. I'm sorry for the countless things I've said or done to hurt you, during and after your life." I shivered. "Betraying you on July twenty-fifth of the eighty-seventh age. Serving in the System Water Forces. Designing the spectral weapon that injured Cease and killed thousands of his people. Vehemently hating the love of your life and projecting that venom on you. Being wholly unsupportive during your pregnancy. Leaving you alone the night you were assassinated. Working to diffuse your aura in the ages that followed..." I gasped, overcome by the volume and magnitude of my offenses. I was supposed to be her best friend, for Tincture's sake. Her sister. The only family she had. Apparently, I'd been nothing but a thorn in her side, from the start. And, yet, she still loved me. Her devotion never wavered. "Please forgive me, Scarlet, for repeatedly turning my back on the one person who never lifted a strand of hair against me, her entire life."

I got to my knees and bowed, briefly touching my nose to the ground. Then, I lay down, staring up at the woolen atmosphere, and spent the next couple hours just talking to my friend, filling her in on everything that happened since she left this world. It almost felt like old times, when the two of us would chat in our tarps until the wee hours of the morning. Except, this time, the conversation was one-way.

I told her that I married my teenage sweetheart, Prunus Persica, and that he made me happier than I ever thought possible.

"I understand some of your old choices and actions a lot better now, Scarlet," I chuckled. "It was your love for Cease that motivated you to do many of the insane things you did. Back then, I couldn't conceive of why you'd give up so much for him and his legacy. Tincture, you were practically willing to throw yourself in the Fire Pit, for his sake. It struck me as irrational, stupid. Like, when you were determined to keep his baby, despite everything you knew it'd cost. I judged you harshly for that decision, and many others. But, now, I realize that we never saw eye-to-eye when it came to Cease because I'd never loved anybody like that myself… not until I *really* got to know Prunus, after your death. Now, all the wild sacrifices that you made for Cease make a little more sense to me. I get it. I'd do the same for Prunus, if push comes to shove."

Then, I told her all about Prunus's presidential campaign and how bizarre and ironic it was that Inexor Buird, of all people, would be the one to help him out the most. I knew why Inexor did it. Why he put so much energy and effort into securing Prunus's future. He was clearly driven by more than just a typical soldier's dutiful desire to aid a country whose stability greatly impacted international security. Inexor stood behind Prunus because he genuinely cared for me, Prunus's wife. Even after all these ages. Even though Inexor knew full well that he'd never get anything more from me than friendship.

"I used to think that all base-raised Ichthyothians were damaged goods. Broken machines. One of the reasons I gave you a lot of grief over your decision to love Cease was because I thought that you were throwing your time and energy down an outhouse. But, if Inexor is any indication of the kind of man a base-raised soldier can be, against all odds—compassionate, loyal, committed, earnest, selfless—then, I'm sorry for writing off your relationship as bogus or one-way. I can now believe that what you and Cease had was real. Mutual. He loved you, Scarlet, every bit as much as you loved him, despite the Childhood Program's best efforts to freeze his heart solid. Every single move he made in the war since meeting you was proof of that. He gave up everything for you. Willingly. Gladly."

At last, I told her that, though Prunus wanted to start a family, we hadn't yet... because I was terrified.

"I don't mean to point fingers, Scarlet," I croaked, "but, honestly, your tragic fate is what's scaring me away from having children of my own. Every time I consider becoming a mother, all I can think about is the way your corpse looked when I came home, that December morning. But, that doesn't mean that the desire for a baby isn't still there, continually drumming in the back of my heart. Especially when I look at your son, at what a fine mage he's become." I exhaled. "When I see traces of you in him... I just... wonder what it'd be like for myself, you know?" I could just imagine teenage Scarlet sitting here and listening to me now, eyes alight with excitement. "Well, the war's over and I'm still sort of young, right? Who knows what the future holds. I sure as hell don't. Whenever any of us make plans, that's exactly what *doesn't* come to pass."

I was quiet for a while, peering at the stars that managed to poke through the smoky clouds. The Big Dipper and the Little Dipper. Like a mother and son.

I rolled over, face in the sand. It was still warm from the afternoon sun. "If only you could see Commence now, Scarlet. You'd be so proud. People all around the world call him the 'Son of Nations'—isn't that amazing? It's not fair that the rest of the planet gets to have him and you don't."

My lids slowly grew heavy. I yawned, stretched and murmured, "By the way, Scarlet… happy birthday." I pictured her face, forever seventeen, and thought of how she would've been thirty-five now, like me.

Six-hundred-twenty-five nations had succeeded from the Order, already. Out of seven-hundred. Victory was in plain sight.

"Commence is giving the world the best birthday present you could've hoped for," I whispered.

And, with that, I drifted off to sleep, Scarlet's bones only a few feet below me, in the earth.

* * *

Overnight, I had one dream. Not a vision, just a dream. It was too foggy and disjointed to be a message from the spectral web.

In my dream, Scarlet embraced me and told me that she heard every word I uttered to her grave. She granted me complete forgiveness for my countless transgressions against her and spent the rest of the night laughing and crying on my shoulder, until the amber sun rose. I awoke at dawn with tears on my cheeks and a smile on my lips.

Not a vision. Just a dream. More than enough.

FAIR GABARDINE

July twenty-fourth.

Tomorrow morning, Inexor and Arrhyth would return to Ichthyosis. For good. Their work here was done.

For Arrhyth, that meant his service in the Nurro-Ichthyothian military was also coming to an end. With the Ichthyo-Conflagrian War resolved, the World Revolt nearing definite success, and all ballots for the Conflagrian presidency cast, Arrhyth and his fellow Nurian comrades would travel back home to their families, in a matter of days. So, throughout the evening, Arrhyth was extra bubbly and cheerful, bowing and shaking hands and laughing and getting drunk on excitement. And, maybe, on more than just excitement. We mages were accustomed to the berry-wine; we all had high tolerances because we grew up consuming it. But, Arrhyth hadn't touched a sip of alcohol since enlisting in the fleet as a teen, so the stuff went straight to his head.

As for Inexor, his behavior tonight was quite different from Arrhyth's. He had nothing special to look forward to, upon leaving these shores. For him, returning to Ichthyosis meant reverting to a new life of emptiness. No wars, no revolutions, no campaigns. No one *enjoyed* conflict, of course, but base-raised Ichthyothians couldn't deny that it was what gave their lives meaning. They were literally born to fight. And, now, it was all over. It was the moment of victory they'd worked for, since birth. But, once it was finally here, could they help but fearfully wonder: now what?

Inexor brooded in private, refusing to accompany Arrhyth, Ash and Prunus as they traveled from stronghold to stronghold to share celebratory drinks with practically every Red on the island. I found the poor man all alone in Ash's cabin, cross-legged on a mat, staring out a vast open widow while fanning himself with a scrap of parchment. Forehead a never-ceasing fountain of sweat, he used one of Ash's old robes to intermittently dab his brow.

I sat beside him, on the floor. A minute or two passed. Inexor wiped his face, yet again.

"I don't think Ash'll appreciate that," I said, softly.

"Oh, is this his?" Inexor murmured, lifting the soggy silvery thing.

I chuckled, lightly. "Who else around here wears grey robes with huge holes cut in the back?"

Inexor spread it out, on his lap. "Must be nice," he half-whispered, "to have your own wings."

I watched his profile, curiously. "You fly, all the time. All those ships and planes."

He smirked. "I said, it must be nice to have your *own* wings. Not warcrafts loaned by bureaucrats who bought your soul the minute you were born. That way, you could actually go wherever you want, whenever you want. Do the things you love…" His eyes flickered to mine. "Be with the people you love."

I suppressed a flinch. "Inexor," I began.

"What?" he snapped, fierce blue gaze appearing almost purple in the red-brown haze. "I know it's impossible, okay? I'm just saying what I *wish*. Not what I can actually do. What's the harm in that?"

"There is none." I was taken aback. "In fact, it's a wonderful thing, to dream and wish. It's just that… after all you've been through, I guess I'm a little surprised that you still *can*," I clumsily babbled. "I mean, I thought the Childhood Program would've..."

"My training taught me to *suppress* my desires," he retorted, "but, nothing can eradicate their *existence*. I'm a human being, dammit. Not a robot."

"I never denied your humanity," I said, delicately. Well, I never denied it to his face, anyway. "I actually know how it feels, to be brainwashed and controlled. I know how tough it is to resist subjugation. So, I'm really proud of you for breaking through a lot of those walls on your own. The Crystal's end handed me my mental freedom on a silver platter. But, you had no such luxury. Everything you've achieved, you got by your own strength and perseverance."

"Thank you," he said, shortly.

"You're a good guy, Inexor," I breathed, sincerely, "and I really could've fallen for you, back then. But, I didn't let myself, because life was crazy and I didn't want to make it any crazier. I was scared."

Inexor was silent.

"I was tempted by your kindness, really," I went on. "But, our lives were simply cleaving in opposite directions. We're from two different worlds."

He didn't miss a beat: "So were Cease and Scarlet." And, with that, he placed his hand atop mine.

I carefully pulled away. No need for Prunus, Commence, Arrhyth or Ash to walk in on *that* sight.

"Yeah, they were. And, look where that got them. I didn't want that to be us," I sighed. "Their story could've ended differently, if their relationship happened nowadays. Isolationism is dying and the wars are over. But, it's too late for you and me. You've got to let go of me, Inexor. Find someone who'll appreciate what an amazing person you are. Conflagrian, Nurian, Ichthyothian, Orion, Anichian—

whatever. The whole world is open to you now, because all the political barriers are crashing down, as we speak. There are seven-hundred nations full of women; you don't think there's *one* out there for you? Your time will come."

"And, when will my time come, Fair, hmm?" he sharply asked. "When I'm a senior citizen? The whole world *isn't* open to me. You forgot that I'm not a regular guy, I'm an Ichthyothian diver. Second Earth isn't my world, *Icicle* is."

"Inexor—"

"Maybe, I would've stayed happily ignorant if I never set foot outside Icicle's walls until my dying day. But, it's far too late for that, now. Now, in traversing the hemisphere, I got a good look at everything I've been missing. And, guess what? I want it."

"So, let that be your next challenge."

"Let *what* be my next challenge?"

"Reforming the Ichthyothian military, of course." I eyed Ash's robe. "So, you can go get yourself some *real* wings, for a change."

Inexor blinked. "Commence already reformed it. He added a provision to the Peace Treaty that—"

"No, Commence dismantled the *Childhood Program;* he didn't revamp the entire system. The system as a whole is still inhumane. On First Earth, westernized militaries didn't isolate their men like that. Most soldiers had families while they were still young, even those who made a lifelong career of their service. I'm sure it wasn't easy for them, but at least it was possible."

Inexor folded his arms over his knees like a little kid in despair. The sight was almost comical, considering his overall bulk. "There's nothing I can do about the way things are, back home."

"Of course, there is. Commence isn't the only person on Second Earth who can affect change, you know. The war's over; got anything better to do? Make this your next mission."

He was visibly struggling with the idea. Gnawing his lip and shifting about, he finally croaked, "I can't."

"Why not?"

"Because… I'm scared."

I stared. Inexor faced unspeakable horrors, since the cradle. He'd already been to hell and back, countless times. How could someone like him be 'scared' of anything?

"You're afraid of the Trilateral Committee?" I was incredulous.

His head shook. "Not of them… but of… being free. I've never felt real freedom, before. I'm not sure I'd know how to handle it, how to *do* it. Let's face it—I'm socially and emotionally crippled. It's easy for me to sit here and *say* that I want freedom—to wish for it, to dream about it—but, when it comes down to actually *attaining* it…"

"Then, get the Trilateral Committee to establish a recuperation program for retirees. Make them help you all out with the transition from isolation." Remembering what Scarlet once told me about the meaning of the prefix 'Ichthyo,' I half-jokingly added, "You can't just toss a fish onto land and expect it to run and leap, can you?"

INEXOR BUIRD

Fair Gabardine sat beside me now, urging me to pursue freedom.

Freedom. The idea was terrifyingly wonderful.

"War is all I've ever known," I told her. "The only thing I know how to do is fight." I swallowed, thinking of Colonel Austere. "What if I actually go and marry and have kids, then not know what to do with them? I mean, it's one thing to mess up my *own* life, but quite another to bring other people into the mix and screw up all *their* lives, too."

"Inexor," Fair looked at me, "if you're so afraid of women, how on Second Earth did you ever think you could handle *me?* I'm no walk in the sunlight, you know."

Walk in the sunlight. The Nurians had a similar expression: walk in the park. We Ichthyothians had no such idiom; our land was all blizzards and ice and coats and visors and quickly trying to get to where you needed to go before freezing to death.

"Walk in the sunlight," I echoed. "I'm Ichthyothian; I can't tolerate much sunlight. This visit alone nearly killed me." I stroked her cheek.

She laughingly batted my hand away. "You already know how to flirt awkwardly and make a girl blush; you've got nothing to worry about."

I studied my coarse palms. "I've seen more of Conflagria than I have of my own country. Can you believe that? I don't go out into civilian Ichthyosis much, except for rare excursions to the Trigon Center and other such government facilities. Then, right after those meetings, it's straight back to base for me. It's tough to imagine what life away from Icicle would be like."

"So, it's tough. So, what? Scarlet always used to say that nothing worth doing is ever easy."

With that, Fair patted my back, got up and left me alone with my thoughts. With my dreams. Staring at the auburn horizon, I tried very hard to visualize my freedom. I pictured myself skiing down the sidewalks of Glass City, wearing a puffy jacket and thick clumsy gloves rather than a heated arrhythmic suit. I imagined living in a different building than I worked. Traveling not in high-speed warcrafts, but in clunky snowmobiles and semivowels, on crowded streets. Sitting cramped at a desk all day, staring at a computer, only using my muscles to walk to the bathroom or the lunchroom or the parking lot. Going to the grocery store to get food rather than just eating ready-made meals in a mess hall. Setting an alarm to wake up in the morning rather than listening for a trumpet sound. Rising whenever I wanted on my days off, not when I was told. *Having* days off, in the first place. Every single week. Paying for everything with money, worrying about taxes and bills. Residing in a small private place rather than a large smoothly-operating facility, paying mind to upkeep and repairs.

The hot sandy breeze stung my nostrils. In many ways, Icicle made its soldiers lazy and dependent on the care of others. To enable us to focus our undivided attention on the war, Icicle provided for our every other need. In all my ages on base, I never spared a single thought to the maintenance crews who made sure the plumbing always worked and the power was always on, or the cleaning staff who scrubbed the showers and polished the floors, or the cooks who fixed our every meal, or the maids who changed our sheets and laundered our uniforms…

It would be strange indeed, to manage these things myself. But, I supposed that without a great international conflict to occupy my mind and energy and time, learning shouldn't be too hard.

And, I wouldn't be doing it alone. Not if I could help it. Because, with a smile, I imagined what it'd be like to come home every day to a wife. *A* wife. Not Fair. I was too late for her. But, there had to be someone else out there who could see in this tired, jaded, emotionally-crippled vet what Scarlet July saw in Cease Lechatelierite.

FAIR GABARDINE

Prunus was out on presidential business; I was alone for the night. It was late. I lay in bed, scrolling my PAVLAK through this week's top international headlines:

July 26th, 12th Age, 8th Era

REDS TRIUMPH OVER GREENS IN INAUGURAL PRESIDENTIAL ELECTION OF 'SOUTH CONFLAGRABLAZE REPUBLIC'

Interim Conflagrian President Commence Lechatelierite (Rd) stepped down from executive office yesterday, passing the baton to skin-mage Prunus Persica and his leg-mage running-mate Gel Kylarks of the Red Party.

The elections took place on July 24th with results announced yesterday morning. Persica and Kylarks secured a 77% majority vote over their Green-Party opponents, hand-mage Auld Wolley and hair-mage Bleu Brine.

"We've had a lot of help, of course," Persica stated in his acceptance speech, referring to Commander Inexor Buird and Unit Leader Arrhyth Link of the Nurro-Ichthyothian Diving Fleet, both of whom spent considerable time on the island to campaign with the Red Party and assist with the World Revolt. "We couldn't have done it without these two officers and their Alliance."

"It's been a real honor to work so closely with the Reds," Link stated. "When I enlisted in the Diving Fleet almost two decades ago, I thought I was giving myself to war. Never in a thousand ages did I imagine that I'd get to be a part of something like this. The restoration of a nation. Of a world."

"We ran our race void of cheap endorsements," Wolley (Gn) stated in an interview yesterday afternoon, when asked to give his opinion on the participation of Buird and Link in the Persica-Kylarks campaign. "Globalization doesn't mean the right to manipulate uninformed foreigners to your advantage."

In addition to the officers of the Nurro-Ichthyothian Military, Persica won the endorsement of 'Son of Nations' Commence Lechatelierite, who decided not to run for reelection due to his growing involvement in foreign affairs.

"I'm not going to live here [in Conflagria] much longer, I'm afraid," Lechatelierite said. "Duty is calling me elsewhere. And, besides, I was never elected in the first place, so how could I possibly run for reelection?"

ORDER SUCCUMBS TO 'WORLD REVOLT': ISOLATIONISM YIELDS TO NEW GLOBALIST POLICY

On July 25th of the 12th age, the Socialist Republic of Anich and the Free Peoples of Oriya became the 699th and 700th nations to join the World Revolt, effectively turning Second Earth over to the reign of the new Globalist Earth Order (GEO).

"We really have no choice at this point but to sign the New Globalist Policy (NGP) Doctrine," stated Kaerb Breach, the Former Second Earth Order Chairman, when announcing his country's decision to become the final member of the GEO. "We live in a world where the majority rules. The Tri-Nation Campaign turned the tables so that we essentially became the blacklisted ones. And, it hasn't been easy. I can't believe that Nuria and Ichthyosis were able to last so long without international trade; we're on the verge of economic ruin, already. I guess we could call it a taste of our own medicine."

"This is quite possibly the most significant event in Second Earth history, if not human history," stated Fair Gabardine, the First Lady of the South Conflagrablaze Republic, when asked her opinion on the erection of the GEO. "It's important to note that, while the new policies are ecumenical, they are still far less invasively globalist than that of First Earth. Commence [Lechatelierite] was adamant about preventing extremism of any kind, and I think that he's done a fair job at constructing a system of moderation."

"I've done a fair job?" Conflagrian President and Ex-Nurro-Ichthyothian Diving Commander Commence Lechatelierite reacted to Gabardine's words. "This was the labor of billions, not of one man. But, if we're looking for a single soul to attribute the most credit, don't look at me. Look at Scarlet July. None of us could've done this without her. She primed our every step."

The NGP Doctrine was originally authored and proposed by Lechatelierite and championed by the blacklisted Tri-Nations: the Democratic-Republic of Nuria, the North Ichthyosis Island and the South Conflagrablaze Captive (now, South Conflagrablaze Republic). In a matter of months, the Campaign swept across the globe, gathering the support of nations large and small—many of which were on the brink of civil war themselves, to the great surprise of many.

"Virtually no one was aware that Aissur, a small nation in the southeastern hemisphere, was on the edge of collapse at the time the World Revolt found them," Lechatelierite said. "I think it came as a shock to most, to learn that Conflagria wasn't the only state on the map with such a tumultuous history. Aissur's condition—and that of several other countries in similar positions—came as a rude awakening to all of Second Earth. But, I think it's fair to say that it was well worth our naiveté, to help save all their lives."

The morning of July 25th, immediately following the conference in which the delegates from Anich and Oriya ratified the NGP Doctrine, Lechatelierite was quoted to have said to his Primary Advisor, Conflagrian wing-mage Ash Argent, "I can hardly believe it myself, that the Order now stands to unite, not divide. I could die now, I really could. My life is officially complete."

"Clearly, that's not the case," said Senator Dink Innoc of Nuria, upon learning of Lechatelierite's words. "If he died now, who'd be the GEO's first Chairman?"

Indeed, Lechatelierite has accepted Kaerb Breach's offer to succeed him as Order Chairman. With Lechatelierite's appointment, the torch of 'Authority Nation' will pass from Oriya to Conflagria, though the Sequest Center in Constellation City, Oriya, will continue to serve as Headquarters.

"Commence [Lechatelierite] is actually excited to move to Oriya," Argent said, laughingly. "It'll be his fourth country of residence, and the kid's not even eighteen. I guess they don't call him the 'Son of Nations' for nothing!"

July 27th, 12th Age, 8th Era

NEW GLOBALIST POLICY ENABLES SCIENTIFIC BREAKTHROUGH INVOLVING CONFLAGRIAN 'SPECTRAL WEB'

Physicists and astronomers from the Free Peoples of Oriya are teaming up with Conflagrian spectroscopers to unleash new possibilities involving the Fire Island's 'spectral web.'

"You see, the [spectral] web isn't exclusively 'Conflagrian' by any means," stated hair-mage Fair Gabardine, one of the world's leading spectroscopers and the inaugural First Lady of the South Conflagrablaze Republic. "The Core Crystal—the web's generator—is physically located in Conflagria, but its irradiation spans the entire planet. Every living being is connected to the web, whether Conflagrian-born or not."

"Any entity with a temperature above zero Kelvin radiates black body energy," said Dr. Kaew Link of the Orion Institute of Physics and Astronomy (OIPA). "The 'non-magical' human body typically has a temperature of 310 Kelvin and emits black body radiation in the infrared part of the electromagnetic spectrum. That's how infrared security cameras detect burglars and mosquitos track down flesh in complete darkness. Whether infrared or optical, all human beings have electromagnetic fields and, therefore, a place in the so-called 'magical' network."

While non-magical beings generally have wavelengths in the infrared range—above 700 nanometers (nm)—'mages' have wavelengths in the visual spectrum—between 400 and 700 nm.

"Everybody 'glows,'" stated Gabardine, "everybody has an 'aura.' But if your 'color' is infrared—which is the case for most people around the world—then, the human eye can't see it and you can't use it. For a wavelength to function in a 'magical' sense, it needs to be in the optical range. Conflagria has a high birthrate of individuals possessing visible auras, perpetuated by an isolated reproductive pool. But, with the Isolationist Laws abolished, humanity can anticipate an increase in international mobility, leading to the birth of 'mages' all over the world, in the future.

"As for the existing non-mage population, do not despair. It is possible to change your wavelength, to shorten it enough to transition from the infrared to the optical range. It's been done before. Twice, actually, by two different Nordics."

Reportedly, Ichthyothian-born Diving Commander Cease Lechatelierite developed a black wavelength, and Nurian-born Diving Commander Nurtic Leavesleft, a yellow one.

"Their auras were faint," recalled Gabardine, "barely visible and hardly usable. But, with training, both had the potential to become as powerful as any mage who was born as such."

The question that follows is: how exactly does one practically go about altering his or her wavelength? The answer is found in a spectral phenomenon known as 'lifeline twining.'

"What happened with each Lechatelierite and Leavesleft was kind of an accident," said Gabardine. "They weren't aiming to modify their frequencies; it was only a side-effect of their emotional proximity to Scarlet July, the Conflagrian Dual-Source Enchant."

"It's an elementary fact of physics and astronomy that spectral lines do not exist in impenetrable isolation," said Link. "They can hit other lines, mingle and merge. The lifelines—our lifelines—that make up the spectral web are no different. These lines can 'twine'—or, adopt one another's characteristics. In fact, all lifelines touch, to some degree. But, through prolonged interpersonal interaction, we can choose whose lines we bind closest to. Leavesleft and Lechatelierite each attached their frequencies to that of a mage. Their wavelengths became shorter, to match hers. They didn't match completely, of course, because they developed different colors. But, they made it in the visual range nonetheless, which is all that matters when it comes to practical 'magical' use. In sum, any 'Infrared,' through twining and training, can develop visible auras and hone magical powers."

What are the large-scale and long-term implications of this discovery?

"The creation of international magical education programs, of course, to teach non-mages how to shorten their wavelengths below 700 nanometers," answered Gabardine.

The new Globalist Earth Order (GEO) is seizing the idea of 'public wavelength modification education' with enthusiasm.

"Ideally, 'mage training' will become a standard part of school curriculums worldwide, as well as offered at institutions of higher learning and public community colleges," said Commence Lechatelierite, the inaugural GEO Chairman. "Of course, this raises countless ethical, practical and safety concerns, but the GEO is committed to addressing all of them before actually launching any such programs. As one can imagine, it'll be an extensive effort, to raise a workforce of magical tutors and install them in schools across the globe. But, it will be done—eventually. Just don't expect 'Wavelength Modification 101' to appear in your local institution's course-offering catalogue for maybe a decade or so. But, just ask any Conflagrian mage and they'll tell you that 'superpowers' are well worth the wait."

NEW GLOBALIST POLICY ENABLES ADAPTATIONS OF ICHTHYOTHIAN WAR TECHNOLOGY: THE BIRTH OF A MANNED SPACE PROGRAM

The Trilateral Committee of the Nurro-Ichthyothian Military is channeling much of its wartime production into a new international manned space program.

"Nurro-Ichthyothian military ventures, like weapons-productions, navigation-system-development, soldier-training curriculums and warcraft design, have laid the foundation for a prosperous manned space program," Admiral Oppre Sive said yesterday.

One of the first projects will be to modify the most versatile of all Nurro-Ichthyothian air and sea vessels, the Vitreous Silica, Sive claimed. The prospective space shuttle has been named 'Vitreous Astroloma.'

"Adapting the Vitreous Silica for spaceflight shouldn't be too difficult," Sive stated. "There isn't much to change. The PAVLAK navigation system can be reconfigured. The body of the vessel is nearly durable enough, in its current form. It is airtight, pressurized, heavily shielded and has enough life-support to sustain an entire army for months. It can already fly to the edge of the atmosphere. So, it shouldn't take much more to get that thing into the black."

And, what else would a spaceship require but a spacesuit?

"As it is, the diving suit is almost a perfect spacesuit prototype. Of course, we're going to have to make it a little thicker and heat to a higher temperature," Sive continued, "but, you can't really ask for more than oxygen-bead technology and the near-indestructibility of 'arrhythmic' fabric."

Sive estimates that the military may be ready for its first manned space launch in only five ages—a prediction that is sending shockwaves of excitement throughout the world. Anticipation is so great, in fact, that it has already spurned talk on who should pilot the inaugural flight of the Vitreous Astroloma.

"I cast my vote for Nurtic Leavesleft," said Commander Inexor Buird of the Diving

Fleet. "I can't think of anyone better to entrust a mission of this magnitude."

Buird certainly isn't alone. The Nurian Silver Triangle Recipient's name has been circulating throughout the ranks of the Nurro-Ichthyothian Military.

"He's the most versatile pilot Second Earth has ever seen," agreed Diving Officer Arrhyth Link.

"Yes, if there's anyone who could exceed expectations as the world's first astronaut, it's him," concurred Diving Officer Dither Maine.

Globalist Earth Order (GEO) Chairman Commence Lechatelierite declined comment when asked his opinion on Leavesleft's likely selection.

"I never thought that, when I took my first piloting lesson in an old prop plane as a teenager, that I would one day be asked to fly a spaceship," was Leavesleft's dazed reaction to the hype.

In addition to being reconfigured for spaceflight, the PAVLAK system will eventually be adapted as a tool for the average civilian household. It has been tentatively named the 'PAVLAK Home Universal System,' or 'PHUS.'

"Just imagine everything you could ever want in a computer and more, and this little hand-held interactive holographic device will have it," Buird said. "Instant audio/video communication to anywhere in the world, internet, television, radio, video, GPS with three-dimensional maps and voice dictation, home security, baby monitors, tutorial driving simulators for teens—you name it, PHUS will have it. It's about time that some of these war-gadgets got used to improve the quality of life for the everyday family."

I clicked off my PAVLAK, slid it under my tarp, rolled over and closed my eyes. I was already half-asleep when I realized with amusement that July twenty-fifth was the official date of the GEO's establishment. The date that once brought so much pain to a certain red girl was now the birthday of a better world.

And, her son, Commence, was no longer just a child of war, but the child who *ended* war throughout the earth. The Son of Nations wasn't just the son of two nations, anymore. Smiling, I curled beneath my blanket. He was the son of the world.

INEXOR BUIRD

The last day of July.

My Nurian comrades were leaving Icicle before dawn tomorrow, heading home to the nation they left nearly eighteen ages ago, when they were only children themselves. The mess hall was loud with chatter. Appetite prematurely shot, I carried my half-full trey to the dish-return—the Recycling Center was no longer necessary, thank heavens—finding myself behind Arrhyth Link and Dither Maine, already in line. I noticed that their plates also bore lots of leftovers.

"You two hardly ate a thing," I commented, sentimentally choosing to speak in Nurian. Starting tomorrow, I'd never have a real reason to utter a word of the language again. It was hard to believe.

Arrhyth grinned. "Why should we fill up on this crap when we'll be eating *real* food in no time?"

"Real food?" I scoffed. "You mean fried carbohydrates and saturated fatty acids?"

"We mean anything except salmon paste on stale crackers with rusty water straight from the tap," Dither snorted.

"Your bodies are used to a regulated diet and a ton of exercise," I pointed out. "When you revert to fries and couches, you'll balloon like blimps."

"And, it'll feel damn good, too," Dither said.

"It's not like we have girlfriends awaiting us in Alcove City; there's no one we need to keep looking good *for*," Arrhyth grumbled. "But, as for you, Commander, your stellar physique has got the ladies lining the hall, huh?"

"Of course." I gestured to the table behind us, at which a few dozen Nurians still sat. "Don't you see them?"

Laughing, they socked my stomach.

"That was low, sir," Dither hooted.

"I operate a facility that socially and emotionally castrates hundreds of men," I grunted. "I'm a low kind of guy."

"You didn't invent this twisted system," Arrhyth remarked.

"But, I sure as hell know how to run it, don't I?"

They chortled again, but with much less heart, this time. Then, there came a heavy silence.

"So," Arrhyth sighed, "we're leaving, again."

"Yes," I said. "Again."

"Only, this time, it's for good," Dither added with a little too much satisfaction. For some reason, that really pissed me off.

"That's not the only difference," I hissed, viciously. "This time, you two aren't blubbering like little civilian girls. What, aren't you going to miss us?"

Dither tossed his plate rather unceremoniously onto the conveyor belt. I was surprised it didn't break. "Last time, we weren't crying because we were sad to leave *you guys,*" he snapped. Hmm, did I wound his pride or maybe compromise his manhood? That was something I always found amusing about Nurians; they acted like their masculinity was constantly in jeopardy. Like it was a 'card' that could be revoked at any minute. Perhaps, they thought this way because they were used to living in a coed society, where it could potentially be difficult to tell who was which gender. Not really a concern, around here.

"Yeah," Arrhyth chimed, sounding more hurt than angry. "We were upset because we thought Nurtic Leavesleft was dead."

"Oh." My tone went hard. "So, you never cared for *us*, to begin with."

"How could you say that?" Arrhyth deposited his dishes with a loud clatter, fork hopping to the metal floor. "We gave you nearly two decades of our lives—we continued to stay here for a while even after the war ended—because we wanted to. Because we've always cared."

"I know," I said, retrieving his fork. "Even though you weren't born into this disaster like the rest of us, you've always been deeply concerned about the fate of my people. That's something I never understood, something that always amazed me. I'm going to miss that. Miss *you*."

They froze, eyes like shuttle-lights.

"Okay, now, I *am* going to cry," Arrhyth murmured.

"Me too," Dither whimpered.

I forced myself to smile. Smiles did wonders for Nurians. The sky could be falling, but as long as someone grinningly told them that everything was going to be alright, they kept their cool for the most part. Smiling didn't come instinctively to me—it was a learned behavior, and it took effort. But, in situations like this, it was more than worth it.

"So, what are you going to do, once you're home?" I asked them, as we left the dining hall. "I mean, besides suffering tremendous reverse-culture-shock. What will be your..." I struggled to find the proper Nurian words, "your life's work?"

Dither blinked. I could immediately tell that I used the wrong expression, after all. It was incredible how, even after all these ages, I still sometimes managed to mess up on the basics of Nurian vocabulary and idioms.

"Our life's work?" he echoed.

"Silly us." Arrhyth smirked. "Here we were, thinking that our life's work was helping end a terrible war, followed by saving the world from a destructive political ideology."

"Sorry to melt your icecaps, but your ages of service here won't feed you for the rest of your lives," I snorted. "Your pensions aren't going to be great; the alliance is only *beginning* to emerge from a severe economic depression, you know—"

"Yes, we know," Arrhyth interjected. "We're fully aware that the alliance is being fished from a smelly sewer-hole, right now. You meant to ask us about our next *careers*, not our life's work. That's already over and done."

"Do you really believe that?" I asked.

"Don't you?"

I shrugged. "Human nature is funny. We all *say* that we want to accomplish our hearts' desire, but deep down, I think the struggle is what we truly enjoy. It's not enough to have everything already. We prefer if our goal stays *just* out of reach, so we can keep fighting for it."

"Half of me agrees with you," Arrhyth said, "while the other half really does want to be finished."

"Which half is that?"

"The tired half. The half that's ready to go to sleep and *not* get startled half to death by a blasting trumpet at the crack of dawn."

I chuckled, since that seemed to be the reaction he was going for. "I think I know what you really want."

He cocked a brow. "Is that so, Commander Seer?"

Who's 'Seer'? "You want to leave the arena of geopolitical affairs only to tackle life's *next* big obstacles: getting married and having children and finding a job."

"Except, not in that order," Dither said. "I think it would be best to find a job first, especially since our military pensions will apparently suck."

Arrhyth ignored Dither, eyes studying my face. "How do you know that's what we want?"

Easy. "It's what anyone in your position would want, isn't it?"

"Is it what *you* want?"

I shrugged. "I've been trained not to want."

Arrhyth's arms folded. "That's bull and you know it, sir. No human being can be taught not to want. You can learn not to *act* on your desires, but that doesn't make them go away."

He was right, of course. I'd recently told Fair Gabardine the very same thing. In many ways, it was a big mistake for Cease to bring Nurians into the Ichthyothian military, because their presence opened our eyes to a whole universe of things we otherwise wouldn't know to want.

"To answer your initial question: yes, over the last eighteen ages, we've obviously had plenty of time to agonize over our potential post-military careers," Arrhyth plowed on. "But, we have no idea if our notions are feasible. Will we need to go back to school for them? I hope not. It'd feel a little odd to sit in a college classroom with kids half my age but with ten times the sexual experience."

"That's what community college is for, I suppose," Dither mumbled. "Hmm, you know, regardless of our career-paths, we should totally take wavelength-modification classes, as soon as they're available..."

"So, what *are* your career ideas?" I asked.

"Business," said Dither.

"Computers," said Arrhyth.

I blinked. "Do *what* exactly with business and computers?"

Arrhyth exhaled. "I don't know. Those are the answers we gave our high-school guidance counselors, back before the military became an option." He looked away and added,

"Never in a million ages did I think I'd be just as lost in my late-thirties as I was in my teens."

"Your service here must've given you *some* marketable skills," I insisted.

"We can shoot, fly, swim and hack the net," Dither rattled.

"Wowie, what a stellar resume," Arrhyth sarcastically whistled. "The employers will be lining up, just like the ladies."

"Come on, you aren't being fair to yourselves," I objected. "You can lead. You know how to communicate effectively, inspiring others to follow you to the ends of the earth. You've been taught to think critically on your feet, when it's a matter of life and death."

"Literally," Dither grumbled.

"Isn't that more than enough for a businessman?"

He nodded, slowly. "Yeah… I guess."

I turned to Arrhyth. "You're a whiz at calculus, physics, geometry, vectors. You know seven different computer languages and can fix a broken terminal in your sleep. And, you're telling me that you're unsure you can 'work with computers' in some Nurian office?"

"I suppose I could," Arrhyth said, cheeks adopting a slight pink twinge.

We made our way down the corridors. Not since Cease was around did I engage in casual chat with other divers. It felt good.

"I think that none of you Nurians have a damn thing to worry about. We've trained you as well as any university. Maybe better, because we taught you real endurance. If your lives don't go smoothly, you won't panic and roll over like any old civilian snowflake. You can take a little hardship—a little hunger, cold, sickness—and pull through, in the end. You've been to *war;* you've already seen the worst that mankind has to offer. You've fought Conflagrian mages at sea, then went on to overthrow the world government—

and you're telling me that you're afraid of some soft-bellied corporate-heads who spent *their* last eighteen ages in a cubicle-farm, drinking coffee and eating sugar?"

Arrhyth and Dither were howling, by now.

"My, sir, I never knew you had such a sense of humor!" Arrhyth exclaimed. "And, wherever did you learn the expression 'cubicle farm'?"

"I'm not trying to be funny," I breathed. "I'm telling you what I genuinely believe. You say that life out there is tough? Well, I say that you're a hell of a lot tougher."

"Well, when you put it that way, sir," Dither grinned, "I guess we'll be okay."

"You'll be better than okay," I fiercely declared. "I didn't train my men to be content with mediocrity."

"Don't worry, sir." Arrhyth patted my arm—another thing I hadn't experienced since… well, maybe, never. "We'll take the corporate world by storm, we promise."

"And, if that doesn't work out for us," Dither chimed, "we can always become athletic trainers or competitive swimmers or something."

Arrhyth's gaze grew pensive. "You know, we always *could* become airline captains or delivery pilots. That's what Nurtic did, according to Commence. It's really not a bad idea. I mean… it's just awful to think that we may never drive anything more interesting than a flivver, from now on."

"So, what *are* you going to do, now that everything's over?" Dither suddenly asked me. "What are *all* of you base-raised Ichthyothians going to do, every day from here on out?"

What kind of question was that? "Keep on training and maintaining."

He was bewildered. "What for?"

"To stay battle-ready, of course."

Dither was visibly disturbed. "We've done everything in our power to *prevent* further conflict from happening."

"Yes, but, you never know what the future holds."

"There isn't going to be any more war!" Dither burst.

I put a hand on his shoulder—and the gesture felt even weirder to initiate than it was to receive. "I never said there will be. The Peace Treaty that Commence and I wrote is as airtight as humanly possible. But, after everything that's happened to Ichthyosis in the past era, how can we help but remain cautious and vigilant? And, if another war *does* break out, who better to rise to the occasion than us?"

"Than *you*, not *us*." Dither's arms folded. "If a third war gets started, I'm not coming back."

"Because it'll be so far in the future, we'll all already be dead by then, from old age," Arrhyth added.

I exhaled. "I certainly hope so."

There was a pause.

"I know you must be very happy about the victory, but," Arrhyth swallowed, "I imagine that it's still going to be tough for you, to be a warrior without a war."

A warrior without a war. "Catchy phrase," I commented. "What's it from?"

The Nurians—and the two surviving adult Ichthyothian recruits from the Trilateral Committee's brief onboarding experiment, several ages ago—were always quoting famous people or making pop-culture references. It was difficult to tell how many of their thoughts were their own and how many were just rote repetitions of civilian media slogans. I'd come to realize over the ages that, contrary to my initial perception, my non-base raised comrades actually weren't very creative on their own accord. Then again, that begged the question: what was creativity, but the ability to pick up the finest concepts from your surroundings and uniquely assimilate them into your own designs? Was there even such a thing as an original thought, in the first place? Wasn't every idea in existence just a variation of another concept that someone else happened to think of first? Research was the foundation of scholarship, the key to humanity's advancement, yet all it ever entailed was finding and restyling data that someone else already gathered.

"It's from *The Great Santini*."

"Who's that?"

"*What's* that, you mean. It's a First Earth movie." Arrhyth's hand waved. "Don't bother; it's just another facet of the vast world of civilian entertainment. In other words, it's something you'll never have to worry about again, now that we're leaving."

Now that they were leaving. The Nurians, my window to the outside world.

"I hope you have a good trip home," I said. "Someday, I'd also like to go home."

They stared.

"But, you are home. Right here," Arrhyth blurted. "Isn't Icicle your home?"

"I'm not sure where my home is, yet. But, I promised myself that I'm going to find it. Soon."

They gaped at me, without comprehension. I didn't elaborate. I didn't want to tell them that I planned to pursue further military reform, because I didn't want them to offer to stay longer to help me with it. They'd already done more than enough for me and my people. They'd earned their freedom. I didn't want to perpetuate their isolation, a moment longer. Yet again, isolationism was the enemy. It was ironic that the Nurro-Ichthyothian military—an epitome of radical isolationism, in itself—was such a strong opponent to the isolationist Second Earth Order. To use a ridiculous Nurian expression: we were the pot, calling the kettle black.

The Nurians were ready for the real world, now. So, I'd let them go and live, so that one day my base-raised comrades and I may do the same.

ARRHYTH LINK

Their names hovered in the air, above my PAVLAK. I stared with an unhinged jaw. Apparently, I only needed to make *one* call to reach both my best friend *and* my sister. I dialed with trembling hands, suddenly glad that the Trilateral Committee was being stingy by only allowing voice-calls today, rather than full audio-visual interfaces. I sat on the locker-room floor, having fled the barracks for privacy. I didn't want to have my first contact in nearly eighteen ages with my loved ones in a packed hall of dozens of others doing the same. That'd be way too much emotion for one room.

The line only buzzed twice before someone picked up. And, it wasn't the someone I expected. Neither of them.

"Leeeeeeeavesleft home, Ehud speaking!" cried a boy's voice.

I held the PAVLAK away from my ear, startled. Nurtic and Linkeree had a *child?* The very thought made my stomach flip. It was silly of me to be so startled—they had eyes for each other since, well, forever, and were now in their thirties. Just because *my* sex life stayed on hold for nearly two decades didn't mean the rest of the world also remained abstinent, all that time.

"Um, hello." Sweat broke out on my forehead, as though System ships were hot on my tail. "May I speak with Nurtic o-or L-linkeree Leavesleft?" I stammered. Goodness, that address sounded so weird.

"Who is it?" Ehud asked, conscientiously.

"Arrhyth Link."

There was a pause.

"Uncle Arrhee?" he gasped.

"Um, yeah, I guess," I murmured, unsure how to start being an uncle to a kid whom I didn't know existed until about thirty seconds ago. Icicle may've trained me to handle enemy ambushes, but nothing could've prepared me for surprise family.

I heard the noisy clatter of a receiver hitting the floor, followed by the thunder of feet. "Daddy! Daddy! It's Uncle Arrhee! Uncle Arrheeeeee!"

This was getting freakier by the minute. After living with the same group of freeze-dried men since my teen ages, I wasn't ready for the craziness of the civilian world. Like best friends and sisters and children. Moreover, best friends and sisters *having* children. I had a brother-in-law and a nephew. Holy crystallines. I suddenly grew scared of Nurtic, scared that he'd be a completely different person than the buddy I once knew. He was a married man with a family, while I was a thirty-eight-age-old virgin living in a catacomb. I fought the strong irrational urge to hang up and toss my PAVLAK out the window.

"Arrhyth?" It was Nurtic. He sounded like… himself. Not sure what I was expecting instead, but the familiarity of his voice almost made me cry with relief. "Arrhyth?" he repeated.

Answer him! I urged myself. Open your mouth and talk, you socially-crippled idiot!

"Nurtic," I breathed, "it's really you." I was horrified to find my throat tightening. Wait, why was I horrified? I didn't have to suck up my emotions, anymore. I was leaving Icicle, forever. The taboo against acting, well, *human* was gone. Civilians didn't perpetually cork their feelings, for no good reason. Speaking with my best friend for the first time since age twenty was a valid reason to get worked up. "W-was that your son?" I asked, eyes burning.

"Yes. Mine and Linkeree's." There was a pause. "I hope that's alright with you," he added, uneasily. Wait, *Nurtic* was intimidated by *me?*

"Of course, it's okay. Are you kidding? Linkeree had such a huge crush on you in high school, I wanted to whack you upside the head with your lacrosse stick to make you ask her out, already."

"High school," he croaked. "Arrhyth, that was so long ago."

"Not much longer than when I last saw you, so excuse me if that's the way I remember you." I exhaled. "The war's over, Nurtic, it's finally over; I can't believe it," I cry-laughed. "I didn't think I'd live to see it, I really didn't. I was prepared to spend the rest of my life here at Icicle, indefinitely separated from my family, as the northwestern hemisphere slowly wastes away before my eyes."

"Here at Icicle," he echoed. "So, you're still in Ichthyosis."

"Yes, but not for long. They're sending us home tomorrow."

"Tomorrow!" And, he also laughed until he was weeping. "How come we weren't notified?" he inquired, once he finally regained composure.

"This *is* your notice, silly. I'm calling my parents, next. Instead of sending out letters or emails, the TC configured our PAVLAKs to reach civilian numbers."

"About time."

"The first and only time. Anyway, I'm going to need you to pick me up, tomorrow. Okay, I don't *need* you to, because I could always take a train or plane or something. But, I'd *prefer* if you came. If possible. By now, my parents are probably too old and tired to make the trip themselves."

"Sure, no problem," Nurtic put an end to my rant. "What time and where?"

"Seven o'clock at the Nurian Diving Academy." There was a pause. "Sorry for the extremely short notice," I quickly added. "I would've called sooner, if the TC allowed it."

"It's okay, don't worry. Seven's just a bit… early. But, we can do it, of course. we wouldn't miss it for the world."

Seven was early? "I can tell that you haven't been in the military for a long, long while."

"Seven's not early to be up and working, but it's certainly early to get your family literally across the country."

"Still got a plane and a pilot's license?"

He chuckled. "Does a vitreous silica have fins?"

"It sure does, future Vitreous-Astroloma-astronaut!" I exclaimed. He was the first Nurian to lead the Ichthyothian Resistance, one of the first Nordics to modify his wavelength, and now he was going to be the first spaceman since First Earth. Some people had all the luck. "So, I'll see you, bright and early, at the northern shore?"

"You bet."

I hugged my knees to my chest. "I'm going home to live with my folks, while my best friend and my sister are married parents."

"You didn't miss the bus, Arrhyth," Nurtic spoke, quietly. "You're still young."

"Still young? We're almost forty."

"Don't you know? In this day and age, forty is the new thirty."

"The new twenty, you mean. Because thirty became the new twenty, a long time ago."

"Oh, yeah."

We laughed again, but only briefly.

"But, really, though," Nurtic continued, seriously, "you haven't been cheated out of life. You've just been living a different kind of life—one of sacrifice. Your country is grateful, Arrhyth, more than you think. We won't soon forget it."

After all he'd been through himself, he was able to speak so calmly and easily of sacrifice. Would I someday feel as light and free? Would I also grow so glad to have given up so much?

"You also sacrificed," I reminded him.

"No more than you."

"But, you don't see me with a Silver Triangle."

There was an uncomfortable silence.

"I was the first to come home," Nurtic broke the ice, "so, they made a big deal out of me. That doesn't mean that I paid a price any higher than the rest of you. On the contrary, in my opinion."

"Well, you *were* the Resistance Leader, for a while. And, then, a System POW… then, a wanted fugitive… then, you saved Scarlet's life in the Fire Pit while she was unknowingly pregnant with the future savior of mankind… then, your college education almost got shot to hell by the First Tri-Nation Campaign… and, in the end, you didn't even have any family to come home to."

I had to be fair. Nuria didn't fuss over Nurtic just because he came home first. He did more for Second Earth in a mere handful of ages than most of us would in a lifetime. Nurtic was just being humble. As usual.

"Well, when you put it like that," Nurtic snickered.

"You were marooned in a desert, for crying out loud," I breathed. "You lived with a huge bounty on your head, in an entire nation of mentally-enslaved magical warriors. And, your country didn't even look for you. If you didn't save yourself, no one would've come for you. You could've died, out there. You almost did."

"Fond memories," he giggled. He actually *giggled*. I was appalled.

"You're not bitter?"

"Why would I be? All that'd do is transform my sacrifice into something ugly."

I shifted my PAVLAK to my other ear. "You're a better person than me, Nurtic."

"No, I've just had more time than you to get over my junk."

Aha. "So, you *were* upset, at one point."

"Oh, yes," he said, darkly. "'Upset' would be putting it lightly. I spiraled into a raging depression. I even stopped piloting, for a time. Completely."

"You *did?*" The only thing crazier than Nurtic grounding himself would be Nurtic cursing God.

"And, I got mad at God. So mad. I think I might've… hated Him, for a while," he half-whispered.

"What?"

"But, as life went on, I started to realize that though my past was glum, my future didn't have to be. I realized that moving forward was possible."

"So, time does heal all wounds."

"I didn't say that. Not *all* wounds."

"But, enough of them?"

"Enough to willingly get out of bed, most mornings."

I thought about that, for a while. "Some people never recover. Some people get post-traumatic stress disorder and spend the rest of their ages running from their own shadows."

"I pray that you won't become one of those people."

"And, if I do?"

"We'll still love and take care of you, anyway."

I forgot how sappy and cheesy Nurtic could be. Damn, I missed that. People around here were always so cold and jaded. It was a miracle that my own soul wasn't dead already. It was hard work, maintaining some semblance of a heart and a sense of humor, all these ages. If I didn't have Dither, fighting for sanity alongside me, I probably would've receded into terminal stoicism, by now.

"So, how come you never joined the Second World Revolt?" I changed the subject. "Fair Gabardine was asking about you."

Nurtic was quiet. Shoot, did I just unintentionally embarrass him? I didn't mean for my words to sound like an accusation, like: *how dare you stay idle all these ages, you selfish lazy civilian.* For goodness' sakes, he probably couldn't pitch in because he was too busy having a career and raising his son.

"As much as I hate it out here, extending my stay for the Tri-Nation Campaign is something I'll never resent," I babbled, more to end the silence than anything. "It's Commence's fault, really. He's an amazing kid. Who would've thought? I mean, he was a total bastard when he was the Leader of the Nurro-Ichthyothian Resistance. A volatile ill-tempered tyrant. We *hated* serving under him. But, then, he went to Conflagria for a while and came back totally different. Because he talked to Scarlet's aura. She whipped him into shape, I suppose. I still can't believe it. I mean, now, he's... *good.* You know? Like his mother and father. He's got the best of them both. Brilliant, courageous, inventive, passionate. He's everything we loved about Scarlet and Cease. It's tragic that they'll never know how awesome their kid turned out. But, I guess that means it's up to the rest of us to be proud *for* them, right?"

"Yes," Nurtic agreed, sadly.

Oh, crap. Of course, this would be a touchy subject for Nurtic. Whoops. Arrhyth, you inconsiderate imbecile!

"Nurtic... have you spoken to him since... since *then?*" I didn't know any detail. The little I *did* glean about Nurtic and Commence's rocky relationship came from snippets uttered here and there by Illia Frappe and Inexor Buird.

"Not since he left my home, no."

"He's never tried to find you?"

"No."

Wow. "He will," I reassured him. "I'm sure he will. One day. He's been really busy with setting up the GEO and everything. But, once things stabilize, he'll come for you."

"I hope so."

"He's probably scared of you. That may sound crazy, but just trust me on this one. I know Commence pretty well. He boldly tackles the future without hesitation, yet trembles in his sandals when asked to merely glimpse backward."

"That's what I figured."

"Have you ever considered looking for *him?*"

"After he left, that's all I did, for months upon months. And, I mean that literally: searching was *all* I did, day and night. Then, I saw footage from his academy graduation."

"Ah. What about since then?"

"Since then, I've thought a lot about reaching out but, in the end, decided against it. I think it'd just make things worse, to force him to face me before he's ready."

I grunted in agreement. "That makes sense. He doesn't know how to handle *not* being in control. No one can make him do anything against his wishes. Pushing the envelope only brings out his dark side." That was one way that Commence strongly reminded me of his father. Scarlet deserved a Silver Triangle just for being brave enough to attempt—and, apparently, succeed at—relational closeness with Cease.

"Exactly. So, the ball's in his court now, not because I want it to be, but because that's the way his world works. I can't take the reins without hurting him. And, heaven knows, I've scarred him enough already."

"Oh, Nurtic," I sighed, "the boy can cure a sick world, but he can't sort out his own head?"

"That's the way it always works, it seems. Just look at Scarlet. She and I grew close during the First Tri-Nation Campaign, much more so than when we were fleet comrades. And, the Scarlet I got to know back then was just… really broken, inside. Insecure, afraid, lonely, confused. Back when we were divers, I always thought that she was bulletproof. Unstoppable. Self-assured. Decisive. The epitome of warrior. I think that's how everybody else always saw her, too. Because, somehow, through it all, even as she was dying inside, she excelled at every challenge she took on, striving to stay strong for her people."

"Strong for the world, you mean."

"She always thought of the whole world as her people."

"Yes, she did. And, look how the world repaid her."

My chest tightened.

"We've been talking long-distance for a while, haven't we?" Nurtic asked.

"Let the military pay. It's not like they don't owe us big."

"Um, alright, I guess…" he murmured, uneasily. Ugh, apparently, even after all these ages, Nurtic was still the same absurdly-polite doormat I grew up with.

"Believe me, we've given them more than enough for a damn phone call," I growled. "And, yes, I know I sound bitter, so shut the hell up."

"I didn't say anything."

"Yeah, but you were going to."

"No, I actually wasn't."

"Of course, because you never mean anyone any harm, do you?"

"And, yet, I can't seem to quit gunning people down with friendly fire, can I?"

I was taken aback. "I should stop. I'm being a jerk."

"Yes, you are."

"Hey, you're not supposed to say anything mean."

"I'm not supposed to lie, either."

I'd forgotten how far up the wall Nurtic could drive me. Man, I missed that.

"When my nephew hits his teen ages, he'll drop out of school in favor of a drug-dealing flivvcycle gang," I spurted.

"What? Why?"

"The rule-follower's kid always rebels hard. Ehud won't be able to stand having an angel for a dad."

"What about an old senile soldier who's forgotten how to be civil, for an uncle?"

I laughed, heartily. "Can I talk to Linkeree?"

"She's not home—she's actually over at Bay River Secondary, coaching swim-team practice."

Nice. "Ah, well, I'll see both of you tomorrow, right?"

"Not a moment too soon."

But, maybe, a couple decades too late.

EPILOGUE

August seventh of the twelfth age.

Commence sat in his mother's old rickety cabin, the feeble structure that once served as the Red Revolution Headquarters. The floor before him bore a distinct green ink-splotch—a relic of the days when Scarlet July designed the incendiary that would wind up in the hands of double-agent Ambrek Coppertus. A few yards away, a bloodstain graced the wooden boards—a permanent reminder of the day, not quite eighteen ages ago, when Ambrek both took and rescued a life.

The barely-five-foot, sub-one-hundred-pound seventeen-age-old leader of the free world sat on folded knees in the very room where his life began, lime eyes downcast, auburn hair hanging over his melancholy face. As night fell, he did not bother to use a photon of spectrum to see through the darkness. He simply sat there, helpless and blind.

It was his moment of victory. But, it was empty. It was overshadowed by the tremendous guilt he still felt, for his messy past. It was dwarfed by his fearful uncertainty for what was yet to come.

His seventeen ages of life seemed to stretch behind him like seventeen eras. He had seen and embodied unspeakable horrors, tormented and hurt countless people. He lived in the Democratic-Republic of Nuria, the North Ichthyosis Island, the South Conflagrablaze Captive-turned-Republic and, in a matter of days, would move onto the Free Peoples of Oriya. Conflagria was his mother's home, Ichthyosis was his father's home, Nuria was his long-lost legal guardian's home… but, none of those nations ever felt like home to Commence. For a fleeting moment, he dared to wonder: would Oriya?

Yet, that was the least of his concerns. He now held the entirety of Second Earth in his small hands. He was literally changing the world. And, there was no one around to reassure him. No one to tell him, well done. No doubt, there was a certain thirty-eight-age-old, blonde-haired, hazel-eyed warship-pilot-turned-astronaut watching the work of his prodigal son from afar, proud of everything the young man did and stood for.

But, that wasn't enough for Commence. Nurtic Leavesleft's approval wasn't what Commence hungered for. Because, by now, Nurtic was a stranger. Just one of the faceless millions whom Ence gunned down, on his warpath. Once upon a time, Nurtic fought hard to be Ence's family. But, Ence wouldn't let him win. How deeply Commence regretted that, now. Someday, though, Commence was determined to reach out to Nurtic again, if only to apologize.

But, Commence knew, no matter what, that he would still be alone at the end of the day, even if he made amends with Nurtic. He would still feel isolated. Because of the pain of his past. Because of the shame in his heart. And, the crimson on his hands. And, the covalent blood running through his veins. And, the iridescent photons igniting his multi-sourced aura. In numerous ways, he was hopelessly separated from every other soul on the planet.

Seventeen ages ago, there lived two people who may have been able to comprehend the unique struggle that Commence currently faced, because they were among the first in this lonely planet to defy similar boundaries and borders, against all odds. Maybe, Commence thought sorrowfully, they could have understood him.

But, they were gone forever.

"Commence Lechatelierite," called a man's voice, imbued with throat spectrum.

Commence dared to lift his eyes. Brilliant light flooded the open door before him. In the center of the illumination stood two small figures, one in a white military uniform and the other in a red mage robe.

Cease Terminus Lechatelierite and Scarlet Carmine July.

The Ice and the Fire.

Commence's breath caught in his chest. But, alas, he was all too aware that they weren't real. Just a spectral mirage. He knew better than to run to them; he'd tried to hold Scarlet's hand once before, clasping nothing but cold air. His gaze dropped back to his knees.

"Why won't you look at me?" Cease's aura demanded. "Why do you bow your head in shame, Leader of the Earth?"

Commence trembled. "Because of *that*. What you just said. 'Leader of the Earth.' It… it isn't a role I deserve," he choked. "Believe me, I'm trying every day to be *him*—the 'Son of Nations,' the man worthy of your legacy… but… honestly, on the inside, I feel the same. I feel like Ence, the oppressive Principal of the South Conflagrablaze Captive who burned civilians alive on stakes. Ence, the tyrannical Diving Fleet Commander who mercilessly tortured his own subordinates for sport. Ence, the nobody from the Alcove City Orphanage who killed a kid in a fit of rage at age four."

"When I was ten, I strangled a comrade to death in fifteen seconds, then left his corpse to chill overnight in the snow," Cease suddenly spouted. "Yeah, he may've struck first, but I sure as hell didn't have to strike last."

"And, when *I* was ten, I set the entire Ardor Village square ablaze," Scarlet piped. "Sure, I had System warriors on my tail, but there were also dozens of innocent bystanders milling around. Who knows how many got hurt or killed."

Commence froze.

"Your identity isn't defined by where you've been or how many mistakes you've made in the past or how you feel about yourself when you get caught up in your own head," Scarlet went on. "If that were the case, you wouldn't look up to either of us, believe me. You wouldn't secretly wish, right now, that I could take your place as the Multi-Source Enchant."

Commence didn't dare to breathe.

"Yes, Commence, I know that, deep down, that's what's been troubling you the most, all this time," Scarlet said, somberly. "You believe that I should be the one in your position, as we speak. That I'm better suited than you to lead Second Earth into the future. That I'm worthy of the responsibility and you aren't." She took a step forward. "But, my child, you don't see yourself clearly—your sight is stuck in reverse. You're not Ence, anymore, and you haven't been, for quite some time. You need to let him go, as the rest of mankind already has. Accept that he was a part of your history—a part you can't erase—then leave him behind, once and for all. You have the chance, today and every day, to define the man you are now. Commence. The Son of Nations. The mage who fulfilled the prophecy because he genuinely cares for humanity. The mage who changed the world because he wanted to and knew how, not because he felt like he was supposed to. Unlike with me, the prophecy was never an obligation to you. Never a chore. It was an occasion you rose to, naturally. Because you're the one it was written for.

"I spent my whole life trying to understand what it meant. I struggled and strove to do everything I could to cover every possible base. But, I never pulled through, like you have. Because, it wasn't my burden to bear. I was a dual-sourced enchant who played a crucial role in the story of this planet, no doubt. But, I was never meant to finish what I started.

"You did it, Commence. You took from all the fallen children of Second Earth what wasn't rightfully theirs to uphold. Isolationism. A world system that was killing mankind. You're the one. The Multi-Source Enchant."

Commence shook his head. "I'm a covalent half-blood who was totally infrared, up until a few months ago," he croaked. "I woke up one day with an iridescent aura whose origins I can't explain."

"That aura always belonged to you, since birth." Scarlet smiled. "Until recently, I withheld it from you. I bound up your lifeline in the spectral web, preventing you from accessing the full extent of your powers. It wasn't easy. Every day, you fought hard against me and nearly won. You're far stronger than I ever anticipated."

Commence felt as though whacked upside the head with an enormous slab of ice. "But… w-what about covalence…?"

"If Nordic genes hampered magical potential, how come *I* became a throat mage with a black aura?" Cease cocked an angular brow. "Blood-spectrum-content makes no difference. So what if yours is a point-seven? Mine is zilch."

"I was waiting to release your wavelength to you, waiting for the day you'd deserve it. The day you'd prove that you understood the magnitude of the responsibility it entailed." Scarlet beamed. "January seventh of the twelfth age was that day."

Commence couldn't speak. He knew that Scarlet was right to restrain him, all those ages. He didn't want to imagine all the terrible things that Ence would've done with complete access to his multi-sources. Most of all, he couldn't believe that Scarlet thought him worthy by now.

"Stand and look at me, son." Cease ordered, quietly.

Commence was compelled by Cease's magical voice; he immediately got to his feet and met the eye of the legendary military commander whose sacrifice, eighteen ages ago, freed all of magekind.

Without another word, Cease walked right up to Commence and put his arms around him. Commence went rigid for a moment, then clung to his father, breaking into sobs. Never before had Commence felt accepted. Never before had he perceived that he belonged anywhere. Until now. When Cease pulled away, Commence saw, with great shock, that his dad's silver eyes were also wet.

His mother embraced him next. She was so small, so slight. Several inches shorter than her son. Forever seventeen.

The moment Scarlet released him, Commence could already feel their presence begin to slip away, their photons receding into the spectral web.

"No, please," Commence objected, fresh tears paving their way down his flushed face. "Don't leave me. Not again."

Even as the words left his lips, Commence knew that he was not being fair. His parents never *left* him. They were taken. Just as Cease was taken from Finis and Qui on December twenty-second of the seventy-fifth age, seventh era. Just as Coronet, Melanize, Amytal and Caitiff were taken from Scarlet on July twenty-fifth of the eighty-seventh age. Just as Finis and Qui were taken from Cease on January seventh of the ninety-fourth age. Just as Cease was taken from Scarlet on May twenty-fifth of that same age. And, just as Scarlet was taken from Commence on December twenty-second.

Loss was a part of life. Loss helped to shape the people it left behind. Loss helped sculpt Commence into the man he was today—which, in turn, helped Commence transform Second Earth into what it needed to become, to truly flourish.

"We're not leaving you again," Scarlet declared, as she took Cease's hand. "We never did, in the first place. Not entirely. Because both of us live *in* you, Commence. I think you can feel that, in your iridescent aura."

"We're proud of you and we love you," Cease said, finally speaking the words that Commence longed most to hear. "You've done well, my son."

* * *

So, it was written: the greatest military Commander in Second Earth history, Cease Terminus Lechatelierite, and the legendary Dual-Source Enchant, Scarlet Carmine July, had a son, and that son was the beginning of the end of Second Earth's darkest days. Commence July Lechatelierite, the first Covalent to walk the planet, was the true fulfillment of the prophecy and the author of a new chapter for all mankind. The chapter of the reacceptance of the Island of Fire in the international arena. The chapter of the abolishment of worldwide isolationism, an ideology that stifled humanity's progress since its inception. The chapter of travel among the stars. The chapter of universal wavelength modification, as great friendships blossomed between longtime enemies. Commence himself was a symbol of this newfound unity, as he was the Son of Nations—the miraculous fusion of the opposing elements of fire and ice. Covalent and Iridescent, he was the first of his kind, but undoubtedly, he would not be the last.

And, as Commence went on to become the leader of the united democracy that was Second Earth, he always kept his parents' smiling faces at the forefront of his eidetic memory. The red and black ones stood there in his mind's eye, hand-in-hand, and told him every day that they loved him, were proud of him, and that he was, in fact, doing alight.

* * *

"Fear not: for I am with thee:
I will bring thy seed from the east,
and gather thee from the west;
I will say to the north, Give up;
and to the south, Keep not back:
bring my sons from far,
and my daughters from the ends of the earth…
Let all the nations be gathered together…"

—Isaiah 43:5.9

NURTIC LEAVESLEFT

Dear Reader,

You did it. You made it through my series. I'm honored and humbled and quite thoroughly shocked, to say the least.

Allow me to backtrack a bit.

It's been roughly a decade and a half since commence July Lechatelierite left my home. As I started a family and became increasingly immersed in my astronaut training, many of the scars of my past finally began to fade.

Until, one summer three ages ago, my mind suddenly went into reverse.

Whenever I slept, impossibly-clear dreams of my service in Nuria, Ichthyosis and Conflagria blazed through my brain like a vitreous silica on full-throttle. The same handful of nightmares recurred, over and over, as though badgering me to take action. Desperate for an outlet, I began to write them all down, reopening each wound yet again, one by one. And, sure enough, this proved to be the remedy—once I documented a specific dream, it never came back.

It got replaced by a new one.

After several months of regurgitating my own past, I started having dreams of things that I'd never experienced. I'd wake in the middle of the night, panicked and terrified, wondering how these haunting, unfamiliar images found their way into my head.

I had memories of spending endless aimless days in a wooden cabin, painting parchment with berry-ink and dwelling over my Circle Trial condemnation. I had memories of sleeping behind a dumpster on cold Nurian nights, with nothing but a tattered robe on my back and a rotten apple core in my belly. I had memories of standing up to a high-ranking military officer in front of all my peers, arguing that mages were human beings who deserved recuperation rather than annihilation. I dreamed of losing my first sea battle at seventeen and waking in a hospital bed, paralyzed and nearly blind, but only concerned with the loss of my best friend. I dreamed of circling the Nurian Trade centerscraper in a stolen plane with an incendiary in my bomb bay, shaking and crying and warring with myself over what I was about to do. I dreamed of splicing the stomach of a seven-month-pregnant mage with a rusty sword, weeping and screaming and pleading for the forgiveness that she'd already granted me, warm blood gushing onto my glowing hands.

It took me a while to understand what was happening to me—what it meant for me to remember being a child-soldier, System warrior, nurse, businessman, dual-sourced enchant, infrared, useless, covalent iridescent, multi-sourced enchant, war-crimes convict, widow, orphan, little sister...

Somehow, someway, these memories were being delivered to me through the spectral web. They weren't dreams, they were visions. Images of reality. And, so, it suddenly became a serious responsibility to continue writing. I was no longer doing it just to relieve myself, but to preserve countless priceless true stories that would otherwise be lost forever. I had the privilege and honor to be the voice of dozens. I had the opportunity to speak for numerous remarkable individuals from all around the world.

While I wrote, I cried often, overcome by the great and terrible emotions and experiences encountered by my friends, comrades, acquaintances and enemies. As I ventured into the psyches of those whom history condemned, I came to understand their hopes, desires, beliefs and motivations. And, even though I could never condone my enemies' evil actions, it was impossible for me to live in their minds and feel the aches of their broken hearts without growing to love them the way they loved themselves.

Of course, I also saw my younger self through others' eyes, saw how I was so gullible and idealistic. I watched myself make the same mistakes all over again, except this time, my blunders were narrated by a chorus of external criticisms. I also cried for this younger Nurtic Leavesleft, the naïve boy who grinned in the face of death and longed to change the world. Sometimes, I found myself nostalgically wishing to be that kid again, with all his wonder and purity, now forever lost. But, most of the time, I just wanted to reach into the memories, grab his shoulders and shake him hard, jolting him from his foolish stupor. I often found myself longing to go back in time so I could redo segments of my past with the knowledge I had now. But, alas, in the end, I don't doubt that everything happened for a reason. Every trial and triumph had to have unfolded in the way they did for all of us to be where we are today—myself included.

For ages, I wrote during my every spare moment, in-between mission trips and astronaut-training sessions, at night and during stolen moments of the day. I was never a dazzling author like Scarlet or Linkeree, but I was stricken with a sense of urgency and revelation that propelled me onward, just the same. It was an enormous task, to organize and compress the thoughts of so many into a few hundred pages with some semblance of a coherent plot. Some visions I may have failed to properly transcribe, despite my best efforts. For example, Scarlet generally thought in pictures, so I fear that a few of her stories may have gotten lost in translation.

As I wrote, I wondered how the public would react to my words—to the fact that I dared to speak from the first-person point-of-view of major historical figures. I knew that my narratives would be rejected by many, deemed as a fictionalization or mockery of the truth, considering how little 'solid evidence' I had for much of it. Indeed, there are plenty of professional historians out there who've written exactly the type of material on the wars that the scholarly world desired. I tried to pick up some of these texts. And, they told me, in their utter failure to say anything at all, that people as wild, self-contradictory, peculiar, terrible and wonderful as Cease, Scarlet, Commence, Fair, Ambrek, Spry and Terminus could never really be put down on paper. Nothing I ever read did them justice, and I doubt my own work does either.

In the end, I broke up my writings into six books of varying lengths, each recording a distinct phase in the life of Second Earth. I gathered everything about the First War into one installment, and spent the next five on the Second War and the World Revolts. My format was scattered, disjointed and hardly chronological, with each chapter in an alternating point-of-view. No doubt, a literary critic would have a field day with my work. But, that's alright; I figured that if I managed to stir a single reader's heart for a moment, then I have achieved my purpose. I don't have any personal ambition for these books; I don't dream of moving the world with them or gleaning fame or fortune. These stories aren't even mine, after all. I was merely a passerby in the larger tale of Cease, Scarlet, Ichthyosis, Conflagria and the world in-between. My dear reader, all I want is for you to feel touched by the countless tragic and beautiful sacrifices that were made for the freedom that mankind presently enjoys.

And, so, I ask you to carry these tales in your heart, wherever you go, until your own eyes close in death. Never forget the numerous souls in history, soldier and civilian alike, who gave up so much to build our world into what it is today. Though the earth is far from perfect, we currently enjoy a lot of liberty and luxury not afforded to our predecessors. I thank you for finishing my series rather than casting it aside, and I ask you to consider all the truth buried behind the 'FICTION' label and pen-name of 'Samantha Mina' that my publishers, in their wide-eyed disbelief, insisted on placing upon the spines.

Love,

Nurtic Ehud Leavesleft

July 25th, 15th Age, 8th Era

1 age until the inaugural launch of the Vitreous Astroloma

7 ages until the institution of public wavelength-modification education

Made in the USA
Middletown, DE
29 July 2021

44749372R00245